# TUCKET'S TRAVELS

ALSO BY GARY PAULSEN

*Alida's Song*

*The Beet Fields*

*The Boy Who Owned the School*

The Brian Books: *The River, Brian's Winter, Brian's Return* and *Brian's Hunt*

*Canyons*

*The Car*

*Caught by the Sea*

*The Cookcamp*

*The Crossing*

*Dogsong*

*Father Water, Mother Woods*

*The Glass Café*

*Guts*

*Harris and Me*

*Hatchet*

*The Haymeadow*

*How Angel Peterson Got His Name*

*The Island*

*The Monument*

*My Life in Dog Years*

*Nightjohn*

*The Night the White Deer Died*

*Puppies, Dogs, and Blue Northers*

*The Rifle*

*Sarny: A Life Remembered*

*The Schernoff Discoveries*

*Soldier's Heart*

*The Transall Saga*

*The Voyage of the Frog*

*The White Fox Chronicles*

*The Winter Room*

Picture books, illustrated by Ruth Wright Paulsen:

*Canoe Days* and *Dogteam*

# TUCKET'S TRAVELS

Francis Tucket's Adventures in the West, 1847–1849

## GARY PAULSEN

A DELL YEARLING BOOK

Published by
Dell Yearling
an imprint of
Random House Children's Books
a division of Random House, Inc.
New York

This edition contains the complete and unabridged texts of the original editions. This omnibus was originally published in separate volumes under the titles:

*Mr. Tucket* copyright © 1994 by Gary Paulsen
*Call Me Francis Tucket* copyright © 1995 by Gary Paulsen
*Tucket's Ride* copyright © 1997 by Gary Paulsen
*Tucket's Gold* copyright © 1999 by Gary Paulsen
*Tucket's Home* copyright © 2000 by Gary Paulsen

**Visit us on the Web! www.randomhouse.com/kids**

**Educators and librarians, for a variety of teaching tools, visit us at www.randomhouse.com/teachers**

ISBN: 0-440-41967-0

Reprinted by arrangement with Delacorte Press

Printed in the United States of America
September 2003
10 9 8 7 6 5 4 3 2 1
OPM

# CONTENTS

Mr. Tucket

Call Me Francis Tucket

Tucket's Ride

Tucket's Gold

Tucket's Home

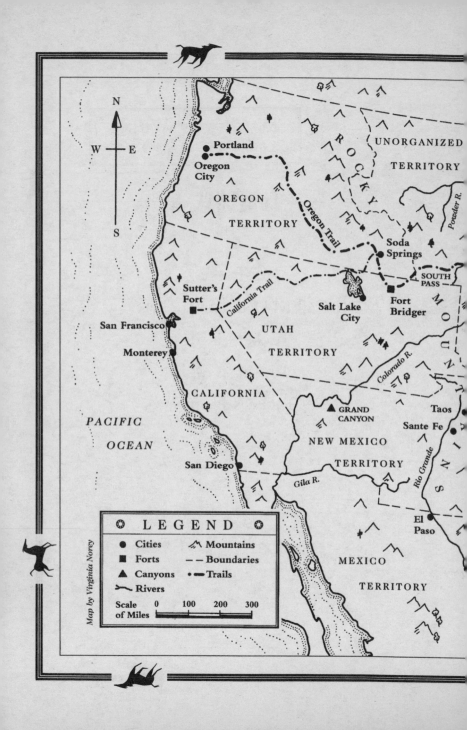

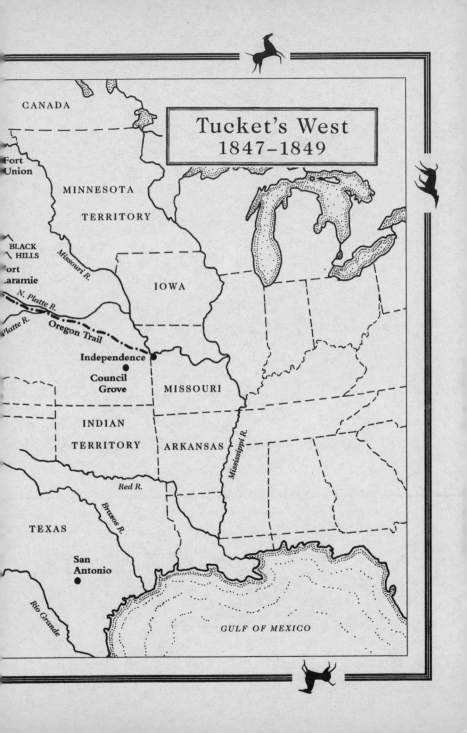

# MR. TUCKET

*To Angenette*

# Chapter One

FRANCIS ALPHONSE TUCKET came back to life slowly. He didn't open his eyes. He didn't want to open his eyes until he remembered everything that had happened.

Yesterday had been Francis's fourteenth birthday, and he had celebrated it quietly. Usually his mother and father—and even his nine-year-old sister Rebecca—made a big thing of birthdays. They had friends in, and a giant cake cooked to perfection on his mother's huge wood-burning stove, and by four in the afternoon everybody was so full of homemade ice cream and cake they couldn't move.

But that was how it had been on the farm in Missouri, where they had had the big house and barn. Yesterday they had celebrated Francis's birthday on the tailgate of a Conestoga wagon at the foothills of the Rocky Mountains. It was June 13, 1847—a warm summer Tuesday in a new country and they were with a wagon train on its way to Oregon. Francis, on awakening that morning, thought that even without any sort of birthday party, it would be his best birthday yet. How many boys of fourteen had ever seen drawings of the Rockies, let alone the real thing? That was an adventure in itself, not to mention crossing the great Kansas plains and watching the train scout, Mr. Ballard, hunt buffalo for the wagon train.

But then there had been a party—or at least a sort of party. As the wagons had squared away for the day's journey westward, Francis's mother called him from helping his father hitch some oxen to the yoke and tongue of the wagon. He went to the rear, where she was, and there, sitting on the tailgate, was a cake. He had no idea how she had done it—her stove was way back in Missouri, too heavy for the wagon. And he had not seen her doing anything special on the buffalo-chip fire that morning—but there it was, a cake. And easily one of the nicest cakes he'd ever seen.

"Happy fourteenth birthday, Alphonse," she said, with a smile. She had always called him Alphonse. His father always called him Francis.

For a long moment he didn't answer, just stood staring at the cake. Then he thanked her, knowing it would do no good to ask her how she'd done it. She would just answer, "Where there's a will, there's a way," as she always explained things that seemed impossible to Francis.

"Would you like a piece now?" she asked. "Or would you rather wait until tonight? The train is going to stop early today. Mr. Ballard wants to check all the wagons before we get to the mountains."

He wanted a piece so badly his mouth was watering, but he knew that wasn't what she expected, so he hid his eagerness. "We could have a sort of party," he suggested. "I could ask Ike and Max over and maybe offer them some cake." Ike and Max were the only other two boys in the train. There were five girls, but they kind of kept to themselves after Max threw a garter snake on one of them.

"That's a good idea," his mother said, nodding. "I'll wrap it in muslin and save it for this evening."

He could tell that he had pleased her. In all

truth, he didn't really want to share the cake with Ike and Max. Oh, they were nice enough, but they weren't really friends. It just happened that they were the only other boys, and Francis was more or less forced to do things with them. Ike would have been all right except that he talked funny and did things in an odd way. He said "thee" and "thou" and his folks always made him wear black clothes and a black flat-brimmed hat. Francis's father had said they were Quakers from the East somewhere, and that they all talked like that, but Francis still found it hard to get used to somebody calling him "friend" all the time.

Max was an out-and-out bully, and Francis wouldn't talk to him at all under normal conditions. But in the wagon train he had to. Max kept finding him when the wagons stopped for the night, and it was either talk or fight. They had fought several times, before Francis had found it easier to talk.

And in fighting they were pretty evenly matched. Their worst fight had taken place the time Max had teased Ike—short for Ichabod. Ike wouldn't fight, no matter how many bad names Max called him. Finally Max had hit Ike on the shoulder. That had made Francis mad and he'd torn into Max and given him a bloody nose, which got him a licking from his father that night, but he didn't care. The licking hadn't been much—he knew his father was doing it because there was no other way to keep Max's mother from complaining all over the train—and his father hadn't used a switch the way he did when Francis did something really bad. He had used his hand, and had smacked only twice, lightly, hiding a grin.

So Francis wasn't all that eager to share his cake with Ike and Max, but it pleased his mother—and he hadn't expected a cake anyway.

The idea of getting a present wasn't even on his mind that Tuesday morning. The nearest store was over five hundred miles away and he knew, or thought he knew, every item in the wagon. He'd helped load it, and there hadn't been any presents, or anything that had looked like presents. But they'd fooled him again. When he got back to the front of the wagon, to help his father finish with the oxen, he was handed a long, thin bundle wrapped in butcher's paper.

"Happy birthday, Francis," his father said, smiling. "We figured that it was about time you had one of these."

Francis was really puzzled, until his fingers tore away some of the paper. He didn't need to unwrap it all to know what it was. Already the sun hit a brass fitting, some dark, hand-rubbed walnut, and the brown sheen of polished steel.

"A rifle." His voice was soft. "A *new* rifle. But how . . . I mean, I helped load the wagon, and I didn't see it."

"The Petersons carried it in their wagon for me," his father said. "I brought it over to ours last night while you were sleeping. Do you like it?"

By this time Francis had torn off the rest of the paper and was finding it hard to keep from bouncing in excitement.

"It's a Lancaster," his father explained. "I think probably the only one of its kind. I thought about buying you a Hawkens in St. Louis, but they only make heavy rifles that fire heavy balls. When I talked to Mr. Lancaster, he said that a smaller caliber was more accurate, and with just a bit more powder, gave as much power as a big ball. Oh, the bullet mold, percussion caps, and powder flask are still in Mr. Peterson's wagon."

Francis could do nothing but stare at the rifle. Its stock, going only halfway up the barrel and bound to the metal with hand-forged brass bands, was of burled walnut. The lock, hammer, and trigger had been case-hardened in new oil, so they looked like etched marble instead of steel, and the barrel was the deepest, richest brown he had ever seen. The whole weapon had been made smaller than a full-sized rifle—just right for a fourteen-year-old boy. Even the sights, full elk-horn design for easy sighting, seemed to be in miniature.

"You mean . . ." Francis hesitated. There was really no way he could express enough thanks. "Did you really have this made just for me?"

"Then you do like it," his father said, smiling again. "I was worried about that. I thought maybe you wouldn't think too much of owning a rifle." His eyes crinkled. "I'm sure there must be a couple of thousand things a boy would rather own than a rifle—"

"I don't know about other boys," Francis interrupted. "But there isn't even one thing *I'd* want before a rifle. I've been wanting a rifle of my own ever since Mr. Ballard took me out and taught me how to shoot his buffalo gun."

They laughed, both of them remembering how the first shot Francis had taken with the scout's big .60-caliber gun had knocked him back on his rear.

"Well, you don't have to worry about getting knocked over with this one," his father assured Francis. "This is only a .40 caliber. Mr. Lancaster said it was fast, but wouldn't kick too much. The only way to find out is to shoot it, I guess. Why don't you go over to the Petersons' wagon and get the mold, caps, and powder? There's also a bag of lead balls already molded. Then when we pull out, you can drop back of the last wagon and practice shooting buffalo chips."

"Alone?" Francis asked.

"I don't see why not. You know how to handle a weapon—I watched you the other day with Mr. Ballard. Just make sure you don't shoot toward the train. It wouldn't do to break somebody's prize punch bowl."

Francis grinned. The only one in the wagon train foolish enough to carry a punch bowl had been Max's mother—and she bragged about it every chance she got. No, it wouldn't do to break it—especially if *he* did it.

"I'll be careful," Francis said, and started for the Petersons' wagon.

"And make sure you don't stray out of sight," his father called. "Mr. Ballard says there've been some Pawnee in this area. They might like to get their hands on that little rifle of yours."

This time they both smiled. The idea of Indians being around was pretty funny. All across the Kansas plains there had been talk of Indian trouble, and everybody worried about the Comanches. And they hadn't, not once in the whole trip, even seen a feather—let alone an Indian. Francis was almost disappointed. He had looked forward to seeing Indians nearly as much as seeing the mountains.

Francis dropped back from the rear of the train, and failed to notice that he was falling too far back. His forgetfulness was caused by the little rifle. Shooting it was a dream. He couldn't seem to miss, and it didn't kick at all. He got so engrossed in firing it that he didn't see the last wagon pull far ahead.

He lay still now, and tried to remember exactly what happened. He had fired about ten times, he knew, liking the little rifle more each time. On the eleventh or so shot, as he was loading, a large brown hand had clamped itself over his mouth.

His rifle had been grabbed first. There had been seven Indians—six young men and an older warrior. Probably a hunting party, because they hadn't been wearing paint. Then Francis made his first mistake; instead of just relaxing and biding his time until he could get a chance to escape, he fought them. Kicking and swinging and biting, more out of fear than courage, he had given the seven Pawnees a rough few minutes. Finally they'd hit him, just a little tap in back of his ear with his own rifle butt, and he had fallen like a stone.

They had ridden all that day, with Francis draped head-down across the old man's lap, bouncing like a sack of meal. He had passed into and out of consciousness on the trip, and had no idea where they finally dropped him—except that it was a dark and smelly place.

Now it was time to open his eyes. He opened them—then shut them as fast as he could.

Sitting above him, giving him a toothless grin, was the ugliest old person he'd ever seen—he couldn't tell at first if it was a man or a woman. Just a wrinkled face and toothless mouth that smiled when Francis's eyes came open.

# —— Chapter Two ——

FRANCIS'S CAMP LIFE with the Pawnees began that very morning. The old woman—as it turned out—was the wife of the old man who had been with the hunting party. She tied a rope around his neck and dragged him around the camp like a new puppy. At each lodge she would stop and call the whole family out. Then she would point at Francis and gabble something he couldn't understand. He guessed that she was bragging about her new "son." But he didn't much like what followed. The women would pinch his arms and push his lips back to look at his teeth, while the children—if there were any at the lodge—came out and kicked him.

Francis didn't stand for it at first. When another boy his age kicked him, he kicked right back, and landed a fairly good blow. This made all the adults laugh, but his "mother" shook her head and pulled his neck rope so tight it nearly strangled him. He figured finally that it was easier to play along and let them kick him. For the present it was enough just to stay alive and learn as much as possible about the Pawnees. He might need the information later to escape. And he would escape; he was sure of it. Either alone, or with somebody from the train—probably Mr. Ballard—who would come to rescue him.

In the meantime, he might as well make it as easy as possible on himself. To this end, he smiled at his new "mother."

That was his second mistake. Immediately she returned the smile and took the rope off his neck. That much he liked. But before he could get accustomed to the freedom of movement, three young Indian boys jumped him, and he had to fight like a demon just to stay on his feet. It would have been pretty fair if just one of the young Indians had tackled him. But with three of them climbing all over him Francis had no choice but to fight back any way he could—which meant hitting, biting, and kicking.

What surprised and angered him most was that none of the elders—not even his "mother"—made any move to stop the fight. Instead they just gathered around and cheered. None of them, it seemed, was on Francis's side, and this didn't help him keep his temper. Neither did the fact that he knew he couldn't win against the three boys. After the first five minutes, he decided that if he was going to lose anyway, he might as well do as much damage as possible on the way down. He picked the largest of the Indian boys and went after him. The other two might as well not have been there. One jumped on his back and another grabbed at his legs, but it was all too late to save the boy Francis had concentrated on—he was underneath Francis when the other two forced him down. And for every blow the two boys should have landed, Francis gave the Indian boy under him one on the nose. Even if they killed him for it, he was going to make that boy sorry he'd ever picked a fight.

"Hoka-ha!"

Francis didn't hear the yell, but the two boys on top of him jumped away. Francis just kept hammering away at the boy beneath him, who had now curled into a ball and covered his head with his arms.

"Hoka-ha," came the gruff voice a second time.

"It is enough! You fight with fists—the way a girl fights."

Francis felt himself lifted roughly by the back of his belt and dropped in the dirt. Immediately he swung around and attacked the man who had lifted him. He was struck such a blow that it knocked him head over heels.

"It is *enough*! I will not say it again."

Francis wiped his eyes with the back of his hand. He had expected to see a tall, or at least a strong-looking man. Instead he found himself looking at a short, wiry Indian with his hair in one braid. At the bottom of the braid there was one feather, hanging straight down. The man wore plain buckskins, un-beaded moccasins, and carried a rifle in his left hand. It was Francis's rifle.

"Enough my foot," he said, glaring up at the Indian. "They started it, not me. You want to start knocking somebody around, why not give *them* a lick or two? And if you're so tough, why do you have to steal rifles from boys?"

In a sudden hush of the people gathered around the fighting area, Francis watched in horror as the Indian raised the muzzle of the rifle until it pointed dead between his eyes.

"Bravery in youth is a good thing," the Indian said. He wasn't smiling. "It is not good to be stupid, little white-eyed wolf. It is stupid to insult the man who holds your gun. It is stupid to insult your elders. If you do it again, I will kill you."

The Indian let the rifle down easily and spun away. Francis watched him go, kneeling there in the dirt. He had never seen such a pure, cold look in a man's eyes, and he knew that he would have to be very careful whenever the one-braided warrior was around.

# —— Chapter Three ——

THREE WEEKS AFTER he came to the Pawnee camp, Francis learned that the brave who had threatened to kill him, and had purchased the rifle for two good horses from the old man who had led the party, was named Braid. Braid was a war leader. He was not a chief, but any time there was a need for a raid, Braid was the man who led the war party. In camp he was just another warrior, except that he was so mean that many people feared him. He had the scalps of many "victories" braided around the doorway to his lodge. He did not dress in finery, the way many warriors did, because he didn't need to impress anybody. His scalps did that for him.

Francis hated Braid more than anything on earth. He watched him lead out a big party of more than forty warriors. They were gone all that day and through the night until the next morning.

When they returned it was obvious that they had been on a big raid. Four of the braves were dead, draped across their horses. More were wounded. But even while the women of the dead men sent up their wailing and covered their faces with ashes, the rest of the tribe prepared for dancing and celebration.

One of the braves, Francis saw, had a scalp with blond hair. The party must have made a raid against a group of white people, and the only white people in the area were in his wagon train. It sickened him to realize that Braid had probably used *his* rifle to shoot at them.

Braid sought out Francis immediately upon the return of the raiding party.

"They will not be coming for you," the wiry Indian said smirking. "Not now, not ever. I have given them reason to fear the Pawnees. They will not risk fighting us for one stupid little white-eyes."

Francis knew he was telling the truth. They would not be coming for him. Not because they feared these Indians, but because they would think he was dead. The train would lick its wounds and head on for Oregon without him. He would have to find a way to escape on his own.

But Braid hadn't finished yet. The warrior dug into his buckskins, pulled out something, and threw it down in front of Francis.

"I brought this for a girl child," he said. "But perhaps you would enjoy playing with it more."

Francis stared at the object in the dirt. Only one thing kept him from screaming and attacking Braid —and that was the knowledge that it would do no good.

What Braid had thrown down was a small china doll. It was a pretty doll, fashioned after a woman going to a ball.

There was only one thing wrong with the doll— its nose had been broken off. Francis remembered exactly how that had happened. He had been teasing Rebecca, as he did sometimes, and in a fit of anger she had thrown the doll at him. She had missed him, and the doll had hit the corner of the stove and the nose had broken off. It was his sister's doll—Rebecca's doll.

That night, during the dancing and celebration, Francis tried to escape. They caught him not ten feet from the lodge and tied him up.

The next morning they let him loose, and that evening he tried to get away again. This time his "mother" beat him across the backs of his legs with a dried willow cane.

So Francis gave up the idea of escaping for a while. They were watching him too closely.

After his third week there, a large council meeting was held and the tribe decided to move the village. Francis had to help dismantle the lodge and load it on the travois in back of the horses—normally considered woman work, as was gathering wood—but he didn't mind because the work took his mind off the terrible situation he was in.

He did mind the direction the band took when they had finished packing, however. Strung in a long line, with much barking of camp dogs, the file headed due northeast—away from the direction of the wagon train.

I'll have to get all the way to Oregon, Francis thought glumly as he trudged along beside the travois, before I'll find out about Rebecca. That is, if I find a way to escape.

It didn't cheer him either to find that the movement of the tribe—almost twenty miles a day—almost doubled the speed that the wagon train made.

They traveled for ten days, and then put up a new camp on the southern edge of the Black Hills, the village winter ground—the place of sweet water and good hunting.

Strangely, Francis liked the Black Hills even more than he had liked the Rockies. The Black Hills were not only fine to look at—with their dark ridges and green meadows—but good to live with as well.

And it was here that Francis met Mr. Grimes.

It happened early one morning. Francis had just finished fetching wood and was bending down over the fire, built outside the lodge because the days were still quite warm, when it seemed every dog in camp started barking at once. Francis turned to see what all the noise was about, and there, riding into the middle of the Pawnee camp as though it were the main street of St. Louis, was a white man with only one arm.

It was, Francis learned from one of the Indian boys, Mr. Jason Grimes.

# Chapter Four

THERE ARE CERTAIN THINGS that are always easy to remember because of the way they happen. Francis's first sight of Mr. Jason Grimes was like that. He would remember it always because of the way Mr. Grimes ignored the Pawnees. It was not an easy thing to do. The Indian dogs were snapping at the hooves of his horses and pack mules, and the squaws and children were so thick all around him that he only showed from the waist up. Yet he ignored them, threading his horse carefully, gracefully around the noisy women and children, looking off in space as though they didn't exist. He made quite a figure as he rode, straight backed, moving easily with the horse's roll. Francis got more of an impression of a piece of timber bolted to a saddle than a man—until he looked at Mr. Grimes's face. It was a thin face, and almost as dark as an Indian's, except that it bore a bushy beard and mustache. He had thin lips and washed-out blue eyes, and on top of his head he wore a dashing but dusty derby, set slightly back, with one long feather sticking straight up from the band. He had on fringed but otherwise not very fancy buckskins, plain moccasins, and no belt.

The last thing Francis noted was that Mr. Grimes's left arm was gone. He carried his rifle, wrapped in a buckskin case, with the same hand that loosely held his horse's reins, and the fact that he had no left arm didn't seem to bother him at all. It seemed almost natural, as though he would have looked odd *with* a left arm.

Francis realized suddenly that he was staring with his mouth open. He shut it. He moved forward through the crowd around the mountain man.

"Hey," he called. "Hey, over here. I'm a *captive!*" The word sounded funny when he said it, but he saw that the mountain man had heard, for he looked down from his horse quickly, then back up.

Francis wasn't sure, but he thought the derby-topped head had shaken left to right just once—as though telling him to be quiet.

Then he couldn't see anything more because his "mother" found him and dropped a noose over his head. She dragged him back, cackling happily, and led him into a corner of the lodge.

With his hands tied in back of him and his ankles lashed firmly together, Francis had plenty of time to think. Most of his thoughts were about the mountain man. How could he come into the Pawnee camp and not be harmed? And *why* had he come? Was he a friend of the Indians?

There were no answers in that dark corner of the lodge, but one thing was plain. The Pawnee weren't going to kill the mountain man. Just the opposite—his arrival was to be the reason for a full day of celebrating. Francis heard all the preparations, and with this knowledge, his heart sank. Any man that friendly with the Pawnees wouldn't be likely to offer him help in escaping.

All that day he lay in the lodge, wondering. He got no food and no water. By nine that night, when the dancing had reached its full frenzy, he at last fell asleep.

Francis wasn't sure of the time when he opened his eyes, but it was either very late that same night or very early the following morning. He did know why he had awakened. There was a calloused hand clamped over his mouth, and in the darkness of the lodge, he could make out the shape of a derby.

It was the mountain man.

Francis felt the bushy beard against his ear, and heard a whisper.

"Don't move. No sound. Just blink your eyes if you hear me and are wide awake."

Francis blinked, and the hand was taken off his mouth.

"Can you ride?" the mountain man asked, still whispering hoarsely.

Francis nodded.

"Good. In back of the lodge you'll find a little black mare I swiped from the Pawnee herd. Walk her out of camp with your hand over her muzzle. When you're safely out of camp, get on her and ride as hard as you can with the North Star on your right shoulder—" He stopped suddenly as Francis's "mother," across the lodge, turned in her sleep. In a second he continued, "If you ride hard enough, and don't hit a hole somewhere, dawn will catch you at a small creek. Take the mare right into the middle of the creek and head upstream. Keep going in the water until you think you're going to drop, then go another ten miles. If you stop, they'll get you. Now, did you understand all that?"

Francis nodded again, "Where will you be?" he asked, rubbing his wrists, which the mountain man had cut loose while he was talking.

"Why, I'll be sitting right here in camp," the mountain man answered, chuckling softly, "eating a good breakfast, wondering whether or not they've caught you. If they don't, I'll see you in a couple of days. Now, are you going to sit and jaw all night or get riding?"

Francis took it for the command it was. Thirty seconds later he was leading the little mare quietly out of the village hoping with all his heart that he smelled enough like an Indian not to upset the dogs.

A minute after that he was on her back, wishing he'd never told a lie in his life. The only time he'd ever been on a horse was when he'd ridden a work-horse while his father plowed. That had only been at a walk, and with a lot of harness straps to hang on to.

The little black mare didn't even have a blanket on her back and she only had two speeds—dead stop and full run.

# Chapter Five

FRANCIS GOT HIS FIRST MOUTHFUL of dirt not a hundred paces from where he got on the little black mare. Luckily, he had figured on falling off, and had taken the precaution of wrapping her jaw rope tightly around his hand. When he hit the ground, she dragged him only a couple of yards. He didn't have time to moan about his scraped elbows and knees. He didn't have time for anything but to get on again.

The second time he made nearly three hundred shattering yards before sliding off her side and bouncing on the rocks of a dry streambed. The trouble was that the mare was so fat—it was like trying to ride a nail keg.

He didn't discover the secret until he had fallen off three more times, removing more and more skin from his elbows and knees each time. Then he remembered how the mountain man had ridden—stiff backed, but loose, almost relaxed, where he joined the horse. Francis still bounced around a lot, but all his bouncing was straight up and down—not off to the side. And once he'd learned to relax, Francis found riding the black mare exciting.

Never had he been so purely thrilled. Her dainty head came down, her ears folded back along her flattened neck, and she really flew. Francis didn't try to turn her, as long as she kept in the right general direction—due west—and he forgot everything in the roar of wind and drumming thunder of her hoofs.

Just at false dawn, when the first grayness made faint shadows under trees, the mare streaked out onto a large meadow. It was entirely flat, and she picked up speed when she hit its edge. Francis, content in the knowledge that she wouldn't have to dodge around rocks and trees for a while, relaxed even more and loosened his hold on her mane.

When she hit the water, he went off over her

head, and when he got up, found he was neck deep in muck. The creek ran straight down the middle of the meadow. When he finally managed to scrape the mud from his eyes, the mare was nowhere to be seen. He had dropped the jaw rope, and she had gone on. He couldn't even hear her hooves. He wanted to look for her, then realized he hadn't time for that. This was the stream the mountain man had been talking about. Horse or not, his orders had been definite—head up the middle of the stream, and don't stop.

He stepped deeper into the water, but didn't start upstream immediately. He felt sad that the mare was gone. He would have liked to keep her awhile, and though he didn't think much of the Pawnees he admired their horses.

"Thank you," he said quietly, looking off into the darkness. "Thank you, little mare. It was a good ride."

And he started walking in the water, only vaguely aware of the chill.

Real dawn caught him nearly four miles up the stream. He had long since left the meadow behind, and the stream was now bordered by thick scrub pine trees. He was very tired, and ached all over from his many falls from the mare. But he knew that if he stopped before getting far enough upstream, he might not meet the mountain man again.

So he kept walking; not in miles, or even yards, but in steps. All day long he did that. He quit thinking of food early in the morning; it did nothing but make him hungry. And somehow, without his having been aware of the passing of a day, evening found him still trudging, still moving. He didn't know how far he'd come, only hoped it was far enough.

Just as the first night birds began dipping and wheeling over the stream for insects, Francis Alphonse Tucket pulled himself onto the bank beneath a clump of overhanging willows and dropped like a bag of sand.

In five seconds, wet clothes and all, he wouldn't have heard the Indians even if they beat their drums right next to his head.

# ——— Chapter Six ———

FRANCIS AWAKENED to a heavenly smell—the aroma of boiling coffee. He was afraid that if he opened his eyes, the smell of coffee would vanish. But when a full ten seconds had passed, and the smell was still there, he knew he hadn't been dreaming.

He sat up and saw the mountain man sitting over a small fire about ten feet away. His back was to Francis, but he spoke at once without turning around.

" 'Bout time you opened up a mite—day's half gone already. You sleep like a fancy city man."

Francis stretched, wincing at the pain in his legs. That would be from the little mare, and the pain in his arms would be from falling on them, and the pain in his knees from the rocks he had landed on, but the pain in his stomach was from hunger. "How did you know I was awake?" he asked after a moment.

"Your breathing changed. When you quit sucking wind like an old buffalo, I figured you were coming around."

"You've sure got good ears."

"I'm alive. You don't stay that way long out here unless you can hear a little."

Francis filed away that advice, and got up. Everything in him hurt with the movement. He didn't believe anything could be that stiff and still be alive.

"I thought you said you could ride." The mountain man chuckled.

"I did all right," Francis answered defensively.

"If you mean you made it alive, I guess you did at that. But I wouldn't call what happened to your hands and knees all right. Seems to me you lost a little hide. Still, you pulled a good trick with that mare—sending her off ahead while you came upstream." His chuckle turned to an outright laugh. "I

followed Braid and five or six others for a while
when they came after you. Unless I miss my guess,
they're down on the Powder River somewhere, *still*
after that mare."

"I didn't plan it," Francis cut in. "I fell off."

"Eh?"

"I said I fell off her when she hit the stream. I
fell off and she kept right on going without me."

"That's sort of what I figured, but I thought it
would be better if you said it. Kinda keep the air
clean around here, if we talk straight." He turned
and faced Francis for the first time. "You know, that
lie about knowing how to ride could have got us
both killed last night, don't you? They could have
caught you, and worked you over a bit, and the first
thing you know you would have been telling them
all about my getting a horse for you. Don't go shaking your head. I know you wouldn't want to talk.
But I've seen the Pawnees make a man tell stories
he didn't even *know*. So from now on you just tell
me what you know is straight, and that'll keep us
*both* out of trouble. What's your name?"

"Francis Alphonse Tucket."

"I said it would be better if we kept everything
*straight*, boy. Now what's your handle?"

"I wasn't lying. My name really *is* Francis Alphonse Tucket. Honest."

"Let me put it another way. What do you go by? I mean, haven't you got a sort of short name they call you?"

Francis thought a minute, then shook his head. "My mother always called me Alphonse, and my father called me Francis. I guess you can take your pick."

The trapper shook his head. "I'm sorry, and nothing against your folks, understand, but I don't like either of them. They don't hit my tongue right. Tell you what. My name is Jason Grimes. You call me Mr. Grimes, and I'll call you Mr. Tucket—that should keep us both happy. Is that all right with you?"

Francis shrugged. "Suits me fine, Mr. Grimes."

"Good. Now then, Mr. Tucket, why don't you hobble your crippled body over here and have a sip of coffee? There's nothing like a touch of coffee to take the sharp edge off an empty belly. After that I'll give you a little venison jerky, and while you're chewing that you can tell me how you came to be the son of that old Pawnee lady."

Francis had tried coffee before, stolen from his mother's stove with sugar in it and he took some in a gulp. It was bitter and he nearly spit it out. But the heat of it felt good and seemed to take away some of the ache in his stomach.

The jerky was as tough as an old boot. While he chewed it—and it took *some* chewing—he told Mr. Grimes about the adventure, starting with the wagon train and the rifle.

He finished his tale by telling how Braid had thrown the doll down in front of him.

Mr. Grimes nodded when Francis finished. "That Braid is a mean one. Back before I made friends with the Pawnees by bringing them powder and lead every time I came through, Braid and I had one bush-ripper of a fight. Knives, hatchets—the whole works. I guess it lasted over an hour, and when it was done, he had one scar down his back and I had lost an arm."

"You mean Braid took your arm off?" Francis asked.

"No, he just cut it good. But it got infected later and I had a doctor in St. Louis whack it off before it poisoned my whole body. It makes for some pretty tight talking whenever I come into his village. Braid hasn't forgotten his scar a bit, and every time I come in he asks me to wrestle. Oh, and speaking of wrestling, I've got something for you. Won it from Braid yesterday wrestling—he made the mistake of tying one arm behind his back to make the fight more fair. He was too stupid to realize that I get a lot of all kinds of practice with only one arm, so I whipped him pretty easy."

As he talked, Mr. Grimes went to his saddle and pulled out a blanket wrapped around something. He carefully unrolled the blanket and handed Francis his rifle, mold, powder, and caps.

"My rifle!"

"Yup, and a sweet little shooter she is, too. I knew it was yours when you started telling me about getting it for your birthday. Seeing as how it looks like we'll be riding together for a while—at least until I teach you enough so's you can make Oregon on your own—we'll take a couple of days off and I'll teach you to shoot it."

"I can shoot," Francis said.

"Well, maybe you can, and maybe you can't. But just reading signs makes your story look thin."

"What do you mean?" Francis asked.

"I mean if you *really* knew how to shoot that rifle, it wouldn't have been seven Pawnees jumping you that day by the wagon train. It would only have been five, and maybe just four—and those four would have been thinking seriously about going home without you. *That's* what I mean."

# —— Chapter Seven ——

"No-ah, Mr. Tucket, that isn't quite the way it's done."

It was the first time Mr. Grimes used the long, drawn-out negative answer to something Francis had messed up. But it wasn't to be the last. In fact, he would use that long no, as Francis thought of it, about ten times to every short nod, which was the way the mountain man approved of anything.

It was the afternoon of the day Francis and Mr. Grimes had met at the stream. Francis had just loaded and fired his gun as instructed by Mr.

Grimes. He felt that he'd done all right. A piece of wood more than thirty yards distant had turned to splinters with his shot. And it *had* been the piece of wood he was shooting at.

"What did I do wrong?" he asked. "I hit the piece of wood, didn't I?" There was just a thin bit of annoyance in his voice.

Mr. Grimes smiled and hooked his right hand in back of his neck, stretching. "Well, now, that's just about what *everybody* says—when they don't know about rifles." He mimicked Francis, " 'I hit the piece of wood, didn't I?' And yes, you did, Mr. Tucket. You hit the piece of wood. But how many times more can you hit it? Go ahead, load up and have at it. Pick another piece of wood out there and hit it for me, will you?"

Francis loaded, aimed, and fired at a buffalo chip about forty yards away. He missed. He tried twice more and missed both times.

Mr. Grimes nodded. "It's this way. You're holding that thing like it was an old rag. Your arms are loose, you're slopping your cheek against the stock, you're grabbing with your hands—and that's all wrong. You'll hit once or twice that way, if you're lucky. But the real trick of shooting a decent gun is to be able to put about four out of five balls in the same place, or nearly so. Now, Mr. Tucket, we'll see if we can't do a little reshaping of that crippled body of yours . . ."

He wasn't fooling. In the next five minutes Francis felt as though both his arms had been broken. Mr. Grimes pulled Francis's right elbow up so high the shoulder popped, and he jerked the left elbow down, directly beneath the barrel of the rifle.

"And don't grab with that left hand on the stock. Just make a baby cradle with your fingers and let the rifle sleep in it."

Francis nodded. It hurt, standing that way, but he could see how it made for more consistent shooting.

"All right, Mr. Tucket, load up and fire again."

Francis didn't start hitting right away, but at least his shots were falling in the same general area. He turned after four shots. "How's that?"

Mr. Grimes nodded. "All right, but you're taking too long to reload."

"What do you mean, too long? It was just a couple of seconds between shots." Actually it was more like a minute. But that wasn't what Mr. Grimes meant.

"It's this way, Mr. Tucket. What would you do if Braid came riding up the creek right now?"

"Why, I'd . . ." Francis blushed. He was standing with an empty rifle. If Braid, or any other threat, for that matter, came riding up the creek, Francis knew it would take him at least thirty seconds to load.

"That's right, Mr. Tucket. You'd be tied like a cow before you got powder down the bore. Every time you shoot, no matter whether you're shooting at buffalo chips or buffalo, you load as soon as the ball leaves the barrel. Carrying an empty rifle is about like carrying an empty water skin. When you get really thirsty, Mr. Tucket, you can't drink air."

Francis smiled sheepishly. "I guess I've got a lot to learn, haven't I?"

"Ayup, Mr. Tucket, you have a lot to learn, but you're coming along. Now let's clean that little shooter of yours and try some rapid firing. That's what really separates the men, or boys, for that matter, from their scalps in this country—not being able to shoot *fast*."

Cleaning the rifle was easy. Francis just cupped creek water in his hand and poured it down the barrel, swabbed it with a piece of patch on the end of his ramrod, then greased the bore.

"Now this is how we'll do it," Mr. Grimes told him, fetching his own rifle from his saddle. "We'll have a sort of contest. We'll start at the same time, and the one who gets the most shots off while I count to ten will get out of working tonight—getting wood and cooking some of the jerky. Does that suit you, Mr. Tucket?"

Francis nodded. He didn't see how he could lose, shooting against a one-armed man.

"All right, Mr. Tucket. Go!"

"But you don't even have your rifle out of its case, Mr. Grimes," Francis said. "You aren't even ready."

"Just giving you the benefit of a little head start, Mr. Tucket. Ready? Go!"

They both fired at the same instant. Mr. Grimes had just flipped his rifle and fired, one-armed, before its buckskin case hit the ground.

"One," he said, starting the count.

Francis worked frantically. From his flask he poured powder into his cupped palm, then he emptied the roughly measured powder down the bore.

"Two."

As Francis was placing the patch across the mouth of the bore, he heard the roar of Mr. Grimes's Hawkens. He couldn't believe it. He put the ball on the patch, and drew the ramrod from its cradle beneath the barrel. He started the ball down with his thumb . . .

"Three."

. . . and put the ramrod on top of it. As he slammed the ball home he heard the mighty

Hawkens roar again. Mr. Grimes had fired three to his one. Francis capped the nipple, raised the rifle . . .

"Four."

. . . and fired. As his second shot tore a buffalo chip to pieces, the Hawkens belched fire a fourth time. It was too much for Francis. He lowered his rifle and watched Mr. Grimes.

"Five."

Mr. Grimes raised his Hawkens and fired. Number five. Five shots in the time it had taken Francis to make two. Clearly, Francis had missed something.

"Six."

Mr. Grimes lowered the Hawkens and held it between his knees. In one fluid motion he poured powder from the flask at his side down the barrel directly—without measuring—and brought the muzzle of the rifle up to his mouth. From his lips he spit a ball into the muzzle. Without a patch, it slid freely down, needing no ramrod. He slammed the butt of the rifle on the ground, to seat the ball, and from the space between his fingers pulled a percussion cap. It fitted quickly on the nipple, the Hawkens came up, and . . .

"Seven."

. . . smoke again poured out over the grass.

Mr. Grimes lowered his rifle and grinned. "I don't guess I have to go all the way to ten after all."

"But that wasn't fair," Francis said. "You didn't patch your balls, or measure your powder—"

"Now, now, Mr. Tucket. The word 'fair' is pretty loose. What's not fair in St. Louis at a turkey shoot might *be* fair when you're up against five or six Comanch." He cut the word "Comanche" off. "Out here people sort of think of 'fair' meaning the same as 'alive.' Savvy?"

Francis smiled. "Savvy. 'Fair' means that I'm going to gather wood and cook jerky."

"You *are* coming along, Mr. Tucket," the mountain man said, grinning again. "Ten, fifteen years, if you're still alive, you'll be the best wood gatherer in the Black Hills . . ."

# Chapter Eight

THEY LEFT EARLY the next morning. Francis would have liked to stay on for a few more days, but Mr. Grimes saddled his big sorrel gelding just after coffee with the air of a man who has somewhere to go, and Francis, stiff or not, knew better than to make any other suggestions.

"Come on up, Mr. Tucket. Let's see how old Footloose carries double."

As it turned out, old Footloose carried double almost as well as he carried single. Francis was given the job of holding the rope that led back to the pack mules. They followed nicely—showing none of the stubbornness Francis thought mules were supposed to show—and under a lightly clouded sky they made their way at a slow walk toward the southwest.

If Francis had expected a lot of conversation as they rode, he would have been sadly disappointed. Mr. Grimes was of the thinking that when he had something to say, he said it—usually with a bit of pepper thrown in. But when there wasn't anything to talk about, two or three hours might pass without a word coming from his bearded face.

Francis had close to a hundred questions he wanted to ask, but he didn't say anything for nearly two hours. In that time they had passed out of the main part of the pine forests and were winding down a dry-bottom canyon. It was an extremely pleasant place, even without water. Both sides of the canyon were of gray rock, and were high enough to keep the mid-morning sun from reaching Francis's back. Occasionally he could hear magpies chattering, and twice he heard the drumming of grouse, beating their wings on rotten logs. Even the sound of the sorrel's shod hooves, ringing off the rock walls, seemed natural and nice.

There was something bothering Francis, however, that kept him from enjoying these things the way he might have. Part of it was Rebecca—and not knowing about her. But it was Mr. Grimes that upset him more, and finally, as the sorrel brought them out of the canyon and back into the sun, Francis spoke up.

"Mr. Grimes, how is it that you're so friendly with the Pawnees—I mean, with Braid having caused you to lose your arm and all? I would think you'd be downright mad, or at least not friendly enough to bring them powder and lead."

Mr. Grimes snorted, and Francis could see the mountain man's back jerk as he began to laugh. "Honestly, Mr. Tucket, you do ask the mulish questions, don't you? I'll bet you spend the rest of your days looking gift horses in their mouths."

"What do you mean?"

"You want me to answer that? Or would you rather figure it out for yourself?" the mountain man said. "It seems simple to me. If I hadn't been 'friendly with the Pawnees' as you put it, you'd be back there with a rope around your neck, getting whipped."

"I'm sorry," Francis murmured. "It was a dumb thing to ask—"

"But since you asked," Mr. Grimes cut in, "I think maybe I ought to answer it. You think I ought to be mad at Braid on account of my arm. Well, Braid can't help the way he was made, no more than you or me. The Pawnees call themselves 'The People.' They live with the land. If you put it in our talk, that means they live by nature—the same nature that makes a she-bear gut you if you mess with her cubs. Braid costing me my arm is about the same as if a she-bear took it. I couldn't get mad at a bear and I couldn't get mad at Braid, and I couldn't hate the whole Pawnee tribe because of a mistake."

"You call losing an arm a *mistake*?" Francis asked.

"Yes, sir. I should have got Braid before he got my arm—not doing it was a mistake."

"How can you talk about killing Braid when you don't hate him, aren't even mad at him?"

"Now be careful, Mr. Tucket. Asking a question is one thing—even when it's a dumb question. But now you're picking, and picking is what St. Louis city folk do . . ."

"No—I mean it. In the wagon train and at Braid's village, I fought a lot. But I couldn't *really* fight unless I got good and mad. Now you make it all sound so cool and calm—I just don't understand, that's all."

Mr. Grimes laughed. "Let me put it another way. I live by trapping, mostly beaver. Sometimes I trap on Pawnee land, sometimes not. When I *do* trap on Pawnee land, it figures that I'd want to do it without getting my hair lifted, so I bring them something they need—powder and lead—and I don't get mad. I get something—beaver pelts—and the Pawnees get something. We all stay happy. Well, maybe not happy—but alive."

Francis couldn't help himself. "Why do you have to bring them powder and lead? They turn right around and use it on white people—like my folks. That doesn't seem right to me . . ."

Francis felt the trapper stiffen in the saddle. He bit his tongue, and thought that he fully deserved getting knocked on the ground and left for the Indians.

Gradually the stiffness went away. Without turning, and in a dead-even voice, Mr. Grimes said, "I guess we'd better ride quiet for a while."

For nearly an hour there was only the sound of the sorrel's hooves and bird calls and their own breathing. Francis called himself many kinds of a fool in that time.

When the silence was at last broken, it was Mr. Grimes who spoke.

"You've been through a lot in the past month or so, and I guess maybe I ought to take that into consideration a mite—"

"No," Francis interrupted, glad of the chance to

speak. "I was dumb. I'm sorry—I shouldn't have talked that way."

"Well, I'm going to say something to you that I shouldn't have to say. I'm not a war maker. I don't want to kill Pawnees, and I don't want to kill whites. If they want to kill each other, that's something else again. I ride right down the middle. And if my powder and lead is used to kill whites, I'm sorry. But it's not my fault. That same powder and lead would kill a lot of buffalo and antelope—and that's how most of it is used. Some mountain men and traders bring the Indians whiskey—if you want to pick yourself a *real* fight, go after those men."

"But I didn't mean—"

"And don't come clawing at me. I've killed a few Indians in my time, and I'll probably kill a few more. I may even put Braid under, someday, or he may kill me. But you can make money on this: If I *do* kill Braid, it won't be because he has something I want, like land. I'll leave that to the farmers—your people. And that's the last I want to hear about it."

He quit talking as suddenly as he'd begun. Again the silence was thick and painful. There was nothing Francis could say, and he knew it, and the knowledge made him even sadder.

"Mr. Grimes," he asked, "where are we going?"

"You mean today, or next month?"

"Well, today, I guess. I thought if we happened to be going near a settlement of some kind in the next few days, you could drop me off."

The mountain man nodded. "If that's what you want. We'll be getting to a settlement tonight—or at least the only kind of settlement they have out here. You can drop off there if you want to. I think Standing Bear would be right proud to have you stay awhile—"

"Standing Bear?" Francis cut in. "Who's he?"

"He's the head of the settlement. I was thinking earlier of swinging by there and picking up a horse for you. Of course now that you want to stop, we'll just drop in and forget about the horse . . ."

"What kind of a settlement is it?"

"Well, it's not really a settlement. More like what you'd call a camp. Out here we call it some-thing else."

"What do you call it?"

"A village," the mountain man answered, chuck-ling. "Out here we call it a Sioux village. You sure do pick the funniest places to want to stay, Mr. Tucket."

# —— Chapter Nine ——

FRANCIS TRIED not to be afraid when the Sioux village came into view. He had seen only one type of Indian so far, the mean type. And he knew that the Pawnee tribe was the not-too-distant cousin of the Sioux. Thoughts of recapture took the place of his faith in Mr. Grimes's judgment, and Francis went cold all over.

"Easy, Mr. Tucket," the mountain man said without turning. "This is like a show. You saw me come into the Pawnee village—we do the same thing here. Act easy."

Francis took his cue from Mr. Grimes. He stiffened his back and tried to remember something not related to where he was now. His mind settled on the birthday cake his mother had made, and looking straight ahead—neither down nor left nor right—he pictured it in exact detail.

The clamor in the village was deafening. Chief Standing Bear's group had an even noisier bunch of dogs than the Pawnees, and the children's howling was earshattering. Francis marveled at the sorrel and the mules. They paid no more attention to the screaming than did their master except that once a mule took aim and nearly drove a dog's head through his rear end with a rear hoof.

Finally, when they had woven their way to about the center of the village, Mr. Grimes pulled lightly on the reins and stopped.

"Standing Bear," the mountain man called.

Francis watched as a small channel opened in the crowd to the right and an Indian, who limped, came through. He was short, bowlegged, and stocky, but he moved with a smoothness that made Francis think immediately of a cat. It must be Standing Bear, Francis thought, and he was not smiling. When he was five feet from the sorrel, his right hand came up slowly, and with as much grace as he used walking.

Mr. Grimes shrugged, said something in Sioux to the chief, received an answer, and laughed.

"I *thought* it was a mite tight," he said to Francis. "Braid sent word ahead and asked Standing Bear to hold you if the Sioux found you. That's interesting since the Pawnee and Sioux are usually enemies—I guess he made a small peace with this village because catching you is so important. It would seem, Mr. Tucket, that you hurt his prestige —the black mare was Braid's personal mount. You sure do things in spades when you get loose, don't you? Taking a war leader's prize horse and all."

"*Me?*" Francis said. "*I* didn't take—"

"Now, now, Mr. Tucket. Just leave sleeping dogs alone. Old Standing Bear here thinks you must be one go-getter of a young warrior—bucking a big war leader and all. The Sioux think it's the funniest joke they ever heard, so why don't you just play along?"

All the time he had been talking to Francis, Mr. Grimes hadn't stopped looking and smiling at Standing Bear. He said something in Sioux, laughed again when Standing Bear answered, and nodded. "Raise your right hand, Mr. Tucket, the way standing Bear put up his."

Francis complied. "What did you say to him?"

"I told him you were the toughest fighter in the

Black Hills, that you were clever as the fox, that your heart was the heart of a mountain lion."

"You said all that about me?"

"Don't let it go to your head, Mr. Tucket. Indians don't take anybody's word on anything. Standing Bear says that he has a pretty tough boy in *his* village—"

"Oh, no . . ."

"Oh, yes, Mr. Tucket. It seems that your wrestling days aren't over yet." He turned and again said something to Standing Bear in Sioux.

"*Now* what did you tell him?" Francis asked.

"I just said that you weren't afraid of his boy, sort of."

"What do you mean, 'sort of'?"

"I said you were so sure of winning that you'd bet your rifle against a good pony and a set of buckskins."

"You did *what*?"

"Now don't get rattled, Mr. Tucket. Didn't those Pawnee boys teach you *anything* about wrestling?"

Francis's eyes scanned the crowd around them, looking for his possible competitor. "Yes, Mr. Grimes, the Pawnees *did* teach me something about wrestling."

"Well, then . . ."

"They taught me how to lose."

There were certain formalities that had to be observed before the match. Mr. Grimes had also brought the Sioux powder and lead. Francis watched him loosen the pack on one of the mules and remove a small keg. It couldn't have been more than a two-pound keg of powder, but the way the Sioux carried on, it could well have been two hundred pounds of triple-fine.

"They can't make it," Mr. Grimes told Francis. "So the only way they can get powder is to buy it, or get it as a gift, or steal it."

After distributing the powder there was more talk, and *still* more talk with Standing Bear. Francis almost went to sleep on the sorrel just listening to him. By this time all of the women had disappeared, the children had backed out of the circle of men, and Mr. Grimes seemed to be the only one listening to Standing Bear. The sun set while he was talking, the evening chill seeped into Francis's back, fires began to flare up around camp, the smell of buffalo cooking touched his nostrils, and *still* Standing Bear talked on.

Finally the Indian's voice stopped.

Mr. Grimes said something briefly in Sioux. The Indian replied, just as briefly. Mr. Grimes nodded, and turned to Francis. "Better get down and stretch a bit. Footloose is probably tired, too."

Francis slid off to the left and fell flat on his face. Both his legs were asleep.

Mr. Grimes muttered something in Sioux and all the warriors laughed.

"What did you say?" Francis asked.

"I told them you were saving your legs for the match."

"Well, if it hadn't been for old, old chief wind-bag there, my legs probably wouldn't have fallen asleep," Francis said grumpily, flexing his knees. "What was he talking about, anyway?"

"Well, he said that his lands reach to where it is always cold in the North, to where great waters end the land in the East, as far as all the ducks and geese and small birds fly in the cold of the end of the time of the sun—"

"Couldn't you cut it down a bit?" Francis asked. "I'm hungry."

"He said I could trap beaver on Sioux land. I thanked him. Then he said I was welcome. Then you fell off the horse—"

"All right. I understood that part. Now do I get a chance to eat before I lose my rifle?"

"Sure do, Mr. Tucket, prime buffalo. But I don't know as I like this negative thinking you're doing.

Cheer up a mite. They probably won't have but a midget against you. Why not think instead of owning a pony and some good buckskins?"

"I told you. I'm too good at losing."

Many things were stacked up against Francis's chances of winning the pony and buckskins. First, he was so hungry that when food was finally offered him, in the form of a large slab of hot buffalo meat, he ate until he could barely stand.

Then, too, two days hadn't completely worn out the stiffness in his legs, hips, and arms. And riding all day on the rounded haunch of the sorrel was hardly good training for wrestling. But the main obstacle was the Indian boy Standing Bear had picked to fight him. He was not a midget, he wasn't even small.

Francis stood on one side of a circle of braves. At his side, silent as usual, was Mr. Grimes. Across from him, and just inside the circle, was the Indian boy—a good thirty feet away.

He was about four inches taller than Francis, and he weighed about ten pounds more than Francis's one hundred and thirty-five pounds. And *he* hadn't spent the whole day riding on the sorrel.

"This is going to be murder," Francis whispered to Mr. Grimes. "Pure murder."

"I'm glad to see your confidence returning, Mr.

Tucket. Just a few minutes ago you were ready to give up. Now you're talking about killing him."

"I meant it the other way."

"Oh."

Francis looked across the circle. A large fire had been built to one side, and in the light he could see two men smearing something on the other boy.

"What are they doing to him?" Francis asked.

"Greasing him," Mr. Grimes answered. "And it's about time you took your shirt off."

"You mean I've got to do that?"

"No, you don't, Mr. Tucket. But the grease is going to make it harder to hold him than a wet catfish. It seems sensible to me that you'd sort of feel like doing the same thing."

Francis took off his shirt slowly, and Mr. Grimes covered him from the waist up with cold buffalo grease.

"It stinks," Francis complained.

"Don't say that too loud." Mr. Grimes chuckled. "They think it smells nice—like perfume."

More wood was thrown on the fire. Into the center of the circle stepped Standing Bear. He looked first at the Indian boy and seemed to snort something in Sioux. The Indian boy smiled and nodded. Standing Bear turned to Francis and snorted the same thing.

"Nod and grin," Mr. Grimes told him. "He's asking if you're ready."

Francis nodded and smiled, at least halfheartedly. He didn't really feel ready.

Standing Bear snorted some more, then spoke for a full five minutes.

"He's spouting the rules," Mr. Grimes said. "No biting, no hitting with the closed hand, no hitting with elbows or knees, humph, I didn't know that."

"Know what?"

"They allow kicking, but not with the toes. You have to curve your toes under and kick with the top of your foot. I guess you'd better take your boots off, Mr. Tucket. It wouldn't be fair to kick him with boots on."

Francis sighed resignedly and stooped to remove his boots. You might know they'd allow kicking, he thought. In truth, his boots were in tatters, but he felt odd barefoot.

"The rest of the rules are simple. You fight in the circle and stay out of the fire. If one of you falls or is thrown out of the circle, he gets thrown right back in and the fight goes on. The match ends when one of you says uncle—go." Mr. Grimes pushed Francis into the ring. The other boy had already entered from the other side.

Francis had wrestled a lot with the Pawnee boys, but he was hardly ready for this Sioux terror. With a loud scream the Indian boy, grinning widely, bounced across the clearing, spun lightly on his left leg, and placed the instep of his right foot dead in the center of Francis's still-undigested buffalo, hard.

It was a kick solid enough to drop an ox. Francis went down with his hands doubled over his stomach and a look of complete surprise on his face.

The Sioux boy landed on him like a cougar—a smiling cougar—and Francis's arm was twisted up his back and his face was mashed in the dirt.

A loud collective grunt issued from around the circle. It was going to be a quick fight, and the Sioux boy would have a fine new rifle. This white boy must have been terribly lucky in his dealings with the warrior Braid.

But Francis wasn't quitting, in spite of being out of breath, and having a mouth full of dirt. The arm lock looked wicked but it didn't hurt much. The Indian had failed to twist the arm enough to make it painful, and his mistake gave Francis much needed time to catch his breath. Then he used a trick he'd learned fighting with Max. He totally and completely relaxed, even the arm the Indian boy was holding. It worked. The Sioux wrestler felt the relaxing, and took the opportunity to change his hold.

It was what Francis had hoped for. With a mighty heave, he arched his back upward and threw the Sioux boy. Then he scrambled and landed, as hard as he could, on top of the boy, grabbed him around the neck and leg, and arched his back.

Another grunt came from the crowd. Maybe the fight would go on for a while yet. Francis heard Mr. Grimes on the side: "Well done, Mr. Tucket."

In almost any other match it would have been the end, for the Indian was all but paralyzed. Francis was on the boy's back, pulling him up at both ends, and he couldn't move.

But because of the grease, Francis couldn't maintain his hold. His hand slipped from the boy's neck, the Indian rolled over, and before Francis really knew what had happened, *he* was in the dirt.

This time Francis saw something new in the Indian's eyes. It was respect. Whereas he had jumped in screaming the first time, he now circled warily as the two regained their feet.

This was Francis's kind of fighting. The circling, looking for a weakness, was how he had learned to wrestle with white boys, and he noticed now a weakness in the Indian. He favored his right leg, the one Francis had twisted.

It was simple, then. All Francis had to do was feint to the left, then come in hard on the right.

The Indian boy would be slow that way, and Francis could get a neck hold, usually a match-stopper.

He feinted, and came in on the right, and the Indian boy was waiting for him. The weak leg had been only a bait, and Francis ran straight into a backhanded slap across his windpipe. It stopped his breathing again, and in the brief second that he hesitated, the Indian tripped him and used Francis's own hold—the reverse back arch. But there was a new twist. Instead of grabbing Francis around the neck, the Indian boy wrapped his fingers in Francis's hair, where there was no grease.

Still another grunt came from the crowd. Surely this would be the end of the match. The white boy couldn't move, and he couldn't get away. Some of the men even turned to go back to their lodges.

Francis *couldn't* move. He tried relaxing again, but the trick didn't work a second time. The Indian boy had him. It wasn't over, though, after all. Mr. Grimes leaned over from the edge of the circle and whispered: "Mr. Tucket, there's been talk of keeping you for Braid if you don't put up a better fight."

Francis didn't really believe him. It was the sort of thing Mr. Grimes would say just to get him riled. But he wasn't quite sure. The Indians did some funny things, and the thought of being sent back to Braid's camp was a terrible thought.

The Indian boy did something completely natural. He spat to get the dust out of his mouth. He didn't spit at or on Francis. But the spit landed about four inches in front of his eyes.

Francis saw pink, then red, and finally just fire. "Now you didn't have to go and do *that*," he yelled in English.

Later not even Mr. Grimes could tell how Francis got out of the hold. But get out of the hold he did, and within thirty seconds it was pretty clear to the crowd that one angry white boy was going to be a pony and a set of buckskins richer. His twist to get out of the hold knocked the Indian boy on his back in the dirt, and Francis, acting more from instinct than logic, made what Mr. Grimes later called a "goat leap." He jumped high in the air and, in an almost perfect swan dive, landed headfirst in the center of the Indian's stomach. Before the boy could regain his breath, Francis had flopped down and wrapped a scissors hold around his chest. Five seconds passed, then ten, and on the fifteenth second—Mr. Grimes had been counting—the Indian boy gasped his defeat. "That's enough, Mr. Tucket," Mr. Grimes called.

Francis released the boy immediately, no longer angry. He stood, and was surprised to see the Indian boy smiling up at him. On the spur of the moment, he leaned down and helped the still-gasping boy to get up. Around the circle there were many grunts of approval.

The Indian, as soon as his breathing settled down, began jabbering and laughing right away. Francis turned to Mr. Grimes.

"What's he saying?"

"He's saying it was well worth a pony to learn that new trick—he means that business of butting."

"Well, I'm glad he's happy," Francis said, laughing also. "And you can tell him that I learned something myself." He rubbed his back. "I may have won a pony, but I don't think I'll be riding it right away . . ."

# Chapter Ten

FRANCIS COULDN'T FIGURE OUT what to do. First he decided he wanted to stay on at Standing Bear's village, but then he found that he wanted to go on with Mr. Grimes. He had announced that he wouldn't be able to ride the pony for a while, but even so Mr. Grimes shook him awake at dawn the next morning.

"Come on, Mr. Tucket. There's a horse to be picked out, and we have to be on our way today. I swear, you sleep like a bear in winter."

Actually, there wasn't "a horse to be picked

out." Standing Bear had already done the picking—and true to Indian form, he had chosen the best pony in the corral.

She was a mare, and except for a white splotch of hair across her rump in the shape of a bird's wing, she was as black as the night. Standing Bear pointed to her with pride, smiled, and talked in Sioux to Mr. Grimes, who reported to Francis:

"He says he picked the pony for two reasons. One, she is good. Two, he hears you have a special liking for black mares. That's a joke and you should laugh."

Francis laughed.

Standing Bear talked some more.

"He says that she's been trained to hunt buffalo, and you should steer her with you knees. Nod and smile."

Francis nodded and smiled at the chief. It wasn't what he'd normally call a smiling morning. The sun wasn't warm yet, he hadn't gone to sleep until well past midnight, and he wouldn't have made it from his borrowed buffalo-robe bed to the corral if Mr. Grimes hadn't half dragged him. It seemed like all he had done since getting lost from the wagon train was get stiffer and stiffer.

Standing Bear acknowledged Francis's smile. He said something in Sioux.

"The pony is now yours," Mr. Grimes translated. "You can take her to your lodge—I guess he means where you slept last night, up by old Footloose."

The mare had a rope halter. Francis opened the corral gate and tried to grab the halter. She backed away, mixing in with some other ponies. He looked questioningly at Mr. Grimes. "How do I catch her?"

"You could run her down," the mountain man answered.

Francis gave him a nasty look. He could barely walk. At that moment, Mr. Grimes stepped into the corral with a horsehide rope. He flipped it out once, twice, and on the third try the noose fell over the mare's head. She stopped then at the feel of the rope on her neck and Francis hobbled up to her.

"Come on, Mr. Tucket," said the mountain man. "Climb on. Let's see how she takes to your weight."

"But, Mr. Grimes . . ." Francis complained. "I'm like a board. Give me a day or two to loosen up—"

"The best way to loosen up is to move a bit. Now climb on, before Standing Bear gets the thought you don't *like* his pony."

All the time he had been talking, Mr. Grimes

was fashioning from a second piece of rope a war bridle—a slipknot—around the mare's lower jaw.

In two tries, Francis managed to get his stomach over the back of the mare. He swiveled slowly until his legs hung down either side, then sat up, straight and stiff.

"Please, little pony," he said quietly, "remember my condition."

The strange part was that the pony *did* seem to understand. She didn't move quickly, or buck, or even tremble. And when Mr. Grimes handed him the end of the war-bridle rope, she walked toward the gate as meekly as a kitten.

It was Standing Bear who caused the trouble. Just as Francis and the pony came through the gate, the Sioux chief picked up a switch, moved behind the mare, and brought the switch down across the white splotch on her rump.

"Eeeeyah!" he yelled.

Actually, as Mr. Grimes pointed out later, Francis should have thanked the old chief, because what happened next loosened Francis in a hurry. But when that switch landed, he was too surprised to do anything but grab the mane of the black mare and close his eyes.

The mare became a dark comet, flashing through the middle of the awakening Sioux village like a fast wind. She knocked dogs out of the way and cleared cooking fires—jumping completely over one old woman kneeling over a pot of food. Through all this, Francis managed somehow to stay on her back.

When the mare reached the edge of the village, she stopped. Francis naturally kept on going, and finally *he* stopped with his face buried in a pile of still raw buffalo hides, but his troubles weren't over yet.

Coming hot on the heels of the little mare was the old woman, throwing rocks as fast as she could. Francis might be a good wrestler, and very smart to outwit Braid—but *nobody* jumped a horse over the old woman and her cook fire and got away with it.

Francis was quick to recognize disaster. Forgetting the mare, he made a dash back toward the safety of Mr. Grimes.

Mr. Grimes wasn't offering much safety. In fact, he wasn't offering anything. He and Standing Bear were wrapped over the top of the pole of the corral, laughing till tears ran down their cheeks.

"Keep it up, Mr. Tucket," the trapper said, as Francis ran by. "She's gaining on you."

Within a hundred yards Francis outran the old woman *and* her deadly rocks, and had also managed to kick away about ten of the camp dogs that had been snapping at his heels.

"Jokers," he mumbled, returning to the corral. The mare had walked back, looking as meek as she had before the wild ride. "Real jokers. I bet you get a lot of laughs out of throwing people off cliffs."

"Now, Mr. Tucket. Old Standing Bear just wanted you to know you were getting a pony that knew how to *run*." The mountain man was barely holding back laughter. "Besides, look how loose you are. You might as well be an old washrag . . ."

Francis nodded, looking down at himself. "And I look like one, too." But his anger weakened fast, and he smiled. The truth was he *had* loosened up.

"We'll stop early today," Mr. Grimes said. "I feel like some fresh antelope. And you can just carry your buckskins until then, so you can take a bath and start all new."

"I guess I will go with you," Francis said.

"Oh. Well, that depends, Mr. Tucket."

"On what?"

"On whether or not you can spend half a day riding downwind of me. You smell positively ripe from those hides."

# Chapter Eleven

NOON FOUND THE TWO RIDERS almost ten miles from the Sioux village. They were on the edge of a small stream, and Francis was only too glad when Mr. Grimes called a halt at a clearing.

"While you're stripping and taking a bath," the mountain man said, "I'll scout up ahead for some meat. There's a mesa about two miles on down where there's usually an antelope or two."

Francis nodded. They picketed the mules, and Mr. Grimes rode off.

Warm, with little or no breeze dancing through

the cottonwoods along the stream, it was truly a day made for swimming. Francis hit the water before the mountain man was out of sight. It was cold—spring fed in the hills somewhere—but the cold only made it all the more refreshing. He played around for a while, diving and splashing in a deep pool, and then scrubbed himself, using his shirt for a washcloth.

He climbed out of the stream and let the sun dry him as he lay on his back. He'd come a long way, he thought. Not in miles—he doubted that he was much closer to Oregon than when the Pawnees had captured him. But in time and knowledge, he'd come what seemed like a thousand years. He'd seen and done more than most people did all their lives, and he was only fourteen.

Presently he was dry, so he unwrapped the buckskins from one of the mule packs on the ground. They were plain, like Mr. Grimes's, and for the same reason. You could hide easier without a lot of colored beads to give you away. Actually, the buckskins had been made as a hunting suit for the boy he had wrestled. But they were new and hadn't been used yet and they fit Francis. The pants stopped at his ankles and fitted tightly to his hips and legs—following the principle of most Indian dress that a belt was good for nothing but cutting into your stomach when you bent over. The buckskin shirt had one set of fringes across the chest, was open at the throat, and its bottom fell almost a foot below his waist.

Mr. Grimes had thought ahead. There were no pockets in the buckskins, so he had procured for Francis a "possibles" sack to hold his flask and shooting equipment. This hung from a strap over his shoulder. Mr. Grimes had also picked up a pair of plain, ankle-high moccasins for him.

When Francis finished dressing, he looked nothing like the boy who had left St. Louis with the wagon train. The buckskins, even new, gave him the appearance of belonging more to the plains than to a settlement. His face was weathered and tan, and his hair—usually kept short by his mother—fell well below his ears.

He smiled, thinking of how he must look. It's too bad I don't have a mirror, he told himself. I probably look like a young Mr. Grimes. The idea strangely pleased him, and his smile widened as he carried his old clothes across the stream and buried them beneath a rotten log. He felt as though he was burying his past life.

He came back across the stream just as Mr. Grimes returned. He stopped the sorrel but did not dismount.

"Well, well, Mr. Tucket. I near mistook you for Jim Bridger. Probably would have if you didn't have brown hair. Jim is turning gray at the temples."

Francis felt a blush sweep over his face.

Mr. Grimes didn't miss it. "I was going to ask you to shoot an antelope for me—but now I don't know. A red face stands out just a mite, and you might scare them away. Howsomever, if you can pull yourself up on the mare one more time, maybe I can offer you a little sport."

Francis wheeled away, glad for the chance to do something. Mr. Grimes had the darndest way of *noticing* everything. Francis untied the mare, slipped her war bridle up tight, and with his rifle in one hand, jumped on her back. He took the reins in his other hand.

Mr. Grimes loped out of camp and Francis jabbed his heels into the mare's ribs to catch up. They rode side by side for twenty minutes, and then pulled up sharply on the edge of what Francis first took to be a cliff. Below them lay an immense level plain, as green as a hay field and twice as flat. Far out on the opposite side of the mesa Francis could see fifteen or twenty brown specks.

"Antelope, Mr. Tucket—or dinner, depending on how you look at it. I'd like you to shoot me a nice young buck—"

"From *here*?" Francis interrupted. "Why, they're at least two miles away."

"No-ah, Mr. Tucket. Not from here. You leave your mare up here with me and you climb down there. Then you hide and"—he dug in his saddle-bags and produced a piece of white cloth—"and wave this around for a while. It's an old Indian trick. They get curious about what you're wiggling and come to see what it is. *Then* you shoot one—and make sure he's a young buck. The old ones get old by running a lot—and that makes them tough."

Francis took the rag, slid off his horse, and looked down the cliff. Actually it was a steep slide, and could be descended fairly easily.

"Why are you sending me down?" he asked. "I've never shot an antelope . . ."

"That's just why, Mr. Tucket. That's just why. Now you'd better get going—we've only got about seven hours of daylight left." His voice was sarcastic.

Francis looked across the mesa at the antelope and shrugged. He was sure asked to do a lot of funny things. He started down the slide.

Going down was easy, and it wasn't as far as it looked. In fifteen minutes he was at the bottom, in back of a small rise, and lying on his stomach waving the rag in the air.

Francis couldn't see the antelope, and as the seconds turned into minutes, he wasn't completely sure that the antelope could see his waving rag. He raised carefully up on his elbows in the grass, but could see nothing. Turning, he looked up at the slide—hoping to see Mr. Grimes calling him back. Again, he saw nothing.

This is silly, he thought. I don't even know what's happening. The antelope probably ran off when I started down the slide. He raised up again. Still nothing. The grass was so high—it was like a wall around him. He started to get up, then fell back. The only thing keeping him still was fear of ridicule by the mountain man. Francis's orders had been specific: bring back a young buck. Getting up now could ruin it, but if the antelope *had* run off, it was stupid to stay down in the grass all afternoon. He waved the rag again.

That's when the thought hit him: this was all a joke. Mr. Grimes was a great one for jokes. Like sending him down to wave a rag around in a bunch of grass, telling him, of all things, that the antelope would *come* to him. And he'd fallen for it—lock, stock, and barrel. He shook his head. Wouldn't he ever learn?

Again he started to get up, and that's when he saw the antelope. There were two of them. One was quite a bit larger than the other. They were both males, and they had seen Francis move.

Even so, they stood still, absolutely still, not even blinking their eyes.

Francis took in a shallow breath, held it, and leapt to his feet, swinging up his rifle. But as fast as he was, the antelope were faster. In the seeming twitch of two white tails, they were doing close to forty miles an hour, dead away from Francis.

He fired, remembering at the last second to aim at the smaller buck. It wasn't a particularly difficult shot, but Francis was rattled, and he felt certain he'd missed. Yet the young antelope pitched forward and fell.

Francis couldn't believe his eyes. He reloaded at once and walked up to the buck. No second shot was needed; the antelope had been hit in the back of the head, just below the horn base. Francis grabbed him by the horns and began pulling him toward the slide. It was a long haul up, and he was sweating by the time he reached the top where Mr. Grimes was waiting.

"Well, Mr. Tucket. You seem to have done all right down there." The mountain man was grinning, and he fetched a knife from his saddlebag. He made one neat cut down the middle of the dead buck and removed the entrails. He saved the liver and heart and left the rest. "The coyotes will get the leavings. I wasn't sure how you'd do. You can tell a lot about a man when he's hunting antelope. It's the waiting. A lot of 'em get nervous and start fidgeting around. I've known grown men to actually stand up and scare 'em away."

Francis blushed again. "Well," he began, "I can see how something like that could happen. I mean, I almost . . ."

"Generally speaking, though," the mountain man went on as though he hadn't heard, "if a man makes it through once, you don't have to worry about him. He'll pull his load when the time comes, and that's all you can ask of any man."

"I *was* a little nervous," Francis said quietly.

"Well, it didn't hurt your shooting a lot," Mr. Grimes said, pointing toward the antelope's head. "I'd call that a right smart shot."

"I thought I'd missed."

Mr. Grimes nodded. "That happens sometimes. You never know till the smoke clears." There was something about his voice; he seemed to be talking around something. Francis caught it but didn't say anything. By that time Mr. Grimes had a small, smokeless fire going and had spitted the liver.

They ate it when its edge was just turning brown, cutting it in thin strips with Mr. Grimes's knife. Francis thought he had never tasted anything so rich and delicious.

After eating the liver, they returned to the camp by the stream and roasted a whole rear quarter of the buck. Then they spent most of the rest of the afternoon and evening cutting off slices and eating them. By dark, they had consumed close to twelve pounds of fresh meat. Mr. Grimes wrapped the rest in the main part of the antelope's skin and put it in one of the mule packs.

"It doesn't really get good for two or three days," he said. "And if it's well wrapped, it'll keep for more than a week."

They doused the fire and turned in early. Mr. Grimes was asleep as soon as his head hit the saddle.

Francis lay for a time thinking. There was something bothering him and it took him almost five minutes to realize what it was. Then he got up, quietly, and fished one of his rifle balls out of his "possibles" sack. He found the antelope's head where Mr. Grimes had left it, and in the moonless dark he turned it over and put the ball in the hole in the back of the head.

As he suspected, it was much too large a hole to have been made by his rifle. He dropped the head and returned to his bed. From now on, he thought, if that man says up is down and day is night, I'll believe him. Anybody who can make a shot like that, timing it to go off at the same time as another rifle, and hit a running antelope at two—no, three hundred yards, *can't* be wrong.

It was a comforting thought. Francis went to sleep smiling.

# — Chapter Twelve —

For a week they rode at an easy pace, saving the horses. Still they made close to a hundred miles before Mr. Grimes pulled up on the seventh evening.

"How do you feel about a little night riding, Mr. Tucket?" he asked.

"All right," Francis answered. "Why?"

"I sort of figured we could make Spot Johnnie's before turning in. Be nice to have a decent meal and sleep loose for a change."

Francis had no idea what he was talking about.

Not once had he mentioned this Spot Johnnie, but Francis decided not to question the mountain man.

"And we can grain the horses. Especially that mare of yours."

So they rode on. There was half a moon to furnish some light and sometime toward midnight Mr. Grimes pointed down at a light in a shallow valley.

"Spot Johnnie's," he said. "Now when we go in, you stay right out to the side of me—so's it doesn't look like you're sneaking. Okay?"

Francis nodded. They started down, angled across a flat meadow, and approached three log buildings. When they were still a hundred feet from the cabins, Mr. Grimes stopped.

"Ease that hammer down with your thumb, Spot," he said in a voice so low it was almost a whisper. "It's Jason Grimes."

Francis hadn't seen or heard a thing, so it was to his utter and complete surprise that the figure of a man arose suddenly beside him—not five feet away. He jumped.

"Dang it all, Jason," the man said, laughing and shaking his head. "You sure do ruin a man's fun. I was planning to let you get all the way up to the building, and then take that pretty hat of yours off, feather and all."

"That's why I stopped," Mr. Grimes answered..

"Got me a friend here who doesn't understand that kind of fun. He might just put a ball in your gizzard by mistake."

Rather than stop to talk, they kept on riding slowly, and Spot Johnnie walked between them. They pulled up at the front cabin. Light was leaking out around the hide windows, and in its glow, Francis got his first look at Spot Johnnie as Mr. Grimes introduced them. There wasn't really much to see. He could have been fifty or a hundred. He had a gray beard and long hair that hung well past his shoulders, and he wore beaded buckskins. There was no hat on his head; instead he wore a beaded headband to keep his hair out of his eyes. His rifle was a Hawkens. Francis liked him at once—there was a nice sound in his speech, a sort of easy confidence, and his eyes looked merry all the time.

"Figured you were always pretty much of a loner, Jason," Spot said, eyeing Francis. "How'd you come by picking up a cub?"

While Mr. Grimes explained about Francis, a boy of perhaps ten years of age came out of the cabin and took the horses around back. Then the three of them went inside.

At first, the inside of the cabin made Francis homesick. It was all so warm and cheerful. Two children were playing on the floor beneath a huge wooden table. There was a fire in the fireplace, although it wasn't at all cold. On one side of the cabin there were beds, arranged in bunk fashion, and all around the walls hung blankets and jackets and old moccasins. It looked like a home. And then, suddenly, he wasn't so homesick anymore—leaning over a big kettle near the fireplace was a large Indian woman.

It startled him to see the woman, not in a lodge, but in a house. She must be Johnnie's wife, he knew, but he caught himself staring just the same. She made him think of the Pawnee village.

As if reading his mind, Spot Johnnie suddenly spoke up. "And this is my family, Mr. Tucket. That's my wife, Bird Dance, over by the fire, and under the table are Jared and John, and the boy you saw outside was Clarence."

The boys under the table didn't look out. But Bird Dance turned from the fire, smiled, and said in perfect English, "How do you do. I'm sure you must be hungry after riding all day. Please sit down and have some stew and biscuits."

Francis managed to hide his surprise. He smiled —he liked her at once—and turned to the table. Mr. Grimes was already sitting there with Spot.

"How've you been making out, Spot?" Mr. Grimes asked.

"Fit," came the answer. "Pure fit and prime. Got me a full warehouse of furs and a wagon or two due next week from St. Louis to pick 'em up. Been a good year, and it might be a better one next. And you?"

"So-so," Mr. Grimes answered. "Found me a new hole last winter that I figure on trying before snow comes. What you giving for near-prime pelts this year, Spot?"

"You mean in money or trade?"

"Money."

"Two dollars—if it's a big one."

"Seems kinda low . . ."

"I might go three, if I knew the trapper and knew he wasn't out just to give me his culls."

"Fair enough. You got yourself a deal. Now, about provisions. You got everything?"

"All but sugar. It's running three dollars a pint —*wholesale*. So I've put off ordering it, hoping it would go down a mite."

"Fine. We'll need the usual. Your oldest boy can put it together tomorrow. In the meantime, I've got some questions that need answering."

They had to stop talking to eat the stew and biscuits, which proved to be worth at least a ten-day ride. Francis ate four bowls of stew and half a dozen fresh biscuits before Bird Dance cleared the table.

"Now," Spot said, lighting a pipe and propping his legs on a small three-legged stool. "What kind of questions you got, Jason?"

"About Indians, Spot. There's something downright funny going on and I can't pin it down. Take Braid, for instance—"

"*You* take him," Spot cut in. "I've had enough of that skunk to hold me for all my days."

"What happened?"

"Nothing—to me. But Braid's thinking of taking over the whole Pawnee nation, way it looks, and for nothing but war. He was here a while back asking for things—powder, mostly, and caps. Only he didn't ask for 'em the way a man might. He said, 'The *Pawnee* want powder and the *Pawnee* want caps,' just like he was talking for the whole tribe. I don't like it."

"I thought he was getting a little feisty," Mr. Grimes said.

"It's not just things like taking this boy," Spot said, gesturing toward Francis. "That's bad enough. But Braid's also been raiding. There've been two wagon trains through here, and they both lost some people to Pawnees being led by Braid."

"Those two trains," Francis said, interrupting, "did any of the people in them mention losing a little girl?"

Spot scratched his head. "No . . . mostly they didn't want to talk about those they'd lost, so they didn't talk about the Indians much at all. One woman—I think it was a brown-haired woman—asked me if the Indians always killed captives. She was pretty broken up about losing a boy—"

"I'm that boy," Francis said. "She's my mother." He sighed. Then at least his mother was alive, and most likely his father. "She didn't mention a girl named Rebecca?"

"Nope—at least not that I recollect. But as I said, the people mostly didn't talk about the raid."

They were silent for a while, thinking. Francis was imagining the muscled figure of Braid nestled just over his rifle's sights.

"Braid's stupid," Spot continued after a minute or two. "He's talking about making a clean sweep, or so I hear, and driving all whites from Pawnee territory."

"That's a bit strong," Mr. Grimes said. "He might hit a train or two, but I don't think he'll bother us—I mean you and me. It would only hurt him to put us under—he'd get no more trade."

"All the same," Spot said, "if I were you, and I knew Braid was around somewhere, I'd make sure I had my shoulder blades covered by a tree."

Mr. Grimes shrugged. "I do that anyway—just

natural. But I don't like this other thing much. If there's anything worse than one mad Pawnee, it's a hundred mad Pawnees. Braid's stirring up a war, maybe. Not so good . . ." His voice trailed off.

And that finished any talk for another thirty minutes or so, while they ate and drank *still* more. Francis had thought he was full, but he was fast changing his eating patterns. He was learning that when you *can* eat, you eat. It might be a couple of days before you got a chance to eat again.

"Just one question," Mr. Grimes said around a mouthful of biscuit. "What's the story on the Crows? I spent a week coming across their stomping grounds and didn't see a one. Usually I get shot at at least once."

"I don't know," Spot answered. "But there's been word they found a big herd of buffalo and spent the summer living in back of the herd. I also heard they've broken up a bit—too many war chiefs or something—and that there's a bunch of small bands out, just taking what they can get when they can get it. But you know the Crows: if you see 'em, more'n likely you're going to have to fight 'em." Spot leaned back and sighed. "Enough of that—I think it's time for a game. Or are you scared? I figured you'd probably given up—seeing how bad I whipped you last time."

"*Whipped* me?" snorted Mr. Grimes. "Did you hear that, Mr. Tucket? This old spot-head thinks he whipped me. Waugh! Drag out the plank and we'll see who whips who in this pond."

"Stakes?" Spot asked, laughing.

"One prime pelt—which I haven't got—against three pints of sugar—which you haven't got. Suit you?"

"Why not? I can always use another pelt."

"Ho—you sure are the one for talk. Where's that plank?"

Spot turned and fetched a flat board from the wall. The board was about two feet long, and at either end a heavy leather thong was lashed. Francis could make neither head nor tail of it, even when Spot put the board down in front of Mr. Grimes and seated himself opposite. The children had been put to bed, but Spot's wife came over from a stool by the fire. She was smiling, and kept smiling while she took their right arms and placed them on the board. When the arms were in such a position that the back of Mr. Grimes's hand was against the back of Spot's, she brought the leather thongs up and around and lashed their elbows in place. Now their arms could move neither forward nor backward, nor up at the elbow.

The two men, with their hands still back-to-back, hooked thumbs. Mr. Grimes looked at Spot, Spot returned the look, they both nodded, and the woman said, "Go!"

It didn't seem to be much of a match at first. The object of the contest was to twist your arm and drag your opponent's thumb down to the board by twisting *his* arm. At the start, Spot got the jump. Mr. Grimes didn't stop him until his thumb was almost mashed into the board, and then only by an effort that made all the cords in his neck stand out.

They hung like that for a long time, grinning at each other, their breath coming in rasps. Then, ever so slowly, Mr. Grimes started to push Spot's thumb back up. The thumbs stopped again when they were straight up, swung back and forth for a period of ten seconds, then suddenly plunged down until Spot's thumb touched the board.

"Ahh!" he said. "Where'd you get all *that*?"

"Been practicing," Mr. Grimes answered. "Figuring the way you whipped me last time . . ."

"Ha! Woman?" Spot called. "Fetch this badger three pints of brown sugar—not that he earned it, understand, but a deal is a deal."

"Seems there's a snake around here somewhere," Mr. Grimes said, grinning. "I thought you didn't have any sugar?"

"Nope—said I didn't *order* any," Spot answered.

"Lots of difference. Besides, you trying to tell me you don't have a single pelt out there in your pack somewheres?"

"Nope—got *three* I saved from last year."

Francis stared at them. The betting didn't make any sense. They both bet something they said they didn't have, but which they really did have. He was going to ask about it, but just then Mr. Grimes suggested getting some sleep and Francis, who had been sitting with the warm glow of the fire on his back and an extremely full stomach, realized that if he so much as blinked, he would be asleep.

He staggered to the warm corner by the fire, where Spot told him to go, and was soon dead to the world.

# — Chapter Thirteen —

MR. GRIMES AND FRANCIS stayed with Spot Johnnie for three days. They had meant to leave sooner, but things kept happening. First there was a joke shooting match between Mr. Grimes and Spot —a joke match because neither of them really tried to win. All they did was trick shooting; kind of show-off stuff, Francis thought. Like Spot throwing a piece of mud in the air, then stooping to pick up his rifle and shooting the mud before it hit the ground. And Mr. Grimes shooting a big rock over five hundred yards away, hitting it three times in a row.

Then the shooting match led to a wrestling match, and the wrestling match led to a giant dinner and warm sun to lie around in and a swim down in the creek by the stable, and before Francis really thought about it at all, three days had disappeared. On the morning of the fourth day, they rose early, packed the mules, and started out.

They were about half a mile from the buildings when they saw the wagons. Mr. Grimes saw them first, as usual.

"Farmers, Mr. Tucket," he said, pointing back past Spot Johnnie's place. Two wagons were visible coming down into the valley, crawling along. They were a good three miles away, but Francis could make out the men walking alongside the oxen. "It could be your chance—if they're going to Oregon. Most likely they are."

Francis didn't understand at first. He wasn't really thinking of himself in connection with wagons. And when he finally caught the mountain man's meaning, somehow it made him feel sad. Still, he nodded. "I guess so—that is, if they wouldn't mind taking a boy along."

"I think they'd probably be happy to have that extra gun," Mr. Grimes said, "especially if Braid's going to do some kicking up."

There was a long moment. The morning sun

caught the mare's mane and made it look almost blue. And how would you like to slow down to ten miles a day, little mare? Francis found himself thinking. How would you like to eat oxen dust and be tied with other horses at night? He looked again at the wagons. There were five showing now—five plodding wagons settled into the ruts across the prairie.

And he didn't want to be with them; not with the dust and the slow wagons and all the people carrying punch bowls. There was more to it now—more than if he were just another train boy. He knew more. He knew Indians, and how to shoot, and how to wrestle—

"You sure do seem to be in powerful thought, Mr. Tucket," Mr. Grimes cut in. "A man would think you're having trouble making up your mind . . ."

There was that, too, Francis thought. How can I just keep going with the mountain man? Mr. Grimes has his own way of life. It's a wild and exciting life, but is it the kind of life for me—for the rest of my life?

Francis shook his head in bewilderment. Then, slowly, he turned toward the wagons.

"Of course"—Mr. Grimes stopped him—"you've got to figure those people are maybe pretty dumb. They won't make Oregon anyways—at least not *this* winter. Here it is early fall, and they're only this far. Way I figure it, they'll be spending winter about halfway there—somewhere in the west part of Dakota Country, where it gets cold."

Francis looked at him. Was the mountain man telling him to stay? Or was he just ridiculing the "farmers" for being dumb?

"Now me," Mr. Grimes continued, his face still blank, "I figure on spending my winter not far from here—where the snow won't get *too* much higher'n a horse and I don't have to worry about much except a few stray Crows. If I get lucky and fill out on beaver fast, I just might come down here and spend the winter with Spot."

"Are you trying to tell me that I'd be better off staying with you through the winter than I would be if I joined that particular wagon train?"

"No-ah, Mr. Tucket, that isn't quite right. I'm not trying to tell you anything. It's your mind, you make it up . . ."

Francis nodded.

". . . but I'd hate to think I plucked you from Braid just so's you could turn out dumb."

Francis felt warm all over—warmer than the morning sun could have made him feel. He hefted his rifle, turned the little mare once more and almost—but not quite—laughed in relief. The truth was he didn't want to leave and it had been handled for him.

Mr. Grimes clucked at the sorrel and moved ahead. He didn't look back—not at the wagons or at Francis. He rode straight, his derby and feather aimed dead ahead.

Francis caught up. He didn't look back at the train either. It might as well not have been there. He felt that he should thank the mountain man, but what could he say? A straight "thank you" would probably only make him snort.

"The way I figured it, Mr. Grimes," he said finally, his eyes straight ahead, "if a guy's gotta spend a winter, he might as well spend it the best way he can . . ."

The mountain man smiled.

# — Chapter Fourteen —

Two days away from Spot Johnnie's, Mr. Grimes stopped on the edge of a deep canyon.

"From here on, Mr. Tucket, we'll see no more people—Indians or otherwise."

Francis nodded, and believed him. They wound down a narrow trail to the bottom of the canyon. It was a dark place, with sheer walls and a thick forested floor, and in the bottom was a narrow stream. Mr. Grimes put his sorrel in the middle of this, and instructed Francis to do the same with his mare.

"We go up it awhile," he said, "and that's how we make *sure* we don't see any people."

That "awhile" proved to be two days long. When they camped at night, Mr. Grimes didn't allow a fire. And in the mornings, when they got ready to leave, he went around brushing out signs of their horses and making the campsite look as though they'd never been there.

At the end of the second day, they moved away from the stream. The canyon had widened into a valley more than ten miles across, and Mr. Grimes headed toward the right—or northern—edge. The forest was much thicker, the ground softer, but still he allowed no traces of their presence to remain at any campsite. His sharp eyes missed nothing, and he left no trail. Where the horses' hooves sank into the ground, he painstakingly pushed sticks under the depressions to raise them. When a twig was broken, he rubbed dirt on the broken end to make it look old.

"It's still pretty plain," he explained to Francis, standing over a hoof mark that Francis couldn't see even though he knew where it lay. "But in a couple of days, the best Kiowa tracker in the world couldn't find us—and neither will another trapper."

"Why are you being so careful?" Francis asked. He was tired of going slow.

"You heard the reasons just now, Mr. Tucket. One is the trappers. It's not that I'm greedy, at least no more than the next. But there's just enough beaver where we're headed to keep a man going, so long as he doesn't clean 'em out in one season. I wouldn't clean 'em out—and neither would another *good* trapper . . ."

"Then what are you worried about?"

"Every man who traps beaver isn't all that thoughtful. We come up here and take out a catch, and if somebody follows us who doesn't think about next season, he might clean out the beaver—lock, stock, and prime pelt. So I'm careful. I'm not worried, Mr. Tucket, just careful."

"All right, that's one reason. What's the other?"

"Indians; Crows, to be exact. We're on the edge of their country, and they're kind of unpredictable. We're going to be spread up and down the canyon, traps all over, and if they find out we're up here, they can make it mean for us. So we're careful about them, too. Any *other* questions, Mr. Tucket?"

"No, sir."

When they finally got where they were going— a shallow meadow about three miles wide and ten miles long, leading away from the canyon—Francis could see the reason for caution. Down the middle of the meadow was a long string of beaver ponds, one joined to the next by a short neck of water. Francis knew nothing of beaver, but he guessed there were probably hundreds of them.

Mr. Grimes led the way up the meadow, and it took them one whole day of slow riding to get to the northern end, and the sound of the beaver, slapping their tails against the water, stayed ahead of them all the way.

"Well, Mr. Tucket," the mountain man said, when they finally stopped, "I make it out to be a pretty fair season for us. What say we make a home?"

First they had to build a house, and although it wasn't much more than a large lean-to, it seemed like a house by the time the roof was finally finished. Mr. Grimes gave Francis an ax from one of the mule packs, and he cut all the poles for the lean-to while the mountain man did what he called the "count" on the beaver stream. It took Francis the better part of a week to cut enough long timbers for the walls and roof, and during that time, he saw Mr. Grimes only in the evenings and early mornings.

At first it didn't bother him. There was a job to be done, and Francis, with his two good arms, was better equipped to do it. But by the fourth day he felt irritated because it seemed to him that the mountain man was just taking a vacation while he put up the house. Over morning coffee, he said, "What are you doing out there all day? Not that I really care, understand. But a guy has to learn—"

Mr. Grimes snorted and then sipped his coffee. "Seems to me you *ought* to care. I mean, I'm out there just resting on my stomach along the creek while you slave away on our castle. *I'd* care. But if I tell you, will you promise not to laugh?"

"Sure."

"I'm counting the grown beaver in each pond, one at a time."

Francis didn't laugh, because he didn't understand. "Why are you counting them?" he asked.

"So when we start taking 'em, we'll know how many we can take out of each pond without ruining it. Of course, trapping all the beaver in the world won't help us if we don't have a house to dry the pelts in . . ."

Francis didn't ask any more questions. Instead he got the house up, back in the trees along the meadow, and Mr. Grimes finished his count just in time to help with the last poles on the roof. Then they put up a small pole corral for the horses and mules, and when that was finished, they moved in. Now, Mr. Grimes explained, there was nothing to do but wait.

"It's like this, Mr. Tucket," he said. "There are

two times to trap beaver. In late fall and early spring. In the fall, you catch them when their coats are turning prime—getting ready for the cold. In the spring, you catch them before they lose their winter pelts. Now I prefer to catch them in the fall —and I'll let you guess why."

Francis thought for a minute, then shrugged. "I don't know. Is the market better?"

"True, but that's not really why. If you take a mother beaver in the spring, you might take her just after she's had young. You not only trap the mother, but kill the young because you take away their milk. If I take her in the fall, her babies—the kits— haven't even started yet and I only kill one beaver—"

"But what's the difference?" Francis interrupted. "I mean, she's still gone, and she still can't have the kits."

"Right. But beaver mate up in the fall, and they mate for life. If I trap a female in the fall, the male that would have mated with her goes on and finds another. It all works out, Mr. Tucket, it all works out."

Francis thought about it, nodded, then asked, "When do we get started?"

"About two weeks after the first cold snap, when their pelts firm up. I figure down here, in the bottom of this canyon, we ought to see some cold before long."

It was true, Francis knew. Most of the aspens had taken on a golden hue, and the scrub oaks were already losing some leaves. The days were still warm but the nights had a way of turning cold, and moving out in the morning from beneath the warm buffalo robe Mr. Grimes had given him got harder each day. Also, the fact that there was little to do made it hard to get up.

Francis found you either had too much to do, or nothing. When there was nothing, his thoughts turned always to his mother and father, and he wondered how they were doing in Oregon. He missed them, but for some strange reason, he missed Rebecca more. She had always been sort of a nuisance to him, following him when he wanted to be alone, asking him dumb questions—this made him smile when he thought of some of the questions he asked Mr. Grimes—and yet he missed her.

Finally the cold weather came. One morning, Francis crawled out of his buffalo robe and the world was a land of crisp whiteness. Frost covered everything. Mr. Grimes was already up, humming —of all things—while he sharpened his skinning and fleshing knife.

"To work, Mr. Tucket," he announced. "Our holiday's over."

Now they had just two weeks to cut enough bait sticks—short pieces of green aspen—store them along the stream, plan the trap line, make skin-drying hoops of the same green aspen, and sort and "purify" the traps.

And with all this work to be done, company arrived. Francis, for a change, saw them first, but only because Mr. Grimes was out cutting bait sticks. Francis was in front of the hut, lashing some drying hoops together with thongs of fresh rawhide from a deer that had wandered into their camp. Across the meadow came four horses. Two of them were being led, and two of them were being ridden. They were quite far away, too far to identify the riders as anything but men, too far away to allow any wild guessing. But even so, Francis made a wild guess and decided they were Crows.

All of this took just five seconds. On the sixth second, he was in the house, looking out through an opening in its side. His cheek lay against the stock of his rifle, the hammer was back, a percussion cap covered the nipple, the barrel was charged, and his finger was on the trigger.

The two men rode, as though drawn by an invisible cord, straight toward the cabin.

# Chapter Fifteen

WHEN THE MEN and horses were still some two hundred yards away, they stopped. One man dismounted and studied the soft ground of the meadow. He turned and said something to the man who was still mounted, and then swung back into his saddle. From the way he dismounted and mounted and the way they rode, Francis now realized that they weren't Indians. More than likely, especially since they had pack horses, they were trappers.

He eased up from the rifle, but only a little.

They could still be up to no good, and it didn't hurt to be ready. He watched for some sign of their intentions—and got it when they were just a hundred yards from the house.

One of them slipped his rifle from its buckskin case and laid the gun across his lap. The other then did the same, and Francis could feel the hair on his neck rise. Nobody dropping in for a friendly visit would make a point of coming armed and ready.

His cheek went back to the stock of his rifle. He wanted to run out back and get the mountain man, but he didn't know how far he'd have to go. And if he left the pack mules and all their equipment alone, even for a minute, everything might be gone by the time they got back.

No, he couldn't leave. There was nothing else to do—he would simply have to stay and try to bluff them out.

Approximately thirty yards from the house, the two men stopped. They were about twenty feet apart, sitting their horses loosely, but both of their rifles were aimed in the general direction of the lean-to. Francis could make out their features easily. One of them was rather short and bearded. The other was lean, also bearded, fairly tall, and it was he who leaned forward in the saddle and called:

"Yo, the house! Anybody home?"

Francis said nothing. He watched.

"Up there! The house!" the man called again. "Anybody home?"

They were getting uneasy. Francis could tell by the way the lean one angled his rifle upward as he talked. Even at that range, the muzzle looked like a cave. Might as well say something, he thought, before they just fire away.

"Who are you, and what do you want?" he called, trying to make his voice sound gruff and older.

"Name's Bridger," answered the lean one. "Jim —to people who come into the light. This here's my partner, Jake Barnes. And all we want is a little hospitality."

Sure, thought Francis—you're Jim Bridger and I'm Kit Carson. If you really are Jim Bridger, you sure wouldn't just amble blind into a trap like this. How do you know I'm not an Indian? You could have been following anybody's tracks.

"You lost your tongue in there?" the lean one yelled again. "I said that the name's Bridger . . ."

"I heard you," Francis answered. The man was lying. He was sure of it. He brought up the front sight of his rifle. It made him feel funny, aiming at a man. But he'd been caught off guard once—by Braid—and it wasn't going to happen twice. "I'm not sure I believe it. Can you prove you're Jim Bridger?"

"*Prove?* What's to prove? I'm just sitting here, ain't I? I said I was Bridger, didn't I? What more do you need?"

There it was. He said he was Bridger, but Francis was positive he was lying, and so they were stalemated. There was nothing to do but wait for Mr. Grimes.

"If you're *really* Jim Bridger," Francis called, "you won't mind just sitting there for a while—"

"What for?"

"Until—until somebody comes who can tell me if that's the truth."

"And what if I decide to ride off? Or come plowing *at* you?"

"I've got a gun on you."

"I figured *that.*"

"I'll use it."

"Maybe. When's this man coming?"

"Soon."

"What's his name?"

"You don't need to know."

"All right. I'll wait for a spell. But if he doesn't come soon, and I mean *soon*, you better figure on using that gun."

The minutes dragged. The sun got hotter, and flies began buzzing around the horses.

He had no idea how long Mr. Grimes would be gone, Francis realized. Somehow, half an hour crawled past. It was the longest half hour of his life. And Bridger—or the man who said he was Bridger —didn't help any. If he had gotten nervous, or started to move around, Francis would have felt better. But he didn't. He just sat his horse—cool, calm, waiting. And the smaller man did the same.

Forty minutes passed, fifty, then an hour was gone. And that was enough.

The lean one moved. He straightened in his saddle and called. "Time's up. I haven't got ten years to waste. Now I'm gonna turn around and ride out of here. My partner's coming with me. I don't think you'll touch anything off—but if you do, you'll get only one of us. And the other one will get you, just as sure as winter's coming."

This was it then; the test. Francis reset his sight. It would be suicide to let the man go. He and his partner might ride off a mile, turn around, and sneak back to kill them at night.

Even as the lean one turned his horse, and the partner followed suit, Francis knew he couldn't do it. It was one thing to shoot somebody who was attacking you, but to just come out and shoot a man because you thought he might be lying—

"Jim Bridger!" the voice was loud, cutting through Francis's thoughts. It came from the side of the clearing he couldn't see, but he knew that voice. It belonged to Jason Grimes. "You figuring on riding out of here without taking a cup of coffee with an old friend?"

The two men stopped their horses. "I figured you was up here somewhere," the lean one said. "And to be downright truthful about it all, I *did* stop for some coffee. I figured old Jason Grimes was as good as the next for a free spot of java. But before you get all relaxed about us stopping for a while, maybe you ought to know there's a two-legged terror in that shack over there with a gun on us. Shouldn't we ask *him* about stopping?"

"What . . . ?" Mr. Grimes turned to the building. "Oh . . . how long you been here?"

"Seems like ten years," Jake Barnes said. "Maybe an hour, really."

"And Mr. Tucket kept you at bay all that time?"

"Who?" Jim Bridger asked.

"Mr. Tucket." Mr. Grimes turned again to the building. "Mr. Tucket, come on out here and meet the men you've been holding."

So it *was* Bridger. Francis felt like an idiot. Still,

he couldn't stay out of sight forever. He stepped out of the doorway and walked toward the horses.

"Why, it's ain't nothing but a cub." Jim Bridger snorted. "Jake, we've been sitting here worried about a *cub*."

That broke the ice, and the two men dismounted, grinning at Francis.

"Where'd you get him?" Bridger asked.

While Francis made a fire, Mr. Grimes told the two mountain men about him. By the time the explanation was finished, the coffee was ready, and they all sipped it and chewed on venison. After that, the men smoked and Francis sat quietly thinking. There was something bothering him. Finally he could hold it no longer.

"Mr. Bridger," he asked, "how did you find us?"

"Why, we just followed your trail, boy. Easy as following a herd of buffalo. But don't worry. We covered tracks coming in—ours *and* yours."

Francis looked at Mr. Grimes. He was smiling.

"Ho!" he exclaimed. "You're feeding Mr. Tucket a nettle. Bad for his liver. The fact is, Mr. Tucket, there's another meadow like this up a ways that belongs to Mr. Bridger. I found this one last year about the same time he found his. We met coming out, so he knew I'd be here about now. Unless I miss my guess, he's on his way up there now."

Bridger nodded. "Caught, cold turkey. Boy, never lie in front of Jason Grimes. You'll lose every time. Say"—he turned to Mr. Grimes—"how are you and Braid getting on lately?"

That triggered off another round of talk. They covered the Indian tribes—Pawnee, Sioux, and finally, while Francis made another pot of coffee, the Crow.

"You might be extra careful when you go out," Bridger told Mr. Grimes. "We saw some fresh Crow sign down at the mouth of the valley. Whole tribe—man, woman, child, and dog. Looking for a wintering ground, I reckon, so they probably won't bother you. But I don't think they'd pass up a chance at those rifles if they ran across you."

Mr. Grimes nodded. "The Crows and the weather—you can't tell about either one. But I think I'd take a blizzard to a Crow any day . . ."

Francis listened to them intently. His stomach was full of warm coffee and jerky, evening was coming down, the fire felt good, and he was in the company of a living legend—Jim Bridger. What more could he ask? Why think about such unpleasant things as snowstorms or Indians at a time like this? Better just to listen, because someday he would want to tell his family everything about this meeting with the fabulous Jim Bridger.

# —— Chapter Sixteen ——

BRIDGER AND HIS PARTNER pulled out early the following morning. Before they were even out of sight, Mr. Grimes said, "Back to work. We lost a good part of a day, Mr. Tucket, and we couldn't afford it."

He walked out of camp to get more bait sticks, and Francis went back to work on the drying hoops.

Actually, they were fairly simple to make. He took a slim piece of springy willow or aspen, eight feet long, and bent it into a circle about three feet across. Then he lashed the ends together with wet, green rawhide that seemed to shrink when it dried and made the two ends of the willow become one piece. After a beaver was skinned, the hide was put in this hoop and with lacing around the sides pulled toward the edges so that when it was dry it would be a hard plate of hide with fur on one side.

Mr. Grimes wanted two hundred of these hoops. Francis ran out of rawhide that evening on the fiftieth hoop. He told Mr. Grimes about it.

"Well, Mr. Tucket, the woods are full of deer and you've got a rifle. Seems like a fairly simple problem to me . . ."

So the next morning Francis walked quietly through the pine glades, glad of a chance to get away from the lean-to. Not three hundred yards from the house, he stopped on the edge of a small clearing, just to enjoy the morning, and found himself facing a nice three-point buck.

There was the deer, and there was Francis, with perhaps fifty feet between them. He raised his rifle, aimed at the buck's shoulder, and squeezed the trigger. The little Lancaster cracked sharply—higher and faster sounding than Mr. Grimes's big bull gun —and the deer took two steps forward, sagging as he walked, and fell. Francis reloaded, as cool as though he were shooting buffalo chips, and aimed at the deer's head. He fired again and it was over.

He started forward, then, remembering what he'd been taught, stopped and reloaded again.

And he suddenly started shaking all over, as though he had a chill. He couldn't even walk right and had to sit down. It was silly, but he was nervous about the deer—nervous and rattled. He didn't know what it was—he just had to sit down for a minute.

When he got up, it was as though it had never happened. He grabbed the deer by its rack and dragged it back to camp. There he skinned it and cut the wet hide into strips half an inch wide. By late afternoon, he was again making hoops, the incident all but forgotten.

Mr. Grimes came in at about four o'clock, his arm full of sticks, and Francis told him about the deer.

"Buck fever, Mr. Tucket—or, as some call it, gun jaw. Most people get it the first time they think about shooting anything bigger than a rabbit. Usually it only hits a man once or twice—and then only if he's had time to think about it. You're lucky."

"Why?"

" 'Cause some get it *before* they shoot. They can't even pull the trigger. I watched one man—and this is pure gospel—stand up against a bear that didn't like him at all, and all he did was aim his rifle and say, 'Bang.' "

"You mean he didn't shoot?"

"Nope. Didn't even draw his hammer. If I hadn't been there to kill the bear, that man would have been nothing in a second or two. Unless the bear could understand English. Hah!"

But Francis couldn't laugh at the joke. He remembered shaking all over, and he hoped that when the time came—*if* it came—for him to face something dangerous, he wouldn't do something dumb like saying "Bang."

By the end of the week the hoops were finished, and Mr. Grimes had gathered all the bait sticks. Next came the traps. There were fifty of them—big, double-springed traps with bait-pan trips. They all had to be smoked over a low fire of green aspen to take away the smell of man. So Francis was put in charge of the smoking fire, working ten traps at a time. They were hung over the fire with a long pole and taken off with a forked stick. Once smoked, they could not be touched by human hands.

After the traps were smoked, they were hung three to a stick, so that Mr. Grimes could carry them to the individual ponds without touching them.

About halfway through the second week of

working, as if on demand, cold settled in and held for a few hours. The next morning, Mr. Grimes reported that they'd start trapping that day.

"There'll be ice on the ponds," he said. "That makes it easier. The beaver sort of give themselves away by cutting holes in the ice. All you have to do is drop a trap in the hole and wait. They come right into it. Even if the ice melts off—and it probably will before the day is out—they still use the same place. Sort of like you'd use a hallway in a house."

While he talked, he was working, lashing bait sticks and trap sticks to a long aspen pole. This pole, with twenty-one traps, he handed to Francis. Then he made another one, just like the first.

They rode out toward the first pond well before noon. Francis was almost excited. All this labor, and now he would actually see what they'd been working toward. And, he thought, just maybe, the backbreaking labor would slack off a bit.

They dismounted at the first pond, and sure enough, despite the fact that it was turning out to be a fairly warm day, the pond was covered by a thin layer of ice. At one point, near the dam of sticks and mud along the bank, there was a broken, jagged hole about two feet across. In this hole the mountain man placed one trap, set, on a pole that angled down into the water and stuck in the mud on the bottom. The trap was well under water and above the trap he tied several bait sticks to the pole with rawhide.

"But won't the beaver see the trap?" Francis asked.

"He'll see it, all right," came the answer, gruff and short. "But he won't take *notice*, Mr. Tucket. At least not till he steps in the trap. Old Daddy Beaver goes more by his nose than his eyes, and if you smoked these traps right, he'll think that piece of iron is another hunk of wood."

So it went, pond by pond. It was nearly dark when they finished the fourteenth pond. Francis had done nothing but hand out traps and bait sticks, and yet he was exhausted—and more than ready to head back for the house and a warm fire.

Mr. Grimes headed back to the first pond.

"They're good enough to let us trap 'em, Mr. Tucket," he said. "The least we can do is keep up."

"You mean there'll be one trapped already?" Francis asked.

"More than one, or I miss my guess."

And of course, he was right. The first pond yielded one, same with the second, nothing in the third, one in the fourth and so on. By midnight or so, with Francis all but falling off his mare, they had eleven prime beaver.

Mr. Grimes had reset all the traps, and although he didn't say anything, Francis was living in a quiet horror that they might start all over again, and *again*, and just keep going until they had two hundred beaver.

But the trapper headed his sorrel back to camp. Once there, after the fire was going and coffee started, he went to work skinning the beaver. And Francis, who could think of nothing but crawling into his big buffalo robe and forgetting everything, was told to stay up and stretch the hides on the hoops.

By eight in the morning—with no sleep—they had finished the twenty-six beaver they had trapped.

"We sleep till noon, Mr. Tucket," the mountain man announced. "Then we start over. And we've got more work now, because after this haul, we'll have to move the traps."

Francis didn't hear the last words about more work. He was asleep.

At noon he didn't want to get up. He wouldn't have wanted to rise with fifteen hours of sleep, but with just four, he almost *couldn't* get up. Mr. Grimes dumped cold water on his face and he did get up, sputtering, and after a little fresh venison, they started again.

Francis lost all track of time. It didn't seem possible to him that human beings could live and work on such an insane schedule. Work at midnight, go to bed at dawn. Get up in four hours and work some more. Ride out with traps and bait sticks, come back with dead, wet beaver. Skin and stretch. Sleep. Eat while you worked, while you rode. Set traps. Close your eyes for what seemed like a second, then open them and work again.

Finally, Mr. Grimes stopped. Five days could have passed, or maybe five years—Francis didn't know. All he knew was that two hundred beaver pelts were hanging and drying inside the house. It was impossible not to know that, for their stench was overpowering.

"We sleep now, Mr. Tucket, as long as we want," the trapper said, grinning. Francis was standing in front of him, almost falling down. "The pelts have to dry for a week at least. I'll wake you at the end of the week."

Oh, no, you won't, Francis thought, grabbing his buffalo robe and heading upwind of the building. Not in a week. I won't even be *started* catching up in a week. Wake me in January sometime, or maybe next spring. Better yet, don't *ever* wake me.

# — Chapter Seventeen —

THE WEEK OF IDLE RESTING that Mr. Grimes had promised Francis never took place, but it wasn't the mountain man's fault.

What happened to ruin the week was the sudden arrival of more "company." But this time, the company didn't consist of friends of Jason Grimes. They arrived on the third day after all the pelts had been hung to dry.

Contrary to what he had thought, Francis didn't sleep even for a day. After ten hours of solid snoring, he was up gathering wood. And by the second day, he was practically bored stiff.

"Don't fret on so much, Mr. Tucket," the trapper said when Francis began grumbling. "A man would think you wanted to go back to work. Rest up a mite. There'll be plenty to do."

Francis snorted. "I wouldn't even mind some more trapping. It's better than just sitting around, getting soft."

"Ah, Mr. Tucket, relax. Trap more beaver and you'd just have to sit around for another week. These things take time."

So Francis had dreamed up things to do. He made bullets—when he already had enough to stand off a small army. He took to riding around the meadow along the stream, not going anywhere in particular, just riding.

And he was riding on the morning of the third day, out along the stream, just angling across it, not paying much attention to what he was doing, when something whistled past his cheek, brushing him lightly—almost like a fly. He reached his hand up absently, and at that instant, the horse stepped on a rock and stumbled.

The sudden movement saved Francis's life. The second arrow—which would have hit him squarely in the middle of the chest—whirred past and buried itself in the muck of a beaver dam ten yards upstream.

"Heeah!" Francis screamed, and at the same second fired his rifle in the air. He had two purposes in mind for shooting the rifle. First, it would warn Mr. Grimes. Second, it would get the mare running.

And run she did. Like a little bomb going off beneath Francis, she was out of the stream and at a full gallop in the space of one breath, while he clung to her back like a flea.

She ran straight ahead, and luckily she happened to be pointed toward the camp. But unluckily, she was also pointed toward the Indians, who were hidden in the brush along the stream *between* Francis and the camp, and she took him right through the middle of them.

Francis hadn't seen the Indians, and suddenly he was ten feet away from all five of them. They were five Crows painted for war, ready, and wanting one thing—to make Francis look like a porcupine.

Arrows whistled by him, and Francis felt as though the world had suddenly gone crazy. Painted faces popped up in front of him, screeched, loosed a feathered missile, and disappeared. Somebody fired a gun right by his face, and it deafened him. He felt a hand grab at his leg, and he managed to shake it off. Another hand came up; he clubbed it down with his empty rifle and—he was free!

He was out of the ring of faces and arrows, flying along with the mare.

He looked back. He had seen no horses, but he knew that the Indians wouldn't be too far from their mounts. It was nearly two miles to camp—two long miles. His horse was well fed and with any kind of a lead, he could probably beat them.

He studied the ground ahead. It was smooth, grassy—ideal for running. He looked back again, and saw that two Indians were mounted and starting after him. As he watched, three others burst out of a stand of willows near where they'd jumped Francis.

It would be a chase. Francis studied his lead—a hundred yards, no more. And he was holding an empty rifle. I *have* to beat them, he thought. He had a good mount in his Indian pony, but the Crows were also riding Indian ponies. It stood to reason that out of five ponies, at least one would be as fast or faster than his. He couldn't expect miracles *all* the time.

Sure enough, one of the ponies was as fast as his little mare. But two others were faster, and they gained rapidly. Before he'd covered half a mile, they had cut his hundred-yard lead in half.

Francis leaned forward. "Run! If I ever needed speed, I need it now."

She was full-out already. She put her ears back and stretched an inch or two, but it didn't help much.

Another half mile, he thought, watching the two Indians gaining on him, and they'll be alongside of me. Then what?

Forty yards now, and one of the Indians raised his bow and loosed an arrow.

Francis, looking back, saw the arrow rise in a slow arc and fall toward him. He felt his stomach tighten as his eyes followed its course.

It fell short—by ten yards or so. The Indian fitted another arrow to the bow and aimed.

He's getting the range, Francis thought. Only thirty yards separated them now.

Francis nudged his pony just as the Indian shot his second arrow. The mare veered to the left, still at a dead run, and the arrow missed.

Twenty yards now. They can't miss again, he thought. Not at this short range.

Only fifteen yards, and now two Indians raised their bows.

"No!" Francis cried. "You can't . . ."

Then he heard it. Far off—a noise like the sound of muted thunder. A second later, he heard something whisper over his head, and the lead Indian fell from his horse.

The second Indian veered aside—releasing his arrow at the same time, but missing Francis.

The Hawkens—the great Hawkens of Jason Grimes had done it again.

Francis eased up a bit and looked for the mountain man. It was still almost a quarter of a mile to camp—an impossible range, an impossible shot.

Now Francis saw him—a speck that was leaning against a tree by the camp. At this range it was impossible to tell what the mountain man was doing, but in a moment Francis knew. A cloud of smoke jumped out in front of him, and the sound of a shot followed.

Francis whirled to watch the Indians. One of the ponies somersaulted, throwing his rider heavily.

That still left three. And those three stopped, dismounted, and hid behind the available cover.

Francis dropped down to a canter. It was safe now, and the mare was blowing pretty hard. Even so, it wasn't but a few moments before he was dismounting at the camp.

Mr. Grimes was smiling. "I do declare, Mr. Tucket. You sure pick some mighty funny people to be horse racing with. If you were all *that* hard up for something to do, I might have raced you myself. You didn't have to go and find a bunch of Crows."

"Well, you know how it is," Francis answered, returning the smile, though he was shaking inside and felt a little sick to his stomach. "I was getting pretty bored, just sitting around all the time. A fellow needs *some* action now and then."

"Used to be that way myself, before I lost my arm. Still, I wish you'd come and ask me before you do those things." He pointed at the Indians in the field. One of them had mounted and was heading away at a run. The mountain man shrugged. "No sense doing any more fancy shooting. One of them would be bound to get away."

"Where is he going?" Francis asked.

"For help, Mr. Tucket. And I expect not too far, the way he's riding. Well, you *said* you wanted something to do—some action. Unless I miss my guess, before long you're going to get all the action you ever wanted. Unless . . ."

"Unless what?"

"Unless we run, Mr. Tucket. And stay ahead."

"But we can't run," Francis said. "There are two of them left, watching us. They'd know right where we went."

"I swear, Mr. Tucket, you're getting smarter every day. So it appears that what we've got to do is get rid of those two Indians in the field."

"We?"

"Sure. Were you figuring on doing it all by yourself?"

Francis looked out across the meadow. Two ponies stood grazing almost a mile away. But the Indians weren't in sight. They could be anywhere, everywhere.

"How do we do it?"

"Simple, Mr. Tucket. We just walk out there until they shoot at us, then we shoot back."

Francis suddenly remembered that his rifle was empty. He reloaded it quickly.

"All right, Mr. Tucket, let's go. We don't have all day."

The mountain man started walking out across the meadow, his rifle draped casually across his shoulder. He looked for all the world as though he were just going for a morning stroll, or perhaps to hunt rabbits.

Except these rabbits, Francis thought, hurrying to catch up, aren't like normal rabbits. These rabbits shoot back.

# — Chapter Eighteen —

FRANCIS WOULD NEVER FORGET that morning "walk." He was afraid, and as they walked closer to where he thought the two Indians were, he became more and *more* afraid. His forehead ran with sweat, and it was all he could do to keep from stopping, or turning, or yelling. But he didn't, he couldn't, because the mountain man was really depending on him.

"You take the one on the right when they jump us, Mr. Tucket," Mr. Grimes said, in his usual casual voice, as they walked. "I'll do my best on the left one."

So Francis couldn't afford to let fear dominate his actions. If he froze up, or ran, it could mean the death of Mr. Grimes. If he missed, or shot a second late, Mr. Grimes would be gone.

He tried to calm down so he could watch the grass for movement, or see any signs in the soft dirt. But his fear was too real. And then Mr. Grimes stopped, held up his hand, and said, "Mind now, Mr. Tucket. They're close. I can feel 'em."

Francis couldn't feel anything. All he could think was that somehow, some way, they had walked *past* the Indians and he would get an arrow in his back any second.

"Now!"

That's all he heard—that shout from Mr. Grimes. From then on, everything was automatic. In front of them, not ten feet away, two painted faces and bronze chests rose. Two arrows were pulled back on taut strings. Two Indian throats let out a roaring sound.

Francis fired without aiming. He just pointed his rifle in the general direction of the Indian on his right side and pulled the trigger; then he turned and ran.

He ran until he stumbled and fell, and then he

lay on the ground and was sick. Sick from fear, and sick from having fired his rifle at a man, no matter the man's intent.

Mr. Grimes came up to him a moment later.

"Did—did I?"

"Did you shoot him?"

Francis nodded.

"Yes, Mr. Tucket, and a fair shot it was, too. It kept him occupied long enough for me to finish him."

"You mean I didn't—kill—him?"

"Nope. You only winged him. Creased him along the head. But it was enough to give him something else to think about till I could get in close."

Francis sat up. The grass was still cool, but the sun felt good. Better, far better than it had a few moments before. "We did it, eh, Mr. Grimes?"

"No-ah, Mr. Tucket, that isn't quite true. We did *part* of it. We still have to get out of this place before that brave comes back. And the longer you sit there, the more likely it is some brave's gonna wind up with your hair for a dance tonight . . ."

"Aren't you forgetting something?" Francis asked. "One of those Indians was thrown by his pony and that Indian is still around. He'll follow us."

"Not without a horse, he won't. And we're going to have their horses under beaver pelts. Now quit your jawing."

At a fast trot the mountain man was heading back toward the camp. Francis followed him. Once there, Mr. Grimes started on the beaver pelts, which were still damp, but dry enough to lash into bundles to be tied across the horses. He told Francis to mount up and go after the Indian ponies.

It took only a few minutes. His mare still smelled all right to the Indian ponies, so they didn't shy away when he approached. But he had one bad moment, after he had gathered up the four ponies. While he was walking them back to camp, he rode past the Indian who had been thrown.

He was sitting on the ground, and if eyes could kill, Francis would have been dead. The Indian was trying to draw his bow, but Francis could see that an injured shoulder wouldn't allow this action. In addition, one of his legs was twisted under him. Francis rode past quietly.

Mr. Grimes had been working like a fiend. All the pelts were lashed into bundles of twenty-five, stacked and waiting. The mules had been cut loose and scared off.

"Why don't we use the mules?" Francis asked.

"Too slow," came the quick answer. "And

they'd need grain to move faster. Indian ponies can do it on grass—and we're going to be needing some speed."

That was the last word spoken for over an hour. Working hard, Mr. Grimes and Francis tied the pelts in bundles across the ponies. They were a bit skittish at first—smelling the almost-green hides— but Mr. Grimes kept them tied close to trees until their eyes quit rolling and they stopped blowing.

Then he and Francis mounted their horses and rode out. It had been almost two hours since the brave had gone for help. If the rest of the tribe were within fifteen miles of the camp, the brave and more warriors could be back any second.

Francis and Mr. Grimes rode hard, holding the horses at a steady lope. The Indian ponies kept up easily, and since the temperature had dropped considerably, it was cool enough to allow a decent run without heating the horses too much. South, down the canyon, in the direction they were heading, clouds were building into a gray wall that indicated snow or rain.

Twenty minutes later, back at the cabin, ten Crow braves dismounted and briefly studied the campsite and surrounding area.

They found many things. By feeling the manure

left by the horses and finding it still warm, they knew that Mr. Grimes and Francis had only a short lead. By noting all the beaver traps left behind, they suspected that the two were running in fear.

The leader of the party, an old man—not too old to ride but old enough to have wisdom—smiled at two of the younger men, who were ready to ride their ponies into the ground to catch Mr. Grimes and Francis.

"Let us stay here for a time and help Laughing Pony fix his shoulder and leg, then we will go. We will still have them before daybreak tomorrow."

The young men shook their heads and grumbled but did as he told them to do.

# — Chapter Nineteen —

IT WAS ALMOST as if the storm had been waiting for them. Mr. Grimes led, pulling two pack horses and Francis followed pulling two more out into the prairie away from the mouth of the canyon and the snow took on more force, coming so fast that it quickly covered the horses and packs. Francis looked back and could see no trace of any tracks— the snow blew in as fast as they were made—and he smiled.

It was silly to keep going now, when surely their tracks would be blotted by the snow.

Mr. Grimes rode on. To be sure, he eased the pace a bit—impossible not to, the way the wind was driving at them—but he didn't stop.

Another hour passed. The snow was heavier, thicker. It was hard for Francis to see the short ten feet to Mr. Grimes. The temperature had dropped ten or fifteen degrees, and it was now near freezing. Francis took turns with his hands in handling the reins, holding one beneath his shirt to warm while the other got numb on the reins.

And *still* they ran. The world became a mixture of thudding hoofs, howling wind, and slashing snow. Twice, Francis had to force himself to resist cutting loose the two pack horses following him. He had tied their lead lines around his waist, and they kept pulling at him, holding him back, snagging at him.

There was no telling how long Mr. Grimes would have pushed them. He might have tried to ride the storm out. But finally, the little mare decided for them.

One second she was running almost smooth, and the next she was tumbling down under Francis, throwing him clear as she collapsed. He screamed, and luckily Mr. Grimes heard him.

By the time the mountain man had wheeled and stopped, Francis was getting up from the snow. The mare was on her feet, too, but sagging and with her head nearly on the ground. She had run just short of breaking her heart.

Francis loosened the pack horses' lead lines from his waist and looked up, through the snow and wind, at the mountain man, who was still mounted. He could see the verdict on the man's frost-covered face.

"No!" Francis screamed. "I'm not leaving her!"

"Mr. Tucket . . ."

"I'm not leaving her!" Francis repeated. He knew how foolish it sounded. They were out in the open in a violent storm, but he was going to stay with his horse. He didn't care. She hadn't flinched when those five Crows jumped him. *He* wasn't going to leave her to die in a blizzard just for a few beaver pelts.

"Mr. Tucket . . ."

"No!"

Then a strange thing happened. From what Francis knew of Mr. Grimes, he half expected the trapper to go off and leave him alone. Or hit him on the head and carry him.

Mr. Grimes dismounted, hunched his back into the wind, and smiled.

"I do declare, Mr. Tucket, you sure do pick the funniest times to be stubborn. I just hope that when

I get down, you'll be this hot about staying around with me . . ."

Francis realized he was crying. He wasn't sure why. He was tired, but he had won—at least sort of won. There was a lot of snow, and a lot of wind, and he was cold—but it wasn't that kind of crying. He just felt choked. He turned away.

"And now, Mr. Tucket, if we're ever going to see what the world is like *after* this humdinger, we'd better get to work. Help me get these horses around."

Mr. Grimes put all the horses, nose-to-tail, in a tight circle. Then he cut the beaver pelts loose from the Indian ponies and put the packs in the middle of the circle of horses.

"Now hobble 'em," he said, tying a piece of lead rope around one of the ponies' front ankles. "Hobble 'em tight."

Francis worked fast. In no time, all the horses, including his own, were hobbled tight—front and rear.

Then Mr. Grimes went around the circle on the outside and began pushing the horses over, toward the center. When he was done, all of them were lying on their sides, with their backs leaving only a small circle of empty space around the beaver pelts. Mr. Grimes went around and pulled all the horses' front and back legs together and hog-tied them. Now they couldn't get up, no matter how hard they tried.

"And now, Mr. Tucket, why don't you and me catch up on a little sleep?"

Stepping over the horses to the center, he motioned Francis to do the same. They cleared off the snow in a little empty space, and began covering it with beaver pelts cut loose from the packs.

They used almost half of the two hundred near-dry pelts, fur-side up, and when they'd finished, the circle of space was completely covered with warm fur. They lay down and covered themselves with the remaining pelts.

It was a cozy, warm place. The horses' backs gave off heat and stifled the sound of the wind. Francis was almost asleep as he put the last pelt in place. In a few seconds, just as he was drifting off, he heard the hoarse snore of the mountain man next to him.

# ── Chapter Twenty ──

FRANCIS DIDN'T KNOW for sure how long they slept in their horseflesh shelter. Perhaps ten hours. Then they lay awake for a time, not talking, just listening to the wind whistling, and fell asleep again. The second time he awakened, Francis could hear nothing but his own breathing and the gentle sighing of the horses. There was no wind, no lashing snow. He stretched as much as the cramped space would allow, and felt Mr. Grimes move near him.

"Well, Mr. Tucket," the mountain man said, "should we see what it's like outside?"

Outside it was so white, so bright and dazzling that Francis had to close his eyes for a minute to keep from getting a headache. They had a bit of trouble getting out of their home—the snow had drifted nearly four feet deep over them—but once out, Francis was amazed to feel the warmth of the sun.

Mr. Grimes didn't allow him much time to marvel at things, or even over the fact that they were still alive.

"Come on, Mr. Tucket, we've got to put these horses back on their feet and get to Spot Johnnie's. We're not in clover yet . . ."

Getting the horses up turned out to be quite a job. They were stiff—Mr. Grimes said the only reason they hadn't frozen to death was that the snow had made a sort of blanket around them—and before they could stand, the circulation had to be rubbed back into their legs.

Once up, the mounts had to be walked back and forth through the snow to loosen them up some more. It was nearly an hour before Francis and Mr. Grimes loaded the beaver pelts and started off.

They had ridden hard—even in the storm—and Francis was surprised to find that they were much farther along than he had thought—well out of the main river valley they had tried to follow out of the canyon country and back up on the plains. It was a good thing, too. The deep snow in the bottom of the valley made it almost impossible to ride, and the horses floundered again and again.

Once they had fought their way to the top of the bluff wall—where the wind had swept the snow along—the going was much easier. There were drifts now and then, but they rode around the really big pileups.

It was cold—almost zero—but without the wind, and with the sun on his back, Francis felt fine. His mare was in good shape again, and the world was a bright new land—crisp, clean, alive. Steam boiled out of the ponies' nostrils.

They rode slowly most of the morning, letting the horses stop to graze now and then, and early in the afternoon, Mr. Grimes called a halt near a stand of brush.

"Why are we stopping so soon?" Francis asked. "We could make another ten miles before dark."

"And freeze to death, Mr. Tucket? They wouldn't find us until spring—if then. We're stopping to build a lean-to out of those willows and get a fire going. We're stopping to eat—if you can find some meat around here somewhere—*and* we're stopping to let this sun work on those beaver pelts for a spell. That take care of your question?"

Francis nodded, sliding from the mare. They cut the pelts loose and spread them, fur-side up to dry the moisture out of them. Then they tethered the horses, and Mr. Grimes took his knife and cut small willow poles for a shelter. Francis shouldered his rifle and ambled off in search of game.

They had been seeing rabbits all morning—jackrabbits in the open places, and cottontails in the brushy beds of streams. In only a few minutes he had got two of the bigger jackrabbits and was carrying them back to camp. There he found a cozy, three-sided bungalow waiting, with a roaring fire in front of it.

Mr. Grimes was standing near the fire, warming himself, and Francis smiled. It all looked like a picture his father had hung up in their barn back in Missouri. The picture showed an old lumberjack, in the middle of the woods, standing over a small fire warming his hands and grinning, while in the background, a bear was sneaking out of the lumberjack's tent with a side of bacon.

"You're sure grinning a lot, Mr. Tucket," the mountain man said with a snort. "Especially for someone who couldn't do any better than a couple of scruffy rabbits. I was sort of figuring on you bringing back an antelope or two . . ."

Francis told him about the picture in the barn, and Mr. Grimes snorted again.

"Must have been an eastern bear. Out here we've got grizzlies, at least up in the peaks. If a grizzly decided to take a side of bacon, he'd like as not take it over your body." While he talked, he was dressing out the rabbits and spitting them over the fire. Before long, they were sizzling and hissing.

They ate quietly—the rabbit meat so tough Francis thought his moccasins might be easier to chew—and after polishing off both rabbits, Mr. Grimes gathered up some of the pelts for the lean-to while Francis led the horses to a clear spot nearby so they could graze.

The afternoon turned to dark early, and with the darkness they heaped wood on the fire and went to sleep, wrapped in beaver pelts.

The next morning they were up before the sun. By first light—still stiff and a bit cold—they were riding. They rode at a good clip most of the day. By late afternoon, Francis could see smoke on the horizon, and he pointed it out to Mr. Grimes.

"I see it, Mr. Tucket. Spot Johnnie's, unless I miss my guess or took a wrong turn somewhere. Only . . ."

"Only what?"

"Only there seems to be a bit more smoke than

there should. Let's see if we can get a run out of these ponies."

He kicked Footloose in the ribs and upped his stride. Francis kneed his mare into a following gallop and the pack horses kept up.

There had been something different in the mountain man's voice—a hardness that wasn't usually there, not even when the Crows had jumped them. Francis wasn't sure, but he thought it was the first time he'd ever heard Mr. Grimes sound even a little alarmed.

And the smoke got thicker as they neared.

# — Chapter Twenty-one —

ON THE RIDGE overlooking Spot Johnnie's Mr. Grimes pulled to a stop. Francis reined in beside him a second later. What met their eyes was total carnage.

Down below, *all* the buildings were on fire—including the storage sheds—and they were burning so fiercely that the snow around them was melted for more than a hundred feet.

Around the house area could be seen small humps, like gray rocks, scattered here and there. There were perhaps twenty of these humps, and with sudden shock, Francis realized that they were bodies. They rode down toward the house.

"Pawnees," Mr. Grimes said, examining several bodies. "Braid and his boys."

Above the burning trading post, toward the east about two miles, they now saw a wagon train of twenty or more wagons. These were not arranged in a circle, but scattered this way and that, and two of the wagons were burning. They looked like small torches in the snow.

Mr. Grimes heeled Footloose and started at a walk toward the house. His rifle was balanced across his lap, and his back was slouched in a way Francis had never seen.

Francis followed. The pack horses automatically followed and slowly the procession approached the trading post.

There were bodies of Pawnee Indians everywhere. They lay as they had fallen, some running, some stretched out as though sleeping.

"I count twenty-three," Mr. Grimes said. His voice was hollow. "Old Spot put up one whale of a fight."

They dismounted and searched the ground around the post, but could not find the bodies of Spot or his family.

"Maybe they got away," Francis offered, "and made it over to the wagon train."

"No-ah, Mr. Tucket. That's a nice thought, but there are too many dead braves around here. They wouldn't have let Spot get away."

"But they aren't out here . . ." Francis's voice trailed off as his eyes went to the still-burning house. The fire was roaring now, as the pitch in the log walls started to burn.

"In—in there?" Francis asked, pointing to the flames. "Spot . . . ?"

Mr. Grimes gave a short nod. He stood for a moment, watching the fire, breathing deeply. Then he broke off and studied the dead Indians on the ground.

"What are you looking for?" Francis asked.

The mountain man didn't answer. Presently he finished his examination, looked off across the hills, and mounted.

"C'mon, Mr. Tucket, let's go talk to the farmers."

When they were a hundred yards from the wagon train, three men came out to meet them. Two of them held rifles at the ready; the other one —in the middle—a stocky man with red hair and a red face, did the talking.

Mr. Grimes dismounted again. "They hit you long ago?" he asked.

"Maybe an hour, maybe more. Fifteen or so came down on our wagons and another forty jumped the trading post."

"You lose many men?"

"Two. Thing is, they kept us hopping while they nailed the post. We couldn't get out to help . . ."

Mr. Grimes nodded. "They were after powder. Did—did anyone get out of the house?"

The stocky man shook his head. "At least, if they did, we didn't see 'em. Friends of yours?"

Mr. Grimes was quiet, staring at the snow-covered hills.

"I know how you feel," the man went on. "One of the two we lost was my brother . . ."

There was silence for a while. Francis realized that the stocky man was crying, but that his lips were moving back and forth in anger.

Mr. Grimes broke the silence. "Well, it appears that the time has come to do something about Braid." He turned to look at Francis. "Remember me telling you, Mr. Tucket, that if I ever did kill Braid, it wouldn't be because he had something I wanted. This is different, Mr. Tucket, very different."

He walked over to Footloose, removed the saddle, threw it on the ground, and mounted bareback. "What's your name?" he asked the stocky man.

"Groves. Ben Groves."

"Well, Mr. Groves, I'd take it kindly if you'd keep you eyes on Mr. Tucket, the boy here, for me."

"Now wait a minute—" Francis began.

"There's a fair chance I won't be coming back from this ride," Mr. Grimes went on, ignoring Francis. "Fact is, he's kinda headstrong, and if somebody doesn't watch him, he's likely to do just about anything. Understand me, Mr. Groves?"

The redheaded man nodded. He motioned to the other two men, and before Francis could move, they had grabbed him, pulled him from his horse, and were holding him fast.

"Hey!" he yelled. "Wait a minute! Mr. Grimes, you can't just go out there and jump a whole tribe of Pawnee." He tried to wiggle free but failed. "They'll—they'll kill you. That's dumb. You can't do that, Mr. Grimes. You can't be dumb. You wouldn't let *me* be dumb . . ."

"Now, now, Mr. Tucket. You're rattling on, and that won't do at all. Mr. Groves, if I don't come back by morning, my saddle, all those beaver pelts, and the ponies belong to the boy. I'd be happy if you'd make sure he gets them—not, of course, that anybody'd be foolish enough to try to take them away from him."

"No!" Francis yelled.

"Also," the mountain man continued, "would your train be going to Oregon?"

Mr. Groves nodded. "The Willamette Valley."

"The boy's got folks out there. You might take him with you—maybe make him work his way."

"No! No!"

"I'll do everything you ask," the farmer answered. "I'll hand deliver him, with his pelts, to his folks if you want. But I'd rather be riding out with you . . ."

"No-ah, Mr. Groves. It just takes one. Two, and they'd kill us both. One, and I might get close enough—by insulting Braid."

"No!" Francis screamed again. "Even if you win, you lose. For what? There's no reason to die. It's done, Mr. Grimes—and done is done."

"And now, Mr. Tucket." The mountain man turned at last to Francis. "Before I go—and I don't want you getting some kind of swelled head out of this—I'd like to say it's been sort of fun having you around. Be seeing you . . ."

He wheeled his horse and started off, northeast, riding loose and fast.

"Mr. Grimes, come back!" Francis yelled after him. "Come back, come back, come back . . ."

But Footloose, without the saddle, gained speed rapidly and before Francis could think the mountain man had vanished in the dying evening light.

# — Chapter Twenty-two —

FRANCIS RODE HARD.

It was a strange mount, but he now knew how to ride well enough to stay on almost any horse. This one was a big black—long legged and fresh. And stolen.

An hour after Mr. Grimes had gone, just after moonrise, Mr. Groves had made the mistake of not watching Francis closely. In a flash, he had run to the corral, thrown a war bridle on the black, and with nothing but his rifle, had left the camp.

The trail cut in the snow and lighted by the half

moon was easy to follow. But the hour lead Mr. Grimes had on him worried Francis. Footloose had been tired, it was true, but without a saddle—and considering also that Footloose was a big horse—it was entirely possible that Mr. Grimes would catch up to the Pawnees before Francis could catch up to him.

Francis drove the horse hard. Every time the black even thought of slowing, he laid his rifle barrel with a vengeance across the gelding's rump. What, exactly, he was going to do when and if he caught up with the mountain man, Francis wasn't sure. Try to stop him, of course, but—if he couldn't talk Mr. Grimes out of tangling with Braid, then at least help him. Two guns were always better than one.

Two hours of riding brought the moon higher and made it practically as light as day when it was actually almost ten o'clock at night.

Ten o'clock, Francis thought, goading the black to even longer strides. How I've changed. There was a time when ten o'clock at night meant getting wrapped in a huge quilt and bundled into bed, and feeling the warmth leave my face as the fire in the wood stove died. Died. There was a time when I didn't even think of things that died. I didn't know anything about all this killing. Nothing died, ever, except a farm animal now and then.

He pushed these thoughts from his mind. They were making him afraid—afraid that he might not catch up.

There would be times, later, when he would wonder about all the little things that kept him from reaching Mr. Grimes in time. If he had beat the black harder, or tried to make his break from the wagon train earlier . . .

As it was, he was only a split second late—the time that it takes a man to pull a trigger. He rode over a rise, and there, in a small, flat meadow, were Braid and Mr. Grimes.

They were riding hard at each other and, in the moonlight, the snow flying up around their horses as they closed looked like the fine spray thrown up in front of a ship. They were both stripped to the waist and carrying rifles. When the horses were fifty feet apart, the two men fired. Francis saw the rifles flash and both men tumble from their horse.

They had fired at the same instant, and the one-armed and one-braided men landed within ten feet of each other.

Francis's mind went blank when the mountain man fell from his horse. He rode up, dismounted, and if he noticed the fifteen mounted warriors on the other side of the battlefield, he gave no sign of it. He didn't care.

"Howdy, Mr. Tucket," the mountain man said, wincing as he pulled himself to a sitting position. His shoulder was turning red. "I sort of figured you'd be along. Glad you could make it in time for the fun . . ." He winced again.

Francis tore his shirt off and wrapped it around the shoulder. Mr. Grimes pushed him away. "No-ah, Mr. Tucket. Not done yet." He propped himself on one knee, then slowly stood, grunting, weaving.

"What do you mean?" Francis asked. "Braid's dead." He pointed to where the Indian lay in the snow. The mounted warriors were now around the body in a half circle. "It's done."

"Not done yet," Mr. Grimes repeated, stagger-ing. He pulled out his skinning knife. "One more thing to do." Weaving drunkenly, he made his way to the body of his enemy. Then he leaned down.

"No!" Francis screamed. "You *can't* . . ." He ran and pulled the mountain man away. This, some-how, was worse than all the rest. To kill Braid was one thing, perhaps even right, in the cold-blooded justice that ruled the prairie. But not this—this ani-mal thing.

"*Can't*, Mr. Tucket?" Mr. Grimes said, laughing

hoarsely. "And why not? He would have done the same to me . . ."

Francis stared in horror, then turned away. Many things were suddenly clear to him, and the biggest was that Mr. Grimes was right. He *could* do what he was doing, simply because he was ruled by the same law that ruled Braid. He was of the prairie, the land, the mountains—and was, in a way, a kind of animal. It was not wrong—not for Jason Grimes.

But for Francis Alphonse Tucket? For someone from a farm in Missouri? For someone with a family waiting in Oregon?

There were different rules for different people. One set for Mr. Grimes, but, Francis thought, as he reached his horse, there was a different set for him. He was *not* and did not want to be a "mountain man."

He mounted the horse. Mr. Grimes would be all right, he knew. The fight had been fair in the Indians' eyes, and besides, they wanted to keep on trading for powder. No, the Indians wouldn't kill Mr. Grimes, and his shoulder would heal. Soon he would be trapping again.

But this time without me, Francis told himself, squaring his shoulders. He wiped his eyes with the back of his hand. A boy named Francis Alphonse Tucket might stay and live wild and follow the beaver ponds. But Francis Alphonse Tucket wasn't a boy anymore. Jason Grimes had made that boy *Mr. Tucket* and Mr. Tucket was going to Oregon, to his family, to his kind of life—to his set of rules.

Francis slapped the horse as hard as he could and headed for the wagon train. And somehow he knew he'd better not look back at Mr. Grimes—not even to wave a good-bye.

# CALL ME
# FRANCIS TUCKET

Dedicated to Jeff Edwards and Joe Fine for their devotion to excellence, and to Sequoyah, Cimarron, Summit, and Central middle schools and all their students and faculty

# Chapter One

Francis Alphonse Tucket sat the small mare easily, relaxed in the saddle, his legs loose, the short Lancaster rifle lying casually across his lap, and looked out at the edge of the world.

The prairie stretched away to the horizon. He felt strangely settled, quiet, in a way he had not felt in many months. It had all begun with this very rifle, the beautiful little Lancaster Pa had given Francis on his fourteenth birthday. June 13, 1847. Somehow Pa had managed to hide the rifle with another family in the wagon train that was taking

Francis's family—Ma, Pa, Francis, and Rebecca, who was nine—from Missouri to Oregon. Francis had dropped behind the train to practice with the rifle and he'd been captured. Taken prisoner by Pawnees. It was Jason Grimes the mountain man who had shown up in the Pawnee camp and rescued Francis, taught him to survive as they traveled together. But they had parted ways just the day before, after Grimes's brutal fight with Braid, the Pawnee brave.

Now Francis was on his own. At that moment he felt a kind of peacefulness he had not felt since he'd first taken up with Jason Grimes.

Or boredom, he thought, sitting in the late-afternoon sun. He felt not peacefulness so much as boredom. When he had left the mountain man he had ridden back to meet up with a wagon train waiting at the burned-out hulk of Spot Johnnie's trading post.

They had welcomed him with open arms and had themselves left early the next morning. The wagon master approached him as they were lining out the wagons in the predawn gray light.

"Do you wish to be assigned to a wagon?"

Francis had been looking at the wreckage of Spot Johnnie's post, burned by the Pawnees, in the same direction as the place where he had left Jason Grimes. "What?"

The wagon master smiled and put his hand on Francis's shoulder. "He seemed like a good man . . ."

"Who?"

"The mountain man. He seemed good, a man you would miss being around . . ."

"Well, he wasn't," Francis said curtly. "He wasn't worth spit." He turned to look at the wagon master. "And I don't want to talk about him anymore. What was that about a wagon?"

The wagon master sighed. "Do you wish to be assigned to one?"

Francis looked at them, lumbering along, kids and loose stock running alongside. They were already raising clouds of dust, and there were masses of flies around the horses and oxen—hungry, biting flies. "No, thank you. I'll just free range, if that's all right."

"Maybe you could ride wide and hunt for us as well."

Francis nodded. "I figured on it." He suddenly realized he was talking a lot like Jason Grimes—short, almost cutoff sentences—and he smiled and shrugged. "I mean it seemed the best way for me to help as we go along. Just until we get out farther west and I can get some word about my folks. I'll have to be leaving you then . . ."

"Of course."

The wagon master had ridden off then, riding a Morgan horse that could either pull or ride—a lummox kind of horse, Francis thought—and Francis checked his rifle, made sure the percussion cap was on the nipple tightly, and wheeled the mare toward a ridge off to the north.

If the truth were known, he was glad to be away from the train. He had often been alone in the last months—even when he was with Grimes. Sometimes when they were trapping he was alone for a full day, now and then longer. He had in some ways come to enjoy it. He didn't have to talk to people and it gave him time for thinking.

And he needed to think now. He let the mare pick up the pace to a trot—she wanted to run but he held her back in case he needed speed later— and guided her with his knees until they were on the ridge. Then he eased her over and down the side a bit so he wouldn't be outlined against the sky. It was something Grimes had taught him. Against the sky it was too easy to be seen—either by game or by enemy—and when he was well down from the edge, he swung the mare left and headed west.

He worked his eyes and ears automatically and let his mind start going over the problem.

He felt as if his life had a hole torn in the middle of it—almost the same feeling he'd had when he was taken from the wagon train—and he realized with some surprise that it came from leaving Mr. Grimes.

Francis had not thought they were that close and in some measure hated the man and now this, to feel this . . . this missing the one-armed mountain man.

It made no sense.

The mare slowed and Francis saw her ears perk forward, and she looked suddenly to the right front as a covey of quail jumped from some brush.

Francis was sliding off the side of the horse and halfway to the ground, the rifle cocked and swinging up under the mare's neck when he saw a coyote come out of the brush with a quail in his mouth.

"Could have been anything . . ." He smiled, eased the hammer down to the safety click and remounted. "Anything . . ."

His feet found the stirrups and he kneed the mare into motion once again. The ridge he was riding alongside started to rise and in front ended where it hit a shallow bluff. He could not see over the bluff and moved back up the ridge to the left and made sure there was a place where the wagon train—now moving slowly about two miles to his left and rear—would have room to get through the bluffs.

He still did not ride the mare to the top of the

ridge, but moved up just until his head was high enough to see and then back down.

The bluff ahead beckoned him more. Grimes was, for the moment, out of his thinking—there was something about seeing over the next hill, some need—and he heeled the mare to pick up the pace.

She stepped into an easy canter and climbed the shallow back of the bluff and stopped just as she came on top, and it was here that Francis saw the edge of the world.

Spread out below, reaching away to the horizon and beyond, reaching away west forever, the land, flat and impossibly large, lay before him.

"It . . ." Francis did not finish.

Even the mare had stopped, seemed to be staring at the view, her ears twitching to knock off flies.

"It's too big," he said finally, and realized he meant it. The land was just too big, too big to see, to own—too big to cross. Too big for anything.

It's bad enough on a horse, he thought, how could the wagons, the mile-an-hour wagons, ever hope to cross it? It would take them years . . .

The prairie he had already crossed was enormous—newspapers in the East called it a sea of grass—but Francis had never seen more than a hill or two at a time. This way, from the bluff edge, he could see it all, or a large part of it, and for a moment the bigness kept him from seeing details.

Then the mare stumbled as a gopher hole caved in under her foot, and it snapped Francis back to reality.

In detail the plain before him proved to be not just empty grass, which he'd first thought. Three or four miles to the west, there was a large, dark smudge that seemed to be surrounded by dust clouds. He thought it was trees or low brush, but as he watched, it seemed to move, crawling slowly across the prairie, and he knew it then.

Buffalo. A herd five or six miles across, grazing and kicking up dust.

Or, Francis thought, food for the wagon train. He had never shot a buffalo—with Grimes he had taken deer and antelope, and they'd eaten a lot of beaver meat when they were trapping, but never a buffalo, and he wasn't sure just how to hunt them.

"Do I just ride out there and shoot one?" The mare twitched her ears, listening to his voice. "Is that the way?"

In truth one would not be enough. There were ten wagons—some thirty people—and they would probably want to store meat for the future.

Two, at least, maybe three or four buffalo.

He looked back and to the left and saw the

thread of dust rising from the wagon train. He could go back for them, bring some men from the train with rifles to help. But few of them had horses, were stuck with oxen, and besides he didn't much want to be with the men from the wagons somehow. And it would take two hours to go back and get them.

So his first thought came back. "We'll just have to ride down there and shoot a couple of them."

It proved to be the second biggest mistake of his life.

# Chapter Two

The mare took over.

Francis checked the cap on his rifle to insure that it would fire and started the little mare down the front of the bluff to the plain below.

It wasn't quite vertical, but very near it, and the little pony squatted back on her haunches to keep from falling forward.

She was nearly running when she hit the bottom. Francis started to hold her back, but she picked up the pace to a canter, then a full lope, and aimed right at the center of the massive herd.

Things started to happen very fast, and almost none of them were under Francis's control.

The mare flattened her ears and lined out at a dead run. The distance to the herd was diminishing rapidly, almost instantly. One second they were stumbling down the face of the bluff and Francis was checking his rifle and the next they were at the side of the buffalo herd.

The mare stumbled, caught her footing and dived into the herd. Francis had one fleeting image of a bull that seemed to blot out the world and then was immersed in a sea of buffalo, so close they were pressing on the mare's side, rubbing against his leg, bellowing and snorting, raising clouds of dust.

The mare, an Indian pony, had hunted buffalo before. The method used by Indians was to get in close so an arrow or lance could be used, and she remembered her training well.

She took Francis in so close she nearly knocked a large cow over, slamming Francis against her side.

Francis reacted without thinking. He was too close to aim, so he just pressed the muzzle against the shoulder of the cow where he guessed her heart would be, eared the hammer back with his thumb, and fired.

The effect was immediate and startling. The cow went down, caving in and cartwheeling, dead almost before she hit the ground, and the rest of the world blew up.

The herd had been made nervous, at least those near Francis, by the horse running into their midst. But there were wild horses everywhere. The buffalo were used to seeing them all the time, and while the mare running into the herd startled them, they did not really see Francis, only the horse, and would quickly have settled down.

The gunshot ended any chance of peace. They had never heard gunfire before, but they had heard thunder, which meant lightning, and thunder and lightning terrified them.

They panicked, instantly, and within a moment of the panic the entire herd—forty to fifty thousand buffalo, had Francis been able to count them—broke into a thundering stampede.

By this time, Francis and the mare were near the middle of the herd. Francis had half a second to grab the mare's mane, wrap his fingers in the hair and hang on before the herd took her.

It was like being caught in a living river. The buffalo had been aimed south while they grazed and that was the direction they ran. It was impossible to see. Dust rose in an almost solid mass, so thick at times Francis couldn't see the mare's ears, and within moments even the sky was gone.

Without seeing the sun, Francis couldn't tell direction, but it didn't matter. They were caught in the herd, and he let the mare run. She stumbled several times at first, until she caught the stride, but the close press of the buffalo seemed to almost hold her up.

They ran forever.

Or so it seemed. In the thick muck of dirty air, the deafening bellowing of the stampeding buffalo, and the constant push of the animals, Francis forgot time, place, anything and everything, trying to stay on the mare and stay alive.

An hour passed, he was sure of it, and the buffalo kept running. They slowed, or started to, then something would restart them and they'd be off again. The mare settled into the run, covered with sweat, her shoulders pounding. Once the herd seemed to turn, seemed to be wheeling in a huge circle, but he still couldn't see the sun, still couldn't tell what direction they were moving. When they finally stopped, blowing snot and wheezing, the mare staggering with fatigue, Francis didn't have the slightest idea where they were, how far they had come, or in which direction.

They had turned once. He had felt the herd move, swinging around to the left. Or was it right? He sat on the mare, catching his breath while she *whooshed* beneath him, blowing to recover from the run.

Except for the dust, which was rapidly settling, it might not have happened. Buffalo grazed peacefully around him while he looked this way and that, trying to locate himself. His left hand was still clutched in the mare's mane, and he released it, the knuckles aching. He had carried the rifle in his right hand, and he remembered now that it was empty from when he had shot the cow.

He blew dust from the nipple and action and reloaded, sitting on the horse. Powder, patch, and ball, then the ramrod, all done carefully, slowly so as not to bother the buffalo close around him, though they seemed to have forgotten he was there.

With the ball seated firmly on the powder, he took a cap from his possibles sack, pinched it to make it fit tight, and put it on the nipple, eased the hammer slowly to the safety notch.

"There," he said aloud, then winced when a cow standing nearby started at the sudden sound and turned her massive head toward the mare. He had to remember to keep quiet while he worked his way out of the herd.

The problem was which way to go. He guessed they had been running at a good fifteen miles an hour for over an hour.

He thought they had come south. But the dust had covered the sun and now there were low, thick clouds over it, and Francis had no way of knowing direction.

The dust settled as he thought on what to do and with that he saw that he was near the edge of the herd. Scattered groups of buffalo stood between him and clear prairie. He silently nudged the mare into movement—she staggered a bit but kept walking—and moved through the buffalo to the clear area.

The mare was still breathing heavily, and he knew whatever he wanted to do, he would have to give her a rest first—at least four or five hours, better to let her rest all night.

He pulled her up when he was thirty yards past the edge of the herd and dismounted.

He was almost viciously hungry—had not eaten since the previous evening and then had only a tin cup of thin soup and some pan bread the women with the train had made up. There were buffalo nearby and he hadn't had red meat in over a week, so he picked a young bull forty yards off and dropped him with a shot through the neck.

The herd immediately stampeded again as Francis had figured—but he was well clear of them and they ran in a direction away from him. The mare jumped with the shot, but he held tight to her catch rein and there was no problem.

This time he reloaded at once, recapping the nipple before approaching the downed bull, carefully ready to give it another shot if it came at him.

Francis poked the bull with the muzzle of the rifle, but it had been a clean shot, breaking the bull's neck, and it was dead.

Still, some instinct, some wariness made him stand back from the bull, sweep his eyes around, noting every small bush or depression, anywhere anybody could hide. He smelled the air, listened, but there were no strange odors—just the smell of the buffalo—and no sounds but the horn rattle and coughing bellow of the herd, now half a mile away where they had stopped from the run after his shot to kill the bull.

He used the catch rope to make a twist hobble for the mare, took the saddle off, and let her go to graze. She had been hobbled before and moved her front feet in small steps while she fed. Francis would have liked to let her roll, but the hobbles prevented that and he didn't dare let her go loose. She'd take off and he would be afoot.

With the mare settled in for rest and grass, he turned to the dead buffalo. It had fallen straight down, on its chest, its chin furrowed into the dirt.

He had never skinned a buffalo, and when he tried to turn it over to get to the underside, he found it was impossible to move it. The bull was too heavy to even roll over.

For a full minute, he studied the carcass and finally decided he wouldn't be able to skin and clean it as he had done with deer and antelope when he was with Jason Grimes.

As much as it bothered him to waste any part of the animal, he would just have to take meat from the dead bull the best he could. He had sharpened his knife the day before on the small stone he carried in his possibles bag, and he leaned the rifle carefully against the front shoulder of the bull—where he could reach it fast if he needed to—and pulled the knife from the leather scabbard he had on a strap over his shoulder.

He cut down the center of the back, surprised at how easily the skin opened to reveal the yellow-white back-fat and rich meat. The meat was still warm and the thick smell of blood came up into his nose and caught. It made his hunger worse, and he cut a chunk of meat from the back and ate it raw, chewing it only a few bites before swallowing it.

"Good," he mumbled to himself. "So good . . ."

It took him less than half an hour to peel the

hide down both sides and cut a large portion of meat from the hump and tenderloin and set it aside.

Clouds of flies surrounded him. They were part of the buffalo herd anyway, laying eggs in the fresh manure that covered the prairie wherever the herd moved. They were drawn by death and the fresh smell of blood, and within a few moments Francis couldn't see anything through them. They carpeted the meat he set aside, covered his hands, face, were in his eyes.

"Fire . . ." He knew that smoke would drive them away, and he found some dry grass and twigs, poured a tiny amount of powder from his horn in the middle of the pile—noted that the horn was less than half full—and struck a spark with his flint. The spark hit the powder, flashed it, and the heat started the grass and kindling. He quickly added more sticks, dry grass, and some larger pieces he found nearby.

When the fire was high—uncomfortable in the heat of the evening—he propped a six- or seven-pound slab of meat up on sticks close to the flame to cook and went to gather more wood.

He had decided to spend the night and he wanted enough wood to last until morning. The dead wood was sparse, however, and by the time he had made a pile large enough to last it was nearly dark and the smell of the cooked meat was driving him crazy.

He had never been hungrier and he sat by the fire on his rolled-out bedroll, leaning against the saddle and ate the entire piece of meat, taking small sips from his canteen between chunks.

As soon as it was hard dark, coyotes came in to the dead bull—not thirty yards away—and ate. He could see their eyes shining in the light from the fire as they tore at the buffalo but he knew they would not bother him and he paid them no mind.

With his stomach bulging and the warm fire on his face sleep hit him like a wall. Something bothered him and he couldn't quite pin it down—something that he was doing wrong—but the feeling wasn't strong enough to keep him awake.

He pulled his rifle in closer, added wood to the fire, rolled his blanket over to make a cocoon and within minutes was fast asleep.

# Chapter Three

"Ahh, see here, Dubs, what fate has provided for us . . . ," a deep, professorial-sounding voice boomed.

It was a dream, Francis was sure of it. It simply wasn't possible that a human voice could be speaking and for a full five seconds he refused to open his eyes and lose the relaxing comfort of sleep.

"Come now, lad. Don't be lazy. We have business afoot. Wake up."

Francis opened his eyes.

At first it didn't matter. The sun was full up and when his lids opened the brightness blinded him.

He blinked, let his eyes adjust, turned away from the sun and opened them again.

He was staring at the dead fire, or more accurately across the fire. There was a man sitting, squatting back on his haunches. He looked old to Francis, over forty, and was so heavily bearded Francis could not see his face for the hair.

But the clothing was more startling. The man was short, almost fat, and dressed in a black suit including a black vest, black boots, black trousers and black frock coat, and a full top hat on his head.

"See, Dubs, the lad awakens." The man smiled—his teeth broken and jagged; a bit of tobacco juice oozed out the side of the lip into the beard and the lines around his black eyes did not match the smile.

Francis slid his hand toward the rifle. Or where the rifle had been. He could not find it.

"See, Dubs, even now he reaches for his weapon. A true child of the frontier." The man spoke to somebody else—Francis couldn't see anybody at first—but kept looking at Francis. The smile widened. Like a snake getting ready to hiss. A hair snake. "I have your rifle—and a nice piece it is, too."

"What . . . who are you?" Francis at last found words. "What are you doing here?"

"Exactly!" The man nodded, waved a filthy finger. "That's exactly what *I* said, wasn't it, Dubs—when we came upon the lad, didn't I say just that? We came over the hill at dawn and I saw you sleeping there and saw your horse and I turned to Dubs and whispered—so as not to disturb your slumbers—and I said: Who is this, and what is he doing here?"

Francis sat up, or tried to. Something heavy, like warm iron, descended on his head and shoulders and pressed him back down. He swiveled his head back and saw that he was looking at a giant—a true giant. It was a man in crude buckskins, so large he seemed to blot out the sun, and Francis saw that the giant had put a hand down to keep him on the blanket.

"Dubs," the man across the fire said by way of introduction. "Isn't he something? There are some who have questioned his humanity, thinking he was of another species—men, I should hasten to add, who are not with us any longer, Dubs having sent them to the nether regions—but I do not question him. I am grateful that he is my partner, my right hand. He is Dubs. I am Courtweiler, although most call me simply Court. And you?"

Francis stared at him. Part of his mind was still trying to awaken and part of him was trying to accept that apparently these men meant to harm him. If they had been friendly they would not have taken his rifle. He realized that what had bothered him last night was his acting like an amateur, a greenhorn. He should have placed his bedroll well away from the fire, hidden so he would have time to react if enemies came. Stupid. Well, nothing for it now. He had to buy time, time to think, time to come up with a plan. "Francis," he said. "My name is Francis."

"Ahh—a proper name, that. Francis. I would have liked to have been named Francis but my ancestors came into it and I had to take the family name. Courtweiler isn't bad, but Francis—now that's a name, isn't it, Dubs?"

Francis looked up again and if the giant was listening at all he gave no indication. He held Francis down with one hand while staring out across the prairie.

"It was a stroke of good fortune coming upon you this way," Courtweiler added. "For us, that is. Not so good for you."

"What do you mean?" Francis looked at his rifle, which was across the fire on the ground leaning against Courtweiler's leg while he squatted. He couldn't reach it. And his possibles bag and knife were somewhere in back of him—he'd never get to them before Dubs landed on him.

"I mean, Francis, that we have a specific need for just about everything you have. Our equipment has run into the ground and we aren't halfway to that golden coast we aspire to. I'm afraid we're going to have to relieve you of your belongings."

"My belongings?"

Courtweiler nodded. "Exactly. Gun, horse, saddle—essentially everything. I think I could even fit into that buckskin shirt."

"My clothes, too?"

"Except your pants. I think we'll leave those in the interests of propriety. But everything else. And I don't want you to think I'm ungrateful. Indeed, if you will turn and look," he made a sign to Dubs, who stepped back and let Francis rise, "you will see that I am in desperate straits indeed. Even my mule suffers."

Francis rose to his knees and looked to the rear where an old mule, so skinny its ribs stuck out inches, stood with its head hanging nearly to the ground. On its back was a blanket worn until there were holes through it, no saddle, and instead of a bridle a loop went around the lower jaw. The miracle, Francis thought, was that the mule had gotten this far.

"You see what I mean." Courtweiler pointed to

the mule. "Dubs prefers to go afoot, and by the third day will outrun a horse. But given as I am to more intellectual pursuits and less of the physical I need to ride. And so we must have your horse."

"I have kin," Francis said. "Just over that rise. They'll be looking for me . . ."

Courtweiler shook his head. "Dissembling won't help, my boy. We came from there. There are no people there, no tracks, nothing. I do not know how you arrived here but let me assure you, there is nobody close to help you."

"I'll die if you leave me here with nothing."

Courtweiler sighed. "Indeed. There is that possibility. Still, life on the frontier is very hard and we must expect these little setbacks and somehow muddle on, don't you agree? Now, please take off that shirt before I have to ask Dubs to assist you . . ."

Francis hesitated, saw Dubs move and decided not to anger the huge man. He shrugged out of his shirt, felt the morning coolness on his skin.

"Off the blanket, please."

Francis moved from the blanket and Dubs snaked it off the ground and rolled it up in one fluid motion and stood again, still, waiting.

"And now, Francis, as fruitful as it has been to meet you, I'm afraid we must be off . . ."

Dubs had already caught the mare—Francis

could not believe they had done all this without awakening him—and they saddled her, left the mule standing and rode off, Courtweiler holding Francis's rifle across his lap as they rode away, headed west while Francis sat next to a dead buffalo, a nearly dead mule, and watched them go.

# Chapter Four

For a time Francis stood in a kind of shock. He could still see them when they were a mile away, heading toward the tail end of the buffalo herd, and then two miles, small dots on the prairie.

My life, he thought. I'm watching my life leave. For that time he couldn't, or wouldn't, think. He knew there were bad men in some of the wagon trains, had heard that some of them were kicked out of the trains and he thought Courtweiler and Dubs might be two of those men. Perhaps they had stolen, or worse, and been forced to leave.

It didn't matter. Francis shook his head to clear his thinking. What mattered was that he was in the middle of God knew where, did not have any sure idea of which way to go to find the wagon train he had left the day before, was nearly naked with no weapons and no tools, and his life, his horse and rifle and all that he needed to live, was riding over a rise two miles away. That was what mattered.

As he thought, Dubs and Courtweiler vanished, hidden by the land, and Francis looked around, half expecting somebody to step forward and say it was a joke, or to help him.

There was nobody and he frowned, thinking. There was an answer here somewhere, something they had said, or Courtweiler had said. What was it?

Was it about Dubs? Dubs didn't use a horse. He just trotted alongside, moving forward in a step shuffle—he looked almost exactly like a bear moving—and he easily kept up with the mare.

Something about the horse, some comment. What was it? Oh yes, by the third day he could outrun a horse. Wasn't that it? Francis looked north again. He guessed that north was the direction he'd have to walk—twenty miles or more—to find the wagon train. But it was only a guess. If the buffalo herd had turned in the dust while they ran—and he had no idea if they had or not—he would be wrong and miss the train. If he missed the train he would almost certainly die—unless he ran into Indians who would help him. The problem was that some of the Indians might *not* help him.

Three days, he thought again. And there it was—the answer. If that big ox could outrun a horse in three days Francis should be able to do it in two. Wearing nothing but moccasins and leather leggings he should be able to do it in one.

He should be able to keep up with them. That was the answer. He would follow them and wait, hang back where they couldn't see him and watch and wait and maybe, when they slept, he could turn it around—do what they had done to him.

He shrugged, loosened his legs from days of riding and when he turned he saw the mule. For half a second he thought of trying it, riding the mule bareback until he played out and went down. But the animal was too far gone—looked out on his feet—and Francis shook his head.

"Sorry, mule—you'll have to stay alone." The wolves would come for him, Francis knew. It was pure luck they hadn't found the dead buffalo yet. Coyotes had come during the night but not the wolves—huge, gray, slab-sided beasts that followed the herds of buffalo to get the old and sick and young. They would make short work of the mule and Francis felt sorry for it; to have come this far just to get torn apart by wolves seemed a cruel fate.

But again he shook his head. His own situation wasn't much better. He'd never heard of wolves attacking men but he would have felt much more comfortable about it if he'd had a rifle or even a knife.

"Enough . . ."

He started off, following the mare's tracks in a shuffle that approximated Dubs's—his toes in, feet almost not leaving the ground.

There was still morning coolness, but the sun was well up and felt warm on his back, and inside of fifteen minutes he was covered with sweat. He watched the tracks moving through the torn ground where the buffalo had gone, fixed on them and kept up the pace for an hour—he figured maybe five miles—when he breasted a rounded rise and could see out ahead again for several miles.

He stopped, catching his breath, and squinted, trying to see ahead as far as possible. For a full minute he stood, could see nothing except small stands of buffalo—two here, three there—and then way off, so small it seemed like bits of dust on his eyes, he saw them. He thought he might have gained—he guessed them to be three miles away— and it was unmistakably the mare with Courtweiler on top and Dubs trotting alongside.

"Good . . ." He took another deep breath and was just ready to step off into the shuffle again when he heard a sound to his rear and turned to see the mule standing there, its head down, eating grass.

"You followed me?"

The mule twitched one ear but kept eating and Francis shook his head. He'd heard that mules were tougher than horses, but this was an old mule and it didn't seem possible that it could have stayed with him, or that it would want to.

"Well, it's good to have company . . ."

He set off again in the easy trot and when he looked over his shoulder he saw the mule take one last bite, raise its head and start off, moving in a shambling, fast walk-trot that easily kept up with Francis.

He must be made of iron, Francis thought. Iron and leather.

He thought of slowing some—he didn't want to catch up to them enough for them to know he was following and the mule, which stood taller than Francis, would show from a long way. But he figured he would slow naturally as the day went on and he didn't want to fall far enough back to lose them.

So he kept the same pace, trotting along. Another hour passed and he saw them again, estimated that he hadn't gained and from then on there was nothing but running.

At first he grew tired. At midday when the sun was overhead, it seemed that he would drop. He was viciously thirsty and it would have stopped him —sweating without water—but he found a small spring on the side of a mud buffalo wallow and he drank enough to slake his thirst. It restored his energy and picked him up enough that the ache in his legs and thighs turned to a dull burn and then, finally, disappeared entirely.

By midafternoon he felt as if he could run forever. The exhaustion had gone, was replaced by a lifting of spirits that almost made him happy—or as happy as a half-naked, unarmed man in the middle of the wilderness can be.

The mule was still with him, shambling along, and as evening approached he found another spring and drank and the mule drank with him, next to him, and Francis realized that he'd told the truth earlier; it *was* nice to have company, even if it was just a mule.

A very old, very tough mule. And as it turned out, a very dangerous mule. Just before dark Francis stopped. He felt sure Courtweiler and Dubs would camp for the night and he didn't want to run up to them.

As soon as he stopped the wolves found them. It

was not a full pack, just three young ones. But they were still dangerous, at least to the mule, and there was little Francis could do. They came in on the mule, who stood, his ears laid back and his head down. Francis threw rocks at them but they merely growled and didn't run and grew bolder with each moment and one of them, the largest, finally had enough of waiting and went for the mule's rear end.

It was his last act on earth.

Francis had never seen anything like it. The mule raised one back hoof when the wolf made his move—Francis thought later it was like cocking a rifle—and kicked so hard and fast Francis couldn't see it move. One instant the wolf was making an attack and the next the whole front of his head was caved in and he hit the ground a full ten feet back, absolutely stone dead. He didn't even twitch.

The other wolves saw it happen; one of them went over to the dead wolf and smelled the body, then looked at the mule, shook himself, and the two trotted off into the evening.

Francis watched them go and smiled at the mule. "Well, if I can't have a rifle or knife you're the next best thing—like a cannon."

He stood close to the mule. In the evening the heat of the day was going fast and he had perspired all day. A chill came into him and he found that by standing against the mule while it ate he felt warmer, and listening to the mule pull grass and chew somehow made it more peaceful, protected, and let him think on his next move.

It would be dark soon. He didn't know how close he might be to them, or even if they were going to stop for the night—although he somehow couldn't see them traveling hard—but he thought they might be fairly close. A mile or less.

Just before the wolves had come he had moved to the top of a low knoll and scanned ahead. A mile to the west there was a streambed thick with low trees running along its side, and if it were his choice he would camp there where there was wood for fire and water for the horse.

He leaned against the mule—which was still, and Francis guessed would forever be eating—and absorbed the warmth from the bony shoulder and waited.

Finally, when it was pitch-dark he left the mule and climbed the knoll again, looked in the direction of the streambed. For a second there was nothing. Then he saw it.

A flicker, then, when his eyes locked on it he could see the full glow of a campfire.

He had found them.

Now all he had to do was wait.

# ──Chapter Five──

It was a wonderful dream. He had dreamt many times since Braid had taken him from the wagon train and he had trapped with Jason Grimes, most often of his parents. Some of them were nightmares, some were happy. But this one was best of all.

He dreamt about beans. His mother had a large pot of beans on the stove and she had put a ham hock in them so the fat and taste went into the beans and it had cooked to perfection, and his mother had ladled some into a bowl and put a chunk of butter on top and was handing it to him, just handing it to him . . .

His eyes opened.

He had no real way to tell time but there was a sliver of a moon and it had risen to halfway across the sky. He guessed that half the night was gone and if they were ever going to sleep they would be by now.

Francis had been sitting on a rock dozing and he rose, stretched, rubbed his arms and set off in the dark. The day's run had worn a hole in his right moccasin and it kept scooping dirt which he shook out periodically. When he stopped to shake his moccasin the third time he turned and saw that the mule was with him.

It is one thing to sneak into camp and try to steal my stuff back alone, he thought, looking at the mule. It is something else again to do it with a whole mule walking in back of me.

There was a very real danger. If the mare smelled the mule she might whicker or whinny and the sound would awaken the two men. If they were asleep. If he could get close enough. If. If.

He couldn't stop the mule if it wanted to follow him and he finally decided to chance it. He would need luck but the way it was going he would need all the luck in the world anyway. He might as well push it.

He turned and trotted off again, sensed rather than heard the mule following him, clumping along.

Things looked dramatically different in the dark. Twice he saw coyotes, once a single wolf that moved off into the darkness, and several times he passed buffalo. A rattlesnake buzzed as he passed, but it was well away from his path and stopped as soon as he was by. The streambed didn't show at all at first, and then when he thought he would never get to it he was suddenly in the trees and low brush that grew along the watercourse.

He stopped, listening, but could hear only the sound of the mule eating in back of him. The mule ate every time he stopped, had been eating all day every chance it got, but the sound wasn't loud and after a moment he moved on.

There was no fire to see now—which was a good sign and he hoped meant both men were asleep. But it made things difficult as far as finding the camp. He didn't want to blunder into them but he was running out of time. It would begin to get light soon—within the hour—and they would awaken.

His nose finally did the trick. As he turned, looking for some glow of embers and trying to see the mare in the dark, he smelled the smoke from the nearly dead fire.

Left, to the left it was stronger and he moved that way and hadn't gone twenty yards when he found them.

It was hard to see in the darkness but he made out the shape of the mare off across the fire. She either did not see the mule or didn't care and was silent.

The men were harder to locate. He stood for a full three minutes studying the campsite and finally saw them against the dark brush around the fire clearing.

Dubs was to his left, lying on his side with no blanket over him, sleeping like a great bear, and Courtweiler was across the fire pit, on his back with Francis's saddle for a pillow and Francis's blanket and bedroll for covers.

They were both snoring, but so lowly that Francis had to concentrate to hear it and he smiled. Good. They were asleep. Now if he could locate his rifle. None of this would work without the rifle —actually both rifles. He needed his and Dubs's. Two men, two shots.

He had no real plan except to get his rifle and force them to give his equipment back.

There. His Lancaster rifle was next to Courtweiler, the muzzle across the saddle by his head. Close. Maybe too close.

How would it go? He tried to imagine it, plan it.

He would get his rifle, then cover them and somehow get Dubs's rifle.

And what, shoot them if they made a try for him? Shoot them? He hesitated. He'd never shot a person, or at least didn't think he had. He had aimed at an Indian who was attacking him, but he thought Jason Grimes had done the shooting and he'd missed, or maybe wounded him.

On the other hand they had left him for dead, these two men. They could easily kill him, and would if they got a chance.

That's how it might play. He'd get his rifle, try to get Dubs's weapon, and shoot the big man if he had to. He took a breath, held it, worked his way softly and quietly around the side of the fire until he was standing over Courtweiler.

He squatted, reached forward, and gently, so gently wrapped his fingers around the stock of the rifle just ahead of the hammer and lifted it away from the saddle, stood back with it.

I missed you, he thought, holding the little Lancaster. He felt to make sure there was a cap on the nipple, then eared the hammer back slowly, holding the trigger so it wouldn't make a clicking sound when it cocked.

So far so good. He stood back and away and moved around to Dubs. The giant's rifle was next to him on the ground and Francis leaned down carefully and reached for it and happened to look at Dubs's face and nearly screamed out loud.

Dubs's eyes were wide open staring at him. Even in the pale light from the partial moon Francis could see the whites, the glare from them, and he thought, I am dead, this instant I am dead.

But Dubs didn't move and when he peered closer—something it took his whole heart to do—he saw that the eyes weren't truly on him, were just open.

Dubs slept with his eyes open.

It was enough to stop Francis. He stared at the man, moved his hands back and forth in front of his eyes, and there was no reaction. Nothing.

But the delay was nearly fatal. He had a firm grip on Dubs's rifle, was lifting it away when he heard a small sound in back of him, a rustling, and something grabbed his hair.

"Ahh, it's you, Francis. How good of you to call . . ."

Francis tore free but the sound had awakened Dubs and both men came at him. He somehow didn't remember that he was holding two rifles and could shoot them. And in any event it was all happening too fast.

Dubs came out of sleep instantly, animalistically,

ready for battle. He rolled to his feet, towered over Francis, reached for him from the left while Court-weiler reached from the right.

They would have him. In a second or less they would have him. He fell backward over the dead fire and his fall saved him.

Dubs was nearly on top of him but overshot when he reached for Francis. The hulk went over Francis, a good two feet beyond, and ran squarely into the mule, who had been following Francis as before.

There was a sound like someone splitting a wa-termelon with an ax and Dubs dropped as if he'd been shot with a howitzer. The mule swung a bit to the side, aimed quickly and caught Courtweiler dead in the middle of the stomach with another well-aimed kick and Courtweiler went down wheezing for breath. Suddenly Francis was the only human able to function.

He stood quickly, aimed the rifle at the two men, but it wasn't necessary. Dubs had taken it directly in the head, and while he was still breath-ing it would clearly be some time before he regained consciousness. Courtweiler still couldn't breathe and was only half conscious himself.

"I guess you must have been hard on the mule," Francis said aloud as he gathered his gear. "I hear they've got good memories . . ."

He moved from the fire pit to the mare, caught her and led her back by the camp to saddle, watching the two men all the while, the Lancaster still cocked and ready to fire. In the east there was a gray softness to the dark and he worked quickly. He wanted to be well away from these two before they could react, and he tied his bedroll in place in back of the saddle and laid his shirt across his lap as he mounted—he didn't want to lower his guard long enough to pull the shirt on over his head. He had taken what equipment there was that belonged to the two men as well and he draped it across the mare's neck.

"You're . . . leaving . . . us . . . like . . . this?" Courtweiler gasped while he spoke, still fighting for breath.

Francis nodded. "You're lucky I don't put a ball in you." He used his legs to back the mare away from the camp. Before turning her he said softly: "Don't come at me again. I won't be so easy to catch off guard and I *will* shoot you."

Courtweiler said nothing and Francis turned and rode away, smiling to himself when he saw the mule take one last bite of bunch grass and rush to follow him.

When he was half a mile from the men he stopped and pulled his shirt on, lashed the extra rifle—which turned out to be a crude version of a

Hawkens, with what appeared to be a half-inch bore—to the saddle horn so it hung down the mare's side and tied his canteen and the one he'd taken from Courtweiler so they balanced one on either side.

Then he set off again, the sun coming over his back. He needed miles in case they decided to follow him as he had done with them so he heeled the mare and picked up the speed, the mule shambling along in back.

He caught himself humming in time to the mare's movement and smiled openly. Where he'd been alone he now had two friends—one of them, the mule, a definitely powerful friend. Where he'd been without anything he now had two canteens, two rifles, two possibles bags, and an extra horn almost full of powder.

He was rich.

Now all he had to do was find the wagon train and get out to Oregon.

# Chapter Six

In one sense his situation hadn't improved. He really didn't know where he was, or which direction to take to find the train.

He decided to head west and cut north when the country to the north looked like easier going. Now it seemed to be made up of bluffs, some fifteen miles distant, and he didn't want to try work the mare and mule over them.

He rode west and angled north slightly, figuring if he missed the train at least he might hit the tracks they left going by.

The riding was easy, especially after the run the day before. His legs still ached and he kept falling asleep in the saddle, particularly when the afternoon sun began cooking his back.

In midafternoon he ran into a small stream where he watered the mare. The mule drank as well—it was actually looking better all the time—and Francis decided to run in the water for a mile or two to help throw the tracks off.

He set the mare in the middle of the stream and was surprised to see the mule mimic her, stepping into the water and putting his feet nearly exactly where the mare stepped.

He left the stream in half an hour, continuing west and slightly north, and he was just thinking he might catch the train tonight, thinking maybe they would have some fresh bread made, or stew, or maybe coffee with sugar in it . . . just letting himself dream of food when the rain hit.

He hadn't noticed the clouds. They had come up in patches, blown away while he rode-dozed, and somehow they had come together again without his realizing it.

At first it sprinkled and he hunched his shoulders and took it. But in a short time the clouds became more dense and the rain came harder and then it roared.

He would have gotten off the mare but there was

nowhere to go, no shelter. He was soaked instantly, and getting cold and hoping it was a short storm and would stop, but it didn't. It rained in a wide belt of dark storm clouds for close to three hours, poured like somebody was dumping giant buckets.

At one point it came down so hard he could not see the mare's head only three feet away, and he lost sight of the mule for the entire storm. He put both powder horns inside his shirt to keep the powder dry but everything else was soaked.

When it stopped, close to evening again, he dismounted and unsaddled the mare and hobbled her. In the evening light he spread his blanket on some brush to dry and by reaching up under the side of a streambed above the water he found some dry bits of wood protected from the rain.

He used a tiny portion of powder and his striker to make a fire, fed it with more small bits of dry wood until the heat could dry out some larger pieces and settled in for the night. There was no food—not in his own possibles bag and not in the one he'd taken from Courtweiler and Dubs—but there was a small metal pot and he made hot water and sipped it, pretending it was coffee with sugar.

"At least," he said aloud to the mule, which was standing nearby while the mare grazed off a bit on her hobble, "any tracks we've left are wiped out. If they're following us they'll never find us . . ."

He trailed off as what he said sank into his thinking. It was true that any tracks he'd left would be gone and he would be impossible to find.

But that held true for *all* tracks. His tracks would have been wiped out by the storm. But not only his tracks.

The wagon tracks would be gone as well. Even if he hit their trail he wouldn't find their tracks. He wouldn't find the wagons unless he ran into the train itself, and the chances of that happening—hitting them exactly right in the enormous area of the plains—were somewhere on the scale of finding a needle in a haystack.

He prepared for bed, rolled in a damp blanket well away from the fire—he would not make the same mistake twice—with the mule standing near him, and as he felt the exhaustion of the past two days take him, he could not stop thinking the word *lost*.

I am lost.

# Chapter Seven

After a time, a day, a month, years—a time he could not really measure—it did not seem as if he were moving but that he was standing in one place and the prairie rolled by beneath the mare.

He arose and left camp without a fire, stretching the stiffness out of his bones while he saddled. He remembered that, getting up. And then mounting in the coolness and being hungry. But after that everything blended into a sameness that defied memory. He kept the rising sun on the back of his right shoulder and rode, and rode, and rode . . .

It was the prairie, the grass sea, and it was end-less. He began to look for things to break the mo-notony. A buffalo here, a jackrabbit there, but he had left the area where the buffalo herd passed and ate the grass down, and the grass here was so high—at times even with his waist sitting up on the mare—he could see nothing smaller than a full-sized bull buffalo.

A day passed. He left in the morning and eve-ning came and it was time to stop and there was no change. He found a spring—there were dozens of them, seeping into wallows—and refilled his can-teens and let the mare drink. The mule took a sip and at once began eating, and watching him eat made Francis's hunger worse.

It was going on two days since he'd eaten from the bull, two days and many hard miles and he was so hungry his stomach seemed to be caving in.

He drank large quantities of water to swell his stomach but it didn't help.

He would have to find something, hunt some-thing. The mare was hobbled and the mule seemed to have changed his loyalties and was content to stay with her. Francis eyed the sun. There were probably two or three hours until hard dark, and around the spring there were dozens of fresh deer tracks.

They probably came in for water in the evenings

before heading back into the grass to eat and avoid the wolves.

He checked the cap on his rifle and put his possibles bag over his shoulder and headed into the grass.

It was like stepping into a different world. On the mare he had been above it, but now the grass was as tall as he was and he couldn't see more than a few feet and it was alive with sound.

He moved slowly, listening intently. There was a constant scurrying of mice and rabbits and twice he heard things move, heavy things, and he thought they were probably deer and he had decided to give it up, that it wasn't going to work, when he came upon the trail.

It was made by deer coming in to water and the ground was churned to powder by their sharp hooves. Francis stopped, studied the trail and decided the best way to hunt in the grass was to sit next to it and wait for something to come along. He certainly wouldn't have any luck blundering around the way he had been doing.

He found a small clearing—more a dent back into the grass than a true clearing—and he settled in and down, sitting with his thumb on the hammer of the rifle and his finger on the trigger.

He hadn't been there five minutes when a fawn came past. It was growing out of spots but still small and in back of her came her mother, a young doe, sleek and fat from the grass and leaves.

He could have shot either of them easily but something wouldn't let him fire at the fawn and the thought of killing her mother was just as bad. As it happened his hesitation was rewarded. Within minutes a young buck, three points on each side, stepped cautiously down the trail not five feet from Francis.

Francis waited until his head was past, raised the rifle, cocked it and fired, aiming just in back of the shoulder where he knew the heart lay.

The noise was deafening in the grass, seemed to fill the space around him, and he blinked. When he opened his eyes the buck was gone and he stood slowly, reloaded and listening, trying to locate it by sound, but all he could hear was a ringing in his ears from the crack of the rifle.

The buck hadn't gone far. Francis's shot had been accurate, and it had taken only three steps before settling into the grass with its head laid back on its shoulders.

He poked it with the muzzle of the rifle as he had done the buffalo, but it was gone and he set to work at once, gutting the deer and skinning it. This time he would not be so wasteful.

He took the back meat and tenderloin, then the

meat from the back legs, leaving the bones for the coyotes. It took him only a few minutes to make a fire from some dead brush near the wallow, and he cooked strips of venison hung over green sticks and ate them when they were still nearly raw.

He thought there'd been a lot of meat on the buck, but he ate over fifteen pounds, ate until his stomach hurt with it, ate until he couldn't get another bite in his mouth, and by that time there were only another ten or so pounds of meat.

This he cut into strips—the way he'd seen his Indian "mother" do when he was a captive—and hung them over the fire but away from the flames to dry them out and keep the flies away while the meat hardened into a kind of quick jerky.

He built the fire up some to keep it going for a while and took his bedroll back in the grass a good twenty yards from the fire, carefully closing the grass back in place as he moved. After his bedroll was spread out, he sat quietly for fifteen minutes listening, his mouth open, holding his breath again and again to hear anything that might mean a possible problem. But all he heard were the scurryings of small rodents, two coyotes already working at the deer carcass, and the sounds of the mule and the mare eating nearby.

Finally satisfied he put both rifles by his side,

checked them to be sure they were loaded and capped correctly one more time, pulled the blanket over the top to keep the night chill out, blinked once and was sound asleep.

# Chapter Eight

The next morning was different. He started right, ate some meat and drank water, made sure all his gear was finally dry, and was moving well before dawn.

Morning light revealed that the line of bluffs to the north had come to a shallow end and he swung straight north on the off chance that he would run into the wagon train.

It was a beautiful day and the mare was frisky, so he let her run for a mile to burn it out, loping easily, and was amazed to see the mule keep up handily.

"Whoa . . ." He held the mare down and studied the mule. It had filled out beautifully in just two days of constant eating and wasn't breathing hard though it had loped a mile. "You actually look younger," Francis said aloud. "Maybe we can rig a pack saddle up later and use you."

He set off again, holding the mare to a fast walk, his eyes sweeping the grass in front of them, and in two hours he found a track.

Actually, if he'd blinked he would have missed it. It wasn't a track so much as a faint line across the prairie, heading west, a blemish in the grass that could only be seen when the light was exactly right.

It was not left by a train—probably by a single wagon—but it was something, a track, which was better than he'd had before, and he turned to follow it. It must have been made before the rain, and the grass the wagon had run over had been broken enough to stay at least partially down. When Francis dismounted and felt down in the grass he could feel slight indentations in the prairie sod, barely half an inch deep.

He remounted and followed the track, which seemed to go west by slightly south, and tried not to hope.

It was only midday, but by late afternoon the tracks seemed to have faded more and he was having trouble following them. It had struck him as odd that a single wagon would come out here alone, but there was something drawing him on and he decided to give it another hour or two before turning back to the west.

The country was the same. Rolling flat, or what seemed to be flat with shallow dips into more flatness. He thought he could see for miles, and he couldn't see anything like a wagon, and at last he decided to end the run and cut north again.

His turn to the north took him onto a low rise, and at the top of the rise he happened to glance left and something caught his eye.

He stopped and studied it. Way off, over a mile, there was something round sticking up out of the grass. It wasn't white, quite, but a gray color. A gray spot and he realized it was tarp, canvas, and that he was looking at the top of a covered wagon.

The mare turned west again without his meaning to turn her—answering pressure from his knees—and he nudged her into a fast walk.

If it was a wagon it would have people. And if there were people they might know where they were, or where the main wagon train was.

But as he drew closer he felt a strangeness about the wagon. It was stopped dead, as if camped. But he could see no stock, no sign of life, and there wasn't any smoke from a cook fire.

He stopped a hundred yards from the wagon and sat on the mare, his thumb on the hammer of the rifle. "Hello!"

No answer.

"Hello at the wagon—is anybody there?"

Silence. For a second he thought he heard a small sound, almost a whimper, but it could have come from the mare or the mule breathing.

"I'm coming in and I'm friendly!"

Still he sat, tensed, waiting for any sign of movement or threat. Again he thought he heard a small sound, but it was so soft he could not be sure and other than that, nothing.

The mule ended it. He had been standing in back of the mare, but he saw the wagon and decided to investigate and walked past the mare and went up to the wagon.

Nothing happened, and Francis took it as a good sign and thumped his heels against the mare's ribs and moved to the wagon.

"Hello!" he said again, but there was no answer. He could find no sign of life until he came to the rear of the wagon and looked inside.

There were two children sitting on a quilt, a girl and a boy, their eyes wide with fright. The girl was eight or nine, wearing a sunbonnet with most of the stiffener out of the brim so it drooped. The boy was five or six. Both of them were blond and covered with freckles. As Francis stared at them—finding children was the last thing he had expected to do—the girl made a sound, a cry, and Francis recognized it as the sound he had heard.

"Where are your folks?" Francis looked around the wagon and could see nothing. "And how did the wagon get here? Where are your animals?"

The boy jumped at the sound and stuck a thumb in his mouth and started sucking. The girl seemed startled as well but seemed to have more spunk than the boy.

"Are you a savage?" she asked. "Are you one of them savages?"

Francis shook his head. "I don't think so. My name is Francis. What's yours?"

She relaxed. "I'm Charlotte, but folks all called me Lottie. This is Billy. Of course, it's William and not Billy, but Billy is the short way of saying William just like Lottie is short for Charlotte, and ain't that the strangest thing? Who would think Billy would come from William instead of it being Willy or just plain Will . . ."

Francis held up his hand. "Easy, easy."

"I like to talk," she said. "Sometimes it gets away from me a little."

Francis nodded.

"It's like there's a place in me full of words and when I open the door to the place they just start coming and I can't seem to stop . . ."

Again Francis held up his hand. "We have other things to talk about now. Where are your folks?"

"Folk," she said. "It was just Pa. Ma went on must have been two years ago when some croup came and took her. Pa decided to go West, but he got the water sickness and they made us leave the train."

"Water sickness?" Francis stopped her again. "You mean cholera?"

She nodded. "That's the one. He was taken sick, and we came out here so he could get well except that he didn't. Get well I mean. It started to take him down, and he left us with some flour and biscuits that he made and took off walking until he got over it so we wouldn't take the sickness from him."

"How long ago was that?" Cholera, Francis thought. Cholera. They said it came from drinking bad water, but nobody was sure and he wondered if he could catch it just by being close to the children. "When did he go off?"

"It's been two days and a little more now." She hesitated, and Francis saw a tear come down her cheek and saw that Billy was crying as well, and

perhaps had been the whole time. "He ain't coming back, is he?"

Some died in a day, Francis had heard. Some had
a fever in the morning and were dead by noon.
The man had gone off to die alone to protect his
children, although leaving them alone in the prairie
was close to a death sentence. Pushing the sick ones
out was the only protection wagon trains had, getting the sick ones away from the unsick people. But
it still seemed a brutal thing to Francis, pushing
these children out with their sick father when they
obviously weren't sick, making them go it alone.

Except, Francis thought, they weren't alone.
Not now. He couldn't leave them. They wouldn't
last a week. And they weren't sick, or didn't appear
to be.

"Wait here," he said. "I'm going to look around
a bit. I'll be back."

He left them in the wagon and started searching
out and around the wagon. He was looking for the
father on the off chance that he had survived—
some had, he knew, although it left them sickly—
and he didn't want to leave the man here if he
wasn't dead.

He found the father on the fourth circle around
the wagon. He had gone a good distance—two
hundred yards—before settling into the grass. Fran-

cis read the sign. He was flat on his back and very dead, although the coyotes and wolves hadn't been at him yet. His arms were at his sides and he had a peaceful look on his face—if, Francis thought, dead people can have any look—and it looked like he'd been sitting and just laid back when death came.

I should bury him, Francis thought, but he knew he couldn't. He shouldn't even be this close and he backed the mare away shaking his head. He hated to leave but the sickness could still be here, still be around the body, and he didn't want to take any chances. He'd have to leave the body.

He went straight back to the wagon where the children still sat inside on the quilt.

"Did you find Pa?" Lottie asked.

Francis didn't answer the question but instead scanned the prairie around the wagon again. "Didn't you have horses or oxen when you came?"

Lottie nodded. "Two horses. Buck and Booger. But Pa he let them loose just before he got bad sick and something run them off."

Wolves, Francis thought. They're probably dead and if not they're so far away I could never find them.

"What are we going to do?" Lottie asked, and Francis thought, That's it, that's it exactly, as Courtweiler would have said. What could he do?

Suddenly he was not alone. He had two children

to care for and nothing else had changed. He didn't know where he was or where to go, didn't know anything except now there were three of them instead of just one.

He shook his head. It would have to be taken a step at a time and one thing was sure, they couldn't stay here.

"Get your stuff together," he told Lottie. "And Billy's, too. We're going to go."

"Where?" Lottie asked.

Good question, Francis thought—and I don't have the tiniest part of an answer. But he smiled, a smile he didn't really feel, and pointed with his chin.

"West," he said. "We're going to go West . . ."

# ─── Chapter Nine ───

Again the mule saved him.

It was one thing to say they were going to go West, something else again to do it. The children were small, but they could not have all three ridden the mare and they couldn't have walked. Francis could have walked and led them on the mare and was thinking of doing just that when he saw the mule standing by the wagon.

"Could you carry them?" he said aloud and Lottie misunderstood, thought he was talking to her.

"You mean me? Could I carry Billy? Well, for a little ways . . ."

"No, no. I was talking to the mule."

"The mule? You were talking to a mule? Do they know how to talk? They look so dumb the way they just stand all the time except this one seems to eat more than anything I've seen . . ."

"Is there a halter in the wagon?"

"Yeah. Pa he kept extra ones for the horses but I'm not sure he'd want you taking them . . . Oh. I guess it doesn't matter, does it?"

She climbed into the wagon and came out in a moment with a halter. Francis tied the mare to the wagon wheel and dismounted, walked up to the mule with the halter and was surprised when the mule stuck his head through it and let him buckle it in place.

"I thought mules were s'posed to be fractious," Lottie said. "Pa he said mules were all the time being fractious but your mule seems to be a right nice fellow. Time was I saw a mule belonged to our neighbor, her name was Nancy and she had red hair and lived a mile away down a rocky road and worked all the time. Anyway she had a mule name of Plover and he could kick so fast he'd kick a rock if you threw it at his back end . . ."

Francis let her talk and used a rope to tie a folded blanket from the wagon on the mule's back. It was

makeshift at best, but it would give them something to sit on.

He had thought fleetingly of trying to harness
the mule and the mare to pull the wagon, but it was
too heavy and they were much too lightweight to
take the load for very long. And besides, he didn't
want to be encumbered with a wagon. They might
hit rough country where a wagon couldn't go.

There were other things he took from the
wagon. Another rifle, and under the seat wrapped
in a grease-stained sack of soft leather, he found a
.44 Colt's cap and ball revolver. He wasn't much
on handguns—they were mostly inaccurate and
didn't have any range or punch—but it held six
balls and he thought there might come a time
when he would need to shoot without reloading so
he took it, along with a bullet mold and a box
of caps and a full flask of powder. There was
some flour—he ate half a handful raw—and some
matches and salt and a cast-iron Dutch oven with a
lid. All of this he placed in a canvas bag he'd found
in the wagon, which he hung on the mule.

He took two more blankets and the quilt to
make a bedroll for the children, cut a large piece of
canvas from the top of the wagon for a tent or lean-
to, rolled them all and tied them across the mule's
shoulders and stood back to look at it. It was bulky,
but light, and the two children together wouldn't

make half a man—they were skinny as well as small—and he thought the mule would not have any trouble carrying them.

He led the mule up to the rear of the wagon and reached in, loaded Billy and Lottie onto the mule's back. The mule took the load easily and didn't flinch or buck, for which Francis was thankful.

Then he mounted the mare, took the mule's lead rope in his hand and left the wagon. He did not look back for some time and when he did the wagon was a spot in the endless grass and Lottie was looking straight at him. But the boy had somehow turned around on the mule and was sitting backward, sucking his thumb, still silent, staring at the wagon.

# Chapter Ten

The Indians found them in midafternoon.

Or, in reality, Francis and the Indians found each other.

Francis and the children started from the wagon about noon, working west and slightly north. He could think of no reason for the northerly movement except that it seemed right, a hunch, and he decided to follow it, hoping to cut a wagon train—the one he'd left or the one that had set the children and their father out. But he understood there was little chance.

The boredom set back in. There were long silences while they rode. Francis thought of his family, his mind triggered by the two children with him. Ma. Pa. His little sister Rebecca. He kept wondering how she was doing. He could not remember her face, how she looked, and found himself thinking that she must look a lot like Lottie.

Billy seemed to prefer sitting backward on the mule, sucking his thumb. The only time he changed was when Francis gave them each a piece of the venison jerky he'd brought from the deer he'd killed. Billy grabbed the meat like a puppy—revealing a thumb that was amazingly white and clean—and almost swallowed it whole before going back to thumb sucking.

The silences were punctuated at intervals by Lottie, who would "go off," as Francis came to think of it, at the slightest provocation, the sunbonnet wobbling as she talked.

"See that buzzard up there? How can they fly like that without ever moving their wings, just hang there like they was floating on the air? Is it like they float there, like sticks float on water? How can the air be thick enough for them to float that way when it's still thin enough to breathe? I wish I could do that, just float up there and see it all forever and ever . . ."

The talk had a lulling effect and between the

boredom of the prairie—which he knew was deceptive—and Lottie going on, he soon fell into a kind of haze.

He should have known better. Every time he'd let his guard down something had come at him. But he rode and dozed, the mule following easily, and Lottie was talking about the neighbor Nancy. ". . . she goes to making things that are so pretty they take your breath away. Things to put on shelves and just look at, little boxes with trees on them and designs and colors—Oh."

The stopping startled Francis. His eyes had been half closed, his body rolling with the motion of the mare, his mind on a million other things and when she stopped talking he snapped his eyes open, but it was too late.

In front of him on either side were two Indian men. One had a rifle and the other a bow with an arrow in the string and they were both on foot— almost unheard of on the prairie. The one on the left was older, a grown man, the one on the right was young—fifteen, sixteen—and they were standing looking at him.

Francis's rifle was across his lap. The handgun hung in the sack off the saddle horn. The two extra rifles were back on the mule.

All of this, the Indians, the way they looked not twenty feet away, their weapons, his own weapons not being ready—all of this he registered in half a second. And at the same time he knew that there was no time. Even if he could swing the rifle up and get a shot off at one of them the other would get him.

It could have gone in any direction and for a full five seconds—it seemed like an hour—the tension was wound so tight Francis could hear his heart beating. He stared at them, they looked at him.

Then two things. He saw they were not wearing paint, which they would be wearing if they were looking to war, and at the same time the older of the two smiled and said something to the other who smiled as well.

They were looking back at Lottie and Billy—who was still sitting the mule backward, ignoring the Indians. Lottie had seen them but she had to hold her head back to peer out from beneath the flopping rim of her sunbonnet.

"Are they savages?" she asked.

"Be quiet," Francis said.

"Because if they are, you know, savages, then I think maybe you should do something. Of course I never have seen no savages and only heard about them in the wagon train where everybody said if they come upon you they'd cut you open and eat your heart and I don't want nobody cutting me open and eating my heart out so maybe . . ."

The older Indian's smile widened and he made a sign in front of his mouth, his fingers fluttering and moving away. Francis knew some sign from when he'd lived with the Indians, and literally the sign meant butterflies or birds flying. But in front of his mouth it meant words flying, and Francis nodded and smiled back and imitated the sign in front of his own mouth.

The young Indian put his bow down, took his fingers off the string and Francis knew it was over.

"English?" Francis asked, using sign. "Do you talk English?"

The boy shook his head, but the man nodded.

"Speak small, not big. Why you here?" His hands moved when he spoke, making sign to back up his spotty English.

"I'm looking for a wagon train. I've been lost." Francis also made sign, but he was not as good as the Indian and much slower.

"Young lost, too?"

Francis nodded. "I found them back almost a day. Their father died of the water sickness and I brought them with me."

Both of the Indians stepped back at this. They knew of cholera—Francis had heard of whole villages being killed in two or three days—and like Francis, they did not know how it spread.

"It's all right now," Francis said. "Good, good. They're not sick now. But that way a day"—he pointed in the direction they'd come—"that way there is a wagon where the sickness came from."

The man nodded and made a sign for peace—his palm up and facing out—and the boy did the same and Francis raised his hand and showed his palm.

"Hunt," the man said, pointing south, "that way."

Francis nodded and pointed west. "We go there." And because he couldn't resist it—the thought had been on his mind since he'd first seen them—he asked: "Why no horses?"

From living with and watching the Indians he knew they wouldn't move fifteen feet without a horse under them. They were all—man, woman, and child—better riders than Francis, and Jason Grimes had told him he thought they were born on a horse. Two men hunting on foot was rare.

But the man made the sign on his head for antlers. "Deer, better on foot, low, in grass. Closer. Shoot more. Horses back there with family." He made the sign for children and women. "Waiting for meat." He smiled.

Francis nodded, remembering the buck he'd killed by waiting in the grass. He started to say more but the mare moved under him, making him look down and when he looked up they were gone, vanished in the grass.

"I guess they weren't savages," Lottie said.

"No." Francis squeezed the mare with his legs and she started forward, the mule keeping up. "They were people, just like us, looking for food . . ."

The thought seemed to quiet Lottie, and Francis set the direction back to north and west but determined not to lose his alertness again.

The children posed a real problem. Alone, if something bad *did* happen he could cut and run and have a chance of getting out of it. There were horses faster than the mare, but not many quicker or more sure of foot, and that gave Francis some advantage.

But Lottie and Billy changed everything. The mule couldn't move fast, wouldn't carry them out of danger if it came, and that made it doubly important for Francis to be aware of what was coming to get time to react or hide.

Then there was food. He could go two, three days without eating but he didn't think it was good for young to go that long. They had to eat on a more regular basis. All he had left was the semi-dried venison and they ate from that most of the day, riding along—both children had been nearly starved and ate ravenously to make up for it—and the jerky was nearly gone.

He would have to hunt soon, get another deer or better yet a buffalo, which would slow them down, and at first that irritated him until he remembered that there wasn't a hurry to get anywhere because he didn't know where he was or where to go.

The problem was that suddenly the prairie was bare. Where he'd been seeing small groups of buffalo out ahead there didn't seem to be any for miles and he couldn't see deer or antelope.

They rode the rest of the day, Francis alert and looking for game and finally just before dusk he shot a jackrabbit.

"We'll stop for the night now," he said, lifting the children off the mule. "Gather wood for a fire so we can cook this rabbit . . ."

Lottie stretched and helped Billy take a few steps to shake his legs out. "Pa he tried to cook one of them once when we were with the wagon train and we like to broke our teeth chewing. We need some good meat, some more deer meat, that's the kind of meat we need. Some good red meat with fat on it to make drippings . . ."

She talked constantly, but she worked as she spoke, finding dry wood and sticks, and Billy helped her, and by the time Francis had finished hobbling the mare—the mule would stay without it—they had a stack of wood large enough to last all night.

Francis took some kindling sticks, shaved them with his knife to get curls, laid a fire and lit it.

"You keep wood on it," he told Lottie. "I'll clean the rabbit . . ."

He quickly gutted and skinned the rabbit and cut it into smaller pieces. There was no water where they stopped so he poured some from a canteen into the Dutch oven and put the rabbit into the water. He added a handful of flour for thickening and cut three chunks of venison to drop in on top. Then he put the lid on and shoved the cast pot into the fire.

"Stew," he said. "An hour or so . . ."

"I like stew," Lottie said. "I didn't mean back then that I didn't like stew and such like. I'm not a picky eater like some, being as I'll eat almost anything though I'm not fond of bugs nor the reptile along the ground. Billy here will eat a bug in a second. He just loves 'em. Not me, though . . ."

Billy was sitting on a blanket staring at the flames and Francis studied him. "Doesn't he ever talk?"

Lottie nodded. "Sure. He just don't have anything to say. Sometimes he'll talk your ear off. I remember once, I think it was last week, he looked me right in the eye and said 'I'm thirsty,' plain as day, must have been six, seven days ago . . ." She trailed off and the quiet was so sudden Francis thought she must have seen something. But he looked at her and saw she was crying quietly looking into the flames. "It was to Pa he said it. I miss Pa . . ."

Francis tried to think of something to say but there was nothing. He remembered when he'd first been kidnapped and then seen a toy that had belonged to his sister Rebecca and thought Rebecca was dead. The empty feeling. The numbness. No words could help.

So he put more wood on the fire and covered the two children to get them to sleep, and when they were at last both sleeping, he moved away from the fire to doze back in the grass with his rifle across his lap and a blanket over his shoulders. Twice in the night he heard wolves—they sang deeper and longer than the yipping coyotes—and he tried not to think of the children's father alone on the prairie.

# Chapter Eleven

Lottie awakened early. Francis heard her as she broke small sticks and found red coals to blow on to make morning fire. They had all slept through the night without eating, and Francis decided it might have been the best thing possible for the meat stew he had prepared. It had cooked until the fire was out and when he came in by the fire Lottie had pulled the pot over to the flames and warmed it. Francis lifted the lid and the meat had become tender and fallen away from the bones.

He let the two children eat—Lottie was quiet

and he thought it was because she wasn't fully awake yet—and then finished what they did not want.

All of it didn't take an hour and it was just getting light in the east when they packed the bedrolls and loaded the mare and mule for the day. Francis helped them up on the mule—smiling as Billy turned around to sit backward—and mounted the mare and rode away from camp.

The day went smoothly. Clouds held to the horizon and then vanished and the sun was hot and welcome. A small breeze kept the flies down, and Francis figured Lottie's talker must have played out because other than ask a question now and then she was mostly quiet.

They quickly settled into the routine of riding, covering ground. Francis had turned straight west—had given up on hitting tracks—but in the middle of the afternoon they came to a ridge that was impossible to climb that stretched far away to the south and they had to turn north.

Fifteen or so miles north Francis could see the end of the ridge, and as they moved slowly in that direction, he could see dust near the end of the ridge. Lottie saw it as well and told him about it.

"Dust up there, you see it? Reminds me of the time when we were crossing that river just after we started before Pa he got the sickness. All the wagons had to wait in the same place so they corralled the stock until everybody was ready to ford the river and they raised *such* a cloud of dust . . ."

"It's buffalo," Francis said, squinting. "I can see them . . ."

But he was wrong.

Lottie was right, or partially so. As they moved closer—at a crawl, or so it felt to Francis—he could see the dust wasn't from buffalo but from moving wagons. It was a full train. But they weren't fording a river. When they were a mile off he counted twelve wagons, and they were bunched at the bottom of a steep upgrade with the horses and oxen corralled in a rope enclosure. The stock milling around was making the dust.

Whoever the train was made up of, he could travel with them. And somebody would take in the children.

They were nearly a quarter of a mile from the wagons—Francis could see individuals and hear the cracks of their whips as they worked the stock —when somebody from the wagon train noticed him.

There was a sudden movement that Francis thought looked like ants scurrying when an anthill has been kicked, and four men came running from the wagons to meet him.

They were all carrying rifles and they stopped

when Francis was still a hundred and fifty yards away, stopped and stood four abreast with their rifles across their chests.

They probably think we're Indians, Francis thought. Probably a mistake.

"I know those men," Lottie said suddenly in back of him.

"What?" He turned and the mare kept walking.

"That's the wagon train that drove us out when the sickness came. I know those four men. That's Peterson and Ellville and Johnson and McIntire and they were the ones to push us away and make us be where you found us and saved us . . ."

Francis turned back to the front. Pushing the sick ones out wasn't maybe nice, but it was the only thing they could do to save the rest. He understood that. But the sickness was past. Surely they wouldn't cause problems now.

When they were fifty yards away, the men leaned in together and spoke quickly amongst themselves, then faced Francis again.

"You can't come in to the wagons," the man on the left said. "Those children might be infected. We had to send them out."

Francis stopped the mare. Twenty-five yards. The one who spoke actually moved his rifle so the barrel was on Francis, and he thought, This is crazy. I'm not trying to hurt them. "They're all right now. It was their Pa who . . . took sick. These two are fine. And so am I."

"Just the same, we can't take the chance. We'll set some food and water out here for you and you turn and head out on your own." The man spoke to one of the others, who trotted back to the wagons and came back in a moment with a bucket of water and a loaf of bread.

All this time Francis sat holding the mare and the mule back. They had seen the stock and thought it was where they would spend the night and were anxious to end the day's ride.

He couldn't believe what he was hearing.

"I'm not . . . geared . . . for children. They need to be with wagons, people . . ."

The man shook his head. "I'm sorry but we can't. We have other children to think of and if they have the sickness and bring it back in . . . I'm taking a risk just standing here talking to you. It might blow on me and I could carry it back to the wagons."

"That's the same trash they talked when they sent us off before," Lottie said suddenly. "Just the same when Pa tried to get them to take us in and let him go off alone to be sick. They wouldn't do it then and they're talking the same trash now. You're just dirt, Frank McIntire. Just pig dirt and you know it."

Francis held his hand up to quiet Lottie and tried one more time. "I can go off alone—in fact I'd rather. I don't want to be with your train." Or, he thought, with any other train if they're all like this. "But these two are too young . . ."

"Just the same." McIntire stopped him. "We can't let you in. Ride on around if you like and pick up the trail, stay a quarter mile out, and God-speed to you. There's a trading post three days west by wagon. Maybe you can find help there, though I doubt it. When they find you're carrying the sickness, they won't let you come in."

"And if we push it?"

The man raised his rifle, as did the others. "We'll do what we have to do."

"Shoot us?"

"We'll do what we have to do," he repeated. "And be sorry for it later."

It was hopeless. Francis turned the mare to the side and began the long circle out around the train and back to the trail, the mule plodding behind.

He did not take the food and did not take the water and thought if he lived to be a hundred he would never take anything from people—good or bad—again.

# ——— Chapter Twelve ———

It wasn't much of a trading post. In fact it wasn't much of anything.

They rode a full day in what looked to be permanent ruts. After they rode around the wagon train—and the armed men followed them all around to make certain they kept going—Francis led the mule up the grade the wagons were trying to climb.

It was too steep for a wagon and they were using two-hundred-foot ropes and a triple team of horses on top to pull the wagons up one at a time.

But the grade didn't bother the mare or the mule at all and when they came out on top where there was a stony ledge Francis was amazed to see that the trail was so used it cut into the stone itself.

Grooves left the top of the ridge and headed west into the prairie, grooves a foot deep in the hard sod, and the grass was eaten down so much along the way that the ground had turned to dust. It almost made Francis smile—he'd been worried about losing the trail. He couldn't have lost this if he were blind.

It was absolutely flat. Even the small rolling hills seemed to have flattened out and the three days it would have taken a wagon to get to the post were only a day and a half on the mare and mule.

They stopped for the night in a dry, fireless camp. There were no springs, and preceding wagons and people had burned every available stick of dry wood or even dry buffalo manure so they couldn't build a fire. There was also no grass for the animals anywhere near the trail. Stock from wagon trains had eaten it down so low that even the roots were gone and the earth was a dry, empty powder.

Francis almost smiled that night, again thinking of his worry about finding the trail. Camp was a miserable affair, dark and with no fire to cheer them. They ate the last of the venison jerky—both Lottie and Billy sneezing from the dust that seemed to fill the air, even at night—and Francis slept fitfully because there was no way to conceal himself in case trouble came. It was like trying to sleep on top of an immense, dusty table.

They were out of everything but water and flour in the morning so they drank water and each took a mouthful of raw flour, and they started before sunup, the dust coming up from the hooves, clogging their nose and eyes.

Francis tried swinging away from the main part of the trail but many had already done it, thousands—Jason Grimes had said they were coming from the East so thick it was like swarming bees—and the dust was everywhere so he wrapped pieces cut from the tarp around Lottie and Billy and just kept slogging.

The "trading post" came as a complete surprise. A small breeze had come up, making the dust worse, and Francis had been looking down to keep his eyes from filling when suddenly the mare stopped.

He nudged her without looking up, but she didn't go and when he looked up he saw it was because she had her shoulders against the top rail of a fence. Actually it was less a fence than a crude collection of broken wagon parts—tongues, boards from the sides, old wheels, all lashed together to make a ramshackle corral. To the right was a gate made from the large rear wheel of a wagon and over the gate a rough sign lettered in what looked like charcoal said:

STOCK BOARDED
TWENNY SENTS THE NITE

Francis doubted that the board included anything like feed or grass in this stripped land.

He raised his eyes and squinted and through gusts in the blowing dirt he saw a series of small shacks arranged on the other side of the corral. Like the boarding pen they were made from old wagon parts gleaned from wreckage on the trail. It looked more like a junkyard for old wagons than anything else.

And it also looked deserted. He peered inside the huts as best he could but couldn't see anything for a full minute and a half.

Then a tarp curtain over one of the openings—it couldn't be called a door—was pushed back, and a face showed for a moment, then disappeared and reappeared a moment later with a hat on.

A thin man, tall and sunken, with a dark beard trimmed short and pointed on the end came out of the hut and approached Francis. He put one hand on the mare's bridle, and she pulled her head away and wiggled her ears, a sign of nervousness.

"You'll be wanting to board the animals?" He spoke in a low voice, almost a hiss, and Francis suddenly thought of snakes and Courtweiler in that order.

Near the huts the wind had died and Francis could see better. He shook his head. "I don't have any money. But I need a home for the young ones. I found them in a deserted wagon on the prairie—I think their father was killed by a bear." (A white lie can't hurt, he thought.) "Is there room for them here?"

"Cholera, you mean." The man smiled shrewdly and inspected Lottie and Billy more closely. "Don't make no never mind to me. I've had it and so's my missus. Onct you've had it you cain't take it again." He pushed the tarp back and looked at Billy and Lottie more closely, pinched their arms. "They don't look sickly. 'Pears they could pull their own weight, anyways. Good, I'll take 'em."

He lifted them off the mule and carried them into the hut without another word and Francis sat feeling uncomfortable. On the one hand he wanted a home for them, but the man was . . . was so wrong somehow.

He shrugged the feeling off and dismounted. They would have a better chance here and maybe a train would come along after the one that shunned them that wouldn't mind taking them on. They would be better off, he thought again, but he tied the mare to the corral fence and made his way to the hut to lift the tarp sideways and peer inside.

The man was in there, doing something with a bucket and a water barrel, his back to the opening. There was also a woman, the man's wife, and she was as thin as the man, had the same angular look about her, a sunken hungry look. But she had Billy in her lap and was pinching Lottie's cheek and smiling, and Francis dropped the tarp back and returned to the horse.

It would be all right. They'd be safer here than trying to ride with Francis.

The man came out of the hut with a bucket of water. "Your stock will need water," he said.

"Thank you."

"It's four cents the bucket," he said quickly. "You got four cents?"

Francis stared at the man. Four cents for a bucket of water? Then he shook his head. "No. I don't have any money."

"You got something to trade?"

"For four cents?"

"For the water."

"I need some supplies and I've got two rifles to trade." He thought suddenly of the pistol and added, "I've got a pistol as well, but it belongs to the children."

"I'll take it for 'em," he said. "And you know, keep it. For them. What supplies you need?"

"Flour and sugar and some bacon . . ."

"How many rifles did you say?"

"Two."

"You don't know the prices here, do you?"

"No."

"A rifle will bring you flour, or sugar, or bacon. Not all of them, just one of them. Ten pounds of flour, five pounds of sugar, five pounds of bacon."

"For a *rifle*?"

"Ayup. Which do you want?"

Francis shook his head. It was robbery but he had no need for Dubs's rifle and he did need flour. "Flour. One rifle's worth. And you throw in that bucket of water for the mare and mule."

"Would you be looking for getting shed of that mule? It seems about to die on you."

Francis looked at the mule and thought how much better it looked now than it had when he first saw it and smiled. "That mule will still be going when you're done, mister. He stays with me."

"Just as you say."

"I could work for you," Francis said. "To pay off other supplies."

"Don't need it now."

"Well then, that's it."

The man went back into one of the huts while

Francis watered the mule and mare, and he came out in a couple of minutes carrying a cloth feed sack with ten pounds of flour and handed it to Francis to tie on his saddle.

Francis handed him Dubs's rifle and mounted the mare and took the lead rope from the mule and rode off into the dust without looking back, forcing himself to not look back.

# Chapter Thirteen

He made it nearly ten miles. The wind stopped and the dust abated somewhat and he kept riding until just before dark. He had angled north, still following the trail but looking for grass and water, and when he was some five or six miles north of the trail, he started to find grass for the animals, and just before dark he hit a spring.

There was wood for a fire, and he shot a rabbit on the way in to the spring and made stew and sat by the fire and was miserable.

Jason Grimes came back to him, the memory of

the man, his rough humor and final viciousness. It seemed years ago yet it wasn't a month since the fight with Braid, and Francis had changed almost daily.

He was nothing like the boy who had started West and he thought of that, was dismayed to realize he couldn't remember how his mother and father looked, how his sister Rebecca sounded. They'd had a dog, a little feisty dog, and he couldn't remember how the dog looked.

Lottie and Billy were there suddenly, cutting into his thoughts. He lay back and looked at the stars—they seemed to be all around him, somehow under him as well as over—and he thought of Lottie with her sunbonnet flopping down all the time and Billy sitting backward on the mule and they were more real to him than Jason Grimes or even his family.

And something the man had said. What was it? Something he had said about Francis working to pay for trade goods. Francis sat up, trying to remember, but it didn't come and he finally could fight the exhaustion no longer.

He put more wood on the fire and took his bedroll and moved back in the grass with his rifle to where a small hummock provided cover and settled in for the night. I am fourteen, he thought, no, wait, maybe I'm fifteen. I'm fifteen and I sleep on the ground with a rifle and I am alone in the world and I am ready to rest . . .

But sleep wouldn't come, didn't come, and by the time the eastern sky started to gather light he was already saddled and moving.

If I keep going, he thought, and get farther away, if I just keep going it will go away, this feeling. But it didn't. The uneasiness grew until it became real, something in back of him, and he actually turned twice to see the mule plodding along expecting, fully expecting to see Lottie riding and Billy sitting backward.

But of course they were not there and he went another mile, riding more and more slowly and finally without meaning to his hand pulled back on the mare's rein and she stopped and he sat. Thinking.

Then it hit him. What the man had said. He'd said he didn't need any help *now*. It was a strange way to put it and Francis remembered how he had pinched the children's arms, how the woman felt them as well.

They were going to work the kids, just use them. Like stock. He was sure of it.

He turned the mare. It was wrong, leaving them. Francis should have found them a good family or should have stayed to protect them.

Should protect them now.

He kicked the mare in the ribs and took her up to a distance-covering trot. He had come slowly after leaving the post and if he kept her moving they should get back in three or four hours.

He'd just make sure the children were all right and then he could turn around and come away again. And if they weren't . . . well, he'd cover that when he got there. He was probably wrong. They were probably fine and it was all in his head.

But soon the mare was moving faster, into a canter and the mule thundered to keep up.

When he was still four or five miles from the post he could see that it had all changed. The wagon train that had forced them to stay out had come to the post and were pulled up to camp nearby. There was no wind, but the stock had churned the ground and clouds of dust floated in the air obscuring the people.

As he rode closer he could see that the wagon train was keeping well away from the compound. They must have found out that Lottie and Billy were here, he thought, and they're scared of taking the sickness. He smiled.

Then he rounded a corner near the corral and saw Lottie and Billy, and the smile died. They were each carrying two buckets of water—in Billy's case the buckets looked as big as he was and he dragged more than carried them—and they were both crying. Even in the endless dust he could see streaks down their cheeks, and when Lottie saw Francis she dropped her buckets and ran toward him.

Francis swung off the mare and she hit him about when he hit the ground. Billy had done the same—both his buckets spilled—but he stopped about three feet away and turned his back.

Lottie moved back and pushed her bonnet up. "It's right good to see you. Time was I never thought it would be good to see someone again, except Pa, of course, and Ma, but then you went and left us here . . ."

"What's the matter? Why were you crying?"

Lottie shook her head. "No reason. Just happy to see you . . ."

"He beat us." Billy spoke with his back to Francis. "He took a cane rod and he beat Lottie and when I tried to stop him he beat me."

"Beat you? Why?"

"For not working hard enough," Lottie answered. "I wasn't moving buckets of water fast enough out to where the train people could get them for the stock and like Billy said he took a cane to me. But it wasn't much. Like a bee sting . . ."

She stopped talking because Francis had picked her up and put her on the mule. Then he reached for Billy and had him halfway up when a voice stopped him.

"What you doing with them children?"

Francis finished setting Billy on the mule—backward—and turned. The trading-post owner was there, twenty feet away. His wife had come out of one of the huts as well and stood with one hand on the doorway, staring at him.

"I'm taking them."

"No, you ain't. Them are my kids now and I'll keep 'em. You gave 'em to me fair and square and I've got an *in*vestment in them. I'll be taking them back now. They got to work off their 'debtedness. It's the law."

Francis was by the mare and he stopped with one hand on the saddle horn, his rifle in the other, half turned toward the man. "You touch them, either one, one more time and you'll pull back a bloody stump."

"Oh, you're tough, are you? Just a regular bobcat."

And it all swirled through Francis then. Captured by the Indians, beaten, escaping, living with Jason Grimes, trapping, blizzards—all in a sudden flash it went through him. All that, and he was still alive and had both arms and legs and he smiled. "Why, yes, I believe I am."

He swung up on the mare and caught up the mule's catch rope and they rode away silently and they were a good two miles away from the trading post, angling north to find the grass and water so they could camp, just over two miles when it hit Francis.

"Billy talked," he said to Lottie. "Back there he talked just fine."

Lottie nodded. "It was the first time he felt like he had something to say. I told you he could talk, but you don't listen to me. Just like I told you it was wrong to leave us with that awful man . . ."

"You didn't tell me."

"Yes, I did. Or I meant to and it's the same thing. I meant to tell you and you should have known it. But it doesn't matter now 'cause we're back together and the whole thing reminds me of the time our neighbor lady, Nancy, lost all her chickens and thought it was a wolf come to her coop but it wasn't, it was one of the Mayfield boys took 'em as a joke except when Nancy found out she put a load of rock salt in his butt with a shotgun and he didn't laugh so much. She was something, Nancy. I recollect the time she made biscuits and didn't get the shortening right and they were so heavy they would sink in water . . ."

Francis steered the mare with his knees, his rifle across his lap, and smiled, letting the words wash over him. Away from the trading post there was no dust, the afternoon sun was warm on his back, and the weather looked to stay good for some time. He had no plans other than to keep moving west and no hurry to get anywhere. He'd take meat later—maybe a buffalo—and they could stock up.

It was all in all, he thought, his smile widening, a good day to take his family for a ride, maybe go see the country.

A very good day.

# TUCKET'S RIDE

*For Angenette, still.*

# Chapter One

Francis Tucket lay on the ridge and watched the adobe hut a hundred yards away and slightly below him. He had his rifle resting on a hump of dirt, the sights unmoving, pointed at the doorway to the hut.

"Are we going to stay here forever? I mean it's really cold. I've been cold before but not like this." A small girl and boy stood ten yards to his rear with the horse and mule, all hidden below the level of the ridge. "It just seems that since you haven't seen anything, we could go down there and get warm. There might be a stove . . ."

"Please be quiet, Lottie." Francis turned and held his hand out. "Now. We're going to wait. I heard something somewhere down there that sounded like a scream. We're going to wait and watch. Be quiet."

There was a horse in front of the hut, tied to a half-broken hitch rail. Some chickens walked around the sides pecking at the dirt. There was no dog. Three goats were tied to stakes in back of the house. The horse had a familiar saddle on its back—military cut with the bedroll in front. The horse didn't look wet, so it hadn't worked hard getting here. Then, too, Lottie was right—it was cold, so the horse wouldn't show much sweat.

All this went into Francis's eyes and registered in his thoughts automatically—along with the direction of the wind, the fact that a coyote was off to the side a couple of hundred yards away eyeing the chickens, and a hawk was circling over the yard doing the same thing. All of it in and filed away.

There. A scream—short but high. Not a man. Maybe a child or a woman.

Well. That was all Francis thought: *Well.* If it was somebody needing help, he was in a bad place to give it. One fifteen-year-old boy, a young girl and a boy with him, a horse and a mule and one rifle.

Still. He couldn't stay and not help.

It was what he got for not going west, he thought—for not taking the two children and just heading out along the Oregon Trail to find his parents and the wagon train he had been kidnapped from more than a year ago. He and the children had made a good start west, then had gotten sidetracked as they crossed the prairie, and before he knew it an early fall had caught them short of the mountains. Snow had filled all the passes.

Somebody at a trading post on the trail had said that there was a southern route down in Mexico that stayed open all year, so Francis had started south. They couldn't hope to winter in the northern prairies. He hadn't realized that taking on Lottie and her little brother, Billy, would slow him down so. He had found them, alone on the prairie, after their father had died of cholera.

It had grown warmer as they had moved south along the mountains. Still cold at night, but they had picked up some wool blankets at the trading post, and Lottie had sewn pullover coats for all of them as they moved down into the territory belonging to Mexico.

*There*. He heard a thump, then a scream.

"You two stay here," he called softly to Lottie. "And I mean *stay* here. I'll be back."

He slid to the left where there was a thin brush line and followed it down to the hut. The building did not have a window, which was good, because the brush line was sparse scrub oak and the goats had long before stripped away the leaves.

Now Francis was barely concealed, and ran quickly, trying to keep his moccasins quiet.

He held himself still at the side of the hut, listening. Again, a muffled sound. He checked the cap on his rifle, cocked it, and moved to the side of the door.

He was five feet from the door when he noted that the saddle on the horse had a large US stamped on the sides, and the horse had the same brand on its shoulder. It was a United States Cavalry mount. Half a question formed in his mind—what was a United States Cavalry mount doing in Mexican territory?—when the door blew open and a young woman ran out, a large man behind her. He grabbed her shoulders.

"Get back in here!"

Half a second: Her eyes were wide with terror; she had a scuff on her face where she'd been hit. The man's blue uniform shirt was ripped. He had a bloody scratch on his cheek. He was wearing a military belt with a flap-covered holster, and he saw Francis, threw the woman aside, and clawed at the holster.

"Wait . . . ," Francis got out, then saw the flap of the holster come up, the hand catch the butt of the revolver, the barrel swing toward him as the man cocked it, an explosion of smoke and noise.

Francis felt the ball cut his cheek and burn past and he shot from the hip. His rifle recoiled in his hands and he saw the ball strike the man high in the chest. He saw everything: a little puff of dust from the blue shirt as the ball hit; no blood, but dust, and then the man went backward and down to a sitting position. He looked up at Francis and said, "You've killed me," and settled on his back slowly and died.

All in three seconds. Francis stood in silent horror. He felt the sun on his back, the terrified woman standing in front of him, the goats bleating nearby, the smoke from the shots drifting off to the side. He stood there and knew that nothing would ever be the same again.

He had killed a man.

# Chapter Two

"Oh, Francis, what have you done? I knew I shouldn't have let you come down here alone. Seems like if I take my eyes off you for a minute you get into all sorts of trouble. It reminds me of a cousin I had. He was always . . ." Lottie had come down the hill and started talking before she'd seen what had happened. She stopped when she saw the body.

Francis stood, still in shock.

"*¿Habla español?*" the woman said.

Francis looked at her. "What?"

"She's speaking in a different tongue," Lottie said. "Could be French. I heard a man talk French once back home. He could rattle it off so fast it made your brain blur . . ."

"Is Spanish," the woman said. "Do you speak?"

Francis shook his head. "No. Just English." He was still staring down at the dead man. "What happened here? I mean why . . ."

"He is soldier from the north." She spat the words. "He came wanting me. Dirty pig. I say no, Garza fight. He hurt Garza. Help me with him."

She moved into the hut and Francis followed. Inside there was only the light from the door. There was an earthen floor packed hard and swept, whitewashed walls, a small fireplace in the corner, a table, two chairs and a bed. A young man lay on the floor unconscious.

"Help me," she said. "He is hurt . . ."

The woman and Lottie took the man's legs and Francis took him by the shoulders. They put him on the cot. He was breathing but had blood on his head. A piece of firewood lay on the floor with blood on one end.

"Husband," she said. "Man hit him with *piñon*." She went to a shelf in one corner where an earthen jug held water. She poured some into a clay bowl, dipped a rag in it, and began wiping away the blood and dirt.

"I don't understand," Francis said in bewilderment. "What is an American soldier doing here?"

She stopped wiping and squinted at him in the dim light coming through the door. "It is the war, no?"

"War? What war?"

"There was war between Mexico and the United States."

"A war? But how can that be? I mean—"

"You did not know?"

Francis shook his head. "Never heard a word about it."

"You know," Lottie started, "come to think of it I believe I did overhear some men talking about trouble with Mexico at the trading post. Of course they weren't talking to me. Nobody talks to me. But I think one of them said to the other that he'd heard there was a problem with the borders or something. I couldn't hear well because *someone* was telling me to hurry up and leave. But I think they were—"

"And you didn't tell me?" Francis turned to her. "We're riding down into Mexico and you didn't say a word?"

"It slipped my mind. What with having to hurry and all the time having to keep quiet about things it just slipped my mind."

"Where's Billy?"

"I left him with the horse and mule."

"Maybe you'd better go check on him."

"You're just trying to get rid of me."

"No I'm not. Now go check on him while I try to figure out what to do."

"Do? Why, you've got that huge body out there to deal with, *that's* what you've got to do. I don't see any muddle on that score. Have to dig a big hole and bury him."

"Lottie . . ."

"I'm going."

Francis turned back to the woman. Her husband was breathing more regularly and starting to move his arms.

"When did the war start?" Francis asked.

She shrugged. "One day Mexican soldiers come by going to Taos. The next day *norteamericano* soldiers come by and say there is war. I hear of big battle between Santa Fe and Taos. Mexican soldiers leave, *americano* soldiers stay. Then this pig"—she pointed out the door at the body—"he came back for me. Then you come and shoot him. And now it is now."

And now, Francis thought, I have killed an American soldier. He was a bad man, true, and he shot first, but even so, I have killed him.

"You are bleeding." The woman came to him and used a clean corner of the damp cloth to wipe his cheek where the bullet had creased him.

"It's nothing. Nothing at all." Francis pushed her hand away and tried to think.

What to do?

Bury the soldier and *run*. It came into his mind as if it had always been there. Hide your tracks and cut and run. Get out before somebody finds out what happened. No one knew his name.

No. He couldn't run from *this*. Not *this*. He had to settle it first or it would be hanging over his head for the rest of his life. He leaned against the wall and moments of all that had happened to him since he had lost his family came back to him in flashes. Kidnapped by the Pawnees. Escaping them with the help of the mountain man, Mr. Grimes. Jason Grimes had rescued Francis and had taught him most of what he needed to survive, yet they had parted. Parted ways because of a killing.

"Where is the army?" Francis asked the woman, who had gone back to work on her husband. "How far are they?"

"They are in Taos. Where the pig came from."

"How far is this Taos place?"

"One day of walking not so fast."

He thought about distances. You could walk thirty miles a day without working too hard. Walking not so fast might mean a lot less. Fifteen or twenty miles. An easy day on horses.

There it was then. He'd have to take the body and find the army and explain what had happened.

Stupid, he thought. No, much more than that. The man had come here alone to do a stupid, terrible thing, then had made it worse by shooting at Francis without thinking and Francis had made it worse by getting involved in the first place. I should have kept riding, he thought, not come when I'd heard the scream.

But he couldn't have done that either.

He beckoned to the woman to follow him outside. "Would you help me? I have to roll his body in his blanket and tie it over his horse."

"Drag it out to the desert and leave for coyotes."

Francis shook his head. "No. I'll need to bring the body back to Taos."

He started to untie the blanket from the soldier's bedroll on his saddle.

Crazy, all of it. Just plain insane.

# —— Chapter Three ——

As it turned out, they didn't have to go all the way to Taos alone with the body.

Loading it had been hard, but finally, with the woman and Lottie helping while Billy held the trooper's horse, they had boosted the dead man belly down over the saddle and tied him in with rope. The horse didn't like it much, didn't like the smell of death, and Francis had to keep him on a short lead as they left the adobe hut and headed south.

The country was dry but pretty. There were high bluffs on the left, and they had not gone more than five miles when they came on a small settlement along a flowing river. There were no people evident, though there were tilled fields and some goats and pigs in pens. Francis stopped to water the horses. They could not set too fast a pace with the dead soldier's body bouncing across his horse. Several times Francis had a struggle to keep the trooper's horse from running away.

"It's spooky here," Lottie said, and even Billy, who sometimes went two or three days without saying a word, said, "Ha'nts."

Lottie took a deep breath and began, "I remember one time when Ma and Pa were both alive and we were back east somewhere, we were pulling the wagon and saw all kinds of shooting stars, and Pa thought they were spooky but Ma didn't and they had an argument about it that lasted nigh on three days . . ."

Carrying a body didn't help, Francis thought—it made everything spooky. He gigged the horses to get them going again; they thought they were going to spend the night in the settlement and were reluctant to leave. He had to kick with his heels and jerk on the horse carrying the body until he finally got them going. The mule came along peacefully, for which Francis was grateful.

Three miles out of the settlement, still a solid ten miles from Taos, they ran into the patrol of soldiers.

There were seven troopers and an officer leading. They came in from the west out of the desert, not on the north-south trail. Their mounts looked done in. Even at a distance Francis could see the horses wobbling, walking too loosely.

I could still run, Francis thought, watching them come toward the trail. We have good stock, fresh horses, and the mule would outdistance any horse alive. I could still run.

But he knew he wouldn't.

The troopers cut the trail half a mile and more ahead of them. They started to turn and head toward Taos. Then one of them saw Francis and called to the others, and they all turned and waited, not wanting to push their horses any more than they had to.

When Francis was still fifty yards away one of the men said, "Hey. He's pulling Flannagan's mount. I know the blaze and one white stocking. And there's a body on it!"

The patrol kicked their exhausted mounts into motion and approached Francis and the children with weapons ready. With a start, Francis remembered that he had never reloaded his rifle. He had been so distraught that he had forgotten all about it. Not that it would help him much with eight soldiers, all weapons ready. He'd be dead before he hit the ground.

"What is all this?" the officer asked, pulling up across the trail in front of Francis to block his way. As Francis stopped, the officer rode closer and looked under the blanket. "It's Flannagan all right. How did this happen?"

For once Lottie was quiet. Francis thought quickly. If he told the truth, would they just shoot him? Or should he lie now and tell the truth later, or would that make them even angrier?

He decided to tell the truth.

"I shot him."

"*You* shot him?"

"Yes, sir. He was trying to force a Mexican woman and I surprised him. He drew his cap and ball and shot at me and I just pulled the trigger. I didn't want to shoot him. It just happened."

"It just happened . . ."

"Yes, sir. In self-defense."

"Self-defense . . ." The officer looked at the body on the horse again, then back at Francis. "Who *are* you?"

"My name is Francis Tucket. Over a year ago I was with my family heading west on the Oregon Trail and I was kidnapped by Pawnees. I escaped and tried to head after them, and on the way I found these two young ones . . ."

The officer shook his head. "Just the name for now. And one more thing. We're still fighting the Mexicans. What are you doing here, in the middle of it?"

"I didn't know there was a war . . ." Francis told him how they had hit the closed passes of the north and drifted south looking for a way through to the West.

"Some drift. You must have come five hundred miles."

"Closer to six, I think. I've been keeping track by day."

"Well, Francis Tucket, I'm going to have to take that rifle and put you under confinement until we can get to the bottom of this."

Francis shook his head. "I'll take the confinement, but I can't give you my rifle."

It was a tight moment. The rifle had been with him constantly, except for when the Indians had captured him and again when two men had surprised him sleeping. It was like an extension of his arm, his mind, and he had no intention of releasing it again, voluntarily or otherwise.

The officer moved to the side to give his troopers a clearer field of fire if they needed it. "I can't have a man under arrest with a loaded rifle . . ."

Francis nodded. "It's not loaded. I didn't reload it after I killed . . . after I fired it last."

The officer thought, looking at Francis and the children, then nodded. "All right." He turned in his saddle. "Sergeant O'Rourke!"

"Sir!"

"Form an escort around the prisoners."

"Sir!"

"Trooper Delaney!"

"Yes, Sergeant!"

"You will take the mount with Flannagan's body in tow!"

"Yes, Sergeant!"

The troopers moved their tired mounts to a line on each side of Francis and Lottie and Billy, who were still on the mule. The trooper named Delaney took the horse with the body from Francis and they all moved out. The officer started in the lead but soon dropped back alongside Francis.

"You say Flannagan was forcing a Mexican woman?"

Before Francis could answer, Lottie cut loose. She'd been silent all this while—an unnatural state for her—and she blasted the officer.

"He was being 'rageous, that soldier, simply 'rageous. Back home in Esther County they would have just taken him out and let the pigs eat him. Francis here saved that woman something awful and it ain't right you come along with all your guns and 'rest him like he was bad. He isn't bad. He's good. And that man shot at him, look at his face, see? He saved us from a fate worse than death and he saved that woman the same way. Seems like you ought to give him a medal for shooting—"

"Lottie, hold it, all right?" Francis turned and held his finger to his lips. She stopped.

"She's something when she gets going, isn't she?" The officer smiled. "Reminds me of my sister. Always knows what's right and not afraid to tell you."

Francis nodded. "She's right most of the time. Just sometimes she takes a while to get it all out."

They rode in silence for a bit. Francis's horse fretted at walking slowly with the tired cavalry mounts, and the mule picked up on it and tried to get ahead. Francis had to fight him back.

"Mules," the officer said. "Good until you need them and then they get stubborn."

"This one is all right. They just don't want to go slow. Your horses are shot."

The officer nodded. "We've been almost a hundred and fifty miles on this patrol. Looking for the Mexican Army. I told my commandant they had gone south but he still wanted to check to the north."

Francis nodded. "I haven't seen any sign of an army." He looked at the officer. "What's your name?"

"Brannigan."

Francis shook his head. "Brannigan, Flannagan, O'Rourke—why all the Irish names?"

"We're an Irish militia out of Missouri, called up for the war. We're coming through here on our way south."

"Why were we at war with Mexico?"

Brannigan snorted. "The truth is, we just want their land. They own the whole West, including California and up into the prairies, all of Texas. Those rubberneck politicians back east wanted it so they trumped up this war. It wasn't much of a war. But there are still skirmishes going on."

More silence. Francis broke it this time. "What will happen to us?"

Brannigan shook his head. "I'm not sure. Flannagan is not from my troop. He's over at K Troop so I don't know much about him except that I've heard he's a bad one to . . ." He looked around at Lottie and Billy. "A bad one to do what you caught him at. He probably deserved shooting ten times over. So I expect there won't be a problem. Still, it's not my decision. The commanding officer will have to decide."

"Oh. Well, I'm sorry I had to do it but the way it happened . . ." Francis trailed off. In the distance he could see what looked like a large earth-colored building, or many buildings tied together, some on top of others. Like adobe huts stacked up.

"What's that?"

Brannigan squinted. "That's the Taos pueblo. Just on the other side is Taos. That's where we're going."

"Who lives there?"

"The Taos Indians."

"Indians?" Francis thought of the Pawnees, and then how he could load his rifle.

Brannigan saw the concern and chuckled.

"They're not like the Plains Indians. These are more settled. They farm instead of roam and hunt."

"More civilized?"

Another laugh. "In many ways they are far more civilized than we are . . ."

# Chapter Four

"Take him out and hang him."

Francis stood, not believing, almost not hearing.

They were in the commandant's office in a building on the side of the central plaza. Except that to Francis it seemed more like a saloon. The room, the building, and the man sitting in front of him were entirely devoted to drinking. Bottles lined every shelf on every wall. There was a barrel of whiskey in one corner and a rack filled with bottles of wine in another.

Francis had seen men drunk before, and he'd

seen men swill whiskey like water at the trading posts, but he had never seen anybody as drunk as the commandant. Or maybe he should say as drunk and still alive. The man wasn't sitting at his desk so much as weaving at it and his speech was slurred.

"I think, sir, that under the circumstances, we should waive . . ." Lieutenant Brannigan was standing next to Francis, and he spoke in a slow, measured tone. Lottie and Billy stood back by the door.

"Right now. Take him out in the plaza and hang him from one of those big cottonwoods out there."

"But, sir . . ."

"No buts. What are the rules if a Mexican partisan kills a trooper?"

"Sir . . ."

"The rules?"

"Summary execution, sir."

"And did this boy or did not this boy shoot and kill Trooper Flannagan?"

"Yes, sir, but . . ."

"By his own admission?"

"Yes, sir, but there were extenuating circumstances . . ."

"Doesn't matter. Take him out and hang him."

"What about the children?"

"Hang them as well." The commandant took a long swallow of something in a tin cup that looked and smelled like tequila. "Hang everybody in the plaza for all I care. It would clear the plaza of riff-raff . . ."

He leaned back and closed his eyes and for a second Francis thought he was thinking. But his breathing grew regular, and after a few moments Francis realized he had passed out cold.

"Well," Brannigan said in a low voice. "I thought that went well, didn't you?"

"Went well?" Lottie had been silent throughout, mostly because she was in shock. She took a deep breath. "He's going to have us hanged. I wouldn't call that going very well for us. I'm never going to see eleven years old and you think that's a good way for things to go? I haven't even learned how to . . . how to do anything, and they're going to string us up. You call that going well? I don't think so. Going well would be if Francis took us out of here. I just wish he hadn't had to shoot that stupid soldier . . ."

"You're not going to hang." Lieutenant Brannigan held his hand over her mouth. "He won't remember a thing he said tomorrow." He turned to

Francis. "Just keep her quiet now and let me handle this."

He turned to the door and called, "Corporal Antrim, come in here, please."

A redheaded trooper whose face was covered with freckles came into the office. "Yes, sir?"

"Commandant Donovan is napping, as you can see."

"Yes, sir."

"He was very tired."

"Yes, sir. He often is."

Brannigan nodded. "Yes. He works very hard. But just before he went to sleep he disposed of the difficulty of the shooting of Trooper Flannagan. Since the situation was to all events and purposes a tragic accident, Commandant Donovan has decided to let the matter drop."

"Yes, sir."

"Flannagan will be buried with full military honors."

"Yes, sir."

"Write up a report that states what the commandant has done for his signature when he comes to . . . awakens, will you?"

"Yes, sir."

"That will be all, Corporal."

The clerk left, and Brannigan looked at the commandant with open disgust, shook his head, and turned to Francis. "You mustn't think all officers are bad because of him. Some are very good at what they do. Well, he won't remember any of this. He'll think he made all the decisions himself when Corporal Antrim gives him the report to sign."

Brannigan opened the door again and led them outside. It was late afternoon, coming in to evening, and the light filtered through the cottonwoods on the plaza in the center of town. The leaves were gone because it was fall, but the hazy light seen through the limbs had an eerie quality.

Francis shivered. For a few moments he'd actually thought he was going to be hanged. He could feel the rope tightening around his neck. He couldn't shake the feeling. "What happens to us now?"

Brannigan stood by the horses with one hand on the mule's forehead, rubbing it idly. "You are free to go, and I do mean go. Flannagan was by all reports a complete scalawag, but he may have a friend or two who will think poorly of you for killing him. And it's best if the commandant never sees you again. No sense reminding him of what has happened."

"I understand."

"I will arrange for some grain for your stock and provisions for you. Then you just keep on going. Head south and west. In about thirty miles you'll come to a river, and you can follow it to Santa Fe. You will find the western trail you were looking for out of Santa Fe."

"Is there danger from the Mexicans?"

Brannigan shook his head. "Not for you and the children. The fighting has moved to the south and we've been left behind to administer. Generally people have just gone back to living their lives—most of them didn't want the war in the first place and are glad to have it move on. Stick to the traveled roads and you'll be fine."

He turned and pointed. "Take your horse and mule to the livery and freight area south of town and they'll give you some grain and food. Tell them Lieutenant Brannigan said to provision you."

"Thank you—for everything." They shook hands. Then Francis put the children on the mule.

"No trouble," Brannigan said, as Francis mounted. "Flannagan brought it on himself. It's too bad you have to leave in a hurry. I think you would benefit from a visit to the Taos pueblo. They are a remarkable people. They have learned how to live and flourish in a place most people couldn't even pass through. You could learn much from them . . . Well," he said, "good luck to you." He saluted as they rode away. "Have all the luck there is . . ."

# Chapter Five

Francis wouldn't consider going out to the pueblo to visit the Indians. He knew that not all Indians were bad, that in fact most of them were just decent people, but he had been captured by some, and held prisoner by some, and had fought some others in his mind, and he found that he was just more peaceful if he went his way and let them go theirs.

He couldn't shake the feeling of the noose around his neck, and he kept thinking about it. Wondering. What if the commandant hadn't been that drunk, and hadn't passed out, and remembered when he had come to, and decided to find them and hang them anyway? Francis paused before they left the plaza to reload his rifle, setting the butt on his left stirrup while he pushed the ball home with the ramrod. When they were moving again the thought of being hanged came back. Fretful thinking. He kept shaking his head to clear the thoughts out.

"What's the matter with you?" Lottie and Billy had been on the mule's back so long that they had almost evolved into a part of the mule. Lottie would often sit sideways on the packsaddle to "keep my autheritis from acting up." Sometimes she lay across the mule, sometimes sat forward on his neck. Once Francis had looked back to find both Billy and Lottie standing up on the mule's back, smiling at him. It just kept plodding, following Francis's horse. "You look like you up and died. . . ."

"I keep thinking on being hanged."

Lottie shrugged. "That's all done now, way I see it. Ma used to say when a thing's done it's done and it doesn't do any good to fret on it and the hanging business is all done. Besides, we're gone from it now anyway and where are we going to sleep tonight?"

Lottie had a way of running things together that made them seem somehow logical. To be done with getting hanged and worrying about where to sleep seemed perfectly natural.

"Want to eat." Billy spoke, and Francis smiled. That was two days in a row. Billy was getting positively talkative.

"We'll get some grain for the horses and then find a spot with some wood and water and make camp."

"I don't think so." Lottie looked at the country around them. "I believe the last time this country had water was when the great flood happened and you know when you think about that it makes you wonder on who's telling stories. I mean, how big would an ark have to be to get *everything* in it? And not just one, but two. Two buffalo, two mountain lions, two coyotes, two gophers, two ants, two mosquitoes, two horseflies, two ticks—and why did he include mosquitoes and ticks, I ask you? Seems Noah must have been stupid wanting to keep flies and ticks and mosquitoes around. Don't you think he was crazy? I mean, if it was me and I had a chance to get rid of horseflies, I'd drop them in a second. Right over the side. Did you ever watch them bite? They take a real chunk out of your arm, kind of twist and pull . . ."

Francis saw the livery and the freight yards ahead and kneed his horse into a trot before Lottie drove him into *wanting* to be hanged.

A sergeant met them. He had no neck, as near as Francis could tell, and was pouring sweat, though it was barely above freezing.

"We're here to be provisioned," Francis said. The sergeant hesitated until Francis told him that Lieutenant Brannigan had said it was all right.

"Fine, lad. You should have said so in the first place. There's grain in those bags, and bacon, and flour; beans and dried beef in that shed over there. Help yourself to what you'll be needing."

Francis took him at his word and loaded the mule down with sacks of flour, bacon, sugar, beans, and close to thirty pounds of oats for the stock. He also took several boxes of matches, two pounds of black powder, three tins of caps and a couple of five-pound pigs of lead. He had a mold and ladle to make rifle balls, but finding lead and powder was always a problem.

The mule didn't seem to mind the extra load, and they set off with perhaps another hour of daylight left, Francis feeling positively rich.

We're moving about four miles an hour, Francis thought, sitting on the walking horse. It was a mind game he played constantly. He factored in the speed and would look ahead to where he would be in an hour, see what was there to help him or hurt him.

In an hour we'll be by that ridge on the left. There are some thick trees along the base. Maybe there's water there. If not we can make a dry camp for the night. We have two canteens, and the animals can go a day more without water since the weather is cold.

Just thoughts rumbling through his mind all the time, information about his surroundings and what to expect. Sometimes he felt like a wolf. He'd watched them hunt several times and they didn't miss anything—they heard, saw, smelled everything around them. They'd stop and eat a mouse, a bug, a rabbit or a deer, then move around a rattlesnake—they just *knew* what was nearby. He tried to do the same, and to be alert, to not miss anything, and so was utterly surprised when the Mexican found them.

# Chapter Six

They discovered a small stream. Francis suspected that it was dry most of the year, but with the snow in the mountains feeding it, there was a flow of water about five feet across, running through the trees and rippling over rocks.

They unsaddled and watered the horse and mule, gave them each about a quart of grain. Francis had some concern about giving them too much grain; they hadn't been fed anything but grass in so long he felt that they might founder on grain—but a small amount would certainly keep them in shape.

When they were fed he rubbed them down with the back side of the saddle blankets, inspected them for any sores or rubs, and then went to the camp.

Over the months the three travelers had become a team. As soon as they stopped Lottie picked a campsite and started a fire, and unpacked their tin plates and cups; Billy started gathering the large pile of wood it took to cook a meal and get them through a night—especially a cold night.

As soon as the fire was going well, Lottie put the large cast-iron pot onto the coals and started cooking. They had no game tonight, so she sliced bacon and put it in to fry, and used a second pot to start water boiling for "coffee." They didn't have any real coffee, but she would heat the water and sprinkle dry pine needles in it to make a kind of tea. When they had sugar, as they did now, they would sit after the meal and drink sweetened "tea."

Francis took his rifle and moved out away from the fire for a time. He circled, looking for tracks in the dying light—human or game—and sat off fifty yards under a *piñon* tree, hidden in the shadows for more than half an hour, waiting for something to move. When nothing seemed to be there he walked silently back to the campsite. Lottie had set the finished bacon on a tin plate and was cooking a kind of cornmeal mush in water and the bacon fat that was left in the pot. When it had thickened enough to "hold a spoon" she ladled it and three pieces of bacon on each plate, poured "tea" into each cup along with generous helpings of sugar, and set them by the fire. "Food's done."

They ate in silence—even Lottie—although she started to talk while they were sipping the tea. In the evenings Francis didn't mind her talking, for it was nice, almost a kind of music. He leaned back on his blankets, feeling the warmth of the fire and hearing every fifth word or so. His face ached where the ball had grazed him.

"I honestly don't understand why everybody gets in such a snit over land as to fight a war. I mean look at all this land around us that nobody is using. There's no need to fight. Just take some that isn't being used and get to living . . ."

It was difficult to stay awake. Finally, after throwing more wood on the fire, he rolled himself into his blankets and closed his eyes. Billy was already asleep and within a minute, while Lottie was still talking, Francis slept too.

FRANCIS WASN'T SURE what had awakened him: a sound, or the absence of it. Perhaps a chill. He opened his eyes to see a man wearing a *serape* squatting across the dead fire from him. The man smiled when he saw Francis's eyes open.

*"Hola, amigo."* He said it softly and did not awaken Lottie or Billy.

Francis didn't speak. He felt for his rifle. It was still there. The man didn't appear to be armed—at least he couldn't see any weapons—but still, he was there. Francis sat up.

"How did you get here?" It was the second time Francis had been surprised on awakening. The first time had been when two men named Courtweiler and Dubs had come upon him and taken everything he owned. Nowadays Francis slept lightly, and he wondered that the horse or mule hadn't made a sound. "Without me knowing . . ."

"I followed you. And I am quiet," the man said in English. Not perfect, but better than many Americans. "It was not hard to track three children, a horse and a mule."

"Two children."

"Ahhh yes, there is that. You are now a man. A young man, but a man. You have killed another."

Francis looked to the fire. There were still a few coals faintly glowing; he put some twigs on them and blew them into flames. He added wood. In the dark it had been hard to see the man. Now Francis studied him in the light. He had a revolver on his belt, partially hidden beneath the *serape*. It glinted now. The man's hand was not near the butt of the gun; but still, the gun was there.

"Why are you here?"

"So blunt, the Americans. That is not the Spanish way. We should have talk and work up to the reason. First, we must introduce ourselves. I am García."

"I am——"

"I know who you are. That is why I am here. You are the man who shot and killed the American soldier yesterday."

"It was an accident. Or almost. I didn't mean to shoot him——"

"You do not understand. I am not angry. I am grateful. The woman you saved was Carmela. She is Garza's wife. Garza is my brother. I am here to help you because Garza has a dizziness in his head from his wound, so he could not come himself."

"Well, thank you. But I don't need any help."

García smiled and looked at the flames for a moment. "You do not need help. So confident. So young." He looked again at Francis. "You are very rich. You have a horse and a mule and food and a rifle and two children who have value, and so you have much wealth. You are traveling through a country that is very poor. There are some who would simply take what you have. Garza has asked that I accompany you for a time until you learn our ways and can take care of yourself . . ."

"But we're doing good."

"No, you're not. You think you are but you need guidance and I will provide it. If I do anything less Garza will be disappointed. A disappointed Garza is an angry Garza, and an angry Garza is . . . well, let us say it is not good when he is angered."

Francis thought and decided García was telling the truth. If he had wanted to steal anything he could have cut Francis's throat and been done with it. Francis nodded. "Well, as easy as you sneaked up on me, I guess you're right. I need the help. Go bring your horse in and tie him with ours. There's some grain in a sack by the packsaddle."

"I do not have a horse."

"Well, mule, whatever."

"I am on foot."

Francis shook his head. "With us riding and you on foot I don't see how you'll be able to keep up."

"I will stay ahead of you. That way I will know what is coming."

Francis leaned back on his blanket and smiled. He had started to say that García couldn't hope to keep up with people on horses but then remembered that he himself had caught up with Courtweiler and Dubs on foot when they had been riding.

"Let us sleep now," García said. "There are still three hours of darkness for resting. I will be over by the horse and mule if you need me."

And he was gone. Francis had done no more than blink, and when he looked again, García had disappeared.

A ghost, Francis thought. He hadn't even awakened the children. Just there and gone—I'm sure glad he's on our side. Francis closed his eyes and let the warmth of his blankets and the glow from the fire take him back down again.

# Chapter Seven

The country they moved through the next day was in some strange way the prettiest country that Francis had ever seen. They moved down into a winding canyon that ran along the Rio Grande river, which went from cascading through narrow clifflike rocks to spreading wider and rolling through gentle rapids.

It was still desert, or near-desert, with scrub *piñon* and juniper and odd stands of prickly pear cactus, but the nearness of water made the desert seem more beautiful. When they came into a shallow valley full of small farms on narrow tracts of land with irrigation ditches running across the ends, it all looked like a picture.

"Ma, she had a calendar with a picture on it looked like these farms," Lottie started. "All set so nice and neat . . ."

Francis had seen the farms and the river moving through them, but he had been spending most of his time watching García. It was amazing. The Mexican carried a small bedroll over his shoulder and had his revolver—a Colt cap and ball—in his right hand. He ran in a kind of loose shuffle that left the horse and mule trotting to keep up. Since trotting was so uncomfortable that Francis and the children didn't want to do it, Francis kept the stock at a walk, and García, as he'd said, quickly left them far behind.

García had not been there when they had awakened in the morning and had not showed himself until they were two miles along the road. The first Lottie knew of him was when he stepped softly out of some *piñon* along the trail next to the mule.

"*Hola, señorita,*" he said to her. For once she was speechless. "A very good morning to you . . ."

"Francis!" Lottie called ahead to where Francis was riding. "There's a strange man here."

"He's not strange," Francis said without turning. "Lottie and Billy, meet García. García, meet Lottie and Billy . . ."

"Where did he come from?" Lottie asked. "You have friends I don't know about out here? I don't think that's right . . ."

"He just showed up. A brother of the man where I had to shoot the soldier. He's here to help us, guide us."

"When did you meet him?"

"He came last night while you were sleeping. If you didn't sleep so hard you'd know these things. I tried to wake you, shook you, poured water on your head, but you were out like a light. I've never seen anybody sleep so hard. I thought you'd died. I woke Billy up and he tried to get you awake too and you wouldn't—"

"Stop that. You're just making up stories."

But it quieted her and Francis used the silence to talk to García. "I saw tracks," he said to García. The Mexican had moved up alongside Francis, holding onto the stirrup on the left side of his saddle and letting himself be pulled along.

Francis had seen a wide band of tracks come in

from the south side onto the road. They were all unshod horses and he couldn't tell for certain how many but he thought more than ten. They moved out ahead of the direction in which Francis and the children were traveling, and they were fresh. Some of the dirt cut by their hooves still looked damp in the morning cold and hadn't frozen.

"I have seen the same. There are many horses. Seven, perhaps ten, it is hard to tell when they all run together."

"They aren't army."

"No, the army horses have steel shoes. These have nothing."

"What do you think?"

García frowned, a quick flicker of concern. "I think it is perhaps not good. Nobody of any worth would be out riding around with seven or ten men on horses. If they aren't army then they must be somebody else and a group of men that large is usually up to no good."

"They're out ahead of us."

García nodded. "I will move off the trail and catch up to them and see. Keep moving but go slower and I will be back to you when I find out more." He slid off into the *piñon* and was gone, and Francis checked the percussion cap on his rifle, cleared a bit of dust off the front and rear sights, and wished he knew more about the tracks.

"What was that all about?" Lottie had seen them talking but hadn't heard what they said.

"García asked if I wanted him to find a good place to camp tonight and I said yes. He's gone ahead to locate water."

"Hmmm."

She didn't believe Francis but that didn't matter to him. He couldn't shake the feeling of worry about the tracks and had just decided to obey his instincts and stop altogether when the sound of gunfire came from ahead.

One shot, then two, then a whole ripping tear of them, and then nothing for a moment; then one more. Then silence. All in the space of four or five seconds.

It had to be García and he had to be in trouble. "Take Billy off the trail and head back up into the trees and hide," Francis said.

"Where are you going?"

"Just move! I'll be back . . ."

He kicked his horse in the ribs and slammed her into an instant gallop. It couldn't be far. García hadn't been gone that long. By her fourth jump he had taken three lead balls out of his possibles

bag and put them into his mouth, took three percussion caps and stuck them between the fingers on his left hand and brought the rifle up to be
ready.

It wasn't enough.

# Chapter Eight

For a moment Francis thought he'd ridden into his own private war.

He came around a corner in the trail, the mare running wide open, his rifle ready, and found himself in the middle of what proved to be twelve men on horses.

Francis had flashes of images. Somehow all twelve men looked dirty at once, covered with trail dust, all riding scruffy Indian-style ponies—wild stock, very small and very tough—and all wore what he thought of as mixed Indian clothing. Leather leggings; wool blankets with holes cut for their heads; some had feathers, some wore old felt hats; some had no shirts on at all in spite of the cold. They were all covered in weapons. All had rifles or shotguns; some had bows and quivers full of arrows tied to their backs; others had one, two, even three revolvers in their belts. Francis saw tomahawks in belts. They were all shooting into the brush on the left side of the trail.

García, Francis thought; they must be shooting at García in there. And then a second thought: I have made a terrible mistake. There was no time for any other thought. He raised and cocked his rifle and picked a target. But before he could pull the trigger, what looked like all the guns in the world seemed to be aimed at him and they all fired at the same time.

He had time to see one ball crease the mare's neck, another nick her ear, and then something slammed into the side of his head and he had nothing resembling thought after that.


HE WAS SURE he was dead. There had been times before when he thought he would die—several times—but this time he was certain, and so when there seemed to be things happening in his mind, he thought he was either in heaven or hell. And whichever it was, Lottie's voice was there.

"I think it's disgraceful the way you just tied him up and dumped him across a saddle like a piece of meat. His head is all bloody, and I think I see his brains in there ready to leak out, and you're just letting him hang like that where they could flop out in the dirt . . ."

It all faded then into a kind of redness that covered him and he stayed that way until something jerked at him, pulled him sideways and threw him down to the ground.

"He might be dead already, for all you care. Look at him, he's all shot to pieces. What's he going to be worth to you if his brains flop out?"

This time Francis tried opening his eyes. He was on his back, and when he opened them the sun was shining directly into them and seemed to shoot a hot spear into the center of his head. He jerked his eyes shut. It did not stop Lottie's voice.

"Where are you taking us? All I see ahead is mountains and brush. Nobody of a civil nature would take two children into a wilderness—ummph!" There was a thump and Lottie's voice stopped. This time Francis turned away from the sun a bit and opened his eyes and kept them open.

His head was exploding in pain; waves of it came from the left side over to the right. He started to reach up and feel it but his hands were tied together. When he tried to roll and free his arms, somebody in back kicked him in the ribs hard enough to make the breath whistle out of his nose.

He lay still on his side and tried to focus on what he could see. A forest of horses' legs was there, standing still. There was a smell of horse sweat, so they had been working hard. Men moved back and forth tightening cinches and checking hooves. They were stopped in a small clearing in a stand of *piñon* and juniper. The ground was rocky. He could not see Lottie or Billy or García without moving, and he was afraid that if he moved, the men would kick him again and he would pass out. It had all come back to him now, riding into the men, raising his rifle, getting shot at. García. What had happened to García? Probably dead.

Aside from the pain in his head and what he thought was dried blood caked there and down the side of his face, he had another burning pain across his left thigh. It looked like a ball had creased there, only slightly breaking the skin. That must be the problem with his head as well: A ball had creased him. How in heaven's name could all those men shoot at him and miss? And after not killing him in the first place, why did they keep him alive and not just shoot him and be done with it?

"Up," somebody said in English and kicked Francis again, this time in the back.

Francis rolled onto his stomach, worked his knees beneath him and levered himself up. His head was on fire. He didn't move fast enough and somebody kicked him again.

"Francis, you have to get up and get on a horse. These men will shoot you sure if you can't ride." Lottie's voice sounded on the edge of crying. "Please get up . . ."

"Lottie?"

"Shut up!" Another kick, but this time the force of the blow helped him move up and he gained his feet. "Mount."

There was the mare standing next to him. She had a bloodied ear and blood down her neck from the wound there but was apparently not hit in any other place. It was a miracle, he thought—that he hadn't been riddled and that somehow they hadn't hit the mare solid either.

He grabbed the saddle horn and pulled himself

up, foot in the stirrup, leg up and over, sitting there, on the edge of vomiting with pain but sitting there hanging on to the horn with his tied hands and weaving slightly.

Now he could see better as well.

They had been climbing into a shallow pass, heading south by the direction the sun stood. He had been facedown over the saddle; his stomach was bruised, and his shoulders and arms were sore from bumping against the side of the horse. How long he had been unconscious he couldn't guess.

The men worked on in silence. They were, now that Francis had had time to study them, very hard men. Some of them looked to be full-blood Indians and some appeared to be mixed, but they all knew horses and wasted no time checking their mounts. There was no water but some snow in patches. They rubbed the snow up inside their horses' lips to moisten them. They had ridden hard, Francis thought, and planned to ride harder.

Lottie and Billy were still on the mule ahead of him three or four paces, Lottie looking back with worry in her eyes. She had a bruise on the side of her face where she'd been struck. Billy had been crying but he seemed quiet now and was looking at the men the way Francis had studied them—checking their gear, their mounts, the way they looked. Francis almost smiled. Billy was growing faster than he'd thought.

He started to say something but Lottie saw his face and shook her head, held her finger to her lips and whispered, "They don't like it if you talk."

"Shut up," a man mounted next to her said. "Or we will leave you tied to a tree for the coyotes . . ."

There was no chance for talk after that. The men mounted, spread out in single file with Francis on the mare and Lottie and Billy on the mule in the middle and set off without speaking another word.

Headed south. Away from any civilization, away from the trail west, away from help.

Away.

# Chapter Nine

Francis had done some long riding in his time, hard riding and hard living, but he had never experienced anything like what these men did now. He didn't think men could stand it. Even more, he didn't think horses could take it.

They simply didn't stop.

As the day wore on Francis felt the pain diminishing to a steady throb that kept the side of his head burning. The dizziness left him, and he worked his wrists to loosen the tie there so that his blood would circulate better. In spite of her wounds, the mare kept up the pace easily—she was, like the others, a tamed wild horse and had enormous stamina. The mule kept up as well.

Billy stuck to the packsaddle like a burr but Lottie started to have trouble toward the end of the day. She weaved and Francis would see her catch herself to keep from falling asleep and falling off the mule.

In late afternoon, they stopped but not to rest. The men all dismounted and made Francis and the children do the same. Francis thought they would stop for the night but he was wrong. They loosened the cinches on the horses for no more than five minutes, retightened them and remounted.

They can't be serious, Francis thought. They're not going to keep riding. One of the men dug into his saddlebags and handed each of the children and Francis a piece of jerky.

"Eat."

"But I'm thirsty," Lottie said. "And Billy is too . . ."

The man struck her once alongside the head. "Eat."

She started to chew the jerky, and Billy did the same. Francis did likewise and within moments they were riding again.

At first Francis had the strength to think while

they rode. The men were running—he was sure of it. Initially he thought they were Indians but some of them spoke Spanish and several spoke English fairly well, and they didn't seem to be of a tribe. Renegades, he thought.

Afternoon bled into evening and soon it grew dark and cold. The men didn't care. The leader kept the pace, riding somewhere ahead in the darkness. The rest followed with Francis and the children in the middle.

They came out of the mountains in the darkness and started riding across flat prairie. The stars were brilliant enough to give some light, and when a sliver of moon came up it seemed almost daylight.

All night they rode. Just before dawn, when it was coldest, the leader stopped and dismounted and the rest of them did the same. Francis thought surely they will stop now; surely they have run far enough to be safe.

But they did not. The men jumped around and slapped their arms against their sides to get warm. They let the children take care of their "personal business," as Lottie called it, gave them another piece of jerky and a short swallow from a canteen, and retightened cinches before remounting and setting the same crippling pace.

The sun crawled up and by this time Francis was

on the edge of hallucinating. He kept seeing shadows jumping out at the edge of his vision. Billy was fast asleep, somehow maintaining his balance, and Lottie had jammed herself into the packsaddle and was sleeping as well.

It was then, just before the sun was high enough to provide warmth, that Francis found out who had them.

The men hardly spoke, and when they felt it necessary they kept it low, just above a whisper. But as Francis dozed the mare moved ahead a bit to be near two of them and one of them said the word: "Comanche."

Francis's eyes snapped open and he knew instantly who they were. Not Indians, not Comanches—these men were Comancheros.

Francis had heard stories of the Comanches down south—mostly in Texas. They were universally feared and made raids for plunder and prisoners as far as the northern edge of the Texas frontier.

From what he'd heard, they were bad enough. But worse were the dreaded Comancheros, groups of men who traded with the Comanches. It would explain how they worked the horses. At one of the trading posts, Francis had heard mountain men talking of the Comancheros and how they rode.

They said a white man could drive a horse until it dropped, then a Comanche could get the horse up and get forty more miles out of it before it dropped again, but a Comanchero could come along, get two hundred more miles out of it, then eat it when it finally collapsed. Tough men.

When they had stolen stock and goods from raiding, the Comanches would meet bands of Comancheros to trade for ammunition, weapons, flour, sugar, lead, and salt. Sometimes, Francis had heard, the Comanches would keep children to raise as slaves.

The Comancheros had a reputation worse than the Comanches themselves. As near as Francis could figure it, he and the children were being taken by a band of them down into the south country where the Comanches roamed.

Absolutely nothing good could come from it. They would be sold, he thought. Or worse: separated and given to the Comanches.

There was only one way open for them. They had to escape.

But the Comancheros kept driving south, farther and farther away from any possible help, into a country Francis did not know. With every step escape seemed more and more impossible. If they would just stop, Francis thought, give him time to think, to rest.

But the pace never let up. They ate riding, slept riding, and kept moving, somehow keeping the horses going by force of will.

All day they moved, stopping only once to loosen and retighten cinches, to take a sip of water and a bite of jerky. All day and into the night they kept riding until Francis felt like he'd never done anything else; moving until Lottie and Billy became part of the mule and packsaddle. All through the night and into the next day. Finally, out in the flats of the prairie, they came upon a cut, a wide canyon that didn't show until they were almost on top of it.

The leader led them down a winding trail wide enough for one horse along the canyon wall. Far below Francis could see a group of small shacks in a stand of cottonwoods—little more than brush huts covered with skins—and a winding stream. It was too far away to see any people, but he could make out a fairly large herd of horses, and by squinting, he finally saw small figures running back and forth. Some wagons were parked near the shacks. As they dropped down the canyon wall, Francis could hear dogs barking.

It wasn't a village so much as a mobile camp, and if this trail was the only way out, it didn't leave much hope for escape. Not that it mattered so much now. Francis was so tired he couldn't make his brain work to formulate a plan anyway; so tired he had difficulty paying attention to anything but keeping his balance on the mare.

She was tired as well. When they came out into the bottom of the canyon, she began to weave and wobble and he knew she would go down soon. She somehow stayed on her feet until they were near the horse herd, then she settled gently to the ground. Francis stepped off as she caved in, and as if she were signaling, half the other horses went down as well.

The men dismounted and unsaddled, dragging gear off the horses without making them rise. Some other men and a few women—as dirty as the men who had taken them prisoner—came out and greeted them, all without talking except in low murmurs. They spoke a mixture of Indian dialect and Spanish as they helped to strip gear off the horses and drag it to the wagons.

A woman came over to Lottie and pinched her cheek. Lottie kicked her and the woman backhanded the girl, slapping her so hard that Francis heard her teeth click.

"Leave me alone!" Lottie was half asleep on her feet. "Just leave me—"

The woman grabbed her hand and took Billy's as well—he was standing near Lottie, his eyes closed—and dragged them into one of the huts.

"Where are you taking them?" Francis started after them without thinking. One of the men stepped up in back of him and quietly, professionally thumped Francis just under his left ear with the brass butt of his rifle.

Francis went down like a stone.

# Chapter Ten

"Francis! Wake up, Francis! We need you—you have to wake up!"

Lottie's voice, insistent, pushing, pulling him awake. He opened his eyes and saw a dark brush ceiling over him. Then Lottie's face came into view, and next to her, Billy's. Billy was chewing on a piece of jerky.

"What . . ."

"One of them hit you on the back of the head with his gun. Billy and I dragged you in here—the woman let us—and then they went away and they haven't been back, and I untied your hands. I think they're expecting somebody because they killed one of the horses and are cutting it up to roast. I've been watching them through a crack in the wall. It's not hard. The wall is all cracks. There isn't actually a wall at all, just a bunch of sticks you could throw a cat through—"

"Lottie, please. Quiet. My head is killing me and I have to think. I know who they are now."

"So do I. They're called Comancheros. I heard some of them talking and they used the word. Is that a bad thing? I mean I know it can't really be good, the way they're treating us and all. But are Comancheros really awful, like I think?"

Francis shut his eyes. "As bad as it gets, from what I hear. We have to get out of here."

"Not until we get some rest. Billy fell asleep standing up and I'm near ready to drop."

"All right. One of us should stay awake and watch them. I rested some on the mare so I'll take the first watch— Oh, she's not the horse they killed to eat, is she?"

"No. It was a scruffy wild thing they had in the herd."

"Good. I've been through a lot with that mare . . ."

Lottie had settled against the wall. She seemed

to shrink into her blanket pullover and was asleep instantly.

Francis sat and leaned back against the other side of the hut, and turned so that he could see between the branches.

There wasn't much happening. The men who had taken them prisoner were asleep as well, and some older men and women—there were no children—were dragging in wood and making large fires. Francis could see the dead horse where they'd shot it. Two women were cutting chunks of meat from it, hanging them over sticks near the fire.

There were half a dozen mangy dogs nearby. They clearly wanted the meat but stayed away from it out of fear. Francis saw why when one of them came a little too close and a woman hit it with a piece of firewood so hard that it ran off screaming, dragging a leg.

Nice, Francis thought. Really nice people here, these Comancheros.

He dozed. Every part of him hurt: his hips and legs from riding, his head from the bullet strike and the rifle butt, his arms from being tied. He didn't sleep but he dozed, in and out, catching himself when his head dropped and snapping his eyes open. But at last he couldn't stay awake.

He wasn't sure how long he'd slept—several hours—and it was dark when he awoke. Lottie and Billy were still asleep, and he wondered for a moment what had awakened him. Then he heard it. Men and women were running back and forth, dogs were barking in alarm.

Somebody was coming and Francis moved to the doorway of the hut to see.

It was pitch dark, the lowering sky threatening to snow. Aside from the fire there was almost no light.

The dogs were all barking toward the northeast and Francis watched that direction until he saw a figure looming out of the darkness. One man on a horse, pulling two other packhorses with huge loads piled so high that the horses looked like dwarf ponies.

But it was the man who caught his eye.

The man sat straight in the saddle and was wearing a buffalo robe for warmth. He had a rifle balanced across his lap, though he didn't seem concerned that he might be in danger, and the rifle just lay there cradled. The packhorses followed him naturally—he didn't have a rope back

to them—and as he rode near the fire he raised his
right hand in greeting and smiled. His left arm was
missing and he was wearing a derby-style hat with
a feather in it.

"No," Francis said half aloud. "It can't
be . . ."

The man sitting on his horse by the fire, greeting the Comancheros like old friends, was Jason
Grimes.

# ── Chapter Eleven ──

Francis was stunned. Memories roared back. His capture by the Pawnees, Grimes "helping" him escape, their life together trapping until Grimes fought a man named Braid in single-handed combat. Grimes had reverted into a kind of madness as he mutilated the dead Braid.

Grimes had been badly wounded in that fight, and Francis had struck out on his own, angry at Grimes for becoming what he considered so evil. He'd thought it probable that the mountain man had died of his injuries.

Clearly he had survived. And just as clearly he was not trapping beaver any longer. He had become a businessman, judging by the enormous loads on the two packhorses. A trader.

Somebody who traded with the Comancheros.

Talk about stooping low, Francis thought, watching Grimes and the men unpack the horses near the fire. Grimes could crawl under a snake.

"Who is it?" Lottie had awakened and was peering through the brush wall next to Francis. "You *know* him? Is that *another* friend?"

"Not a friend, exactly. He was, but I don't know what he is now."

"Will he help us escape?"

Francis frowned. "I don't know. He helped me get away from the Pawnees once but things were different then. Now . . ."

Lottie sighed. "I hope he will, Francis. I'm ever so worried about us."

"Me too, Lottie. Don't worry, I'll think of something."

The problem was that Francis *had* been trying to think of a way out but it looked impossible. Alone he could cut and run and might have a chance. But with the two children—and there was absolutely no way he would leave without them—it became much more difficult. They slowed him down and there was the added responsibility of having them near; he couldn't take foolish risks that might endanger them.

They had added wood to the fire outside and Grimes was showing his goods to trade, as he had done with the Pawnees. He had powder and lead, but he also had some mirrors and blankets and sugar; some cheap knives and tomahawks; and dried apples, other dried fruit, and some salt. He passed blankets and bolts of material around, spread one blanket on the ground and displayed his wares there. They soon had a brisk trade going. The Comancheros needed the goods to trade with the Comanches when they came. In return they gave Grimes pelts and cash money the Indians had given them previously.

Francis watched all this and wondered how he could get Grimes's attention. If the mountain man couldn't help him escape, maybe he could do something for the children.

As the trading grew more excited, squabbles broke out over items that several people wanted. Two men wanted the same blanket, and they soon pulled knives out and went at it. One man— larger than the rest, the man who had led the raiding party that had taken Francis and the children—held up his hand and stopped the trading.

He said something in broken English to Grimes and pointed to the brush hut where Francis stood watching.

Grimes shook his head and motioned for the trading to continue. The leader made a "No" sign and pointed again at the hut. Finally Grimes stood and walked in the direction of the captives.

The leader grabbed a burning stick off the fire and followed. He stopped at the door of the hut and held the torch up so that Grimes could see in.

"Pasqual, there ain't nothing in here but a couple of pups. I ain't going to give you my whole poke for a couple of sprites. What would I want with pups?"

"Hello." Francis took a step away from the wall into the light. "How are you doing, Mr. Grimes?"

For a full three seconds, the mountain man stood still. Then he took the torch from the Comanchero and held it out.

"Mr. Tucket—is that you?"

Francis nodded.

"Why, I thought you went on west to join them farmers you missed . . ."

"I got sidetracked."

Grimes looked at the children. "I should say so—are these your kin?"

"In a way."

"You wouldn't consider leaving them?"

"No."

"It was a stupid question, knowing you and how much you like the niceties of civilization."

"I don't believe in hacking up dead bodies, if that's what you mean."

"It don't seem like you're in a position to be picking at people . . ."

"I'm sorry. It just slipped out." And as Francis said it, he realized he meant it—he *was* sorry. In a way, he was genuinely glad to see the mountain man, and not just because he hoped to get help. Seeing him now, he felt that he'd missed him. "I'm sorry . . ."

Grimes was silent for a time, the fire from the torch flickering on his face. Then he sighed. "You sure do cause me a peck of trouble."

"I didn't mean to."

"The way the stick floats is me and this Pasqual are friends, ain't we, Pasqual?"

The man nodded, smiling through broken teeth. *"Amigos, sí . . ."*

"He don't understand a whole bunch of English so we can talk a bit. We're friends, but the friendship is on account of what I can bring them when I come trading. If I don't bring them anything my hair will probably go to a Comanche in trade—"

"So you have all that stuff on the packhorses," Lottie cut in. "Give him that."

"Speaks right up, don't she?" Grimes looked at Francis.

Francis nodded. "She doesn't hold back much."

"The problem is this Pasqual is a heap good trader. He wants to keep his gold *and* get the trade goods."

"Ahhh . . ."

Grimes nodded. "So he told me he'd trade all three of you for what I've got and we'd call her square."

"Sounds like a good deal to me," Lottie whispered.

"The tight part is all I own is wrapped up in these goods. I trade for you and I wind up with nothing to keep going."

"I'll pay you back," Francis said. "Somehow. I'll get work and pay you back."

Grimes nodded. "Yes, Mr. Tucket. That would be one way to handle it. And I know you'd hold to it. But I'm about done trading with these yahoos anyway, and I thought there might be another way to make a poke."

Francis waited. The torch had burned down to a small flicker, about the size of a candle flame, and Pasqual took it and swore when it burned his fingers. He dropped it in the dirt.

"Remember when we dealt with them Pawnees?" Grimes spoke out of the sudden darkness.

"Pawnees?" Francis said.

"You know, when you visited them Pawnees for a while and then I came and we met there. Remember how that went?"

"Ohhh. Sure." Francis had been a captive and Grimes had "arranged" for a horse to be ready for him if he got away. "It's a little more complicated now, what with my new family."

"I figured that. Just remember how all that happened and we'll work it the same way now. I'll go trade with Pasqual and we'll open a barrel of trade whiskey and see what happens later."

"Later," Francis repeated.

"Ayup. You just keep your powder dry and keep this little missy quiet, and I'm going to go have me a shindig with Pasqual."

And he left the hut and went back to the fire.

"What did he mean?" Lottie asked. "All that

talking around the corners of things—what did he mean?"

"He meant," Francis said, settling down with his back to the wall, "that we aren't going to get a lot of rest tonight."

# —— Chapter Twelve ——

In spite of what he had said, Francis made Lottie and Billy sleep, or at least try to. The idea of escaping with Grimes made him think of the situation and what they were up against. He could not forget the ride here—the endlessness of it, the way the men kept on going and never quit.

How they could get away from these same men posed a problem that Francis needed to think about. Grimes might be able to set something up, but that didn't mean it would succeed.

If the Comancheros chased as hard as they ran, it would be next to impossible to get away with Lottie and Billy. The mare was done and the mule was not much better, which meant they would have to take different horses from the Comanchero herd. What if they didn't get good stock? What if they didn't get away? What would the Comancheros do to them if they tried to run and failed?

What if . . .

He finally stopped thinking about it. There were too many variables to make any kind of prediction—so much that could go wrong. It came down to a very simple, possibly deadly problem. One: They couldn't stay and get traded to the Comanches. Two: The Comancheros wouldn't let them go voluntarily. Three: They had to run.

Whether they made it or not, they still had to run, had to try, and that was that.

Lottie and Billy finally slept. The temperature had warmed slightly, and they seemed comfortable enough in their blanket pullovers. Francis sat by the wall and watched the celebration through the brushy wall of the hut. Grimes had broken open the top of a small keg of whiskey. He dipped tin cups in the brew and handed them to the men around the fire, and in a very short time they were all as drunk as Francis had ever seen—with the possible exception of the army commandant.

They did not stop the party because they were drunk but kept on until the barrel was empty. Then Mr. Grimes started trading. He pointed at the hut where the children were and shook his head and waved his hands. He didn't want the children. He wanted gold. He would trade for gold. And soon, lubricated by the whiskey, the Comancheros started bringing out gold they had gotten from Comanche trading. And by the time they were all nearly drunk enough to pass out, Grimes had sold all his goods and had a small sack of gold coins.

He had been drinking with the men, taking the cup on each pass. Could Grimes help them escape if he was drunk?

The mountain man was soon weaving and wobbling as much as the Comancheros, and when most of the men left and returned to their huts—falling all over themselves—Grimes was as drunk as the rest. He fell back on his blanket by the fire, rolled up and passed out. The few remaining Comancheros tried to scoop more whiskey out of the empty keg and then drifted off.

And that, Francis thought, watching it all, was that. So much for running. He turned away and settled his back against the side of the hut, his mind full of bitter thoughts. How could it have been any different? Grimes was still Grimes—a rough man in the company of other rough men. Why would he risk it all just to save three kids—one of whom he didn't even like?

Francis let his eyes close, opened them and checked Grimes once more. When he saw that the mountain man was still unconscious, he closed them again. Not to sleep, he thought—just to rest and be ready for what would come the next day. Just a moment . . .

"Were you going to sleep all night, Mr. Tucket?"

Francis opened his eyes slowly to find Mr. Grimes standing in front of him in the darkness of the hut. "I thought you were drunk and I must have fallen asleep . . ."

"I was letting on. It takes a heap to make me drunk even when I'm drinking and I wasn't drinking. And you were supposed to be ready . . ."

"I am."

"Get the sprites up. We have to move *now*." And Grimes disappeared into the darkness.

Francis shook Lottie and Billy. Lottie snapped awake instantly, but Billy took a moment.

"Come on—there's no time to waste. You take my hand and hang on to Billy's with your other one. We don't want to get separated in the dark. Do exactly as I tell you and be quiet."

Francis moved out of the hut. Grimes hadn't said where he was going because he hadn't needed to. They needed horses and that meant the horse herd at the edge of the encampment. Francis dragged the two children at a dead run.

Grimes was already there with his three horses. One was saddled and the other two had packsaddles on them.

He whispered, "You'll have to ride the packhorses. Most of their stock seems awful run-down."

"We rode hard getting here. They haven't rested enough yet." Francis thought briefly of the mare and the mule. He hated to leave them, but they hadn't recovered enough.

"No more talk. We have to ride. Throw the pups up on one horse and you take the other."

When Francis got close to the packhorses, he

saw that they had some gear tied to their saddles. His rifle was there, along with his powder horn and possibles bag. "You got my gun!"

Grimes snorted. "I remembered it from before. Thought you might need it. The man who had it was so drunk he won't know it's gone for a week."

They moved through the horse herd, leading their mounts—Francis pulling the horse with Lottie and Billy on top. For a time, it seemed they would make it. They had cleared the herd and were twenty paces into dark prairie when a dog started barking.

Francis didn't know what set it off but as soon as it barked another joined it and soon every dog in the village was yelping.

It woke some of the drunk Comancheros, who yelled at the dogs. Grimes had stopped, frozen, waiting for the clamor to subside. It nearly did.

But one of the Comancheros was sick and wandered to the edge of the village to throw up no more than thirty feet from the little group.

At first he didn't see them. He finished his business and was turning away when something caught his eye—a flash of metal in the moonlight, the dark mass of a horse against the starry sky. Something.

"*¿Qué?*" He leaned forward, peering into the dark, and still almost didn't see them.

Then Billy sneezed.

"*Hooo!*"

It sounded like a whistle—a big owl hooting—but it got the job done. Drunk or not, the camp lived on the edge of danger every moment, and they came awake instantly with the alarm.

The man who had yelled didn't have a gun, but he had a belt knife. He pulled it and went for Grimes. The mountain man stepped to the side and clubbed him down with his rifle, then swung into the saddle. "We're for it now. Let's go."

And he wheeled and vanished into the darkness. Francis threw his leg up over the packhorse and followed, kicking the horse into speed although he didn't need to. The two packhorses were accustomed to following Grimes and they slammed out at a dead run.

It was hard to stay astride. The packsaddle was covered with a piece of folded empty canvas but it didn't have stirrups. Soon they were at a wild lope through darkness over broken ground and Francis had dropped the rope leading to the second packhorse. He wanted to check on Lottie and Billy but couldn't turn. He yelled back, "Are you with me?"

"With you? We're *ahead* of you!"

And they were. The packhorses had followed Grimes and his mount when the mountain man had taken off. The children's horse was faster than Francis's.

It was a miracle that they didn't fall. Grimes kept them at a hard run for well over an hour, until the horses were snorting and blowing, before he slowed them to a walk to catch their wind.

They had caught up to him and Grimes spoke while they rode. "We don't have much time before they catch us."

"With that ride?" Francis felt his horse heaving, trying to suck air.

"Don't forget who they are. We have the night helping us. They'll track slow in the dark and if we keep moving we might stretch it a bit, but they'll come on hard and we won't have much time."

"What can we do?" Lottie's face looked white in the darkness.

Grimes was quiet for a time, thinking. "I figure we've come twelve, fourteen miles. I know where we are. The river canyon lies just north of here—two, three miles. Maybe four. There's water and game there. You'll be able to hide, get food—"

"What are you saying here?" Francis cut in. "You're going to leave us?"

Grimes nodded. "It's the only way. They're after three horses. If you get off here and walk north and I keep moving west with the packhorses, they'll come after me. You cover your tracks and they won't see them in the dark. With light stock and no pups I can keep ahead of them for days, maybe forever. They'll think you're with me and it will give you time to get away north, get back to help."

"You're deserting us," Lottie said. "Of all the cold things to do . . ."

Francis had thought the same thing at first but now shook his head. "He's right, Lottie. If we stay with him we'll be slower and they'll catch us. It's the only way we have a chance. We have to separate." But still something held him and he thought a moment before he realized what it was—he didn't want to leave the mountain man. At one time he had never wanted to see Grimes again, but now he realized that he had missed Grimes a great deal.

"I don't want to leave you," he said and realized how it sounded: soft, silly. "I mean—"

"I know what you mean," Grimes said, his

voice low. "It was right good to see you again too, although I wish we could meet under some easier conditions. I'd like to ride with you awhile myself, but this is the only way."

"I know."

"And if we waste time jawing and palavering, they're going to ride up on us."

"I know."

"So dismount and go."

"Where are you going? Maybe we can meet up again." Francis swung off and held the second packhorse while the children jumped down; took his rifle and possibles sack; then handed the two lead ropes to Grimes.

"Straight west until I lose them, and then I'll start swinging north. I'll stay where it's warm for the winter because my bones are old and I don't like the cold like I once did. Look for me there. Where it's warm. Cover your tracks as you head north and keep your hair on and your powder dry."

And he was gone before Francis could think, I should have thanked him.

"I don't like him," Lottie said as he disappeared into the darkness.

"I didn't for a while. But I changed. He grows on you. Come on, we don't have time to talk."

As it happened they had less time than Francis had thought. He made the two children walk ahead of him in single file. Following them closely, he broke off a small branch of mesquite and brushed over their tracks as best he could in the dark as they moved.

In not more than ten minutes he heard hooves coming hard.

"Stop now," he whispered. Seeing the children's faces in the dark, Lottie's white and round, he added, "Turn away from the sound, lie down, and not a sound now, not a sound at all."

He actually saw the riders pass. It was too dark to count them—more than ten, maybe fifteen men—but they were pushing their horses and they thundered past the children not sixty yards away without seeing them.

They'll catch Grimes, he thought, watching them fade into the night. Moving that fast they'll come up on him before morning. He has just the one gun, and I should have stayed with him. We'd have taken two of them, maybe four before they took us . . .

Then he shook his head, remembering who Grimes was, what he'd done, how tough he was; he took some catching. If he was caught, he would take some holding. He smiled then and thought Grimes must have been something with two arms, hard as he was with only one. I hope I see him again.

"Come on," he whispered to the children, starting them moving north again, "we've got some ground to cover."

# TUCKET'S GOLD

*To Maddux,*
*who lights up lives*

# Chapter One

If there was one thing Francis Tucket knew with certainty it was that death, brutal death, was close to taking them.

Dawn was coming and here he was, a fifteen-year-old boy in charge of two children, walking across a sunbeaten, airless plain that seemed to be endless. Francis, Lottie and Billy had no food or water or any immediate hope of getting any, and at any moment a dozen or two of the dirt-meanest men Francis had ever seen in a world *full* of mean men could come riding up on them and . . .

He didn't finish the thought. There was no need. Besides, in surviving Indian fights, blizzards, gun battles and thieves, he had learned the primary rule about danger. It would come if it would come. You could try to be ready for it, you could plan on it, you could even expect it, but it would come when it wanted to come.

Lottie and Billy understood this rule too. He had found them sitting in a wagon on the prairie all alone. Their father had died of cholera and their wagon train had abandoned the family, afraid of disease. Lottie had been nine then, Billy six. Francis hadn't thought he and the children would stay together long—after all, he had to keep searching for his own family. He'd been separated from them over a year before, when Pawnees had kidnapped him from the wagon train on the Oregon Trail. But Francis and Lottie and Billy—well, they were used to each other. They stuck together. Unlike Francis and Jason Grimes, the one-armed mountain man.

Jason Grimes had rescued Francis from the Pawnees and taught him how to survive in the West on his own. Then they'd parted ways.

2

Until last night. Last night when Grimes had helped them to escape from the Comancheros. The Comancheros were an outlaw band, ruthless, terrifying, inhumanly tough. To escape, Grimes had had to take the packhorses Francis and Lottie and Billy had been riding and lead them off empty, hoping the Comancheros would follow his tracks westward while the three children headed north on foot in the dark of night.

It was a decent plan—it was their *only* plan—and it seemed to be working. As Francis and the two children had moved north in the dark, they had seen the Comancheros ride past them after Mr. Grimes, tracking the horses. The Comancheros had missed the footprints of the children, partly because it was hard to see them and partly because Francis made Lottie and Billy walk in each other's footprints. He came last, brushing out the trail with a piece of mesquite behind him.

But luck was the major factor in the plan. If the Comancheros caught Grimes or even got within sight of him they'd know that Francis and the children weren't with him. They'd turn and come back for the children. Children meant real money because they could be sold or traded into slavery.

Francis knew that brushing out the tracks would only work in the pitch dark of night. In daylight the brush marks themselves would be easy to follow.

"I'm tired." Billy stopped suddenly. "I think we've gone far enough."

Francis frowned. When Francis had first met Billy, the boy wouldn't say a word. And now he'd gone from never talking at all to complaining.

"If they catch us"—Lottie slapped Billy's head so hard Francis thought he heard the boy's brains rattle—"they'll skin you. They'll make a tobacco pouch out of you and let the coyotes have the rest. Now keep walking. If we don't keep moving they'll be on us like dogs, won't they, Francis? On us just like dogs . . ."

Lottie loved to talk, would talk all the time if she had the chance, seemed to have been talking since Francis had found her in that wagon. Lottie would explain every little detail of every little part of every little thing she was talking about so that not a single aspect of it was missed, and she sometimes drove Francis over the edge. Now, as Billy started moving again, Francis picked up the pace, pushed them as hard as they could stand it and then harder, and Lottie didn't have breath left to speak.

Dawn brought the sun and the sun brought heat. Francis and the children were bareheaded and the sun quickly went to work on them. Billy wanted to complain, especially as the morning progressed and there was no water and the sun rose higher and became hotter, but Francis drove them until Billy began to weave. Then Francis handed Lottie his rifle and, pushing her in front of him, he picked Billy up and carried him piggyback, mile after mile, then yard after yard, and finally, step after step.

Lottie saw it first.

"There," she said. "See the spot?"

Francis was near dead with exhaustion. He had hardly slept at all for the two nights before and had been used roughly by the Comancheros in the bargain. He was close to the breaking point as he said, "What spot?"

"There. No, more to the right. On the horizon. It's trees. I'm sure of it. A stand of trees."

They had seen many mirages—images of trees and water that were not there. But Francis looked where she was pointing and saw it instantly. He stopped and set Billy down. The boy was asleep, and he collapsed in a heap, still sleeping. "You're right! Trees. And trees mean water."

He turned and studied the horizon. He hadn't been able to look up when carrying Billy and he was shocked now to see a plume of dust off to the west and south. It was at least fifteen miles away, against some hills in the distance. It was so far away that it seemed tiny, but Francis knew it was probably caused by riders, many riders.

Lottie saw him staring.

"Could it be buffalo?" She watched the dust. "A small herd?"

Not here, Francis thought. Not here in this dust and heat with no grass and no water. Buffalo wouldn't be that stupid. "Sure. It's buffalo."

"You're lying." She sighed. "I can tell when you're lying to me, Francis Tucket. It's them, isn't it?"

Francis said nothing but his mind was racing. So the riders were heading back eastward. But why would they be coming back so soon? Had they caught and killed Grimes already? If so they'd be looking for the children. Or had they given up the chase or just seen Grimes and found that he was alone and turned back, still looking for the children? Well, Francis had his rifle. He was ready. He would get two, maybe three of them before they were on him, and maybe that would discourage them. Or they might miss the tracks.

He knew this was a vain hope. There hadn't been a breath of wind to blow the dust over the brush marks he'd left, and undoubtedly they had men who were good trackers, men who were alive because they could track mice over rocks. So the Comancheros would find them and he'd get one or two and then . . . and then . . .

He looked to the trees, which were about two miles away. He could carry Billy there. They could get to the trees in time. Then what? The riders would keep coming back until they came to the place where Francis and the children had turned off, about nine miles back. They would see the marks and turn and start north. Nine miles. The horses would be tired but they would make ten miles an hour. They had to ride maybe twenty miles back to the turn and then nine or ten miles north after the children. He let the figures work through his tired brain. Maybe four hours but more likely three. The riders would be on them in three hours.

Francis and Billy and Lottie would need an hour to make the trees and then . . . and then nothing.

It would all just happen later. He'd get one or two of them and then they'd get him and take the children and nothing would have changed except that a few horses would be very tired and he, Francis, would be dead. If he was lucky. He did not want to think of what they would do with him if they caught him alive.

And as for what would happen to Lottie and Billy—his heart grew cold. But there was something else back there, more than just the plume of dust. There was a cloud. At first it was low on the horizon and showed only as a gray line, so low that Francis almost didn't see it. But it was growing rapidly, the wind bringing it from the west, and as it grew and rose he could see that it was the top edge of a thunderhead.

It didn't *look* like salvation, not at first. He had seen plenty of prairie thunderheads but as he watched it he realized two things.

One, it was growing rapidly, roaring along on the high winds, coming toward them at a much faster rate than the horses of the Comancheros. Two, it would bring rain.

Rain that would ease their thirst and cool their burning bodies and, far more important, rain that might wipe out their tracks, erase everything they had left behind them.

Still, it was a race, and nothing was sure. The clouds had to keep coming to beat the horsemen to where the children's tracks turned north. And it had to rain.

If the clouds turned off or didn't beat the Comancheros or didn't leave rain, then distance was all the children had. They needed to get to the trees and build some kind of defense.

Francis picked up Billy, who was still sound asleep and seemed to weigh a ton. He set off at a shambling walk, abandoning the tedious brushing in their race to get to the trees. Lottie shuffled ahead, carrying the rifle and Francis's possibles bag. She was wearing a ragged shift so dirty it seemed to be made of earth. Her yellow hair was full of dust. Francis wore buckskins, but the children only had what was left of their original clothing and what they'd managed to pick up along the way.

We're a sight, Francis thought. A ragtag mob of a sight.

He looked at the trees and they didn't seem any closer.

He looked at the cloud and it was still building,

9

though it seemed to be heading off slightly to the south.

He looked at the dust plume and it was still moving on the same line eastward, getting ready to cross their trail.

He looked back to the trees and thought, I would absolutely kill for that old mule we had. But the mule had been taken by the Comancheros.

# Chapter Two

They reached the trees just as the edge of the cloud caught up with them.

"Ten more feet and I would have died," Lottie whispered, and sank to the ground.

Francis dropped Billy like a stone—the boy fell without awakening—and studied their location. It was a meandering dry streambed with a row of stunted but leafy cottonwoods along each side. There were also stands of salt cedar, thick and green, and while no water was evident the streambed seemed moist. Francis knew there was water beneath the surface or the trees would have been dead.

"Lottie, scoop a hole there, at the base of that rock."

"You want to start digging, why don't you just go ahead? I have more important things to do than scrape at the old ground."

"Water." Francis was so dry he croaked. "Dig down and let it seep in."

"Oh. Well, why didn't you say so?" Lottie knelt by the rock and started digging in the loose sand with her hands. When she was down two feet, she yelped.

"Here it is! Just like you said, coming in from the sides. Oh, Francis, it's so clear, come see." She scooped some up and drank it. "Sweet as sugar. Come, try it."

Francis knelt and cupped his hand and drank and thought he had never tasted anything so good. But he stopped before he was full.

The wind was picking up now, blowing hard enough to lift dust and even sand, and he could no longer see the dust from the riders. The wind was blowing at the coming thunderheads and he smiled because even if it didn't rain there was a good chance the wind would fill in and destroy their tracks.

By now the thunderhead was over them, dark, so huge it covered the whole sky, and the wind had increased to a scream.

"Over here!" Francis yelled to Lottie. "Beneath this ledge." Incredibly, Billy was still asleep. Francis grabbed the boy and shook him until his eyes opened. "Get over by that rock ledge. Everything is going to break loose—"

A bolt of lightning hit so close Francis felt it ripple his hair, so close the thunder seemed to happen in the same split instant, and with it the sky opened and water fell on them so hard it almost drove Francis to his knees. He had never seen such rain. There seemed to be no space between the drops; it roared down, poured down in sheets, in buckets.

Francis couldn't yell, couldn't think, couldn't breathe. He held Billy by the shirt and dragged him in beneath the ledge that formed the edge of the streambed, away from the trees and out of the wind.

Lottie was there already and they huddled under the overhang just as the clouds cracked again and hail the size of Francis's fist pounded down. One hailstone glanced off the side of his head and nearly knocked him out.

"Move in more," he yelled over the roar of the storm. "Farther back—*move!*"

He pushed against Billy, who slammed into Lottie. They were already up against the clay bank beneath the ledge and could not go farther in. Francis's legs and rear were still out in the hail and took a fearful beating. He doubled his legs up but even so the pain was excruciating and though the large hailstones quickly gave way to smaller ones, his legs were immediately stiff and sore.

The streambed filled in the heavy downpour. Luckily they were near the upstream portion of the storm and so avoided the possibility of a flash flood—which would have gouged them out of the overhang and taken them downstream to drown. As it was, the water came into the pocket beneath them and turned the dirt to mud and soon they were sitting in a waist-deep hole of thick mud and water. And just as soon, in minutes, the rain had stopped, the clouds had scudded away and the sun was out, cooking the mud dry.

Aching, Francis pulled himself into the sun. The children crawled after. Water still ran in the stream but was receding quickly. The hot sun felt good, and Francis wanted to take his buckskin shirt off to hang. But he knew that if he didn't keep wearing it the shirt would dry as stiff as a board.

He straightened slowly, working the pain out of his legs. He looked to the west and smiled.

There would be no tracks after *that*. There might not even be any Comancheros left if the lightning hit their horses, which happened often. Horses seemed to draw lightning. Buffalo too. Francis had seen dead buffalo after a thunderstorm, still smoking from lightning strikes, the meat already cooked and ready to eat. . . . Thinking of roast buffalo made his stomach growl.

"I'm hungry." It was the first thing they'd heard in hours from Billy, finally awake, a standing mudball. "I'm *really* hungry."

"Well, I hope you aren't figuring on meat for a meal," Lottie said, holding up Francis's rifle, "because *this* thing isn't going to shoot."

Francis took the weapon and his possibles bag from her. Both were soaked, so he set to work.

He opened the possibles bag and spread his patch material—mattress ticking—and two cans of a hundred percussion caps each on a rock to dry in the sun. The caps had stayed mostly dry in the tight containers but he knew they fired better when totally dry.

He was surprised to find that the powder was only slightly damp. The powder horn was watertight except for the stopper on the pouring end and it had let in only a drop or two, which had been quickly absorbed by the powder near the spout and hadn't penetrated into the rest of the powder.

He thought of pouring the powder on a rock to dry, just to make certain, but decided against it. It was all the powder he had, maybe enough for eighty or a hundred shots, and one puff of wind would take it all away. The balls themselves were of lead and not damaged. He had about sixty left. The ball mold was of brass and would not rust, though he dried it carefully and set it aside.

He checked his grease pouch and found it still in good shape—the water couldn't do much to grease—and with his gear cleaned and drying he

**16**

went to work on the rifle. This rifle, a beautiful little Lancaster, had been given to him by his pa on his fourteenth birthday. The same day Francis had been kidnapped.

Francis stared at the rifle. That birthday was so far away—a lifetime ago.

He shook his head and went back to work.

The rush of water had taken the percussion cap off the nipple and he was certain water had worked through the nipple into the powder inside. This meant that the charge would be much reduced in power, if not completely ruined. He put a new cap on the nipple, went to the ledge where they had sheltered from the hail and fired the rifle into the mud. Nothing happened the first time, nor the second. The third time, the caps had burned enough water out so that the remaining powder charge ignited with a dull *phwonk* that drove the ball less than an inch into the mud of the bank.

"I'm getting hungrier," Billy said suddenly.

"Hush now, lizard gut." Lottie cuffed him lightly across the back of the head. "He's working on his tools. Drink water to fill your belly and leave him alone."

Francis sat on a rock, which was already dry from the heat of the noonday sun. Using only the small knife from his possibles bag, he took the rifle apart. The patch material was also dry and he ran a slightly dampened patch down the bore of the rifle, then a dry one—using the cleaning rag slot on his ramrod—and when it was completely dried out he set it up so that the sun would shine down the bore as directly as possible.

The walnut stock had been well soaked in oil and bear grease over the years, and the water had not penetrated the wood. But he removed the lock. He wiped it dry and then greased it with a touch of grease from his bag until it cocked and snapped with an almost slick sound.

Finally he used a small nipple wrench from his possibles pouch and removed the nipple, greased the threads and screwed it back in place. Then he smeared a tiny amount of grease on a rag and pushed it through the bore over and over until the rifling was entirely greased and there wasn't a chance of rust.

Finally he put the weapon back together with practiced ease. He measured a charge, poured it down the bore, patched a ball with a greased patch and pushed it down on the powder, pinched a cap so it would wedge tight on the nipple and put the hammer on half cock—the safety notch.

"There." He stood. His shirt was dry and the mud had turned to dust and flaked off the soft leather. His buckskin pants were also dry and still soft and he put the strap of his possibles bag over his shoulder and looked to the sun. "We've got a good five hours of daylight left, maybe six. This streambed moves northwest—which is away from the Comancheros, and it's the way we want to go— so we'll follow it until dark. At least that way we'll have water and—"

"I'm hungry." Billy had locked on the one thought. "And my feet hurt."

"—there's a chance we can run on some meat. All meat needs water and they'll be coming to the streambed to drink. And *all* our feet hurt because we're barefoot." Francis looked down at his feet. The moccasins had long since worn off from walking—they were good for only a few miles in sand and rocks. Yes, his feet hurt too, but they would soon toughen up and get callused.

He started off without speaking and for once Lottie was silent. She followed, dragging Billy by the hand, and the three of them shuffled through the mud and sand and water of the quickly drying stream.

# ──── Chapter Three ────

They walked along the stream the rest of the day, and though they saw plenty of tracks—deer and rabbit and coyote and some raccoon—they made too much noise for the game to hold position for a shot.

Francis thought of going ahead to hunt, but he hated the idea of leaving the children alone so soon after their brush with the Comancheros. He had despaired of getting any food. But just before dark, when he walked around a curve in the stream, there was a young spike buck standing angled away with its head down, drinking water.

Francis raised and fired without thinking, so fast Lottie yelled and dropped to the ground. She thought somebody was shooting at them.

For a second he thought he'd missed. The deer made an amazing leap to the side, clearing the edge of the streambed and landing above them, a good eight feet up and fifteen over.

But Francis was sure he'd held true and that the ball had gone into the back of the ribs and out the front, through the heart. When he climbed up the side of the stream the buck was lying there on its side, dead.

Francis paused, thanking fate and the spirits and the deer—his stomach growling all the while—and then handed the knife from his possibles kit to Lottie. "Start gutting it and we'll skin it. We'll stay here a day or two and make some moccasins with the green hide. I'm going to look around and make sure we're alone."

At one time Lottie would have objected to getting stuck with the work, but she was too hungry.

Billy looked like he was going to start chewing on one of the deer's feet any second. It was not a time to be squeamish.

Francis reloaded, put a cap on the nipple and studied the surrounding country. He had two worries. One, that somebody might have heard the shot. The Lancaster had a small bore—.40 caliber—and made a fearsomely high, sharp crack when it went off. Still, the sound probably wouldn't carry more than a mile or two—he had fired in the confines of the streambed—but he wanted to make sure that it was a *safe* mile or two.

The second worry was about a fire. They could eat the meat raw—Francis had done so on occasion and he was sure Lottie and Billy would be able to stomach it—but he longed for a full, hot meal. He also needed to melt some grease off the deer to replenish his supply for shooting and cleaning and to work into their feet and moccasin leather. He needed a day down, and the children needed at least a day of rest, maybe more. He had to be able to make a fire and not have it attract any attention.

The country had changed dramatically as they'd moved up the streambed. It had gone from flat desert-prairie to a rolling terrain with outcroppings of rock. Francis climbed one of these outcroppings and sat on the top.

It was about three hours from dark, and the late light cast long shadows from the hills and rocks. He sat quietly and let his mind go blank, let his eyes study. There, a bird wheeling—a hawk—and there, a deer, a mile and more away. To the right, half a mile on, a family grouping of antelope, three of them, and over there, another hawk diving on something, maybe a mouse, and four crows wheeling in a warm draft of air, climbing and tumbling. Two jackrabbits running from one coyote, a half mile to the left. All normal things, all seen and dismissed.

Francis was looking for the other thing, the thing that didn't match the surrounding country. A bit of sharp line, a movement, a curve that didn't follow nature. He swiveled and studied for a full half hour and did not see or hear anything out of place. He gave it another half hour, not moving except to turn carefully, cradling the rifle across his arms. But there was truly nothing out of the ordinary to see or hear or smell or feel.

At last he was satisfied. He stood slowly, his legs

stiff, and moved down the hill and back to where Lottie and Billy were working.

The deer was gutted and the rear partially skinned. It looked like Billy had more blood on him than was in the deer. He looked like a wild animal. Lottie, who had been doing the real work, had only a spot of blood on her cheeks and some on her hands. But she smiled through a cloud of flies—it was hard to believe how many there could be in such a short time in an otherwise empty prairie—and motioned to a stack of wood.

"I had Billy bring in wood. I wasn't sure you'd want a fire but if you did it would be hard to find in the dark and we might fetch a snake were we to grope around without light. I 'collect the time one of my neighbors, I think it was that one named Nancy, she fetched a snake in the woodpile when she was reaching for some firewood in the dark and that was the last time she brought in wood after dark."

Francis waited. Nothing more came. I know I'm going to be sorry for this, he thought, I know I shouldn't do this, I know it's just the worst thing in the whole world to do. "What happened to the snake?"

25

"She had it by the tail and she took it and whopped it against the side of a chopping block and killed it and then she said, to the snake she said, 'If you want to act like wood you can by jingo *be* wood' and she put it in the stove—it was stiff as a poker because she whopped it kind of hard—and burned it for heat." A deep breath. "Of course that was before she up and took with the ha'nts and could tell about things before they come to be. I remember the time . . ."

Francis let her go. He was used to the talk; as a matter of fact, he was getting fond of it, and recognized that it was not because she liked to talk so much as because she *saw* things. Saw *everything* there was to see and was very, very smart. She missed nothing. And when there was something to be done—gutting a deer, gathering wood, which he hadn't told her to do but she'd taken care of just on the off chance that he would want a fire—she jumped in and did it.

She finished the story about Nancy while she skinned the deer. Billy helped, and Francis took over when the carcass had to be flopped to get the skin free.

"Get some sharp sticks to cook on," he said. "Green so they won't burn."

When the skin was completely off the carcass he draped it over a bush and cut some meat into strips, meat from the back haunches and the tenderloin down the back. These he laid on top of the ribs to keep them out of the dirt. Then he set about making a fire.

He had no flint or striker, but he did have the rifle and powder. He cut slivers of wood from the dry underside of a wet log and found some dead grass already dry in the hot sun after the rain. He arranged the shredded grass and slivers of wood in a small hollow and sprinkled a bit of powder into a tiny pocket beneath the grass, leaving a thin trail coming back on top of a small flat rock. At the end of the powder trail he put a percussion cap, picked up another stone and struck the cap. It went off with a sharp snapping sound; it lit the powder, whose trail acted as a short fuse that set off the bit beneath the grass. Within three seconds he had a small fire going.

"More wood," he called, and Lottie handed him small pieces until they had a healthy blaze.

"Now the meat . . ." He took a strip of venison, put it on one of the green sticks and held it over the flames, so close that the bottom edge started to burn.

Lottie and Billy did the same and when the meat was hot—well before it was fully cooked—Billy could stand it no longer and ate his piece. He immediately started cooking another, by which time Francis and Lottie had eaten theirs and started on more. They sat that way into the night, eating and cooking, grease in their hair and faces, until a large part of the deer was gone and they were so full they couldn't move.

Francis blinked—a bit of smoke in his eyes—and he was so bone tired that the blink was enough. His belly was full and the fire was warm on his face and his eyes didn't really open after the blink. He rolled onto his side, still facing the fire, saw the children do the same and was instantly, profoundly asleep.

# Chapter Four

He slept hard until the sun came creeping into the streambed and warmed his face.

His eyes opened then and he saw the two children lying asleep on the other side of the fire pit. He rose and stood—every muscle in his body seemed to ache—and stretched. Amazing, what a difference a full belly and a drink of water could make.

He picked up his rifle and moved off a bit,

climbed the side of the arroyo and swept the horizon. The sleep had been wrong. In this country, to
not keep an open eye but just drop off by the fire
was insane, but he had been so tired he couldn't
have stayed awake if he'd been lying in broken glass.

Nothing. A clear blue morning sky. Not even a
line of clouds. No dust, no horsemen, nothing. It
was as if, Francis thought, they were completely
alone on the planet.

"We ate most of the deer," Lottie said in back of
him, startling him. "Should we get the fire going
again and cook the rest?"

"Small," Francis said. "A small dry fire—no
smoke. We don't want to attract company. Use dry
wood and keep it little. There were some hot coals
still there to get it going."

"I know. You don't have to be telling me everything, Francis. I know some things. I know lots of
things. There was a man, he came through one
time back on the farm and had a list of questions to
see could a person know things, and I answered
most of them. Although some of the questions were
dumb. One was about horses and fish and
dogs . . ."

Francis let her ramble and make a fire while he

set to work on the hide. Billy was still asleep. They had skinned the deer close so there wasn't any flesh or fat adhering to the hide to scrape off and he stretched the skin to dry in the sun. It would shrink, he knew, but he cut strips from the edge to use for thongs and lacing. He stretched the skin to keep it flat while it dried.

"How long until we can make moccasins?" Lottie asked.

"It should dry enough today if it doesn't cloud up and rain. We can rig something up tomorrow. They'll be made of raw hide but they'll help a bit."

"Good. My poor feet."

Lottie held one off the ground, standing on one foot and tipping the other sole up behind her. Francis could see it was torn and blistered. His were the same and he looked down at Billy, still asleep, and saw that the boy's were the worst of all.

Well, Francis thought, it's a good place to rest. We still have some meat. He marveled that they could have eaten most of the deer, but he'd seen Indians do the same and, after all, they had not eaten properly for days. There's water, he thought, and wood, and we're alone. "We'll stay here two days. Fish me out the deer guts."

**31**

"What?" Lottie said.

"The tube guts from the deer. The intestines. Pull them out of the gut pile."

"Is this some kind of joke, Francis? Because if it is . . ."

"Never mind. I'll do it myself." Francis went to the pile of guts where they'd left them. A cloud of flies came up but he took a stick and fished out the intestines. He had seen Indian women clean them out and hang them to dry with a rock for weight so they would become like string for sewing. But they were too far gone and torn apart when he tried to stretch a piece of them. He threw them back. The stomach, lungs, heart and liver were all still there and he knew it was a waste not to eat them. Indians would have eaten them first and saved the meat for later. He'd seen them, and Grimes too, eat buffalo guts and liver raw out of an animal almost before it was dead. But he couldn't bring himself to do it, though it was always wrong to waste part of a kill.

The next day Francis found that making moccasins was more difficult than he'd thought. He had repaired them himself when they had worn out but he'd never made a pair from scratch.

The hide had been stretched and dried for only

one day in the hot afternoon sun. Unfortunately the hair was still on it. Francis used his knife to cut the hair shorter but they didn't have the week it took to throw the hide in a creek to let the hair "slip" out of the skin. For that matter, Francis thought, looking at the streambed, which had further dried up since the rain, we don't have a creek either.

He made the children stand on the hide's skin side and scratched outlines of their feet. He added half an inch around the sides and cut the sole pieces. He did the same for himself, then set all the pieces on the ground, side by side, and looked at them.

"Well," he said. "Well . . ."

"They need walls," Billy said. "They ain't going to work without they have walls."

"You mean sides," Lottie said, "and he *knows* that. Don't you, Francis? You know how to do that, don't you?"

Francis nodded. "Sure."

Of course he didn't, but if he admitted it to Lottie he'd never get another word in. He studied the hide again, wishing he'd spent more time watching the women work and make things when he was a Pawnee captive.

Billy was right. The soles needed walls. Francis cut long strips of hide about two inches wide, cut narrow laces from the remaining hide and, after boring holes with his knife, laced the strips around the soles so they stood upright. Then he cut toe pieces and laced them to the tops of the walls until he had some version of moccasins.

"They look alive," Billy said. "Like they'll eat our feet."

Francis smiled. They did look odd. He hadn't gotten all the hair off, and even the laces were fuzzy. The end result was comical: hair-covered, fluffy, odd ends sticking out all over the place . . .

"They'll break in soon," Francis said. "Let's get walking. I don't like staying here." He couldn't shake the feeling that the Comancheros had ridden past them—well to the south but past them just the same—and would come back for them somehow.

When Francis was finished, they'd been in camp just over two days. In that time the three of them had eaten most of the good meat off the deer, except for some strips they'd dried in the sun. Francis gave the strips to Lottie and Billy to carry, shuffled his feet deep into the green-hide moccasins and set off.

"Which way are we going?" Lottie held back. "Do we have a plan?"

"Northwest. It's the only way to go." In truth they had no choice. Somewhere to the west of them lay a great desert. He had heard people talk of it, and if he took the children there they would certainly die of thirst. East of them lay a whole area ravaged by the war between Mexico and the United States, an area where bandits ruled the land. And south of them . . . well, that was the way to the Comancheros and he had no illusions about their fate if they went that way.

If they went far enough north they would meet up with the Oregon Trail and maybe get on with a wagon train and head west and he could find his family and . . . and . . . and . . .

It was always there, the dream, the hope. But the truth was he could barely remember them. He stopped walking as the thought struck him: he felt close to these two children, felt that Lottie and Billy were more of a family to him than the one he'd lost when he was taken prisoner.

Lottie and Billy had been trudging with their heads down and ran into Francis.

"Why have we stopped?" Lottie pulled at her

35

moccasins, which were loose and slapped on her feet. "What are you thinking about?"

Francis looked at them and smiled. "Families," he said. "I was thinking about families."

Then he settled his possibles bag, held his loaded rifle loosely and easily in his right hand, the hammer ready on half cock, and started northwest in the easy shuffle he'd learned from the Indians.

It was the only way to go.

# Chapter Five

Francis walked well ahead. He did this partly because the other two had shorter legs and were carrying the dried meat and leftover hide, and partly because he could not stop worrying. Some fears were about the Comancheros, but he worried more about water. They were walking up the streambed and had found puddles here and there, but they were drying up fast, and he did not like the prospect of making a dry camp or of going more than one day without water.

Every now and then he would leave the streambed and move up along the higher banks, or go well off to the side and stand on a hill, careful not to kick up dust for anybody to see.

But there was nothing but a wide, half-desert prairie that seemed to stretch endlessly. He would stand, the rifle cradled in his arm, his eyes moving slowly. Waiting, he studied, and he found birds and rabbits and deer. But nothing human.

Toward evening he roamed wide, moving out carefully half a mile on each side of the streambed, looking for tracks or some sign of movement. Nothing.

He came back into the streambed and walked another hundred yards, looking for just the right place, and at length he found a ledge slightly above the bed with an overhang to catch the light and heat from a fire. In front there was a small pool of water, left either by the rain or, more likely, by a seeping spring. He tasted it. Ah! It was sweet.

"Gather wood," he told the children when they came up. "And dry grass for kindling and for beds. I'm going to look for fresh meat."

"Francis," Lottie began, "we know how to make camp. You don't need to tell us." He nodded and moved off.

Francis checked the cap on the nipple of his rifle, pushed it down tightly with his thumb and moved up the bed of the stream. He had seen many tracks of deer and smaller game. It was time to hunt, even though they had enough skimpy meat to keep them going for two more days and Francis could go days more without eating. He also hated to stop this close to where they'd left the Comancheros. But he had to hunt now in case they came into a country with no game. Cover was thinning and he had to think of three mouths and three stomachs instead of just his own. Lottie and Billy couldn't cope with hunger as well as he could.

It would be wrong to say he hunted. He walked up the streambed, passed two does and an older buck, waited until he saw a young buck, aimed and fired. The deer dropped. It was strange, almost like the deer had never been hunted with a gun. They moved off, away from him, but slowly and only for a few yards, and then they stood and looked at him.

He dragged the deer back to where the children

had gathered wood and grass. It was nearly dark and Billy was chewing on a piece of half-dried venison.

"Here," Francis said, "start gutting and skinning and I'll get a fire going."

"Do we need more meat?" Lottie took the knife he handed her and stood looking at the dead deer with distaste. "It seems as if we have enough meat for a couple of days, and we—"

"We are on foot," Francis cut in. "With bad shoes and two people with short legs. If we had horses or even that mule it would be different. We could pack food or take turns riding and cover some ground. On foot we're going to be lucky to make seven or eight miles a day. I stood on a hill and could see close on to twenty miles and believe me, there is nothing out there where we're heading. So unless we come across some horses we need plenty of food and water now. Start cutting while I get a fire going. Billy, you make us some grass beds up on that ledge. It isn't going to rain tonight so we don't have to worry about flooding. Dig back in a bit and watch for snakes."

Francis shredded dry grass, took a double pinch of powder and put it on a flat stone next to the

**40**

grass, placed a percussion cap next to it and struck the cap with a rock. It snapped and set the powder off; the powder flashed and the grass caught.

He put more grass on it, then small twigs, and soon the ledge and riverbank were lit with a cheery yellow glow. Francis climbed out of the streambed and was pleased to see that neither the flames nor a glow from them showed above the cut bank more than thirty yards away.

He had taken two steps back toward the riverbed when he heard Billy scream.

"Yaaaaaeeeeee!"

Snake. It was all Francis could think of. Rattlers hunted at night and they denned up during the day. Billy must have dug into a den just when one was getting ready to come out.

Francis ran back to the edge of the bank and jumped into the streambed.

"Ha'nts!" Billy yelled. "There's ha'nts back in there. I hit a cave of ha'nts!"

"What?" Francis stopped next to the ledge. He couldn't see anything. Lottie was there, covered with deer blood, holding the knife.

"There be ha'nts!"

"What is a ha'nt?"

"Ghost," Lottie said. "He saw a ghost. That's what they call ghosts back home."

Francis peered under the ledge. "In there? In the dirt?"

"Look for yourself," Billy said. "*I* ain't going back in there."

Francis peered back beneath the ledge at a slab of limestone. Over countless years the water had cut back beneath it, making a small roofed area perhaps three feet deep. It could not, by any stretch of the imagination, be called a cave. Not even a hole. But just above the recess the recent rain and flooding had cut the earth away, and when Billy had started to work back in to make a bed the loosened earth above the ledge had given way and a clump had fallen out. There, in that clump of earth, shining in the firelight as if suddenly come to life, was a complete human skull.

Francis jerked back. Then his common sense took over. "It's nothing," he said. "Just a skull. Probably some old grave."

"It's a ha'nt!" Billy stared wide-eyed at the skull. "It's full of evil luck."

"Only for the man who was the skull," Francis

**42**

said. "It looks like his luck ran out. You can see the hole in his head." He turned the skull slightly with a finger and pointed to a small triangular hole in the forehead. "It looks like a lance hit him, or some kind of sharp club or hammer."

"What's that?" Lottie had come closer and pointed.

"What?"

"Up there, in the dirt. It looks like a piece of steel or something."

Francis put more wood on the fire and in the brighter light he poked back carefully into the dirt the skull had fallen from. He found a metal edge and pulled at it. At first it wouldn't move and then suddenly it came, pulling dirt and what seemed to be the rest of the skeleton along with it. Francis found himself holding—he blinked—a steel helmet. It was rusted and tarnished and somehow looked familiar, though at first he could not tell why. It was round, with a steel brim that came to a point in the front and back, and had a steel edge down the middle of the top.

"It's Spanish," Lottie said. "I remember Pa talked about how the Spanish came to this country before the settlers landed back east, and the Spanish had cities and everything out here. He had a book with pictures and I remember a picture of some men wearing hats like this. He was smart, Pa was." Her voice became sad. "I miss him something fierce sometimes."

Francis nodded and they were silent a moment. He looked down at the helmet. "I remember too. My parents had a book in the wagon, and the pictures showed the Spanish had swords and battle-axes. But no guns." He shuddered. "I wouldn't want to be alone in this country without a gun."

"There's more." Billy had gotten over his fear and pointed back into the cavity left by the falling skeleton. "More metal. See it shine?"

This time he was wrong. Francis reached once more into the hole and tugged at a corner of metal. He pulled out a bar that he took to be lead. Then he dug his fingernail into it, or tried to, and knew. Oh no, this wasn't lead. He took the knife from Lottie, for once speechless, and he scraped a corner with the blade. The metal shone brightly in the firelight.

"It's silver," he said softly. "A whole bar of silver."

"There's more," Billy said, reaching back into

**44**

the hole. "A whole lot more." He pulled at a metal band and a rotten wooden container fell onto the ground, bars scattering around Francis's feet. Not all of them were silver. He caught the sheen of yellow through the dirt and picked one up.

"Gold?" He almost whispered it.

# Chapter Six

"We're rich." Lottie tried to say it aloud but it came out a whisper. "*Look* at it all."

For a moment Francis couldn't move, couldn't think. It had been so long since he'd really considered money. His life had been all powder and lead and hunting and shelter. Money didn't enter into it. He had never had a dream of wealth. All he thought of was getting through the day—sometimes just getting through the next hour—and the constant thought of somehow, someday, some way getting back to his family.

Now this, he thought. It was almost an irritation. Now this . . . as he looked at the bars scattered around his feet. There were four silver bars and five yellowish bars. All crudely cast but in rough rectangular forms. Not big, but big enough. He used the knife again and knelt down and scraped one of the yellow bars and found it softer than the brass of his ball mold. The scraped area emerged a wonderful glistening yellow-gold color.

Yes, he thought. It's gold.

Yes, he thought again. We're rich. And then a third thought came, the first realistic one: the gold and silver didn't mean a thing out here and it was a long way, an incredibly long, dangerous and hard way on foot to anywhere that gold and silver had any true worth.

"I wonder how it came to be here?" Lottie said. "All just in a pile like this."

"Indians," Billy said. "They must have killed him."

"And then buried him?" Lottie snorted. "I don't *think* so."

"There was somebody with him," Francis said.

**47**

"They had a fight but fought them off, whoever they were. Then they buried this man and—"

"Buried the gold with him?" Lottie shook her head. "Why would they do that?"

"—and buried the gold for the same reason we have to rebury it. It's too heavy to carry. Go ahead, pick one of them up."

Lottie hefted one of the bars. "It must weigh close to fifteen pounds."

"And the silver weighs almost as much. Nine bars times fifteen pounds—that's going on a hundred and thirty-five pounds. Even breaking the nine bars between us we can't carry it far."

"I could try," Billy cut in, his eyes shining as he stared at the bars. "We ought to give it a really *good* try."

"No." Francis shook his head. "We wouldn't make five miles and believe me, we have a lot more than five miles to go before we're out of this godforsaken flatland."

"So what do we do?" Lottie asked.

"We take some of it. Two bars of gold. Then we bury the rest in a different place and we mark it well so we can find it again. We head north until we can buy some horses and we come back for the gold."

"We share it?" Billy looked up.

Francis nodded. "Share and share alike. A third each."

Billy smiled. "How much rock candy can I buy with my share?"

Lottie shook her head. "We'll talk about how you're going to spend it later. Help me with the deer. We have to clean it and strip it and hang the meat to dry. And we have to bury this poor man again."

"Bury him?" Billy looked down. "He's nothing but a few bones and some hair."

"He was a real person and he should get a real burial, same as anybody, isn't that right, Francis?"

Francis nodded. "We have to hide all this again so we can find it when we come back, and that includes burying the man. But not here, not here . . ." He clambered up the edge of the streambed and studied the surrounding terrain for a moment in the darkness.

There was a small depression near three large boulders, the depression in the center of imaginary lines drawn from all three stones. X, Francis thought, marks the spot—or a three-legged X.

"We'll bury him in here." He moved to the depression. "The ground is soft and we can find it again."

"We can dig with these." Billy came up holding a sword in one hand and the old helmet in another. They were rusty—the helmet had a couple of small holes where the rust had eaten through—but the sword was in surprisingly good shape. The blade was short, perhaps two and a half feet, and wider than Francis would have thought. The sword he had seen in the book had a long thin blade, very sharp, with a basket handle. This one had merely a crosstree to protect the hand, and the blade was more like a long sticking knife.

But Billy was right. It would make a good digging tool.

"Start digging," Francis said. "Lottie and I will work on the deer meat."

They had a small fire and Francis hung strips of meat on green sticks over the fire to cook. When they were done and still hot he took some up to Billy, who was digging away, loosening the dirt with the sword and scooping it with the helmet.

It was hard dark now, but a full moon had risen and it threw so much light that it was easy to see where to dig.

**50**

"That's close to enough," Francis said. The hole was waist-deep on Billy and about three feet across. "It can't wash out here and the wind can't blow the dirt away down low like this."

Billy put the sword and helmet aside and sat on the edge of the hole, chewing the meat Francis handed him. "Ain't it strange?"

"What?"

"He was rich, that man. He came along here and he was rich and somehow died so he never got to spend it. Then we come along and find his body and now we're rich."

Somewhere off in the distance a coyote wailed— short yips followed by a long high note. Another answered, mimicking the tone. Francis looked around the prairie in the moonlight and thought but did not say what he knew was the truth. They were a long way from being able to spend the money. There were many things that could happen to make them wind up like the Spaniard, wind up in a hole in the ground.

He shook the feeling off. "Come on, let's get Lottie and bury him and hide the gold. We have a lot of work to do."

# Chapter Seven

"How many are there?" Lottie stared down at the tracks.

"More than five," Francis said. "The tracks run together. And they're fresh, since the rain three days ago."

"Maybe only a day old." Lottie looked hard at Francis.

They had walked less than four miles before coming across the tracks. It had been a soft morning. The weather had remained clear but somewhat cooler—perfect for walking—and the moccasins were proving to be better than they looked. They had used part of the hide from the second deer to make a crude backpack for the two bars of gold. Billy had cut a strip to hold the sword at his side, though he was so short that if he didn't watch it, the tip dragged in the dirt.

Francis had moved out beside the streambed a few hundred yards, so Lottie, who was in the lead, had come upon the tracks and called for him.

"Horses?" she had said, and pointed. Billy had crouched down to look.

Francis nodded.

"With riders?"

"It's hard to tell."

"I thought you could track."

"I can."

"They don't have shoes," Lottie said now.

"Maybe they're wild horses and we could catch one or two or even three."

Francis had been thinking along the same lines, only a bit more realistically. Unshod horses were not necessarily wild. Indians did not shoe horses, nor were most of the Comancheros' horses shod, except for those they had stolen with shoes on. And catching wild horses wasn't that easy either. There was a reason they were called wild.

But Francis had learned from Mr. Grimes, the mountain man, who in turn had learned by studying wolves and coyotes, that you always watched everything; and when something came along that was different, you investigated it.

Francis had no intention of running into Indians or Comancheros and didn't have a clue about how to catch wild horses. But it was still very interesting that suddenly, in the midst of this flat, grassless plain, the tracks of five or ten horses came in from the side and moved up the streambed ahead of them.

Francis knelt to examine the tracks more closely and found one, with a slight crack in the forward rim of the hoof, that he could identify and study without confusing it with the others.

They were not moving fast, not even trotting. More strangely still they seemed to be moving in a tight group. There was very little space between the tracks and now and then they stopped or moved off to the side a bit and he could see where they had been chewing at small clumps of bunchgrass.

That was a good sign. Ridden horses were not allowed to stop at every little bit of grass. Maybe they were wild . . . but that didn't explain why they stayed in such a tight group. A single horse never went off to the side to nibble—it was always the whole group.

"We'll follow them," he said after a few moments. "They're going our direction anyway. But keep it quiet in case we come up on them."

And so they walked most of the day, moving quietly, taking turns carrying the pack with the gold. The thirty pounds felt heavier and heavier as the day progressed. They peered around each curve in the streambed as they came to it, and it was nearly evening when Francis, who was walking in the lead, froze and held up his hand to stop Billy and Lottie. He'd seen something, a slight movement. He motioned them to move off to the sides of the streambed and wait for him and he made his way around one bend, then another, and when he came to the third curve, a sharp angle to the left, he saw them.

There were six of them. All small Indian ponies, tied together. Or they'd once been tied. Now they were more or less tangled together in a clump.

Francis stopped and studied them, trying to see how it could have happened. They looked rough, muddy, their hair matted and tangled, and some were bleeding from small wounds. But none seemed to have any broken bones; none was dragging a leg.

But where had they come from, and how could they have managed to get this far (however far it was) without killing each other?

They saw him almost at the same moment he saw them and another strange thing happened. Two of them seemed startled and shied slightly, started to run away, but they were all held by leather-rope halters and some kind of picket line that had become so wrapped and crossed that, though the two wanted to run, they were held back by the other four, which were trying to get a drink from a nearly dried-up pool. One of those ponies actually seemed to want to come toward Francis.

He approached them, walking slowly, keeping his arms still and the rifle down at his side so it wouldn't appear to be a stick or club. They all watched him now, but even the shy ones didn't move away. Wherever they had come from, they certainly weren't wild. Their ears were up—filled with burrs and mud, but up—and they studied him with interest as he moved toward them.

Twenty feet away he stopped again.

"Easy." He spoke low, almost whispered, but did not hiss. "Easy, easy, ea . . . sy . . ."

They held their position. In the end he walked right up to them, held out his hand, took the chin cord on the halter of a compact pinto. Francis grinned when the pinto nuzzled his shoulder.

"You're all sick of this, aren't you?"

Clearly they were trained and just as clearly they were monumentally tired of being tangled in a six-horse knot. They stood gently while he leaned his rifle against a small tree and untangled them, one by one, tying each horse to the tree when he got it loose.

"Oh my, Francis, look what you've found."

Lottie and Billy came up and even that didn't bother the ponies. "Where did they come from?" Lottie moved to the pinto and began untangling its mane and forelock, taking the burrs out of its ears.

"I'd say Indians," Francis offered. "Except that I don't know if there are any around here. They might be from the Comancheros but it's a long way to their camp—unless they broke away from a moving band. Either way I figure they were picketed and pulled loose in that storm, still all tied to the picket line. They must have panicked and run a distance—probably still driven by the storm—and then kept moving in a clump."

"Comancheros." Billy looked over his shoulder. "They could be tracking the horses."

"Could be." Francis nodded. "But that was a powerful rain. Any tracks were wiped out, and even a Comanchero couldn't track in pure mud. Besides, if they were being followed it stands to reason they would have been caught by now, moving as slow as they were."

"So they're our horses." Lottie smiled.

Francis nodded. "We ride, at least for now." He smiled back at her. "Which one do you want?"

# Chapter Eight

They spent that night and the next full day working on the horses. It was one thing for Francis to say they'd ride, another to make certain they could.

The ponies were in a slightly weakened condition at first, and perhaps that was for the best. The pinto still managed to throw Francis twice. Lottie took a small white mare with a circle around one eye, and Billy took a muddy gray pony because he said it reminded him of the mule and he missed the mule.

"Where'd you get that old mule anyway?" Lottie asked. "You never told us."

"Two men named Courtweiler and Dubs came on me and stole everything I had and left me the mule."

"Well." Lottie turned to look at Francis. "I'll bet you fixed those crooks!"

"The mule helped," Francis said. "But that's another story."

Luckily only the pinto bucked. The rest needed care. Francis used some of his deer grease to treat the cleaned cuts and bruises so the flies wouldn't get into the wounds, and spent the rest of the day making usable jaw bridles and reins out of the braided picket lines and halters.

They picked one other horse, a reddish mare, for a packhorse, though they had no true pack to put on her back. They tied the horses to the tree for the two nights they were camped and Francis slept at the base of the tree to be ready in case something frightened them.

At dawn the next morning Francis shook the other two awake. "We're leaving. Come on." They ate cold cooked meat and before true light they headed out, back in the direction from which they'd come, for the rest of the gold.

Francis led at first, riding the pinto and pulling the pack mare with an eight-foot piece of picket line. They climbed out of the streambed and onto the flat of the prairie. He and the pinto had worked out their differences and he found the small horse quick and responsive, answering to knee pressure, so he could steer with his legs and keep his hands free.

"What about the two extra horses?" Lottie followed Francis, and Billy brought up the rear on his gray.

"Enough is a feast," Francis said. "We can't lead them all the time so they're on their own. But I think they'll follow."

And he was right. They fell in behind Billy and walked along as if led.

Francis and the children found that the Spaniard's new burial site had not been bothered. They used Billy's sword—he would not let anybody else carry it—to dig up the gold and silver.

They put it on the pack mare, balancing it on either side in deerskin pouches. There was no cinch and at first the packs would not stay on. Lottie figured out a way to tie it into the mare's mane to keep it centered. Francis took some of another piece of the braided rope that had held the ponies and looped it beneath the mare's belly to keep the packs tied down. It was not truly a cinch but it kept the packs from flopping or coming loose.

They started north again late in the afternoon and by dark they were passing their camp of the previous night.

As before, they began with Francis in the lead. But in time he handed the pack mare over to Lottie and began to range, moving left and right of the centerline of their march.

It felt wonderful to be riding again. The pinto was a good horse and with a little grass and rest and water would be a great one. They had meat left from the last kill, enough for two more days, and now they could cover thirty miles and more a day.

At dark Francis came back to the creek bed where some small cottonwoods stood. They tied the horses to trees, each separately, and gathered wood and cooked meat and ate until they were full. They had to dig a seep pool for water—the stream was dried up—but the water was sweet and there was plenty for all three of them and the horses.

Francis then made a circuit on foot with his rifle, moving out half a mile in the dark, and could not see any sign of light on the horizon or from their own fire.

He had put on a good face for Lottie and Billy, but he was worried. If the ponies had come from the Comancheros, they would be tracking them. But there was no indication that anybody was coming and so he went back to the fire just in time to hear Lottie finish what had apparently been a long story about horses she had known back home.

Billy was sound asleep, and Francis curled up near the tree by his pinto, his rifle in his arms. Soon all three were asleep and there was no sign, not a single indication, that on the following morning Lottie would find the castle in the clouds.

# Chapter Nine

It was strange that Lottie was the one to see it first. She had just been telling about a book she'd read, or somebody had read, that had men fighting with swords, huge swords as tall as the men, and the men lived in castles . . . when she looked up and said, "Like that one up there."

And sure enough there was a castle, or something that looked so much like a castle it didn't matter. It was far off on the horizon, or floating above the horizon, with blue daylight showing beneath the castle and beneath the earth it stood on. It appeared to be made of red sandstone, with buildings on top made from reddish earth and a tower at each end.

"Look close," she said. "You can see the people."

They had been riding close together and at first Francis and Billy couldn't see what she meant. But when they moved their heads closer to Lottie's line of sight the castle jumped into focus. And she was right. Francis could see small figures moving, along the roof or the top of a wall, and around the wall at the base and off to the side was a field of what seemed to be corn, dried and golden.

"It's a mirage," Francis said. "We've seen them before."

"Not like this one," Lottie said. "Not a castle. And not this close."

"A mirage doesn't have to be far away. Mr. Grimes told me once he saw a mirage of a sailing ship on an ocean while he was washing his face in a stream."

"But the people." Lottie pointed. "You can see them so clear. . . ."

They rode in silence for a time—a strange state

for Lottie—and Francis had to agree with her. Mirages usually didn't last long, or they wavered in the light, or shimmered and disappeared. This one did none of those things. Instead the light beneath it narrowed and vanished until the structure was clearly connected to the ground and then it started to grow as they rode through the day, higher and higher until even Francis had to acknowledge that it wasn't a mirage at all but a real castle.

Except that as they grew nearer it became clear that it wasn't a castle so much as a small town on top of a butte.

And with that knowledge Francis realized that he was leading two children and a packhorse carrying a fortune in gold toward a strange village on a strange mountain filled with strange people who might not be friendly.

When evening caught them they were still a good ten or twelve miles from the butte and Francis dropped into a small gully filled with brush and salt cedar and tied the horses.

"We'll make a cold camp. No fire. No cooked meat. Dig a seep hole for water. As soon as it's dark I'm going to move a little closer and take a better look at that place."

"It's a castle," Billy said. "Lottie was right."

"No, Billy," she said. "It's a town on a mountain. I just thought it was a castle."

"Still. They'll have food and water and maybe candy we can buy with the gold. I think we ought to get up there and see if they've got a store."

Francis smiled, though it was lost to the others in the gathering dark. They ate some small pieces of cooked, partly dried venison, and then Francis settled them in, and walked off into the dark.

He set a good pace for two hours and covered five or six miles. Then he slowed a bit and walked another four miles in two more hours. He had been moving in a streambed—dozens cut the prairie surface—and so could not see what was in front, but after walking what he thought might be ten miles he pulled himself up to the edge of an arroyo and took a look.

He was surprised to see that he was quite close to the butte. The moon helped him to see the small adobe houses. They had a soft, curved beauty in the moonlight, and here and there he saw the light of a fire coming through an opening between two houses. There were no lanterns, nor did there appear to be light from candles or anything like a window. He didn't see a horse herd. But there were several fields of corn plants, dry and apparently harvested last fall, and his mouth watered at the thought of corn bread and gravy to go with the venison. . . .

A sound stopped his dream. A soft sound, close, something brushing, no, some sound he'd heard before. Something sliding. Really close. Not sliding either, more slithering . . .

The snake hit him just as he realized what it was and saw it in the moonlight. It didn't rattle, though it was a good four feet long and had close to a dozen rattles. Francis's head had been just over the top edge of the arroyo and his upper right arm lay along the dirt as he held himself there, and the snake hit the muscle in his right arm, down from the shoulder about four inches.

He had some good luck to go with the bad. He was wearing his buckskin and so the fangs did not get in as deep as they might have. And the snake could have hit his neck instead of his arm, which would have killed him pretty quick.

But the fangs did get through into his arm and the snake dropped a heavy dose of venom.

"Ahhh . . ."

Francis fell back into the streambed, six feet down, and for a second raw panic took him. Jumbled images and words. Stupid, he thought—Grimes had told him once that Apaches didn't like to move at night because the snakes hunted then. He knew that. Should have been more careful. Stupid way to die. Couldn't cut up on his shoulder, couldn't get at it to suck it anyway; too far back to Lottie and Billy. He'd never make it.

The pain was immediate and intense: his whole shoulder was on fire.

How long?

Minutes. He'd heard somewhere that maybe half an hour was all it took. And the bite was high on his body. The poison would reach his brain soon. Or his heart.

He could lie down and die right here or he could fight to live. To do that he needed help, somebody to cut the wound, bleed it, poultice it or suck it. Soon. He had to get help. The village.

His mind was fuzzing now, everything becoming blurred as the pain drove him into shock and the venom worked into his system.

He had to keep moving. Make it to the town on the butte. Keep his legs moving. Not running, had to keep it even, keep his blood from pumping hard and carrying the poison, but keep moving.

Colors now, in flashes. He stopped for a moment and vomited. He thought how silly it was to waste all the venison he'd just eaten.

His arm and shoulder were on fire and he kept seeing visions. Lottie and Billy in the wagon. Billy riding the mule backward. More colors. Gold. Gold bars and silver bars and then a sun exploding in his brain, then going out and out, and he was falling now, first to his knees and almost down before somebody was there, a strange-looking man in a strange costume. Not a man, a demon, no, a wild beast with a mask with bulging eyes there in front of him making sounds he couldn't understand.

"Help . . ." Francis tried to speak to the monster. "Snakebit. Shoulder. Two children. Help . . ."

But all that came were more words he couldn't understand and then he was sinking to the sandy floor of the arroyo, first to his knees and then over on his face and then there was nothing.

# Chapter Ten

He could not say if he was alive or dead. It was a dream that became a nightmare, back to a dream, and then to another nightmare peopled with strange beings and spirits, and in it all, through it all, there was horrible pain and sickness.

Later he couldn't remember much—and for that he was thankful. Snatches of scenes came. Lottie was there in front of him, and Billy, and then somebody was turning him over and then there was horrible pain in his shoulder and then something with two heads and corn leaves for hair was looking down at him and saying something he couldn't begin to understand, and then he was sweating, pouring more sweat than he ever had in his life, and something hot was going down his throat, hot and thick and sweet and then salty and then finally, for what could have been an hour or a day or the rest of his life, he went back into nothingness, which at last turned into sleep.

He did not awaken as much as become reborn. His eyes opened the smallest crack and he saw or thought he could see a blurred fence in front of him and that didn't make any sense at all because at the same moment he knew he was flat on his back on some kind of blanket. Ceiling. It was a ceiling with round timbers covered with a latticework of smaller limbs and willows. He was looking up at a ceiling. But how . . . when?

His eyes swiveled slightly to his left and he saw Lottie's face. She was sitting on the floor with her face lying on the bed and was sleeping fitfully. He could see her eyelids fluttering. There was light coming through a small doorway that dimly lit a small room not over ten feet square. He was on a bed made of willows in one corner of the room away from the door opening and for what seemed a very long time he could not think on where he was or how he came to be there. He decided he wasn't dead—he didn't think Lottie would be there if he was dead—but at first he couldn't understand how he'd come to be in a room. How could a room be in the prairie?

Then he remembered the town on the butte with the small adobe houses and he knew. "How did I get here?" He said it aloud, or tried to. What came out was a cross between a crow's rasping caw and a hissing whisper.

It was enough to awaken Lottie. "Francis? Are you talking? Did you say something? Oh, Francis, was that really you? I've been so worried these past two weeks that you were going to die and I would have to live without you that—"

"Two weeks?" That came out better. Actual words, but still rasping and choked off.

She wiped her eyes and sat up and nodded. "Billy will be so glad. He's out hunting rabbits with Two Toes—"

"Hunting?"

"Don't worry, he didn't take your rifle. Honestly, if you asked for that gun once you asked for it a hundred times. I'd bring you the rifle and you'd hold it in your arms like a baby or something and go back to sleep. If I took it away you would wake up and ask for it and go back to sleep holding it. Billy is hunting with a bow Two Toes showed him how to make. I swear, he's been running with that boy so much I think he's turned Indian. He can hit a running rabbit with that thing. They have contests, all the boys, and the winner gets the other boys' arrows to use. Billy must have had close to a hundred and fifty arrows before they quit shooting with him. Then he started hunting and it was him brought in all the fresh rabbits for you—"

Francis held up his hand. "Too fast. Go back. I guess we're in the village on the butte—an Indian village. But . . . how did I get here?"

"Oh. Well, I don't know it all because I still can't talk to them very well because they haven't got a handle on English and I can't get my tongue around their words. Billy has learned to rattle with them, or at least with Two Toes—that's a boy he's gotten to be friendly with—but all *they* talk about is hunting and girls—"

"Just what you know. Tell me what you know."

"Billy and I were waiting with the horses when six men come out of the dark and took hold of us."

"Took hold?"

"Not in that way. Not in a bad way. Although Billy had a pretty good go at them with his sword when they first came out of the dark. But they kind of wrapped him up and then they stopped and made signs that they were peaceful and had smiles and motioned that we should come with them. They let us ride the horses but *they* didn't ride. They trotted along beside us as fast as the horses moved. And they didn't take the pack either, though you could tell they were curious at how heavy it was. When we got here you were already on this bed and there were two old women and a medicine man working on you. I swear, I didn't know *what* to think. It was getting light when we got here and even as dark as it is in here I could see you were in a bad way.

"I didn't know why at first and thought they must have hurt you but then they showed me the marks on your shoulder and I knew you were snakebit. They let me stay with you but they wouldn't let me make none of my spit-and-mud poultice to draw out the poison. It's a shame too;

**75**

I had Billy drink water and spit in a gourd all day. We must have had close to a quart. But they wouldn't have it—they used some junk they made up with water and leaves—so it all went to waste."

"They saved me?"

"Well, them and me and Billy. Billy hunted rabbits and we've kept a clay pot of rabbit stew to mix with the corn gruel they give you."

"They must have carried me here from where they found me."

Lottie nodded. "And there's been at least one old woman with you all the time. They fed you and cleaned you and all but I think they were really just here to keep me from using my spit-and-mud poultice. I tell you, I saw a man bit by a copperhead back home and he was up in two days, not two weeks. He went to a dance and danced the reel all night not four days after he was bit. Of course he was dead a week later but that was because he tried to steal a team of mules and somebody up and shot him and couldn't rightly be blamed on the poultice not working."

"They stayed with me?"

Another nod. "Until this morning. They turned you over and looked at your shoulder and one of them nodded to the other one and they left. I thought they had given up. Oh, Francis, I was so sure you were going to die. . . ."

"I thought I was dead and then . . . I just didn't know. . . ."

"They must have known you were going to make it when they left this morning."

"Well. They were right." Francis took a deep breath. "If I've been in this bed two weeks they must have taken my clothes." He raised the thin blanket that covered him and looked under it. "What have they got on me?"

"Well . . ." Lottie blushed.

"What is this? Some kind of wool diaper?"

"Like I said, we've been feeding you broth and meat for two weeks and you couldn't get up. So we had to—"

"Like a *baby*?"

"Well, yes. I guess you could say—"

"Where are my buckskins?"

"Francis, you shouldn't be jumping up—"

"Right *now*!"

Lottie shrugged and went to the corner where the gold pack lay. She brought him his clothing.

"They cleaned them and smoked them so they smell like new-cut pine."

"Turn around. Face the door." Francis sat up— the effort almost made him pass out—and after much struggle and with many pauses to rest, he took the diaper off and got his clothes on. "There. Now, hand me my rifle, would you, please?"

Lottie brought him the rifle. "The gold is safe here too. Anything else?"

"No. Not now. I have to rest again, just for a while. I'll just close my eyes for a few minutes. Just for a very few minutes." He laid the rifle next to him and closed his eyes, opened them and closed them again. Lottie smiled and tiptoed to the door.

"Lottie?"

She stopped and turned. "Yes?"

"I thought I was dead and all I could think of was you and Billy."

She waited.

"I guess we're a kind of family."

She smiled.

"Thank you . . . ," he said.

"It was nothing."

"Yes. It was. And I'll never forget it but now I have to rest, just a little."

"You go ahead. I'll be right out here by the door on my cot."

"Just for a while . . ."

"Just for a while."

And Francis was asleep.

# Chapter Eleven

More than once Francis thought that if he hadn't been so set on getting back to his folks he would have stayed in the village.

It was, first, one of the most beautiful places he had ever seen—and he had ridden through the foothills of the Rockies—with a beauty that changed constantly. The butte was perhaps a thousand feet high, jutting up above the prairie with sheer walls, and even close it still reminded him of engravings of European castles he'd seen in books.

Up the north side there was an angled road—really a wide trail. It was too narrow for a wagon but two horses side by side could traverse it easily, although that didn't matter because the people in the village neither used nor kept horses. Except for this trail it was virtually impossible to reach the top of the butte.

And on the top the village had been built all around the edge to match the butte so that the outside walls of the houses went straight to the edge of the butte and there were no windows or doors on the outside. Anybody who tried to climb the butte to attack would simply run into the walls and not be able to go farther up.

And the houses lent themselves to the beauty. They were made of adobe bricks covered with reddish mud, and their walls were gently curved so that even when they went two and three stories high they seemed to grow directly out of the ground—almost as if they had been not built so much as planted and grown.

In the center of the buildings was a clearing about a hundred yards across and toward the center of this area were three underground houses with curved roofs that rose slightly above the ground. These were the only houses Francis and the children were not allowed to enter.

"Billy says they're called kivas," Lottie told him the first morning he could walk around and see the town. "It's where they have their church and outsiders are not to go there."

It was not a hard rule to obey, considering it was the only rule. Francis had never seen people so happy or so lacking in anger or frustration. Everywhere he turned he met a smile or a nod or a hand holding out a piece of meat or a thin piece of corn bread or a gourd with soup or water in it.

These Pueblo Indians talked a great deal among themselves but were so courteous that as soon as they saw that Francis and Lottie couldn't understand their spoken language they talked mostly in sign language.

Francis knew some of their symbols, because Plains Indians also spoke a great deal with their hands, and many of the symbols were the same. Soon Francis was able to understand and explain the village to Lottie. Billy could have done it too, since he spoke at about a five-year-old's level, but he was never around. Indeed when Francis first saw him Billy seemed to have become Indian. He was naked except for a clout around his waist and he had a quiver of arrows over one shoulder and a bow in his hand, with the sword carried by a thong over the other shoulder.

Billy had changed. When he saw that Francis was recovering he stood on one leg and nodded and said, "I thought you were going to the spirit world. It is good you are not."

The people in the village lived primarily by farming. There were fields at the base of the butte, irrigated by a ditch system. It had been designed with a system of ingenious gates that brought water to all the fields.

They farmed corn, beans and squash. They ate the squash as it came ready and they dried the corn and beans to eat through the winter and while none of the people were fat, none were starving either. Francis had never seen healthier people.

It was true they didn't have horses, but they didn't seem limited by that. They did hunt in the scrub forest north of the butte—mesquite and pine and cedar—and here they found many deer and turkeys and uncountable rabbits. They hunted with short, strong bows that were so powerful they sometimes drove an arrow completely through a deer and out the other side.

Whenever there was a job to do—as when they got the fields ready to plant or replastered the walls of a house with mud—everybody chipped in. As he grew stronger on the diet of turkey and rabbit and corn and cooked beans, Francis worked with them, and so did Lottie and Billy.

It was nearly spring and there was much work to do. The fields had to be prepared for planting, which involved using wooden hoes to break the soil and make soft mounds for the seeds. The irrigation ditches had to be cleaned and repaired.

In the beginning the work seemed like drudgery to Francis, but after a short time he found himself liking the strain on his muscles. It was nearly two weeks since he'd regained consciousness and his shoulder was completely healed except for a small lump where they had cut across the fang marks so the poultice would draw. Now and then he felt a small ache, but it was nothing, and he became strong again working in the fields and on the ditches. He had also made a corral for the six horses—he was afraid to let them graze freely or on a hobble because he didn't want to lose them—and at least twice a day he went down to the corral and fed and rode them and led them to water.

He found himself staying with the horses more and more, and finally he realized that the north was calling him. It was time to get moving if they wanted to get north and cut into the Oregon Trail. Still, he had found a new kind of peace here and loved life in the village. Lottie and Billy seemed happy too, so he kept quiet about moving until he was alone one day with a man who had become his particular friend.

His name was Kashi and he was about thirty-five years old—considered an elder in the village—and sometimes at night they would sit by the fire and hand-talk. Francis had tried to tell Kashi about the Plains tribes, how they lived and hunted, and about getting away from the Comancheros. Kashi had told him of the history of the village, how the butte had kept them isolated from the Spanish so they still lived the old way.

But this day they were by the ditch and Francis stopped raking and studied some clouds to the north. Kashi came up to his side and made a sign of birds flying north and pointed at Francis.

Francis nodded and mimicked the sign.

One more sun, Kashi signed, then you go? Tomorrow?

And Francis knew it was the truth. He nodded. Tomorrow. The horses were so fat on spring grass they looked greasy; the days and nights were warm; Lottie had made good new moccasins for them, and two new buckskin shifts for herself and a buckskin shirt for Billy, though he rarely wore it.

Tonight, then, Kashi signed, you must all come to my house and we'll feast on rabbit and deer and bread.

Francis nodded and smiled and rubbed his stomach and made signs that he would tell Lottie and Billy. But his mind was already on the horses, what had to be done, the gear to be made ready, food and gold and silver to be packed . . .

He was still in the pueblo but his thoughts were gone, heading north.

# Chapter Twelve

It was evening. Francis pulled the pinto up on the edge of a small rise and looked back on his little caravan and smiled. They were close to thirty miles from the butte and it was well out of sight. They had come into the juniper and rolling hills—a whole new country.

But there had been a few moments when Francis thought he would never get away from the village.

The feast had been wonderful. Kashi's wife,

named something that sounded like Annas, had baked corn bread in the large earthen ovens outside the houses that resembled beehives and they had venison and rabbit stew and hot bread to dip in the gravy and talked, with Billy translating, until after midnight.

That was when Billy had found out they were leaving the next day.

"I'm not going," he had said as they left Kashi's house and moved back to their own room to sleep.

"Of course you are." Lottie shrugged. "You go where we go, that's how it works. And we're leaving in the morning to find Francis's folks."

"Two Toes said if I stay I can hunt deer with them in the fall and if I get a deer I'll become a man, sort of . . ."

"You're *seven* years old."

"They don't go by years. They go by if you can kill a deer with a bow and arrow."

"No." Francis had shaken his head. "They go by many things. Hunting deer is just one of them. You wouldn't truly be a man for at least five years yet, no matter what Two Toes told you. There are many tests to pass."

"Still, this is a good place to live—"

"You're seven!" Lottie had cut in. "You don't leave your family when you're only seven years old."

"I don't care. I'm staying."

Lottie spluttered, "Billy—how can you *think* of leaving me and Francis? Your own sister! Your own . . ." She looked at Francis. "Francis! You tell him!"

Francis had remembered the stubborn little boy who had sat backward on the mule and hadn't talked for so long Francis thought he *couldn't* talk. I could just tie him up and bring him, he thought, if only he didn't have that sword.

But Lottie solved it. "If you stay here there won't be anything to spend the gold on—there isn't a store for a thousand miles and nothing even *like* rock candy."

"Oh," Billy had said. "Well, then, I'll come with you."

And they had gone at dawn the next morning. They took only four horses, leaving the extra two for the village as a token of gratitude for all the help the people had given. The horses could be ridden, but better yet the horses could pack corn and deer meat up the grade to the village. Until now Francis and the children had been carrying by hand.

The weather had been grand all day, and with all the new clothing and gear and a decent buckskin packsaddle they made good time. Francis let Lottie lead the packhorse with the gold and other equipment and sent Billy off to the sides to hunt with his bow. Billy came back about noon with a huge tom turkey in front of him on the pony, and Francis decided to make camp a bit early so they could clean the turkey and cook it.

He saw a bend in an arroyo ahead, down and to the left, with some large cottonwoods that meant water. There had been rain a few days earlier and it made for good grass for the ponies along the bottom of the arroyo. Francis set up a camp beneath the cottonwood. Billy cleaned the turkey and Francis cut it in strips to cook over sticks above the fire Lottie had started and while the meat was cooking he picketed the horses and then took his rifle and headed out to the west to take a look.

Francis smiled when he saw Billy pick up his bow and sword and head off to the east. Billy was still a boy but in many respects he had grown so fast his actual age almost didn't matter. To take a large tom turkey with a bow was a feat. Turkeys were smart and hard to hunt even with a gun . . . his short time with Two Toes had completely changed Billy.

Francis climbed a ridge on foot and looked back on the camp. He was a half mile away and a quarter mile higher and he moved still higher until he could see for miles to the north and east and west. At first he could see nothing unusual but something caught his eye to the east, a strange line in the scrub forest, and he realized after a moment that it was some kind of road or heavy trail. It came straight from the east but before it came to their campsite it curved away to the north and disappeared in the trees about two miles from the camp.

A trail meant people, and judging by how wide and well traveled this one looked, a goodly amount of people, although he could see no dust.

It was getting close to dark and he moved back toward camp warily. Tempers were still flaring over the war with Mexico, and the Comancheros were somewhere to the south. People moving on the trail might not be friendly. He had just decided that it would be prudent to keep clear of the trail as they made their way north when he heard a twig snap behind him and turned in time for somebody or something to hit him so hard on the side of the head that it seemed his brain was torn loose, and he was completely unconscious before he hit the ground.

"AHHH, MY DEAR BOY, we meet again. I must say, though, I didn't think we would again see each other. I had my hopes, not to say dreams. . . ."

Francis swam up slowly from some deep place in his mind.

"You left us in a very sad state, if you'll remember."

He knew the voice but at first couldn't quite place it in his memory. The pain in his head didn't help.

"Imagine our surprise. We were making our way toward that fine trail to see if we couldn't come upon a traveler who would, let us say, help us in our need, when we saw the light from the fire this girl started, and while coming toward the light we found you."

Courtweiler.

And Dubs.

They had come upon him once, before he found Lottie and Billy, and had taken everything he had. He had tracked them and run them down and caught them sleeping and taken it all back, plus their half-dead mule.

"I should have shot you," Francis said. He opened his eyes and tried to sit up but they had him tied wrist to ankle. He stared up at Courtweiler. The little man, in a ragged black suit and top hat, stroked his beard and smiled.

"Yes, my boy, you should have. I won't make the same mistake. What I don't understand is how you seem to come onto such good fortune. This charming girl to cook for you and a veritable fortune in gold and silver. As I think I may have said to you once before, our good luck is your very bad circumstance."

Francis's mind was clearing. The hulking Dubs must have carried him back to the camp—or from the feel of it, dragged him. Lottie was sitting across the fire. There was a welt on her cheek that would soon be a bruise.

Billy. Courtweiler hadn't mentioned Billy. Just

**93**

Lottie. Francis craned around and could not see the boy.

"I told them we were on our way back to our family and that they'd come looking for us if we weren't back soon—"

"Hush, child. Or Dubs will strike you again." Lottie grew quiet.

"Fine. Now, my boy, was there any more gold where you found this?"

Francis didn't answer. Where was Billy? Francis had cast out to the west. The two men had come on him from the west, or maybe the northwest, so they probably hadn't seen Billy. The boy was still out there and might come walking in on them at any moment.

He had to get loose. The two men had turned away to look at the gold and Francis tried his bonds. They were so tight that his hands had gone to sleep, tied with a piece of line from the horse pack, but there was a strand he could feel loosening and he worked at it. He shook his head at Lottie, meaning not to mention Billy, and she nodded, but he wasn't sure if she understood.

"How fortune does change." Courtweiler

turned from the pack. "We were down to eating our shoes again, and on foot, and now we're rich, have a girl we can sell to . . . well, whomever . . . and have horses into the bargain. Honestly, my boy, it's almost worth letting you loose just to catch you again and see what else you can get—"

A whirring went past Francis's face and a stick seemed to pop out of Courtweiler's right shoulder. An arrow! Buried to the bone.

"Arrrrrnnngh!" Courtweiler grabbed at the arrow but before he could pull it out there were more fluttering sounds and three more arrows zipped past Francis.

One hit Dubs in the neck as he was straightening from the pack, the next took him full in the chest and the last one struck him in the stomach.

Dubs reached up and slowly pulled the arrow out of his neck, then actually took three steps toward Francis before he stopped, settled back until he sat, and then slowly went over on his side and lay dead, his eyes never closing.

It wasn't over yet. Francis had been working at getting his hands free the whole time, and he pulled them loose just as Courtweiler jerked the arrow out of his shoulder and started for him, fumbling at his belt for a revolver.

"Francis! Here!" Lottie was up and running. She grabbed Francis's rifle from beside the pack and threw it. Francis caught it, turned and fired without thinking, without aiming, and saw the dust puff out from Courtweiler's coat as the bullet hit his chest and drove him back to fall near Dubs.

Francis pulled the ropes from his legs and felt for his knife at his belt. Gone!

But Courtweiler lay still. It was over. Francis stood there panting and turned and saw Billy beside Lottie.

"Francis!" Billy said. "I saw them, and saw you tied up, and started shooting. I only had four arrows with me. I didn't think, there wasn't time, and then the big one pulled that arrow out of his neck and I thought you were dead for sure! Oh Lord, did I kill him? Just a minute, I'm going to be sick."

Lottie held his head while he threw up and then led him away and held him while he took deep breaths that sounded like crying.

In silence Francis took the sword from Billy's shoulder and started digging two graves back by the cottonwoods, chopping at the sod until he was down to the loose sand beneath and scooping it out until he was far enough down to cover the two men. Then he dragged them over and dropped them into place—after taking the revolver from Courtweiler's belt and a flint and striker from his pocket for starting fires. He folded their arms over their chests and covered them with earth and then with rocks to keep the coyotes out. He didn't feel sorry for them—they would have killed him, after all. But he felt sorry for Billy.

When he was finished he stood over the graves and looked north. He could not see far. It was dark and even the glow from the fire only penetrated a few yards. But he looked north just the same, and thought, Somewhere up there and west a little are my parents.

They would start in the morning when the light was good and Billy was all right. They would start then. It was still a long way and they had seen so many buried from wounds and accidents and cholera and just living, so many, and he hoped there would not be any more graves.

They would start in the morning.

# TUCKET'S HOME

# —— Chapter One ——

Francis Tucket lay quietly, the sun warming his back, and watched a small herd of buffalo below him in a depression on the prairie. There were only fifteen or twenty of them, mostly cows with some yearling calves. Two young bulls were sparring, tearing up the dirt and raising dust in great clouds.

He turned to look behind him, where ten-year-old Lottie watched their horses graze. Her little brother, Billy, crouched beside her, making an arrow. Francis looked down at the buffalo. The sun was gentle on his back, the dust from the fight was drifting away on a soft breeze, and as Francis lay watching, he let his mind wander back over the trip since he and Lottie and Billy had left the Pueblo Indian village.

They'd stayed there a month so that Francis could recover from a snakebite. With the help of some of the Indians, Lottie had pulled him through, while Billy had learned to hunt and shoot a bow and arrow with amazing skill. The village had been a peaceful place.

Now Francis shifted and scanned the horizon. Even in a quiet moment like this one, you had to be alert, ready for anything. They'd all learned that the hard way.

Francis Tucket had been separated from his family more than a year before, on his fourteenth birthday, when Pawnees kidnapped him from a wagon train. Jason Grimes, a one-armed mountain man, had helped him escape and taught him to survive. After they parted, Francis had found Lottie and Billy alone on the prairie, their father dead of cholera. They'd been members of a wagon train that abandoned them when their father became sick, for fear that he would infect others in the train. So the three had stuck together and headed west to the Oregon Trail to find Francis's family.

Lottie had proved to be the best organizer and camper Francis had ever seen, and Billy, now just shy of eight, had become a hunting and scouting machine of the first order. They'd been through some hair-raising adventures: Kidnapped by the Comanchero outlaw band. Storms. Snakebite. Ambushed by the murderous thieves Courtweiler and Dubs. The three had shared plenty, good and bad, and now they shared a secret—the ancient Spanish silver and gold they carried on the packhorse. When they were being chased by the Comancheros Billy had stumbled upon the grave of a Spanish conquistador, buried with his armor, sword and plunder of centuries ago. Of course, gold and silver meant nothing out here in the wilderness. But someday, someday they'd find Francis's family and civilization, though they still had five hundred miles of rough country to cover alone.

Francis had feared there would be problems on this part of their journey, but it had turned out to be nothing more than a camping trip in a country so beautiful that Francis often had trouble believing it was real.

They had started in partial desert, country covered in mesquite and piñons, but it quickly gave way to mountains. Spring had come early and had stayed. Thick, green grass kept the horses well fed and happy; streams ran full of cold water and trout. Billy caught the fish easily, using a skill he'd learned from the Pueblos that required only a bit of line braided from horsehair, taken from the ponies' tails, and a bent and sharpened piece of wire.

Francis had no trouble getting deer with his rifle, and Billy supplemented the venison and trout diet with rabbit and turkey and grouse he shot with his bow. Within a week they were all getting fat, and the packhorse nearly staggered with extra meat as they rode through grassy mountain meadows amid high mountain peaks still covered with snow.

But they hadn't seen any buffalo until they'd come to this rise and seen below them the small herd with the fighting bulls.

"Honestly, Francis, I don't see why we need more meat." Lottie had crawled up alongside him. Billy, his arrow finished, was a hundred yards back, below the ridge, adjusting the make-shift packs on the horses. "We have so much now we can't carry it all."

"Not so loud—if the wind shifts they'll hear us and run," Francis whispered. "The reason is that we don't have *buffalo* meat. Besides that, they're fat and we need the grease for our moccasins and leather and my rifle. So we're going to shoot a buffalo, all right?"

She nodded and became quiet and he studied the terrain around the herd to see how best to approach them for a shot. The buffalo were in a small basin with a series of drainage gullies that fed in and out. Francis saw that the one that ran off to the east seemed to provide the best course. It was deep and wound back toward him in a big loop, with a smaller ditch he could use for access. He nodded and pointed with his chin.

"See that ditch off to the right?" He looked at Lottie, then back. "You go back with Billy, I'll make my way down there and—"

Suddenly, as if by magic, there was a burst of gray smoke below them from the edge of the gully that pointed toward the buffalo. Half an in-stant later Francis heard the crack of a rifle—they were so far away it took that long for the sound to reach them—and one of the cows watching the fighting bulls pitched forward and down onto her side.

"What . . ."

There was another puff of smoke. Another cow went down; then another shot, and another and another, coming so fast they were almost on top of each other, and each time, a cow would drop on her side and start kicking in death. Twelve shots. Twelve cows.

"Francis, somebody is shooting our buffalo!" Lottie punched his shoulder.

"Stay down." Francis watched the basin below. The buffalo had not run but were moving in confused circles. "And quiet—be quiet and let's see what's going on." Twelve shots in perhaps twenty seconds. No man on earth could load and fire a muzzle-loading rifle thirty-six times a minute. There had to be more than one man hiding in the gully. Francis looked to the rear and waved to Billy—who had heard the shooting—to stay where he was with the horses.

"There!" Lottie whispered. "There they are."

Francis couldn't believe his eyes. A tall, thin man in a full dark suit came out of the gully, followed by three other men in tan suits, all wearing strange-looking round helmets. The man in the dark suit carried nothing, but the other three had two rifles each and were festooned with powder horns and belts and ramrods.

"Why, Francis, he's a fancy man." Lottie snorted. "What's a fancy man doing way out here?"

"Killing buffalo, the way it looks." Francis studied them a moment, wondered if there was danger there, decided there could not be and shrugged. "They seem harmless. Let's go down and see why they needed to shoot a dozen buffalo."

# Chapter Two

Francis and Lottie walked back to Billy and mounted up. As they rode down, Francis explained what they had seen to Billy.

The rest of the herd had fled with the approach of the four men, and Francis stopped in front of the man in the dark suit, who was leaning—Francis had to work to keep himself from staring—on a silver-headed cane. Behind the man with the cane, Francis could see yet another man in a tan uniform back in the gully, who had been hidden before. He was holding five horses and two pack mules.

"Oh, I say." The man in the suit spoke in a strange accent. "This is smashing, absolutely *smashing*. What luck. We'll have guests for dinner! Do say you'll join us, won't you? We're going to have a mountain of fresh tongue. . . ."

"My name is Francis, this is Lottie and the boy back there is named Billy."

"Oh, do forgive me. My name is Bentley. William James Bentley the Fourth, actually. And these men are my servants."

Francis nodded, speechless. Billy heeled his horse forward until it was next to Francis. He had become incredibly accurate with his bow—had indeed once helped to save Francis and Lottie from Courtweiler and Dubs. Now Billy sat with the bow across his lap, an arrow nocked to the string.

"He talks funny," Billy said to Francis. "Sort of like them others we had to shoot . . ."

Francis nodded at Bentley. "You do have a kind of . . . accent—"

"I'm English," Bentley said, interrupting. "We're from England on a grand adventure before I take over the estate from my parents."

"A grand adventure . . ." For a second images jolted through Francis's mind. Jason Grimes scalping Braid, Comancheros, the Mexican War; himself being held captive by Pawnee, freezing, being shot at, snakebit. Shooting and burying people.

"Why, yes. Your Oregon Trail is quite the thing in England. Stories of the trail and the wilderness abound. We came over last year and wintered in Independence, where we also outfitted, although I brought my own rifles. They were made by a superb gunsmith named Drills. Then we started west with pack mules. . . ."

This man, thought Francis, actually talks more than Lottie.

"And made rather good time, what with this absolutely capital early spring and all the grass for the livestock, much better time than we would have made pulling wagons . . ."

Francis held up his hand. "Please, just a minute."

"Let him talk, Francis," Lottie said. "His voice is pretty, like a bird."

Francis shook his head. "Do you have a guide?"

"Why?" Bentley shrugged. "One simply travels west."

Francis sighed. He was hoping for a guide to tell him how far north they had to go to hit the trail. "You mean you've come all this way with no guide?"

"Assuredly. Although we may have missed some of the more noteworthy aspects of the journey without proper guidance. We have not, for instance, seen any red Indians. One would like to see some red Indians. Are they, for instance, really red?"

Francis thought back again to Braid, to the Comancheros. Oh my yes, let us see some red Indians.

He pulled his thinking back to the present. "You shot twelve buffalo."

"Quite. My men reloaded for me so that I could just keep firing. Splendid, what? Mind you, it's not as good as back in the grass prairie. We had a day when we shot seventy-two of the great beasts. It was capital, simply capital."

"Why?" Francis couldn't help himself. "What did you do with them?"

"Took the tongues, of course. We dried some

and pickled some and ate some fresh. It's the very best meat, tongue."

Billy couldn't stand it. "All the rest was left to rot?"

Bentley shrugged. "There are millions of them."

We have to get away from this man, Francis thought. He's friendly enough but he stinks of death. Just that—death.

"You will join us for dinner, won't you?" Bentley asked again.

Francis shook his head. "I'm sorry but we have to keep riding." Out of the corner of his eye he saw Lottie throw him a sharp look but for once she remained quiet. "We have to get north and west to Oregon before fall. But if you don't mind, I would like to get some hump meat and grease off one of those buffalo you killed."

"Of course, of course. My men will help you, and you can even take some tongue if you wish."

"No, just back meat and grease. You don't have to help, it will just take a minute."

Francis moved to a young cow. He would not have shot her himself—she was just over a year old and too young to kill—but since she was dead anyway and he knew the meat would be tender, he decided to use her. He cut down the center of the back and took out the hump and the tenderloins that ran down both sides of the backbone. He also removed the skin from both sides—Lottie helped him while Billy held the horses—and then rolled the cow over and cut her belly open and took several long strips of belly fat. The whole operation didn't take fifteen minutes. The meat was rolled in the green hide and packed on the packhorse.

Francis remounted his own horse and stopped in front of Bentley. He felt he should say something to the Englishman. It was a pure miracle the man and his servants had managed to come this far without running into hostile Indians or, worse, scavengers who worked the trail, preying on travelers the way Courtweiler and Dubs had done.

"Mr. Bentley, don't go much more south. If you go too far that way, you will run into the Comancheros."

"Oh, are they red Indians?"

Francis nodded. "There are some Indians with them but mostly they are plain mean and will kill you for your shoes, let alone those pretty rifles. You should head back north and hook up with a wagon train. There's safety in numbers."

Bentley smiled and held out his hand to shake. "Well, I thank you for the advice, my boy, but there are five of us and as you can see we are heavily armed. I don't think we need to fear."

Francis shook his head. "Mr. Bentley . . ." Then he realized it would do no good to say more, so he shook hands with Bentley and nudged his horse and rode away.

Within a hundred yards Billy had moved well off to the side and ahead, scouting, and Lottie had pulled her horse and the packhorse, which she trailed, up alongside Francis.

"I think we could have stayed for food, though to be honest I don't think I would much favor tongue, but he talked so pretty, Francis, I could have listened to him for hours and hours and maybe he would have cooked something other than tongue if we'd asked him nice enough and maybe he even had potatoes. Oh, Francis, wouldn't a potato taste wonderful? I swear, I haven't had a potato in so long I've forgotten what they taste like. . . ."

And she went on and on, but Francis could

not shake the smell of death that had been on Bentley, and he heeled his pony to a faster walk.

The farther they could get from Bentley the better.

# Chapter Three

"I saw dust." Billy came in from the right side, where he had been riding in a parallel line about a mile away. He urged his pony into a lope until he was next to Francis and Lottie. It was late afternoon and his horse was sweating from the heat.

"How far off?" They had come two days since meeting Bentley, and Francis still felt too close to the hunter. He could not help thinking that Bentley would draw something bad to himself, and Francis did not want to be around when it happened.

"I'm not sure. I don't know distances."

"If you're walking a horse, how long would you have to walk to get to the dust?"

Billy frowned, thinking. "Maybe an hour . . ."

Three miles, perhaps four. "Where are they?"

"Off to the side, moving the same way we are, heading north."

"How big is the dust cloud?"

Another frown. "Hard to tell. Maybe the same as three or four buffalo might make walking— more than we make but not a whole lot either."

"What do you think?" This came from Lottie.

But Francis was still intent upon Billy: "How fast are they moving?"

"They came up even with us at a pretty good clip, then they seemed to let up and are holding, the same as us."

"Are they Comancheros?" Lottie looked grim. "Could it be them?"

Francis shook his head. "I don't think so. They usually move in big groups. This seems like a smaller bunch: four, five men at the most." He looked back at their own trail. If Billy can see their dust maybe they can see ours, he thought. But they had been moving largely through grassy meadows where there was no dust, and the other group—whoever they were—were farther east, in the foothills of the mountains where there was less grass and more dry dirt.

"What do we do?" Lottie peered eastward, trying to see the dust.

"Nothing right now. It might even be Bentley and his men taking my advice and going north. We'll wait until dark and I'll sneak over and see who they are."

"I'll go too," Billy said.

"Not this time. I need you here to keep an eye on things with Lottie."

"But I'm good at sneaking. . . ."

"I know. But one is enough for this kind of work. I'm going on foot and you can help keep the horses here."

Billy frowned but at last nodded. "All right, but I don't like it."

"It's for the best, Billy," Lottie added.

And in a terrible way, that proved to be right.

★ ★ ★

THERE WAS A SLIVER of moon, no clouds and a sky packed with stars—enough light so that Francis could see just shadows and shapes.

"No fire tonight," he told Lottie. "Eat some of the venison jerky cold."

She nodded. Billy was near the horses, sulking.

"You watch out for snakes," she said. Francis had been bitten by a rattler while trying to sneak up on a Pueblo village and it had nearly killed him.

Francis nodded, checked his rifle to make certain the cap was firmly seated on the nipple and set off in an easy shuffle. He would have preferred taking a horse, but it would whinny when it smelled the other horses and give him away.

The country was rolling hills, but they were small and well rounded, so the going was easy. He could have made good time but he opted for caution. Instead of making for the strange camp in a straight line he looped slightly north and moved slowly, stopping often to listen and watch the shadows.

When he had walked about three miles, he caught a flicker of light. He stopped and watched it until he knew it was a campfire. It was more than a mile away and he could tell that whoever it was who'd made it had no concept of caution. The fire was huge, and showers of sparks leaped into the air as whole logs were tossed onto the blaze.

Bentley, Francis thought. It must be him. Still, he had to be sure, and keeping a low profile, he worked his way closer until he was no more than thirty yards from them. He crouched in a small ditch and watched.

It was indeed Bentley and his men. Francis shook his head. They must have taken his advice to head north, but their camping methods were nothing short of insane.

Even in good times it paid to be cautious. Always—unless you were in a cave or a well-concealed ditch—you *always* kept your fire small and burning clean. No spark, no light, must get out to show itself to possible enemies. And that was in good times. Right now, in the aftermath of the Mexican War, when the Comancheros were raiding and other scavengers were about, being careful was the only way to stay alive.

Francis lay watching them for nearly half an hour as they laughed and joked, throwing still more wood on the fire. At last he decided he should let them know he was there and tell them how foolish they were being. Then he froze.

At first he couldn't tell what caused him to stop. Some instinct made him hold up, freeze, and then let his eyes move away from the fire.

There.

A soft line that shouldn't be there, a curve of a shadow against the dark. Then a sound, a soft clink of metal against stone. For the time it took to draw three more breaths, there was nothing strange at all.

When it came, it was so fast and so brutal Francis almost cried out. If he had, it would have been his last act on earth.

Out of the shadows, out of the dark night, a pack of devils appeared. Later Francis decided it must have been five men, but it happened so fast he couldn't count them.

At first there was no time to move, to warn Bentley's group, and then, within seconds, Francis didn't dare.

The men were armed with guns at their belts, wearing ragged clothes and old floppy army hats. But they did not use their guns. Three men also carried army sabers, and the two others had lances.

There were almost no sounds. The attackers were on the group in an instant, hacking and stabbing with silent ferocity.

It was a massacre and it was over in moments. Bentley and his men were dead almost at once. Still the attackers did not stop, but kept hacking and chopping and tearing until the bodies were in pieces, the heads chopped off and all the clothing removed. Francis lay in his small ditch in the dark, horrified, not believing what he was seeing, though he knew it was real.

All this time, the men were silent. Then one, apparently the leader, stood spattered in blood in the light of the fire and said, "I wonder who they were?"

Another man answered. "I don't know, but they sure had good rifles. Look at these guns!"

Francis was still afraid to move. He stayed where he was until the men found some whiskey and started drinking. He waited until they were drunk. Only then, a few hours later, did he crawl backward on his belly until he could crouch, then moved along in that crouch until he could stand. And then he turned and started off in a silent trot, which soon became an outright run.

And not for a second could he get the last sight out of his mind: Bentley's head jammed on the end of a lance, the light from the fire giving it a hideous glow that made it look almost still alive.

# Chapter Four

"We have to stop, Francis." Lottie's voice was strident. "You're going to kill the horses!"

Francis seemed not to hear her or to care about what she said—even if there was an edge of truth in it.

He had come back to them just at dawn and found them both dozing, with Billy holding the horses' picket rope.

"Up!" Francis had rousted them out of sleep. "We have to start moving. *Now!*"

"But, Francis . . ." Lottie had rubbed her eyes. "What is it? Why . . ."

Francis had looked at her but all he could see was Bentley's head, all he could think of was the mad dance of the murderers hacking and slashing and stabbing. I am here, he'd thought. With all that I have in the world to live for—Lottie and Billy. The hope of finding my family. All the Spanish gold and silver from the old grave. We are here, and madmen are . . . right . . . over . . . *there*.

Insane butchers are just four or five miles away. They're worse than Comancheros, worse than attacking bears or Indians—they are like wolves with rabies. They kill just to kill.

Francis had hurried to get Billy and Lottie away from them.

"Bad men," he had told Lottie and Billy. He did not tell them what he had seen. He would never tell them what he had seen. Not if he lived to be a hundred years old.

"We have to run. Now!"

He had kept them to grass so there would be no dust as they rode, and he'd driven them hard all day. He thought the killers would head north and maybe a little east to catch the wagon trains, looking for small parties to attack, and so he'd taken Lottie and Billy northwest. At first he'd led them but as the mounts tired, he dropped back and pushed them, whipped them until it was dark. And still he drove them. All night, with the horses staggering, until dawn came again, and he thought they had traveled close to fifty miles. And at last he stopped near a beaver pond in a stand of aspen with the morning sun warming the horses' sweat so that it steamed.

"We stop here," he said. "Cold camp, no fire—eat jerky and sleep. Five, six hours. Billy, you sleep tied to the horses like you did before."

He left them and with his rifle went to the top of a nearby hill and squatted, looking out across the foothills.

He was exhausted, almost staggering, like the horses. But he sat for an hour, not moving, hardly blinking, hearing the flies around him, the birds, the squirrels, beaver—staring at their back trail and the hills to the east.

Nothing. No dust, no movement. Nothing. And finally, while he stared, his eyes closed once, opened slowly, then closed again. He fell backward and slept.

HE WAS NOT CERTAIN what awakened him. It was close to evening; he had slept hard for nearly seven hours and probably could have slept for seven more. Lottie and Billy were still asleep, the horses standing asleep near them. As he watched, a horse awoke and started to move, eating great mouthfuls of grass that he tore off with sideways motions. The horse came to the end of the picket line and jerked Billy—who had the rope tied to his wrist—along in the dirt for a good two feet.

Billy did not wake up, and Francis smiled. All right, the trail seemed clear. The horses needed to eat and rest more and recover. They would spend the night and move on in the morning.

He studied the horizon one more time and found it clear, stood and stretched and made his way down to the horses. They were all awake and whickered softly as he untied the picket line from Billy's wrist—Billy still did not wake—and led them softly into tall grass. There he hobbled them with rope and let them graze.

The beaver pond was nearby, and for no particular reason he walked to it and stood looking into the clear water. He could see trout, their sides flashing in the sun, and as he turned to go he caught another glint.

This was at the edge of the pond near the horses, where the beaver dragged the cut limbs into the water and left a muddy skid trail on the bank.

A gray flicker of light from the sun cut into the water and he knew instantly that it was a trap. He moved to it through the grass without stepping in any dirt, reading signs now, studying. He had trapped beaver with a man named Jason Grimes. Grimes had helped Francis escape from the Pawnees who had taken him from the wagon train so long ago. Mr. Grimes had shown up again at the Comancheros camp and helped the three of them escape and then had led the Comancheros off while Lottie and Billy and Francis ran north.

Francis stopped by the bank and studied the trap in open disbelief.

Because he only had one arm, Jason Grimes had a unique way of tying the small aspen bait stick to the pan of the trap. He used a bit of rawhide in a crisscross fashion because he had to hold the trap with his knee while he tied the rawhide with one hand.

Francis was looking down at just such a knot now. He leaned closer. The bait stick was fresh-cut—not more than two days old—and the trap was not covered with leaves and debris as it would have been if it had been there a long time. Besides, Grimes would never put traps where he couldn't check them every day. It wouldn't be fair to the animal to let it suffer in the trap.

Francis stood, looked to his left carefully and started swinging his eyes to the right, looking into the trees, trying to see past the green leaves of the aspens, then moving to the left again, searching in increments, carefully studying each part before moving to the next, and before he had gone halfway around he heard a soft voice say:

"Well, pilgrim, I see you got clear of them Comancheros."

And Francis wheeled to see Jason Grimes standing in the dappled shade of the aspens.

# Chapter Five

"How—I mean when . . ." Francis shrugged and sighed. "Hello, Mr. Grimes, it is good to see you." He was surprised and shouldn't have been. Nothing the mountain man ever did should surprise him. "How did you come to be here?"

Grimes stepped forward and matched Francis's smile. "Same as you, boy. Same as you."

In the light, out of the shade, Francis saw Grimes clearly, and was shocked to see that he looked thin and wasted, as if half starved. There was a new scar from his left cheekbone up to his hairline. His hair was also spotty and turning white. Francis looked away at once but not before Grimes caught his expression.

"I made it clear of the Comancheros," he said, "when they were chasing us. Or almost clear. Two of them were right pushy and kept coming; I cornered up and dealt with them but one of them caught me with a hand ax while I worked on him. . . . Dust."

For a second Francis didn't follow him. He saw that the ax wound had healed, but that didn't explain the way Grimes looked—near death.

"There," Grimes repeated. "Dust. Coming this way."

Francis turned and looked where Grimes was pointing—three or four miles to the east, out of the foothills on the edge of the prairie—and saw a small plume of dust and he thought, *Oh God*, and it wasn't swearing but a prayer.

"Not like you to pray," Grimes said, and Francis realized he'd said it aloud. "Not over a little dust . . ."

"It's not just the dust." Francis squinted, trying to see better. "It's what's making the dust. Or at least what I think is making it."

"Five men," Grimes said. "Crazy—like wolves with crazy-water sickness. Is that right?"

"You know about them?"

Grimes nodded. "Heard about them. They came from back east—Tennessee or some such hill place. They've been running and killing out here for nearly two years. They were in the army and came out for the war but broke loose and went bad. Real bad."

"I have to wake the others, get the horses ready to run again. You can come with us."

But Grimes wasn't listening. He stared fixedly at the dust plume and seemed to be thinking. Then he squatted on his haunches and smoothed the dirt at his feet and took a stick for a pointer.

"See this canyon here—the one we're in?" He drew a shallow V with the stick in the dirt. "It goes back into the peaks and looks like a dead end, but it ain't. I found this canyon when I came north, after I got away from those Comancheros, and I wintered here, trapped a little beaver just for the meat." He inhaled and for the first time Francis noted how he was wheezing and having trouble catching his breath. "You take the young ones back up the canyon and you'll find a trail out the back. It looks snowed in but it ain't."

Francis nodded. "Good. Let's get going."

But Grimes smiled and shook his head. "I ain't going."

"What do you mean?" Francis pointed toward the dust. "They'll be here in an hour. You can't get away from them by heading out the front of the canyon."

"I'm not going to try to get away from them. Fact is, ever since I heard of them I've kind of been hoping I'd run into them."

"But . . . but *why*? They'll kill you. Believe me, I saw what they do. They'll cut you to pieces."

Grimes nodded. "There's that possibility, Mr. Tucket."

"Then why stay? Come with us, run with us."

Grimes looked at the dust—it was closer now by a mile—and then looked back up the canyon at the snow-covered peaks, seemed to see something up there, up in the mountains. "No. This is as good a place as any to die—better than most."

"Die?" Francis stared at him. "Why stay here and die?"

"Because I'm dying anyway—been wasting away for months. I'm about done now—it's all I can do to walk. I cut my horses loose to run three weeks ago."

"What?" Francis paused, his breathing suddenly shallow. "Not you, Mr. Grimes!"

"I got somethin' tearing at my vitals. At least now I won't have to just rot away. I can get those five scavengers to help me while I take a few of them with me."

"No!" Francis shook his head. "There are doctors. We have money—gold. Lots of gold. We can get help."

Grimes smiled. "Not this time, Mr. Tucket. Not this time. You go wake the children and be on your way now, before they pick up your trail and start to gain on you."

"But—"

"No buts to it. Get to riding if you want to save the young ones. You ain't got twenty minutes left. Besides, I've got work to do. I've got to pick a place to make my last . . . to make my stand."

"I'll stay. Two guns are better than one."

Again Grimes shook his head, this time slowly. "That won't work and you know it. If they get past us they'll get the children. They stay to fight me, that will give you time to run, and even if I don't stop them I'll guarantee you that all five won't be coming on."

Francis stood there for a count of ten, tried to make it work in his mind, tried to think of a way to stay and help, but he knew Grimes was right. Hated that Grimes was right but knew it. He still could not bring himself to leave his friend. "I'll send the others on. They'll get away."

"Get away. Now. Go." Grimes looked at the dust again. "They've stopped." And now a new sound came into his voice. It was as if Francis weren't there and Grimes were standing alone. His body seemed to uncoil in some way, and he stood taller and his eyes grew hard and he squinted tightly. "There, they're coming on. Maybe saw one of your tracks. Five of them. Ready to kill." He smiled. "That ought to be about right. I always said it would take at least five men to finish me. . . . We'll see, we'll see. . . ." He turned and saw Francis and seemed surprised. "You still here? Get gone. Now. It's going to get interesting around here in about half an hour."

Francis hung there for another five seconds,

tearing at it in his mind, and then he knew Grimes was right, and he turned and ran to wake Lottie and Billy.

They were used to reacting quickly now, and within four minutes were mounted and the three of them were riding, with Lottie wisely remaining silent and Billy offering to go back and fight, alone if necessary, and insistent enough that Francis thought he would have to tie the boy across his horse before he could make him come. Billy gave in at last only because Lottie joined forces with Francis and convinced him it would be best to come.

They went past where Grimes had been but Francis could not see him and knew he was getting ready. Francis peered into the trees but couldn't see any sign. That did not mean Grimes wasn't there. The old mountain man would be finding his best fighting ground—his back covered in some way, his rifle loaded and checked, a second and third load of lead balls and patches in his mouth to reload quickly, his knife and ax to hand. Getting ready. Ready.

He looked up into the mountains where the trail Grimes had pointed to worked out of the back of the canyon. He tried to focus on it, see it amid the peaks, visualize how it must lie, and tried not to look back. He rode that way with Lottie and Billy for a time, letting his horse pick out a faint path. At last he could stand it no longer and he looked back.

They had climbed, and the valley lay before him. The dust had disappeared, which meant that the men had either stopped or come into the grass where there would be no dust. He thought they had kept coming, and he tried to gauge how far they had moved and tried again not to think of what was going to happen, to think only of keeping Lottie's and Billy's horses moving ahead of him. He was forcing his mind to look ahead when the first shot came from below and he could not stand it, would not stand it.

"Keep moving up the trail!" he yelled at Lottie and Billy, and wheeled his horse and slammed the barrel of his rifle across her rump and was gone back down the trail.

To the mountain man, to Jason Grimes.

# ───── Chapter Six ─────

The mare ran hard because it was downhill and because she was fresh and because Francis kept hitting her across the rear with the barrel of his rifle. He knew it did not help—she was running as fast as she could, mouth wide, spit flying back—but he could not help himself.

After the first shot there was a small delay— perhaps thirty seconds—and then a second shot. In those thirty seconds Francis's pony covered a quarter of a mile. After the second shot, another short delay, and then a third shot followed by two more in rapid succession.

Francis ran toward the gunfire and came around a small stand of aspen into a long, narrow clearing.

The grass and trees were green. He would always remember the green. The sun came through the trees and the light gathered the color and seemed to bathe the whole clearing in a green glow. Everything else seemed frozen, as in a tableau.

Far down the clearing, near the other end, a horse wandered aimlessly, chewing at grass, still saddled and bridled. The body of a man lay on the ground near the horse.

Halfway down the clearing another horse stood, still saddled and bridled, and beside him another man lay unmoving in the grass.

Closer in, a third horse stood and on the ground near him a man sat, with a red stain on his chest just above the stomach, and he was looking down at it. As Francis watched, he fell over sideways, still looking at the stain.

Closer still, near where Francis and the mare came storming out of the trees, a fourth man lay with Grimes's hand ax embedded in his head.

Nearer yet, almost beneath the pinto's hooves, Grimes knelt with the fifth man, the two of them facing each other, Grimes with his head down slightly, as if working, and his hunting knife deep in the center of the man, holding him up in a kneeling position—though the man was clearly dead.

All five, Francis thought. He killed all five in not one full minute. Two shot long, one closer in, one with his tomahawk and the knife at the end.

"You're . . . you're something," Francis said, sliding off his horse. "You're just something. All five of them—"

Grimes raised his head and Francis saw it: Grimes had been hit. Hit once across his left shoulder, and again through the left side of his chest. When he raised his head Francis could also see the other man's knife in Grimes's side, up under the left ribs into the lung.

"I'm shot and cut to pieces, Mr. Tucket. It appears I got my wish." He pushed the other man away and tried to stand but instead he fell onto his side.

Francis was next to him. "Where . . . what can I do?"

Grimes seemed not to hear. He struggled to rise and at last, with Francis helping, he made it to a sitting position. Francis could see blood coming out of the corner of his mouth now and he knew the mountain man's lungs were gone, knew it was over.

"You lie back." Francis moved to help him. "We'll make camp here and feed you and make some bandages. You'll be good in a week, maybe two. I'll get some hump meat for you. . . ."

Grimes shook his head. "Let me be. Just let me be." He was quiet again, pulling air hard, leaning against Francis, who was crying openly. Grimes's breathing stopped and Francis thought he was gone, but it started again and Grimes said, "Don't you bury me. Leave me for the wolves and coyotes."

"But it isn't—"

"Don't. I want them to have me and take me on with them. Leave me out of the ground."

He was silent for another long time, his breath coming ragged, and then he looked at Francis, into his eyes, and he said, "I wish I could see one more sunrise," and he died then, with Francis holding him in the green light and with the bod-ies he had conquered all around him, died without closing his eyes, and Francis stared down at him and thought he could not stand it. Something, some part of what made him alive, had been cut out of him with Grimes's death and he could not hear and he could not see and he thought of his love for Grimes and his hatred for the men who had killed him, and of the green light and of Grimes fighting Braid and trapping beaver and saving Francis from the Pawnees and again from the Comancheros and from these five men, and he cried and cried, heaving with it, until Lottie and Billy came back to find him and put a blanket over him while he sat for the day and all the night, holding the dead mountain man, crying for what he had lost.

# Chapter Seven

Francis sat his horse on a ridge between two clear-white peaks that shot up into a blue sky and thought of an Indian prayer he had heard.

*There is beauty above me,*
*There is beauty below me,*
*All around me there is beauty.*

The peaks went out ahead of him as if they were marching to the west. Huge, craggy mountains were still fully coated in snow. And he knew that probably no man from the east had seen them except for Grimes and perhaps other wandering mountain men. Grimes had told him once that Kit Carson had said he'd been out here, but that might have been something Kit made up. The word was he made many things up.

"Why are we stopping?" Lottie came up beside Francis. "There's no wood here for a fire and no water for the horses either. Shouldn't we go on down into the valley a little?"

Francis shrugged. It had been four days since Grimes had died and Francis was still, as Billy said quietly to Lottie the first night, ". . . not right in the head."

It was not just the death of Grimes, although that had triggered it. They had done as Grimes had asked and sat him at the base of a tree with his rifle across his lap and his ax and knife close to hand by his side, leaning back against the tree so he could see out across the prairie to the horizon.

The other five bodies Francis had roped and dragged, one at a time, to a gully. He dumped them in and left them.

He'd searched them first. Even in grief he could not bring himself to waste anything. They

had the rifles they had stolen from the Englishman and some gold coins and the odd striker and
flint to make sparks and start a fire but little else.
He did not know what to do with the rifles. He
was used to his own and did not like the foreign
look of them. They were huge long-barreled affairs impossible to handle well on a horse and he
offered one to Billy, who picked it up and found
that it was much longer than he was tall and put it
down.

"I'll stay with my bow," he said. He had
hunted with the bow ever since they'd stayed at
the Pueblo village and his arrows kept them in
camp meat—turkey, rabbits, squirrels and even
one deer.

In the end, they left the rifles near Grimes.
The packhorse was already encumbered with
food and gold and the rifles were just extra
weight they could not carry.

And so they had ridden away from Grimes, but
Francis could not shake the feeling of an end to
some part of his life he could not understand, as if
he had somehow died with the mountain man.
They had followed the trail Grimes had told
them of but had made slow time because Francis
stopped frequently to stare at the peaks and re-

member his life with Grimes, sometimes dismounting and sitting for half a day, holding the reins to his horse, gazing at nothing.

He left everything to Billy and Lottie. Setting up camp, killing and cooking meat, finding the trail—which was not well marked—and even scouting for possible danger. He would stop in the evenings when and where Lottie said to stop, sit while they gathered wood and struck a flint to make fire, eat what Lottie handed him to eat, drink when he was thirsty, or not, if water wasn't at hand.

On this fourth night he did not sleep, as he had not slept the previous three nights, and on this fourth night Grimes came to him.

Francis was sitting, looking into the fire. It had died down to a bed of red coals. Lottie and Billy were wrapped in their blankets, sleeping deeply, turned away from the flames, and Francis wasn't thinking of anything in particular except to wonder if he would ever sleep again, and Grimes came walking in and sat down by the fire pit.

Francis jumped back, thinking: A ghost! But Grimes did not show any wounds. He sat quietly for some time looking at the glowing coals, as Francis had been doing, and then he looked up and said softly, as if worrying that he might wake the other two:

"It's all right."

"What?" Francis leaned toward him. "What did you say?"

But Grimes stood, hefted his rifle so that it lay cradled in his one good arm, nodded at Francis and walked into the darkness without looking back.

Francis watched him until he was out of sight. Then he sighed and smiled and lay down on his side and was instantly, profoundly and deeply asleep.

HE AWAKENED to find himself covered with a blanket, his rifle at his side. It was still dark and Lottie had a fire going and was cooking a whole rear leg of venison on a spit over the flames.

Francis raised himself on one elbow. "That's quite a bit of meat for breakfast."

His voice startled her and she jumped and scowled at him. "You nearly scared me to death. And for your information it's not breakfast. This is supper. You slept the clock around—all night and all day until dark again."

Francis lay back and, looked at the fire silently for a time. He did not feel lost as he had before, did not feel ended. He could hear and smell the meat cooking and could hear the night sounds around them. Nearby the horses were standing, picketed, and he could hear them breathing. Off to the west a coyote yipped. "Grimes came to me," he said.

"Came to you?" Lottie stopped turning the meat. "You mean in a dream?"

"He means a ha'nt." Billy was sitting across the fire wiping grease into his bowstring. It was made from twisted deer-leg tendon and it dried out if not kept greased. "Grimes came as a ha'nt . . . a ghost."

"No." Francis sat up. "He came and sat next to me and told me it was all right. Then he got up and left and then I went to sleep."

"It was a ha'nt," Billy repeated. "He was worried about you and was coming back to tell you it was all right. Ha'nts ain't all bad. Some of them are good."

"What do you know about ghosts?" Lottie said. "It's all stuff and nonsense. If Francis said Grimes came back to him, then Mr. Grimes came back to him, and if he said it's going to be all right, it's going to be all right. You go check the horses, make sure they're still picketed right, while Francis and me think on what to do next."

Billy hesitated, but something in her eye made him think better of speaking and he went to do as she said. She turned to Francis as soon as the boy was gone.

"Are you really all right, Francis? Because you haven't been yourself for days and days."

He held up his hand. "I'm fine."

She turned the deer leg slowly. The fat dripping from it into the open flame sputtered and flashed as it ignited. "I was worried about you."

He lay back and closed his eyes. "I'm all right. Don't worry. I'm fine now. We'll eat and sleep another night and then tomorrow we'll strike north as best we can and see if we can find the wagon trail that Grimes said was there." His stomach rumbled. "But for now, how much more are we going to cook that meat? I could eat dirt."

Lottie smiled. He was back.

# Chapter Eight

Francis held his horse back below the crest of a small rise, dismounted and went to her nose and pinched it so she wouldn't whinny. Two miles back Lottie and Billy were following. Ahead of him, over the rise and a mile away, there appeared to be a man on horseback with a herd of twenty or twenty-five horses that he was pushing ahead of him. The man had a saddle and was not an Indian, but Francis was wary, especially of someone alone out here with horses in a herd.

He walked and led his horse until his eyes came just over the ridge, where he could see without being seen. He watched for a good fifteen minutes. The man wasn't pushing his little herd but seemed to be letting them graze along at their own speed.

Francis heard a sound and turned to see Lottie and Billy approach. He motioned them to stop well back but it was too late. Billy's pony smelled the herd and cut loose with a shrill whinny—almost a scream.

The effect on the man a mile away was immediate and strange.

He galloped his mount around the herd, got them moving straight away from Francis and then he took out a bugle and blew a series of high notes, one rapidly after another, and in what seemed seconds a group of five men on horses came boiling over yet another ridge to surround the horse herd in a protective circle.

It was all done very efficiently and looked so controlled and disciplined that something about it reassured Francis—he even thought they might be Army—and he remounted and showed himself above the ridge. When Lottie and Billy caught up they rode toward the herd.

As they grew closer Francis waved, and one man waved back and came riding out to meet them.

He was not Army but he rode a good mount, well taken care of, had a good rifle, also well cared for—a large, beefy man with rounded shoulders and huge hands—and he smiled when he saw them. "Why, you are but sprites. Are you alone in the wilderness at such an early age?"

Francis said, "We came from south a ways. Did you come from back east this year?"

The man nodded. "I am Orson, and these men are Caleb, Lyle, John, James and Isaiah. We are heading west for the promised land in the golden valley by the Columbia River. Are you children of God?"

Francis wasn't sure how to answer but Lottie came forward and said, "We are all children of God, that's what my mother said before we were attacked and all killed but my brother and me, saved by Francis here."

Francis looked at her sharply. Her mother had died of croup. Her father had taken the children westward two years later and died of cholera; she and Billy had been cast out by the wagon train.

He thought she shouldn't lie but she gave him a look right back as if to say, "Do you *want* me to tell them our father had cholera?" and went on. "Which was over a year ago and since then we've been captured by the army, then the evil Comancheros, escaped at great peril, been attacked by wild men and bitten by snakes. . . ."

The man named Orson held up his hand. "That's enough. You must come and visit with us for a time and tell us the stories."

There was something about the man, something so open and honest that Francis said, "It would be nice if we could team up with you. To get west. I have folks out there somewhere I need to find. I'm a fair hunter and Billy is as good a scout as you'll ever meet and Lottie can help the womenfolk." He got a definite scowl here. "Why, she can run your whole camp."

Orson nodded. "We'd be glad of the company but we have no womenfolk. We left them all back home while we came out ahead to settle the land. They'll come in a year or so by ship, down around Cape Horn and back up, to meet us where the river runs into the Pacific Ocean. And if you can hunt you'll be more than welcome. We can shoot game when it's plentiful but it seems to have pulled back from the trail and we can't get close enough for a shot."

They had been riding while they spoke, and they came up over a small rise now. Francis could see a small group of wagons—he counted six of them—arranged in a circle with oxen herded into the middle. So they were using oxen to pull the wagons and had just brought the horses for . . . what?

"Why so many horses if you aren't pulling the wagons with them?"

Orson smiled. "We were told there's a shortage of good horses out west and we pooled what money we had and brought these mares and some stallions for brood stock. We hope to sell horses as well as to farm."

Francis nodded but thought it perhaps a little bit silly. The West was covered with horses, small mustangs, wild Indian ponies, that were as tough and good as any he'd ever seen, but even as he had the thought he found himself looking at some of Orson's stock with envy. They were large, well muscled and strong-looking, not just for riding but for all-around work, pulling a wagon or cultivator or even a single-bottom plow.

Look at me, he thought, thinking like a farmer. Grimes would roll over in his grave. If he had a grave—the thought jumped into his mind. The way Grimes had looked sitting against the trees, his eyes glazed and staring out across the prairie . . . He shook his head. That was how the mountain man had wanted it and it was right for him, right for the wolves to carry him off.

"We have some hump meat," Francis said. They had taken a buffalo the day before, a young cow with new spring fat on her, and had twenty pounds of fresh meat wrapped in green hide. "We'll cook that for food tonight and Billy and I will start scouting and hunting in the morning."

Orson nodded. "Roast buffalo hump sounds as good as Christmas dinner. We still have potatoes to boil. . . ."

"You have potatoes?" This from Lottie. "Oh my, I haven't had boiled potatoes with gravy for, oh my, I can't remember when. . . ."

And so that night for the first time in what seemed years, Francis prayed before eating (or at least listened to the others pray) and ate meat cut in slices from a pan with a fork, and ate boiled potatoes covered in buffalo-fat brown gravy that Lottie made in a cast-iron pot by burning some flour in grease and adding water to thicken it, ate until he could eat no more and listened to the men talking of the farms they would make when they came to the golden valley, their voices mixing with each other in a kind of low music, until he curled up in the dirt by the fire to sleep.

He supposed that Grimes would have called these men pilgrims, with a cutting edge to his voice. But Francis's last thought was that all of it, the talk and the dreams of farms and the civilized food, all of it set well with him and he didn't mind.

# ———— Chapter Nine ————

He had never seen people work so hard. In truth, everybody who came west on the trains had to work a great deal just to cover the ground, but these men, all big, all happy, ready to laugh or pray, whichever mood took them, worked until he thought they would drop. If something broke they fixed it, and fixed it better than it had been when it was new. Or if something looked like it was going to break, they would fix it. If a horse came to the edge of limping, even hesitated in its step, they were on it and working at the hooves, checking it, rubbing liniment into its skin, slowing its pace, talking to it in low, reassuring sounds that seemed almost like music.

"They . . . they love things," Lottie said to Francis one day when they'd been traveling with the men about a week.

"What do you mean?" Francis was cleaning his rifle and looked up.

"The men. Watch them. They love everything. They love horses and oxen and wagons and when they talk about their families at night they love them and the mountains even when it's hard going . . . they just seem to love things."

And when he thought of it Francis agreed. He never heard a bad word from the men. One morning they were greasing wagon axles, taking each wooden wheel off with the axle propped up on a fork and wiping the wooden axle with buffalo grease, and one of the wagons fell on Orson's foot. It caught the edge of his foot and caused a nasty cut and a huge bruise. Francis thought it must have hurt like blue blazes but Orson merely stood there until they pulled the wagon off him and then he laughed. "It's lucky I have two feet."

And, Francis found, they ate like wolves. He

hunted to feed them and it took three full deer or one small buffalo a *day,* eating three times a day. He'd never seen such appetites and he could remember Grimes sitting down and eating ten pounds of meat in one sitting at one meal.

Lottie changed her mind about doing women's work and cooked for them—though the men washed and cleaned up after she was done—and ten days into their journey together she sighed, looking at the empty pots. "I cook more each time and they eat it all. I don't think I could cook enough to fill them."

It would have been easy to consider them friends. Francis and Lottie and Billy traveled with the men and laughed with them and were close to them, but Francis and Lottie and Billy had the problem of the gold they'd earned. Billy hunted with Francis, using his bow to take turkeys, rabbits and squirrels for what the men called "bites now and again," and that left Lottie alone with the Spanish gold.

What they had amounted to a fortune. Though Francis had not worked it out—sums bored him and for the moment it didn't matter anyway, since there was no place to spend it—the amount was enough to cause greed and desire. So Francis and Lottie and Billy had kept the gold hidden, wrapped in private packs rolled in green hide in back of one of the wagons in a space that the men had provided. But the gold came between them and the men, for it was a secret to be kept, and the more Francis came to like the men, the less he liked the feeling of not being honest.

They had traveled for two weeks. Francis, Lottie and Billy had fallen into the routine of hunting, traveling, cooking and eating, helping with the wagons if it was needed, which it almost never was, and moving slowly through the country.

They covered ground at a snail's pace, rarely making more than ten miles a day, and it often frustrated Francis, who was used to the freedom and relative speed of horseback travel.

"When we get up," Billy whined one morning, "we can see where we're going to sleep tonight."

"It makes no never mind," Lottie said to him, slapping him across the back of his head—though much more lightly than she formerly had. "The company is good and we're moving in the right direction."

In two weeks they had come not much more than a hundred and twenty miles but the country had changed dramatically. They had gone through a small range of mountains, working down several passes that were fairly easy going and came out in some break country that was semidesert. From a distance, it looked almost flat but as they approached it the country turned into a nightmare. The smoothness gave way to steep-sided gullies and ditches that made wagon travel almost impossible. The wagons hung up, tee-tered, fell, crashed down, half rolled over and were jerked to the next gully. Francis and Billy were off a long time hunting. Game had become more scarce as they left the mountains and they had to work harder for meat, and by the time they came back to the camp with two deer and half a dozen rabbits the men had a fire going and were settled into doing camp chores, mending broken wagons, torn harness and the like. But tonight there was a difference; something had changed. They seemed reserved, not talkative— even Billy and Lottie noticed it—and Francis could not see the reason.

He shrugged it off at first, sat by a fire to sharpen his knife, which had hit sand when he was gutting a deer and become dull. He was just finishing it up when Orson came to him.

"Francis," Orson said in his deep, even voice. "We must talk."

Francis looked up. "All right. Let's talk."

"Over there, by John's wagon, where we can be alone."

The hairs went up on Francis's neck and he stood and hefted his rifle, slid his knife back in its sheath. "Why alone?"

"Because I think you would rather be alone for what I have to say."

What on earth? Francis thought. What is he after?

Francis held back and let Orson lead so he could watch him. He liked the man and trusted him, but so much of his life had become a habit of caution, of taking care, that he couldn't help himself.

Orson stopped by John's wagon and turned, and Francis held back a step and a half. "What's wrong, Orson?"

Orson coughed, seemed embarrassed. "You have your goods in the back of John's wagon. . . ."

Francis nodded.

"We are in some hard country for wagon travel."

"I know." Francis waited.

"It is only maybe three more weeks now and we'll turn the wagons into rafts and run down the big river to the settlements. We are nearing our destination. Everybody is anxious."

Francis nodded again. He had heard them talking. They thought to make the Columbia River before long and there they would make rafts to get to the valleys where the farmers had settled.

"But now it is very hard going."

"I understand. Do you want me to stop hunting and help with the wagons? Is that what this is about?"

Orson shook his head. "No. No. It is just that the wagons break. . . . John's wagon broke and your bundle came undone."

Ah, Francis thought. There it is.

"Francis, there was so much gold there in your bundle."

"Yes. I know."

Now Orson waited and when Francis did not come forth with more information he sighed again. "We believe that a man's business is his own and I do not want to pry but the others—"

"Others? Does everybody know about the gold?"

Orson nodded. "We have no secrets. And we do not have a desire to intrude in your affairs but the others have a concern and I must confess I have some of the same feelings. Is the gold, I mean, does the gold—did you come by the gold honestly? We would not ask except that there is so very much of it."

Francis relaxed. Orson was so honest, and so obviously uncomfortable about asking . . .

"Yes. We found it." Francis quickly told him the story of discovering the grave and the Spanish armor and sword.

Orson smiled. "Such good fortune, such very good luck for you."

Francis nodded but thought again, as he had thought many times, that the gold was only good where you could spend it. And while they were closer, they were still many hard miles from where the gold would do them any good.

# ──── Chapter Ten ────

Francis could not believe the river.

He stood with Lottie at his right and Billy at his left, Orson and the men off to the side, and stared at the river in awe. And not a little fear.

It was half a mile across, smooth but with a fast current that made the dark waters roil so that they looked almost alive, and evil. The Columbia.

They had come across the last of the high desert plains with little further mishap and no injuries, now following a trail that was so heavily traveled it would have been impossible to get lost. They set the wagon wheels in the ruts. Game became more and more scarce and Billy and Francis ranged farther and farther afield to get meat, at times going ten or fifteen miles off the track before they found deer or elk. Buffalo had disappeared completely, hunted out in the years the wagons had been passing, as had most other game. But as they came near the river they met Indians of different bands and tribes who wanted to barter tools or steel or guns for food. The men and Francis had nothing extra to trade, but Francis, who knew the more or less universal sign language used by all the tribes to trade or talk war or peace, took some young men aside and they showed him how to catch salmon in the river, using line and bone hooks.

Francis set to fishing as soon as they reached the river. The salmon were so numerous that they seemed to fill the water, and soon he had more than enough fish for everybody. The meat was oily and thick and rich, and while it tasted fine at first, within two days Francis was ready for elk or venison again.

Work on rafts began at once. The wagons were

broken down and taken apart, huge cedar logs were cut from the surrounding forest and horses in harness were used to skid them down to the water. They lashed the logs together with rope and bark twine, and used boards from the wagons to make flooring. Then they built a pen to hold the animals.

But now the Indians, at first helpful, had changed. When it became apparent that the white men had nothing further to trade or sell, the Indians took to stealing. Any tool left lying around, a nail, a piece of rope, an auger bit, was soon gone. They hung around the camp constantly, watching the men work and waiting for a chance to grab something and run. The white men soon learned to keep track of their tools and equipment and stopped losing gear, but they began to distrust the Indians.

While fishing one day, Francis befriended a young man named Iktah. Iktah's language was almost impossible for Francis to learn because there were so many short, guttural, sharply cut-off phrases that were hard to pronounce. But they soon became almost fluid in their sign language and Francis learned to trust Iktah.

They were sitting on the bank one day just

after Francis had set his lines, watching the dark waters stream past, when Iktah pointed down the river and signed, "The water down there is not safe."

Francis signed, "Why?"

He watched Iktah carefully as he answered, "It has been a dry year. No rain, very little snow. The river will not come high as it does sometimes. It is too low. There are places where many rocks stick out of the water like sharp teeth. They will eat the boats and the men and the horses and oxen."

"Is this all true?"

"Yes."

"What must be done?"

"There is a trail back through the mountains. It will take more time but it is safe. My people could help you carry your goods and drive your animals. Do not let the men go on the river."

That night while eating—salmon, always salmon—Francis told Orson what Iktah had said.

"We have not heard of this before," Orson said. "Nobody in any group has left word."

"He says we are the first this year to try the river."

Orson shook his head. "We would have heard.

And now this man says his people will help us carry our things over the mountains? The same people who would steal us blind?"

"He says the river is too dangerous," Francis repeated. "Farther down, miles down into canyons where you cannot turn around, he says there are rocks that will tear the rafts to pieces. You cannot get through."

Orson sighed. He was not tired—Francis did not think he could ever be tired—but there was a sadness in his voice. "I think that we cannot believe what you have heard about the river. I think they merely want to steal more from us and are using this as a way to get what they want."

"Orson, I believe him. I'm going to go around."

Orson shook his head. "You have learned how to make your own way, and you must do what you think is right. We wish you well."

Francis knelt in the dirt and took a stick to sketch a map, and he thought of Grimes as he drew. How many times the mountain man had done the same thing, showing a tree, a river, mountains, drawn in the dirt as Francis did it now.

"Here we are," he said. "Iktah said it would

take seven days by horse to get back to the river below the bad places. Lottie, Billy and I will leave tomorrow with horses, and you won't be leaving for another week at least. We'll stop here, near where Iktah says there are two peaks, and camp by the river and wait. If you're right, when you come along we'll rejoin you."

"And if we're wrong . . ." Orson looked steadily at Francis.

Francis shook his head. "You'll be fine, you'll be fine."

They shook hands, and Francis went to tell Lottie and Billy to get ready. That night they packed and arranged the loads. They left at dawn, and Francis did not look at the river as they rode away. He thought only of shaking hands with Orson.

# ─── Chapter Eleven ───

"I don't think they're coming," Lottie said. "They decided to stay right where they were." Her eyes were hopeful as she poked the fire.

"Or maybe," Billy said, "they haven't left yet."

"Maybe." Francis nodded. "Yes, that's probably it. They haven't left yet."

But Francis didn't believe it. Orson and the other men might have delayed a day or two, but it was going on two weeks since Francis and Lottie and Billy had set out. Once they reached the river, Iktah had left them here to camp and gone back to scout. The men should have come along by now.

The three of them had been waiting for more than eight days. Billy had ranged out to hunt. Somehow he had brought down an elk with his small bow. It was a large bull—more than seven hundred pounds—and they had spent the week in a comfortable camp by the river drying elk meat and eating red meat to get the taste of salmon out of their mouths.

"Should we stop looking?" Lottie asked.

"No." Francis shook his head. They had been taking turns watching the river and standing watch by the fire at night, to keep it going so the men would see it. "Let's keep it up for a while yet."

"Maybe I should look for another elk." Billy pointed at the hills. "I saw fresh signs back about four miles. We could use the meat when they come."

"Good idea. The way they eat we'll need . . ."

Francis trailed off. It was late afternoon and he was watching the river while he spoke. The water was more than half a mile wide here but had flattened considerably and slowed down. The river was still dark, and had what must have been underwater obstacles because it seemed to boil and tumble, almost in an oily way, with thick bulges that rolled up and back under. While he watched, Francis saw the body of a man hit one of the bulges, come upright for a second with his arms up in the air, almost as if waving, and then disappear. It was too far away to tell for certain but it looked a lot like Orson. Francis nearly cried out.

While he watched, he saw the bodies of four horses and one ox float through the same eddy. Then came a large piece of wreckage that was unmistakably part of the raft Orson and the men had made from their wagons and cedar logs.

He dropped to his knees, mutely watching the water.

Then there was nothing.

Lottie and Billy had been looking away and had not seen anything but Francis felt a brush on his shoulder and turned to see Iktah standing there, making signs.

"The teeth of the river have taken your friends."

Francis nodded slowly and answered with shaking hands, "I'm afraid that is so."

"What did he say?" Lottie asked.

"He said that Orson and the rest of them aren't coming."

"Well, we can wait. I like traveling with them, even when I have to cook."

"No." Francis put his hand on her shoulder. "They aren't coming. Ever."

"Oh." Her eyes grew wide, then teared. "*Oh*. All of them?"

He nodded.

"Oh, Francis." She turned and looked at the river, across it, at the mountains behind. "Is it to be like this always? Just always so hard, so that it crushes people?" She covered her face with her hands and began to sob.

Billy had been listening silently, standing on one leg with his left foot on the inside of his right knee. And he nodded now, looking strangely weary and wise beyond his years. He looked up and down the river. "It's always been hard. I guess it always will be hard." He went up to Lottie and put his hand on her shoulder.

Francis felt less grief than a bone tiredness. He

had used up all his grief when Grimes was killed. Now he was so exhausted that even pain was dulled. He just wanted it over.

"We can't travel on the river," he said to Iktah. "Even if we had time and could do it, making the rafts would take more tools than we carry." He looked back into the mountains. "Is there a trail that will take us to what the white men call the golden valley, where the settlements begin?"

Iktah frowned, thinking. "There is talk of such a trail. It follows the river but way off to the side. I have not seen it and do not wish to go to where the white men live. But they say it is easy to follow. Just look for the dead line with the yellow flowers."

"Dead line?"

"There is no grass because the animals of the white men have eaten it all. And where the animals leave their sign in the flat places there are yellow flowers that grow tall and smell bad."

Francis had been speaking aloud, translating to Lottie and Billy as he read sign, and Lottie said, her face still wet with tears, "He means mustard, Francis. Papa showed us how the wild mustard seed is in some of the feed the wagon trains carry.

The oxen and horses eat it and it passes through them and grows where they leave their manure while they walk. We just have to follow the mustard flowers."

"How far is it?" Francis asked. "How many sleeps?"

Iktah shrugged. "Some say three, others seven or eight. It depends on how you work your horses."

Close, Francis thought. I am close to done with this. We are close to done with this. "I thank you for the time spent traveling with us."

Iktah shrugged again. "It was right to do it. Sitting by the fire with you to talk was a good time. Some things are not a good time, but this was. I will go now." And he turned his pony and disappeared. Francis waved a hand in farewell.

Then he looked at the sun. "We can make some miles before dark. You want to keep going?"

Billy was already gathering his things together. Lottie nodded. "I want to get away from this cursed river."

They broke camp quickly. Billy rode first, then Lottie, who trailed the packhorse. Francis mounted and followed them. There had been times when his life depended on water, times when he would have loved to see this river. But now he wanted shut of it. He never wanted to see it again.

# Chapter Twelve

It turned out to be three days to where the settlements began. It was a quiet ride, for Francis hardly spoke, and that silenced Lottie. Francis was getting more and more anxious. Were his parents alive? How did his parents and his sister, Rebecca, look now? How would they feel when they saw him—they would have thought him dead all this time, after all. What would they think of Lottie and Billy?

If he expected to find them at once, he was to be sadly disappointed. At the first settlement they had never heard of the name Tucket, nor at the second, and in the third a man looked at them and said:

"Tucket! Now, that sounds familiar. Let me see . . ."

Lottie clutched Francis's arm.

"I got it!" the man said. "Weren't they all killed on the river?"

After that Francis nearly stopped looking.

But Lottie got her stubborn streak up. "Francis," she said, "you can't stop now. Billy and me won't let you stop."

So they rode on, Lottie talking, talking, to fill the silence.

Nine days later, in the fifth settlement, they stopped at a lean-to that served as a store and trading post. A wizened old man leaned across the board counter and said, "A family called Tucket? Would there be a girl named Rebecca?"

"Yes." Francis held his breath. How long, how many months? All the time he had spent searching now came down to this very second.

"Would she have black hair?"

"She does."

"Is it the family that lost a boy coming across, lost him to the Indians?"

"Yes!" Lottie shouted.

Francis nodded. "Lost me. They lost me."

"Ahhh." The old man nodded. "Then they must be the ones."

"Where are they? Where? Where?" Lottie could stand it no longer.

The old man looked at her, then at Francis. "Pushy little bit, ain't she?"

"Please, sir," Francis said, "where are the Tuckets?"

"The Tuckets!" Billy roared.

The old man pointed to the twin rut road that ran west from the lean-to. "Four miles that way, then one mile off the road. They have a sign with their name on it. You can't miss it."

But the three of them were already gone.

FRANCIS STOPPED HIS HORSE and sat quietly on her for a moment, watching the man in the field, letting the sight of him fill his heart. The man was plowing, working a team of horses, and he had his back to the three of them. Francis clucked to his horse and tightened his heels and the pony moved forward, walking softly but slightly faster than the plowhorses, until she was just four feet in back of the man working the plow. Lottie and Billy followed him, Billy smiling but Lottie oddly serious, with a worried look.

The man stopped and straightened his back and wiped sweat from his forehead and turned and saw what at first he took to be three Indians and a packhorse following him.

They were all dressed in buckskins, seasoned by hundreds of campfires and rain, their faces weather-blasted and burned and blackened. Francis wore his hair tied back in a club with a rawhide thong and he held a rifle that had become part of him, an extension of his arm.

"What . . . ? Who . . . ?"

Francis let him wonder for another beat. Then he slid off the horse and stood, taller than his father now, leaner, and he said, "Hello, Pa. How are you?"

For a second, then two, there was nothing. Then a look, a swift flash in the man's eyes.

"Francis?" A smile, from deep inside, and a bellow: *"Francis!"* And he reached over and jerked Francis away from the horse and was holding him and crying and hugging all at once.

And Francis was home.

# Afterword

After Francis returned, his family was, of course, ecstatic. At first his mother almost could not accept it, and many times, months after he was home, she would come to his bed while he was sleeping and push his hair back from his head, kiss him on the forehead, touch his cheek. At first it bothered him. At first many things bothered him. Sleeping in the cabin his father had made was hard, since he was accustomed to sleeping outside, and having people around him all the time was hard too, and the noise of the farm. But after a time he came to like the closeness, the hard work, the wonderful food made of so many things besides meat. The wonderful food made by his mother and Rebecca.

He liked farming, working alongside his father, the way his father said "son." He liked going for walks with Rebecca, and how she made him laugh. He liked the way Rebecca, Lottie and Billy became good friends.

Lottie and Billy stayed briefly with the Tuckets, then were taken in by another family who had lost their children to cholera on the way across. They lived just over a hill and saw the Tuckets nearly every day.

After they all got settled, there was the question of the Spanish treasure. Francis and Lottie and Billy were almost staggeringly rich, for they had seventy-five pounds of gold and sixty pounds of silver among the three of them. The gold alone was so valuable that the same amount would have made them multimillionaires in modern times.

It's hard to get exact ratios, but it must be remembered that the main reason the Oregon Trail existed, and that such a huge percentage of the population went west (the largest mass migration in American history) was that hundreds of banks were failing and the country was in a severe depression. People had lost farms, houses, land. Nearly everybody was dirt poor—literally.

And this poverty was most extreme in the new West. Everything was done by barter or trade. Money, in the form of currency, hardly existed, and anybody who had money, or gold and silver, was in a very good position to make more.

At the tender age of eleven Lottie became something of a banker. And Francis was glad to leave her in charge. Billy was too. Once he'd bought and eaten his fill of rock candy, the money didn't interest Billy. So Lottie loaned the money at interest, investing and reinvesting, so that in three short years she had nearly doubled the amount they'd found in the Spanish grave. Through defaults in loans she acquired two farms and a sawmill, which she leased back to the previous owners and continued to earn money on.

Meanwhile, Francis worked with his father on the farm. For a time he was content with the work and life as it was.

Then there came a day when he went to see Lottie about something financial and he wasn't sure why, but on the way he stopped and picked some wildflowers and handed them to her when he arrived. And she nodded and smiled in a soft new way and put them in a jar with water.

The next day he brought flowers again. She

smiled. And so, gradually, Francis and Lottie changed the way they thought about each other.

Almost one year later to the day, they wed. The day after the marriage, Billy ran off to sea.

"I want to see more of the world," he said. "I'll be back."

And he did come back. But in the meantime Francis and Lottie set up housekeeping on a farm down the road. Four years later Billy returned. The three of them now owned many farms, several large herds of brood mares and horses, a wagon factory, four sawmills, three small hotels. Billy took some of his money and bought a square-rigged sailing ship and started a shipping line. Within five years he had three more ships and was hauling wood, cut by his own sawmills, to China to trade for tea and porcelain, which he shipped east to Europe, and then brought people back from Europe to the East Coast before starting the circle again.

When he could, Billy returned home. He also married and had children, and Lottie and Francis had children, who in turn married and had children, and much of the states of Oregon and Washington are owned by their children and their children's children and *their* children.

Francis lived to be an old man and died in 1923. Lottie lived seven years longer. They never traveled again. They lived their lives in a small frame house just over the hill from the original Tucket homestead, amassing one of the great American fortunes. Each evening, after supper, Francis would take his rifle and go sit among the trees as the sun went down and think of prairies and storms and Indians and mountain men and herds of buffalo and grizzlies and horizons—oh yes, horizons—and every night the last thought before he went back to the house to drink a cup of warm tea and to sleep, every night he'd think the same thought of a one-armed mountain man leaning back against a tree, dead.

Every night his last thought was of Jason Grimes.

# Author's Note

When we think of the American West, most of us think in images and ideas that come from the time of the cowboys. Countless books (some of them mine), plays, songs, radio programs, television shows and movies have been devoted to it. Actually that period lasted only thirty years or so, from the end of the Civil War in 1865 until about 1895. Yet it often seems that more energy has been devoted to this brief time than to all the history preceding it.

Of course, what we know as the American West is a place that existed long before human beings appeared on Earth. The mountains we see today have been relatively unchanged for millions of years. In prehistoric times, the Western states were a swampy jungle filled with enormous reptiles, dinosaurs and other creatures now long extinct. At another time huge stretches of the West were ocean bottom, a place where sharks as big as buses hunted and killed.

Most of the period since humans first appeared in the West (approximately 28,000 B.C.) is unrecorded. Archaeological discoveries show that people have lived in Western canyons, deserts and mountains perhaps more than twenty thousand years. While much is made of how "new" America is compared to Europe, Native American culture predates much of European culture. Early inhabitants are still a powerful presence in the West today. In my own travels, I've come across thousands of pictographs—ancient paintings and drawings on rock walls—that were created centuries before Christopher Columbus began his voyage to the New World from Spain in 1492. I've seen pictographs that are personal narratives showing people gutting animals after a hunt, or a figure shooting arrows at other figures to frighten them away from his crops—stories of achievement and also, perhaps, a warning to enemies.

Long before the explorers Lewis and Clark made their great expedition from St. Louis to the

Pacific between 1804 and 1806, and still longer before Francis Tucket made his journey, the West was not wild but largely civilized and tamed. Native Americans had lived there successfully for thousands of years. After the Spanish conquest in the 1540s, Spanish soldiers began to explore the West, and Catholic missionaries started to establish a system of missions and churches, many of which are still in use today. The Spanish founded Santa Fe about 1610, San Antonio in 1718, San Diego in 1769 and Los Angeles in 1781. San Francisco was founded in 1776, the year the thirteen colonies declared America's independence from England.

In that same year men left to map a trade route from Santa Fe in New Mexico to Monterey in California to make it easier to transport goods to the coast. A traveler going south from Santa Fe into Mexico would find small inns, forerunners of our motels, at intervals where he could rest his horses and pack mules. These inns were known as *fondas,* a word still in use today.

But to the north there were still vast tracts of wilderness inhabited by Native Americans and a very few mountain men and French trappers. This is where I brought Francis, because I wanted to write about an area and a time largely neglected in history books and ignored by movies and television.

It was a time of great adventure, when you could ride through herds of buffalo for days and when mountain ranges bounded on forever, when everything was new and raw and savage and when Francis was limited only by himself—and by nature.

Some readers have commented on the violence and hardship of Francis's life, the amount of fighting and death and difficulty. Nothing in these books about Francis Tucket is completely fictional—every act of violence, every difficulty is based on reality and actually happened to some person who existed then. This includes the attacks by the Comancheros, the skirmishes following the Mexican War and the scavengers who deserted from the army and roamed and pillaged. The hardships that people faced trying to go west by wagon, on foot or on horseback were staggering. Several people died for every mile covered on the so-called Oregon Trail. They died from cholera, typhus, typhoid fever, gun accidents, simple flu, ear infections, rabies, infections from small cuts, blood poisoning, scurvy and other malnutritional diseases; they died from attacks by bands of robbers, from being run over by wagons, from drowning, from botulism and other food poisoning and from simple childhood diseases like measles and chicken pox.

They did not, however, die in attacks by Native Americans, which is the way Hollywood tells it. In the time of the Oregon Trail the Native Americans were helpful, often providing food and guidance, and there was rarely, very rarely, an attack on a wagon train, and never a time when the settlers had to "circle the wagons" and fight. That happened only in the movies. All the difficulty with Native Americans came later, after they were invaded by the military and their lands were stolen. This happened after 1860, by which time there was a railroad across the continent and the Oregon Trail was a thing of the past.